PENGUIN BOOKS

THE VERY MODEL OF A MAN

Howard Jacobson was born in Manchester in 1942 and educated at Cambridge, where he studied English under F. R. Leavis. His books *Coming from Behind* (1983), *Peeping Tom* (1984), *In the Land of Oz* (1987) and *The Very Model of a Man* (1992) are all published by Penguin. He is also the author of *Redback* (1986). *Roots Schmoots*, a journey among Jews, is published by Viking and forthcoming in Penguin.

HOWARD JACOBSON

———————

THE VERY MODEL OF A MAN

PENGUIN BOOKS

PENGUIN BOOKS

Published by the Penguin Group
Penguin Books Ltd, 27 Wrights Lane, London W8 5TZ, England
Penguin Books USA Inc., 375 Hudson Street, New York, New York 10014, USA
Penguin Books Australia Ltd, Ringwood, Victoria, Australia
Penguin Books Canada Ltd, 10 Alcorn Avenue, Toronto, Ontario, Canada M4V 3B2
Penguin Books (NZ) Ltd, 182–190 Wairau Road, Auckland 10, New Zealand

Penguin Books Ltd, Registered Offices: Harmondsworth, Middlesex, England

First published by Viking 1992
Published in Penguin Books 1993
1 3 5 7 9 10 8 6 4 2

Printed in England by Clays Ltd, St Ives plc

To Rosalin

Contents

1. Cain Remembers a Birthday   1

2. Voices on a Babel Night   21

3. Cain Encourages His Father in a Blasphemy   45

4. Hairless in Kadesh   66

5. Cain Expatiates on the Strange Resemblance that Devotion Bears to Envy   85

6. Openings   108

7. Cain Beholds His Mother Fall to Earth   130

8. Skirting Sodom   151

9. Cain Loses Himself in Pathos   173

10. A Minute Chapter   186

11. Cain Forgets a Birthday   188

12. Yetzer and Yotzer   211

13. Cain Refuses Dominion over the Kingdom of Sin   239

14. Those Lentils . . . That Pottage which Jacob Sod   262

15. Cain Rectifies a Failing in His Brother   295

16. A High-minded Offer   321

17. Cain Accepts the Protection of Y-H-W-H   327

18. Last Words   338

Rabbah b. Bar Hanah said in the name of R. Johanan: One who descants upon the praises of the Holy One (blessed be He) to excess, is uprooted from the world.

The Babylonian Talmud

Then God says to Cain: 'Thou art cursed from the earth which hath opened its mouth to receive thy brother's blood at thy hand . . .' So the unbelieving people of the Jews is cursed from the earth, that is, from the church . . .

Augustine, *Reply to Faustus the Manichaean*

To the life about me, to the people who made up the world I knew, I could not attach my signature. I was as definitely outside their world as a cannibal is outside the bounds of civilized society . . . I should have been a clown . . .

Henry Miller, *Tropic of Capricorn*

1. Cain Remembers a Birthday

The Lord was our shepherd. We did not want. He fed us in green and fat pastures, gave us to drink from deep waters, made us to lie in a good fold. That which was lost, He sought; that which was broken, He bound up; that which was driven away, He brought again into the flock. Excellent, excellent, had we been sheep.

There was no eluding His watchfulness. His solicitude lodged with us, His voice stalked our movements and our thoughts. The walking voice. Wheresoever we went, whatsoever we had a mind to, It followed. No matter the hour, whether in the cool of the day or in the hot, we heard Its step upon our heel, sometimes affecting an idle fitfulness of direction – a voice out for a mere stretch and perambulation – sometimes unable to disguise the predatory intention of Its tread – a prowling, meat-hungry voice; but always we felt Its ancient breath, fiery and sour like an ailing lion's, on our necks.

There was no escaping Him, whatever the occasion. But that day . . . *that* day . . . with lambing going on and the whole of heaven, so it seemed, in a pastoral flutter, He was more than usually in the way. All afternoon His voice paced amongst us, hectoring, fussing, dithering and indecorous –

'Breathe, breathe evenly. In . . . and now . . . out. In . . . and now . . . out. And . . . push. Push! Trust in the Lord thy God, who maketh the hind to calve, to make plentiful thy womb. Breathe and push. Breathe and push. Behold, it opens – thy womb opens!'

1

Until my father, my terrestrial father, could bear It no longer and pleaded with His Great Pervasiveness, His Immanence, to give us respite.

An unwatched hour or so to ourselves? Some consideration for my mother's . . .?

The skin of God was thinner than an idea, His pride easier to pierce than the violet-veined eyelids of a naked new-born babe. 'Oh yes, I forgot – your *modesty*.' His wounded irony rumbled like thunder, now here, now there, now past, now still to come, then fled like a ragged shadow across the sun, and was gone.

Long after dark, though, we could still hear Him pacing the vaults of heaven, cracking His knuckles, chewing at the strands of His beard, a walking voice, predestinating, prognosticating, wretched for news. The Lord of Hosts, maker of behemoth and leviathan, already a doting grandpapa.

It was to have been, for my distraction, a naming day. A lesser christening.

The day after the day after the day after tomorrow, my father with a small *f* had promised, we will go and give names to the birds that swim underwater.

Fish, I said.

Not knowing what amused small boys – for I was the first small boy ever: the pattern, the progenitor of all small boys to come – he took two pebbles from the ground, blew on them (for everything still smouldered from the energy of creation), made them vanish behind his back and appear again in the sockets of his eyes, then shaped a perfect popping circle with his mouth.

Porpoise, I said, watching him pop and goggle, goby . . . gudgeon . . . turbot . . . ro-ro-roach . . . flounder . . . sockle – no, cockle.

He clapped his hands at every fresh invention; blew his

cheeks and bulged the pebbles that were his eyes, marvelling that he in whom language lay coagulate, like the sediment in wine, could have fathered me who flowed as though I were a spring struck from rock. I was his name-boy, his nomenclator, his onomatologist, his word-child. Without me he would never have got around to distinguishing himself from a berry. He would not have laid verbal claim to a single stick or stone, would not have spoken himself apart from his own snuffling pigs. Nature would simply have closed about him. And he would not have had the words to notice.

You are so passive, my mother charged him . . .

You are so existentially compliant, I agreed . . .

You might as well be a jar, my mother said . . .

Or an amphora, I added, or a pitcher or an ewer or a gallipot or – there was no end to my extravagance – or a jeroboam.

His quiescence bubbled like bdellium in the sun. Laughter oozed from him and ran sizzling down his chest. Things and things may break my bones, he sang, names will never harm me. Call me what you like. A jar is good. A jerowhateveritis is even better. That's exactly what I am – an empty earthen vessel, an Adam-amphora, a hollow-pot-man modelled out of clay.

And he would point skywards, celestial shepherdwards, with clumsy mischief, stabbing his accusing finger into his placating palm, so that the divine husbandman and potter who was always watching, insatiably lonely, illimitably lovelorn, should both see and not see.

My father lived in his hands. He could not speak the little that he spoke without them. He knew no method of concealing his guilt or protesting his innocence other than by clenching his fists or holding out his palms. Look: empty! Behold: I am a good man! He became a conjuror and juggler in an attempt to deepen his moral life. He practised legerdemain so that he might complicate his character. Lacking certainty that he could call any of his thoughts his own, he had at last to secrete small tokens of independence and self-esteem about his person. A dried pea hidden in the folds of skin between his thumb and forefinger enabled him to hold his head high.

As for not minding his origins in dust and water – God's *golem* – that was just bravado. The thought that he had been assembled out of paste, on a whim, tormented him. Every night he dreamed and howled, the bristles of his beard starting from his chin as though he were more porcupine than man, his sleep distempered by the termination of his memory in mud.

Not having named emotions he was sensible of no more than he could close a hand around, and a slave to those equally. With the first light his terrors vanished – he was whole again, entire, in possession of a present so blazing it required no explanation in a past; then, either his laughter ran like resin, or his wrath overflowed like lava. I have spoken, he raged, pointing the same finger he employed for mirth. The phrase was filched unashamedly from the All Powerful One. It signified impatience at the highest level; a long rope finally running out. And promised to bring darkness down on all rebellion. Except that whereas He – HE – could punctuate it with spectacular finality, turning on the wind and showing us through a livid tunnel in the clouds His long receding back, my father lacked the machinery of conclusiveness. He could imitate the umbrage, but he had nowhere to disappear to. His rope stretched out for ever. I have spoken, he boomed, and then had to sit the silence out beneath a tree, his jaw set, his fists locked.

Look: closed! Behold: an angry man!

When the day after the day after the day after tomorrow came around and still the fish swam anonymous, I let the top off the volcano of *my* rage. I thought you had given me your word. I thought we had named an arrangement. I thought *you had spoken.*

And into the new, impressionable, still incubating earth, I stamped my foot.

Creation had not been completed in six years let alone six days. I am not saying that He whose reach is beyond measure had overreached Himself; only that the very concept of completion was erroneous. Germination had grown a scaly mind of its own. Breeding bred itself. Worts, pulses, fungi, fantastically fronded euphorbia that were part of No One's grand design sprouted overnight on the instigation of a mere half-finger of spilt fluid. Where we stood motionless for more than a minute, vainly fancying that immobility might save us from His prying, novel vegetation came up between our toes. Bugs, beetles, horned and carapaced monstrosities inconceivable even to *that* Imagination, willed and bestirred themselves into being if we as much as breathed on sand. Merely to walk carelessly was to commit murder; to stamp one's foot was to wipe out whole, untried species. But worse, it was to send an echo down we did not know how far below, and thereby waken to the idea of existence heaven itself could not guess what miscreations.

And I stamped hard enough to invent basilisks.

Fine . . . very good . . . right, my father said.

I braced myself against the coming violence. *Fine . . . very good . . . right.* Scornful though I was of mean words sent on grand errands, I knew the menace that lurked, pretending to be reasonable, in these. *Fine, very, good* and *right.* I had heard them often enough, and in that order, from God's lips too, always charged with a sense of aggrieved honour, of rejected munificence, and always as a prelude to that most diabolic of all punishments – accession to a request, provision of the thing sought, in double, treble, tenfold measure. Should the sun dry up every spring and river and we complain too forcibly of thirst, He would drop a deluge on us that lasted twenty days and twenty nights. If we shivered too demonstrably beneath the naked stars He would make the moon itself scorch us with its light. Once, after the first armadillo had rattled itself upright, horrified by its birth in dung, and sent our hens and plovers scurrying in shock into a desert which the day before had been a bog and the day before that a glassy lake, we raised a query, evinced a curiosity so moderate as to be almost hypothetical – a matter of concern only to some imaginary other family in some imaginary future time. About eggs . . .? We did not mention that my father practised illusions with them; we kept the grounds of our concern nutritional, not conjurational. But at the same time we were careful not to *sound* hungry. About eggs . . .? We could only have said less on the subject had we said nothing. Yet the vehemence of His retort was such that not all our experience of persecution at the hands of His great givingness could have prepared us for it. A sudden change in the direction of the wind, an agitation like a cough in the foliage, warned of the imminence of the walking voice. We threw ourselves to the ground and covered our heads, hoping that It might walk over us without doing injury. But Its tread was heavy and brutal. 'Ye have wept in the ears of the Lord,' It rampaged, 'saying, Who shall give us eggs that we may eat thereof? Your cries have been as the famished, even though the trees are bent double with fruit, and the air is noisy with birds. The lamb skips in the field, and the ox turns his slow head to thee. But thou criest for the shell of an egg. Fine . . . very good . . . right. Therefore shall I give eggs unto thee, and thou shalt eat, not one egg, not two eggs, neither twenty eggs nor an hundred shalt thou eat. But even an hundred times an hundred shall I give unto thee, until they come out at thy nostrils, and thou spittest them from thy face, and they are an abomination unto thee. Now shalt thou see whether or not my word shall come to pass.'

And when at last we dared to uncover our heads, we saw that the earth around us had become an entire roost, a nest stretching to infinity, smelling of sweet straw and droppings and leaking yolk. And when we listened we heard that there was not a sound under the heavens but that of laying.

That would teach us to impugn the bounty of the One True And All Providing God.

And now my father with a little *f* would teach me to impugn *him*.

Fine. Very good. Right.

I saw the magician's hand raised. And I saw that it was closed. But in my fear of it I swung my head away and bent my neck, when all along it was my neck, the back of me and not the front of me, that the hand was after. It must have been the thumb that found me first, for the pain seemed to come from one blunt and persistent point of pressure. Then the other fingers joined in, and my whole head began to throb, and when I struggled I discovered I was without footing, held like a rabbit by someone with murder in his heart.

You can tell when you are the pretext for your father's rage, and not its true object. You sense something stoppered, some bitter failure to find satisfaction, in the violence. A piteous sensation of disappointment, that is not *your* disappointment, runs through you, keener than any merely fleshly anguish. But the realization that you are both victims only increases your shame: there is now his ignominy to suffer as well as your own.

So I was doubly disgraced when he carried me, kicking and sorrowful, to the place I had cried to go to; and, because my desire to name the fish merited, by God-like logic, that I should join them, he pushed me face down into the water.

I flooded. Not only my mouth but all those other parts that God loved to abuse and shame us with when He disowned our making – my eyes, my ears, my nostrils – filled and forgot their functions. Confused their functions, rather; for I seemed to see the smell of my own fear, tasted the sound of it as it swam towards me, dazzling in colour, finned, breathing beads of air as unblinking as blindness, that burst with the salt

7

odour of uncreation around my drowning head. I had no ears to hear with, but my father's words roared like pain through the ruffles of swimming skin by which he held me.

You want to play with fish? Fine. Very good. Right. Here are fish . . . let's see you play with them. You want to know one from another? Go on, then, go on . . . meet them. Introduce yourself. Say, hello Flounder. Hello Gobot, this is Turbey. Go on . . . go on . . . let's hear you!

I came up fighting. Sodden, yes. Fearful, certainly. And with a self-esteem every bit as impaired as my father's. How could it be otherwise? You cannot be granted as a chastisement what you ask for as a kindness, what you understand to be legitimately owing, and still respect yourself. Because his desires were every day a botheration to the Almighty, my father passed on to me – from first father to first son – the burden of unentitlement. So when I say that I came up fighting, I mean with the weapons of the undeserving: sarcasm, irony, contempt. Who but the already defeated looks for consolation in derision?

You bully me, I cried, because I am the one thing crawling on this earth that you are not afraid of.

(Water was still pouring out of me. It's possible that I spluttered more words than I spoke. But my dishevelment was a help to me. It seemed to prove my point.)

The minute the sky rumbles, I went on, you bow your head.

Your heart fails you whenever a leaf falls.

You leap like a grasshopper from every unfamiliar sound – and because you have no memory every sound *is* unfamiliar to you.

You whimper in the night.

You are amazed by the morning.

You are amazed by me too, but because you suspect that in the making of me you might at least have lent a hand you feel you may unmake me when it suits you. I alone am subject to you. And you will damage my spirit for no other reason than that they have damaged yours.

They?

He knew who – he knew *what* – I meant by they.

Them.

Those two.

Their harmony. Their understanding. Their honey-sweet compliance.

Had I aimed a stone at my father's heart I could not have dealt him a crueller blow. We did not mention it, this collusion between my mother and the God who had created her as an afterthought, on a passing fancy, to be a help meet to my father, seeing as he looked lost and lonely. We did not mention that the help meet was no help; that God's afterthought had become His first thought. We looked the other way when He came courting on a thunderbolt, older than time but shining like a lover. Invisible but omnipresent. Athrob.

Athrob – it was my private name for Him. The stress falling on the first syllable, the A as in Ache. Or Babel. *Athrob*. Still, when I come upon the word, I think of mouldering majesty and unseemly passion.

What we did not mention, though, became more evident with every day that passed: woman had grown to be of greater interest to her Maker than man. She who had scarcely figured in the original scheme now occupied the forefront of His attention. She was the gateway to sin, the reason why of law, the coloration of the concept of a fall. He – HE – had only to look at her to see cause for another thousand legislative niceties and prohibitions. A smile from my mother had Him ransacking the storehouses of His moral system. A single bead of sweat upon her downy arm threw His metaphysic into a fever of activity. He could not take His mind off her. And in her belly stirred the future.

Was not the future, you may ask, already on the earth in me? No. I was the past, the punishment and the forfeit for that sin which He That Is Without Sin had hatched out of His consuming jealousy. Fantastical fictions boiled in His brain. Stories of treachery, envy, malice, spite. A whole bubbling mythology of celestial insurrection and perfidy and disguise, all to posit the idea of a grand and *almost* worthy adversary, without whom, as an explanation of my mother's indiscretion, the Lord God Almighty would have been thrown back on the shaming proposition – shaming to *Him* – that she freely chose cohabitation with that inert lump of dough, originally intended as a companion for things bestial and creeping – my father.

At my birth there had been only lamentation.

Hence the stone I aimed at my proper father's heart.

Not another word, he warned me. Not so much as a letter.

He showed me his hands. Closed. Name one more un-namable relation, his hands said, name one more unnamable mother or one more unnamable God, and you will never name anything again.

I submitted – another link in the great chain of submission – lowering my dripping head, bowing my bruised neck, and allowing him to lead me, though I might with as much reason have led him, to where my mother laboured. Or rather, to the environs of where my mother laboured. Not too close. I was on rations as to proximity. His idea. Not his, His. I was to be kept at a distance, out of sight and out of touch, so that I should not breathe contamination on the future. The expedition to find and name the fish had been conceived on high, precisely in order that I should be removed from the scene at the very hour that my mother's swollen stomach was expected to reveal its contents. And, of course, in order that my father should be removed likewise. Very neat. Very tidy. Two tiddlers in one net. Leaving the field free for Him to run errands, boil water, mop brows, hold hands. Bend that mighty back in the exquisite degradation of service. Savour the most corrupt of all inverted rituals – worshipping one's own handiwork. And be the first to see that bloody little head appear. Except that, in the event, my father could not keep *his* distance or *his* nerve; and would rather have drowned me than miss out on his wife's wailing.

Wasn't that what we all wanted, from the first boy to the Only God – to be there when the woman howled?

You will not say anything and you will not go anywhere, my father told me. You will wait here until I come for you. I have spoken.

The rope of patience was running out. Listen to it. *I have spoken.*

The spot he chose for my confinement was sandy, rocky, barren, enjoying the shade of one solitary gasping tree that had not been there a fortnight earlier. Already it was dying – its light stolen by epiphytes, its heart gnawed at by termites. Even here, where there was nothing to envy, enviousness was at its labours.

I was just close enough to hear my mother at hers. Far enough not to see or spoil. A pretty torment they had devised for me. And still my father wasn't satisfied. Sit, he said. And when I sat he bore down on me, his full weight pressing on my shoulders, as though he meant to plant me in the ground.

If I grow here the termites will get to work on my heart, I said.

He looked at me, trying to read my thoughts, then saw something in my eyes for which he had no name but which he must have felt he could not trust. I will have to tie you, he said.

I stopped myself from saying, the word is tether. But once the loop had gone around my neck I did say, first a rabbit, now a goat.

He raised his hand, but this time it was only to run his fingers through his own hair. He had, after all, a christening to attend. It'll get worse than that, he said. Next time it will be man.

I watched him go, his strong squat body uncertain of its purpose; his back, built for resolution, for taking the stress of voluptuousness and conscience, slack with inutility. By his sides his fists, the twin spheres of his moral life, hung like empty sleeves, neither closed nor open.

I cursed him for the pity he cost me. Then, because I knew – although there was no standard for these things, no precedents yet, no jurisprudence of the family – that it could not be good for a son to curse *or* pity his father, I fell to pitying myself and cursing the disheartened tree to which I'd been secured. Hardwood, ironwood, wallow – no, more will . . . willow, *weeping* willow, box, bay, pine, Judas.

Judas.

My mother had usurped the day. All naming rights belonged to her. Except that the category was no longer fish but pain.

I sat, truly at the end of my tether, a small bundle of chafing reproaches, listening scornfully to her limited vocabulary. Oh! Aah! Oufff! Oufff! Aah! Oh! Not only were the sounds insufficiently distinct from one another to contribute to any useful lexicon of agony, they were also not to be distinguished, in accent, in cadence, in sequence, in predictability, from those I had learnt to associate with another category altogether – ecstasy.

Oh! Aah! Oufff! Oufff! Aah! Oh! Many a stewed and sweat-soaked night, under a bilious yellow moon, I had counted her breathings, exhilarated by my exclusion, but transported still more by the knowledge I possessed like marrow in my bones, that somewhere on the other side of that stricken moon, shaken by an extraneity immeasurably greater than my own,

the Lord God Almighty, the volcanic Yahweh Himself, lay
slumped at the pedestal to His single throne, His airless robes
wound and wound again around His all, all-seeing eyes; His
potter's hands pressed vainly flat against His all, all-hearing
ears; a livid, heaving inflammation – the colour of fleshly
covetousness – swelling those lips that had shaped the first
creating Word.

Morality is another name for spite. It was His idea that
every delight my mother had taken in begetting she would pay
for, gasp for gasp, in the sorrow of delivery. In your ends shall
be your beginnings. The mind of a moralist rejoices in the
orderly concept of poetic justice. Without the poetry, where
would be the justice? But making the punishment fit the crime
is only the half of it; whoever would savour to the last drop
the sweets of retribution must understand that the crime already *is* the punishment.

My mother's pain, then, might have seemed to mimic her
former joy; but it was also in the order of things – the only
order conceivable to a Mind obsessively symmetrical – that
her joy should have no other language in which to express
itself but that of pain. She groaned in the bringing forth
because she had groaned in the conception; and she groaned
in the conception in anticipation of the bringing forth. In this
way, from the start, was suffering levied, like a tax payable in
advance, on pleasure.

He – HE would have recanted, for this second delivery, had
He been able. My birth had satisfied the greater part of His
unstable wrath. His jealousy was less vengeful now, more
diluted, more tristful. Even He needed a rest from violent
oscillation. Now a blessing, now a curse. Now a covenant,
now a dispossession. The ordinances of moral rule jangled His
nerves, upset His stomach. He, too, would have liked quiet.
The company of relations. He wanted to hold the baby. The
new baby. But He could not undo His own logic: '*I will greatly
multiply thy sorrow, and thy desire shall be to thy husband;*

thy desire shall be to thy husband, therefore will I greatly multiply thy sorrow.'

And so we each bellowed. Oh! Aah! Oufff! Oufff!

Until finally, a cry weaker and yet more insistent than all the rest silenced us one by one, and alone prevailed.

I strained my hearing. Pulled at the goat-lead, desperate to gain whatever ground I could, for even half a foot's-length might have been enough to give me the one clue I needed to the identity, the sex, the size, the colour and the conformation of what my mother had gasped forth. There is satisfaction to be taken in near-choking, and I took it; luxuriating in a nausea of which I could at least explain the cause.

As the sun set, a suffusion of sugary benign pinks bedaubed the heavens. God's smile. Then a soft humming, like distant wings beating – a sort of crooning of the spheres. God's blessing.

Although, ever since I can remember, I have thrown myself into the arms of sleep more willingly than I have submitted to any alternative embrace, and to this day suffer something close to derangement if I am forced for long to go without her, I did willingly go without her that night, so essential was it to my well-being, or rather to my ill-being, not to miss a single intake of live breath, a solitary endearment, the merest exhalation of a contentment that contained not me. Not for a second did my eyelids droop. I pulled, choked, burned and listened. The night itself held no terrors that could distract me, even though the termites rose against me, and the sand flicked and writhed beneath my knees and elbows, and everywhere in the moon-silvered blackness things blundered up from dew and dirt, so confounded by their function that they devoured their own flesh, consuming themselves out of existence no sooner than they'd entered it.

In the morning my father came for me. I knew that he too had gone without sleep because not once in the night had I heard the accustomed anguish of his suffocation in the mud of nightmare. He did not exactly look tired – although his eyes were bruised, ringed purple, bearing the rotation marks of his own knuckles – more ... I suppose the only word is *sacred*, washed with wonders. Marvel-fatigued.

He untied me – untethered me – with the exaggerated delicacy he usually reserved for magic. I was eggshell and his hands were swansdown. I was the dried pea and his fingers – watch, everybody! – the cones you had to find me under. To say that he untied me belittles his tenderness and dexterity. He spirited me from that tree.

When he saw the marks around my throat where I had struggled, relishing failure, against my captivity, his cheeks turned the same colour the evening sky had been. Joy and pain identical in sound; now rejoicing and remorse identical in pigmentation. We are unsubtly made. We lack the strings to pluck the tunes we hear. I would have liked my father unambiguously contrite that morning, I would have welcomed a symphony of sorrow from him, but the emotion that rattled the phlegm in his chest could have been any one of the four or five with which he'd made himself familiar. After the delicacy he could as easily have thrust my head under water again.

Come, he said. Perhaps I only imagine that he said, my son.

Since I couldn't have out and out contrition, I would have settled for a long sentence. For some sign from him that he at least understood there were long emotions in our vicinity – his and mine – worth trying to make long sentences about. But he was undoubtedly in elemental spirits, his thoughts under the sway of first and last things, and I accepted that I would have to be satisfied with that.

My mother was waiting for me, squatting in shadow, smiling.

Cain, she called. Perhaps I only imagine that she called, my son.

In the few days I had not been allowed to see her (fear of commotion, fear of contamination, fear of pollution: fear,

fear, fear), I had disconnected her voice from her body. I had
carried the sound of her in my head, could conjure her calling
Cain any time I wanted – I still can conjure it, something
between a lullaby and a reprimand, a caress and a call to arms –
but the actual voice was now not as thrilling to me as the
disembodied one; or rather, for it was still the same voice and
still enveloped me in its remembered warmth, it let me down
by virtue of its location, it failed me in proportion as I could
see it, it wasn't the intimate and dignified and *grand* a thing
that I'd been carrying in my imagination now that it was back
where it originated, in her mouth.

In the few days I had been forbidden her I had forgotten
what she looked like. She was heavier than I remembered,
rounder shouldered, greasier, more lugubriously jowled. I had
forgotten that her arms were decorated with bleached bones
and phosphorescent feathers to please my father, and that she
wore anklets of braided vine, although her ankles were often
swollen, perhaps to please God. I had forgotten how plump
and creased her wrists were, and that she dyed the nails of her
fingers and her toes, and that the sight of a painted nail which
was also broken, at the end of a finger or a toe which wasn't
clean, either roused or upset me unaccountably. I concentrated
on her extremities because now that it was before me I did not
after all want to see what she held to the heart of herself.

Look, she said.

I had forgotten the way her mouth worked. How it always
appeared to contain too much moisture or too little, and how
she was always mopping up or watering it with her tongue.

Look, she said. Your brother.

I must have advanced, or made some sudden movement,
because I recall her shrinking from me and holding out a
creased and grimy palm and saying, not too close. Not yet.
Just look. Isn't he lovely? Isn't he beautiful? Your brother.

At the time I wondered why she was so anxious for my
corroboration. Why did I have to say he was lovely? What did

it matter whether or not I found him beautiful? Did she lack confidence in her own judgement? Couldn't he be finally and indisputably lovely in her eyes until I agreed he was? Only later did I understand that it wasn't confirmation she was after from me at all, but remission. Concede his loveliness to me, was what she was really saying, so that I may be forgiven forgetting yours. I must away on another expedition of the affections: wave me off, with your blessing.

Well? she said. What do you think?

What did I think? I thought she ought not to have had him at her breasts. Whatever needs the positioning answered to in him, or her, or in my father, or in God, I thought it was graphically discourteous to me. Would not the ground have done? Was there not space beside her or between her painted toes? Was there no dying tree for him to be tethered to? Could not my father have dangled him from the fold that gathered plentifully at his blood-red neck? Had she truly wished me to scrutinize him dispassionately, estimate his loveliness and beauty impartially, attach myself to him early as an admirer, were there not a hundred other less indiscreet tableaux of the family she might have struck?

Impelled by an unerring instinct for divisiveness, our Creator created in us the right of choice, and in the exercise of hers my mother chose to force a breast on Abel with her right hand while with her left she simultaneously beckoned me and held me back, saying, look, look, look, look, look, your brother.

I looked. Through crumpled, half-closed, old man's eyes he looked back. If you are given to fancy you could say we exchanged a salutation, brother to brother, across whatever distance he had still to travel before he could become as young as I was. Then, his curiosity expended, he returned, all mouth, to what all mothers must ensure all mouths desire.

I will kill him, I thought. I will surely have to kill him when the time comes. Or else I must accept what I cannot, that I alone shall have no bearing on his future.

And because my bowels yearned – I could not have said towards whom – and because such a dispersion of sensation, such promiscuity of emotion, was unknown to me and unnamed, I named it love.

* * *

He sits, Cain the wanderer and reciter, the man of crowds and cities, and wipes his face deliberately on the rich, billowing sleeve of his ornate gown. The robe with which God originally clothed his father, to conceal his father's nakedness, to spare his father's shame, is said to be in circulation, the subject of wrangling and controversy among connoisseurs and antiquaries. But this is not it. Cain's costume is costly in the more worldly sense.

He is jewelled, scented and elaborately sandalled. He is known to be particular about where he sets his foot, fearing not just snakes and scorpions but worms, water, soil – the very feel of bare, unreconstituted earth itself. It is said that his medium is marble and his element is artifice and that the exclusion of all stains of nature from his person is his first concern. To this end he carries with him at all times a large square of spotless cambric with which he removes perspiration and emotion from the corners of his eyes and mouth. The billowing sleeve is a purely theatrical device.

He accepts the approbation of his audience without smiling. There are no lines upon his face to suggest where a smile might form. His mouth has a set and waxen look, not sternness suppressing merriment, but an apparent atrophy of the smiling muscles, a stamp of incapacity, an ingrained physical reluctance as incontrovertible as a birthmark.

In the absence of easy, malleable charm, Cain makes a virtue out of intransigence. Notoriously susceptive, the people of Babel find this intriguing, amusing, even enchanting. They attend politely, bolt upright on the mosaicked benches which ring the recital room, sometimes nodding their agreement, as he berates them for their shortcomings as listeners and – since the art he practises is confessional, or at least memoirist – as confidants. He has been in Babel some weeks, but has so far refused to proceed beyond this point in his narrative. 'You are too eager to discover what comes next to deserve to hear it,' he has told them.

They will have expected some sign of reassurance from him after this. A shadow of a smile, if not a smile itself. A memory of mirth. But there will not have been the faintest movement around the mouth. Not a twitch. Nothing that necessitated so much as a dab from the billowing sleeve.

They will have laughed at his words anyway, taking them to be clues to a joke, if not exactly a joke themselves. Lacking a serious theology, and therefore humour, the people of Babel are always on the look-out for a joke.

'You suppose that a story is like a staircase,' Cain has told them, 'and that you put your foot on one step for no other reason than that you should gain the next. But where is it that you are going? What is *up* there which you are in such a hurry to attain? Is it the wisdom that comes with eminence? Is it the beauty of a panoramic view? Or is it, as I suspect, the simple consolation of knowing that what has a beginning has an end? Mere outcome. Yet how can my words leave you in any suspense as to outcome? Behold: I *am* the outcome.'

They behold him. He *is* the outcome, their looks concur, whether or not they know what to make of such obvious information.

They smile, seeing as they are not to appear suspenseful.

'A story is not a staircase,' he tells them. 'Or if it is, it is a rotten one, with treads missing, and no handrail. And the object of all your climbing – if climb you really must – may after all remain the lowly step you began from.'

A joke? They smile, seeing as they are not to laugh.

He would laugh himself, were he capable of laughter, to

19

hear the word story so often on his lips. I am as crass and false and obvious as the rest of them, he thinks. I am as conceited and banal as they are.

By 'the rest of them' he means those other story-tellers with whom the city teems. In Babel everyone is either a story-teller or a story-listener.

Ever since the small-business deities of Babel, who had managed their temples like bazaars, complained of trade, abandoning the soaring city to its public servants and civil functionaries, its curators and impresarios, the people have abandoned themselves to a love of fancy, a childish play of the suppositional faculties, an orgy of wondering and marvelling which can be satisfied only by the continuous importation of alien jugglers and acrobats and impressionists and haruspicators and monologuists-in-metre. All over town little brown men from beyond the Indus sit cross-legged on the steps of vacated ziggurats, whistling out fairy-tales which uncoil like snakes from writhing baskets, for the diversion of a population that has never cared for fairies. In the parks of palaces, in museum gardens, albino poetesses with streaming hair shrink from the light and hymn creation praises to the sun. Mythologizing is afoot in every rationally laid-out square. An elfin grandiloquence pipes upon the precisely engineered canals. In short, the entire plain of Shinar is jabbering, and Cain is jabbering with it.

But at least tonight he believes he has frustrated the little bit of Babel it falls to him to entertain. He may not have expelled gross expectation from his audience, but he has driven it to the dunce's corner of the room. This means that those who wish to go on listening to him can look forward, inexpectantly, to a further instalment of his narrative – always provided that curiosity and caprice have not, in the mean time, crept back to light their countenances like children's.

2. VOICES ON A BABEL NIGHT

I

East of Eden, journeying without the prospect of change from one ant-hill village to another, he had heard tell of the crystalline cities of Shinar – Ur, Larsa, Erech, Babel, where theatres had been quarried from white mountains, and gleaming limestone ziggurats rose in never ending tiers until they grazed the sky.

The men of Nod were as clay-caked as their habitations; they moved upon the earth ruminatively, indistinguishable from it, with their heads lowered, smelling of their own animals, the straw they slept on, and the silt of rivers. But in the cities of Shinar, a blue-eyed, high-shouldered citizenry walked upright on paved streets and flung ladders to the clouds. Larsa was walled and colonnaded; Erech was so devised that every passage you made across it was a scented promenade through groves of orange trees; Ur had cisterns from which iced water was piped invisibly to your dwelling; and Babel, cut in alabaster, its towers covered with gold and silver, the jambs and lintels of its gates inlaid with worked ivory, its meanest walls set with multicoloured cones like the hats of sorcerers, sent up a commotion, night and day, that was at once the roar of its populace and the exhalation of its self-esteem. In Babel, where you could wear your finery at any hour, without fear of slush or mire flying off the wheels of hand-carts or seeping up through broken flagstones, crowds dressed as though for temple worship gathered around splashless fountains to be amazed by tumblers and troubadors, by balladiers and minstrels, clowns, contortionists, gleemen, joculators, caricaturists, interpreters of archives – any foreigner, in fact, who was willing to please them with a demonstration of such genius as was not native to the city: levity, hyperbole, dissimulation, retrospection.

To the ears of vagabond-romancers such as Cain, stranded in the fuming marshes of Nod, the far-off pavements of Babel rang like music in a nearby room. No two earth-clogged itinerants could talk for long without the topless towers arising between them, even though for some the rumours were altogether too seductive to bear.

No, they said, shaking their heads with a bitterness that belied their certainty. No. No. Those platforms that defied the longest vision, disappeared into the mists of heaven and wore out men's hearts with climbing? They would believe them when they saw them.

The alabaster mountain, whiter than a woman's breasts? Just a grey crumbling chalk cliff in their surmise.

The gold and silver? A trick of gilding.

The multicoloured cones? Botched stone-masonry.

The diversion-thirsty crowds, doling out appreciation and applause as a rich man tosses crumbs? Just the usual street urchins with pebbles in their pockets.

But the possibility that they were wrong, that those who loaded up their asses and headed for the enamelled peaks would find every report confirmed, perhaps surpassed, by actuality, preyed on the minds of the most vehemently sceptical and made Babel blaze even more fantastically in their imaginations than it did for the rumour-mongers and their dupes.

Cain was not proof against the day-dream of performing in shaded squares that never emptied, but his motives for bending all his thoughts on Babel were as much to do with topography as vanity. If he went to sleep with applause breaking like the tide around his head – the secular sound of spiritual adoration, the body expressing the soul's approval – it was to specific images of a place that he woke hungry: the rearing towers, the tiled courts, the streets that never oozed, the barbers' shops, the jewellers, the tailors, the decorated surfaces, the baked imperviousness of the houses, the baths from which you emerged drier than when you'd gone in, and with a skin so soft a breeze would bruise it. To feel hard surfaces beneath his feet, to be free from the demeaning suck and pull of mud, to have his clay mortality barbered off him each morning, to escape the God of leaking creation – were these not powerful inducements in themselves, without entering into professional speculations, for him to turn his back on the bog-men of Nod?

As for whatever other advantages might accrue in Shinar – well, he would leave those to brute chance, if he should be so lucky as to find so Godless a thing, and the passage of pure pagan time.

II

'So, our Edenite friend deems us to be worthy, at last, of hearing the next chapter of his misadventures,' muses – *amuses* – Naaman, the city's most senior official in matters relating to civic buildings and their uses as places of public entertainment and religion. The latter being, in spirit if not in letter, defunct in Babel, Naaman's principal responsibilities are for the issuing or revoking of licences to street performers, the transference of this or that monodrama to this or that theatre, the allocation of tickets to citizens of degree and influence. It falls to Naaman, in other words, to make or to break reputations.

Which might be why there is frequently an expression of merriment on his face – womanly merriment, it should be said; the merriment of languid mothers – and why, as he sits and takes sherbet in the dying sun, he extends his long legs and throws back his head, confident that no attack will be made on his exposed throat.

'It could be,' replies Asmar, 'that he is tiring of our company already and is planning to take leave of us.'

Asmar is Babel's most treasured potter and ceramist, the recipient of a Life Fellowship which entitles him, among other civic benefits, to the best of seats at whatever theatrical representation, recital or dog fight happens to be taking place within the city boundaries at a time when he is not occupied at his wheel. As a rule, Asmar's pots are bigger than Asmar, but for all that he is daintily formed and squeaks like a field-mouse, he too is stretched out in the manner of a sultan on a bamboo elbow-chair, and seems to fear the intrusion of no man's gaze or inquisition.

The custom of discussing absent parties in public places is well advanced in Babel, and is understood to be a concomitant of that broad curiosity which makes the city a haven for wandering actors and musicians.

'I don't th . . . ink so,' Naaman muses lazily. 'I suspect that the instruction he has so kindly given us in the art of listening is not the only business he means to have with us. I have heard it whispered that he may be looking for labourers.'

'To instruct?'

'To labour. And handicraftsmen as well – sculptors, silver-smiths, wood-turners, mosaicists, potters . . . But don't look so alarmed. If he has not approached you, that can only be because he has so far approached nobody.'

Naaman has a mouth which is as soft and perfect as a baby's, but he plumps it wickedly in anticipation of sherbet and Asmar's discomfort. It is well known that Asmar cannot hear of a commission being offered, even for work that does not fall within his scope, without wondering why it has not been offered to him.

'I assure you –' The potter's little voice rises to a squeak, but he is spared having to protest further by the arrival of his tormentor's daughter, Zilpah, a girl paler and narrower than an ear of corn, who wears her hair in a single pigtail, plaited exquisitely, but is otherwise ostentatiously unornamented.

'We are discussing the Edenite,' says her father. 'I believe you know the one?'

She nods, sending a perceptible thrill down the pendicle into which her hair has been woven. 'I have even heard him.'

'What woman has *not* heard him!' observes Asmar.

'We are speaking,' Naaman continues, 'of his rumoured ambition to lure away our artisans for the purposes of building a rival city.'

'Rumours!' retorts his daughter, with a contemptuous survey of the over-peopled square. She is sitting cross-legged in her chair, her toes tucked under her. Bedouin women sit like this, on carpets of shifting sand far from Babel. It is their distant simplicities that Zilpah is pictorially quoting. 'This city is nothing but rumours,' she goes on. 'Especially where the Edenite is concerned. According to rumour he conceals a sulphurous tail beneath his gown. According to rumour he has horns that sprout whenever the moon is crescent. According to rumour a monstrous fiery letter has been burnt into his flesh by a god he's wronged, which smokes him awake the moment he lies down to sleep.'

Naaman smiles at Asmar. 'Now you know why he hasn't approached you,' he says. 'The fellow is queasy around kilns.'

In his amusement he throws back his head again, showing a throat that is arched like a scimitar.

Asmar wipes imaginary clay from between his fingers. 'All I've heard,' he says, 'is some nonsense about his wanting to live higher than any other man. At the top of a temple or somewhere.'

'Then he's come to the right place,' says Zilpah.

'Y . . . es,' Naaman agrees. 'But why does he want it? To enjoy a superior view of us, do you suppose?'

'I'll tell you my theory,' Asmar offers. 'He is looking for a burial plot for himself. He has a mind to lie somewhere conspicuous, and since he has riches – you only have to look at how he dresses – it's my belief he will purchase a mountain as soon as he finds the right one.'

'And how will he know when he has found it?' laughs Naaman, allowing a bubble of mirth to form where his wet lips are fractionally parted.

'By its height. Can you see him consenting to lie lower than another man?'

Zilpah wonders that Asmar can be so sure of Cain's vanity on so brief an acquaintance.

'Vanity! I'd be surprised if this country has a mountain high enough to satisfy him. He'll have to build his own on top of one of ours.'

'So that he can be close to the god who branded him?' Naaman wonders.

'So that he can be as far as possible from you two,' Zilpah says.

The sun having gone down behind a temple, Naaman straightens up in his chair and shakes his shoulders. 'Whatever the truth of the matter,' he reflects, 'the man is without question restless. I don't need to be told that repose is the last quality one should look for in those who choose to earn a living baring their souls to strangers. But I maintain that our Edenite is distracted over and above what is usual even in his profession. Have you seen him eat?'

'Have I *heard* him, do you mean!' snorts Asmar. A simple golden ring hangs from the potter's ear. In appreciation of its owner's jest it swings a little and would sparkle in the sun, were there any sun left for it to catch.

'I do not think it should be held against a foreigner that he is not accustomed to our diet,' says Zilpah. In moments of absent-mindedness she reaches for her plait, pulls it over her right shoulder, and smoothes it. In moments of distress she does the same, except that instead of stroking her hair, she plucks at it.

This evening she does both.

Her father watches her with care.

'I have heard him say,' she continues, 'that until he came to Babel he had never fed on creeping things that creep upon the earth.'

'What, never on weasel or on mouse?' marvels Asmar. 'Never on tortoise or on ferret? Never on chameleon?'

'No, nor on lizard. Nor on snail. Nor mole. And what is more,' she goes on, 'he has never dined on stork either. Nor on heron. Nor on lapwing. And never once, not even as a side-dish, has he tasted bat.'

'You misunderstand me,' says her father. 'When I speak of the perturbation of his temper around food I am not referring to his inexpertness. This can be forgiven on the very grounds you cite. But have you not noticed how he rises from the bench in extreme urgency, on the pretext of some forgotten errand or sudden indisposition, in pursuit of mustard, pepper, bread, more wine, or in order to procure a sharper knife or shorter fork, or so that he may relieve himself – not as you and I might, in advance of the meal's appearance, in that quiet hour given over to preparation and expectancy, but at the very moment, and *only* at the very moment, that his dish is put before him? Precisely as everybody else's head goes down, his snaps up.'

'Might it not be,' suggests Zilpah, 'that he mistrusts communality?'

'Or that his appetite is so stimulated,' Asmar ventures, 'that he wishes to prolong his ecstasy? Think of it, a man who has never before tasted chameleon –'

'No,' says Naaman, 'I have observed him too long to be

satisfied with either explanation. It is not other people he fears. Any more than it is the too quick conclusion of a gratification he wishes to go on indefinitely. I believe it is anti-climax itself he dreads. So intimate must be his acquaintance with disillusion, so complete his foreknowledge of the disappointment which waits on all pleasures of the flesh and palate, it is my view that he would rather never expect at all, than expect and be sorry.'

'You mean he would forestall even anticipation?' Zilpah wonders.

'I'd say your father means that the breast was snatched from the poor devil too early,' puts in the potter, who shapes a hundred unyielding breasts upon his wheel each day.

'More likely that the milk when offered – I'm not entirely sure this is a conversation you ought to be included in, my dear – did not flow as freely as it should have,' says Naaman, staring in stylized embarrassment into the dregs of his sherbet. 'For it certainly appears to be the immediate prospect of delivery, the instant of effusion itself, that precipitates his distress.'

'Then let us hope,' says Asmar, 'that the demons of disappointment are not curdling *his* milk even as we speak.'

'He will be the first man to have eluded them, if they are not,' says Naaman. Then, observing the look of puzzlement on his daughter's face, he explains, 'We have extended a traditional Shinarite welcome to our guest this evening. He has always refused all offers of gentle company in the past, but we felt we could tickle him into a little soothing tonight. Eh, Asmar?'

'As you say, Naaman,' answers the potter, with a brief tug at the ring which dangles from his ear. 'As you say, the demons are doing their worst by him at this very moment.'

Thinking about demons, Zilpah feels her breasts rise.

Thinking about chameleons and bats, Zilpah feels the pulpy lips she has inherited from her father fill with blood.

Thinking about effusion and the unsmiling teller of a single tale who would forestall even anticipation, Zilpah believes she can feel her milk begin to surge.

All the while, Naaman watches her with care.

III

And all the while, the satiric poet Preplen watches Naaman.

He too, although it is not good for him to be drinking anything but water, is taking a light evening refreshment. He is sitting close to Naaman's party and is listening to every word that has been said. This isn't the reason that there is a twist in his spine and that he hunches over himself so that he is at all times in his own shadow. A lifelong habit of sleeping with too many pillows under him is to be blamed for the first condition; suspiciousness of soul for the second. But it hasn't helped to straighten him or lighten him to have heard what he has heard.

As a foreigner himself he is sensitive to local sarcasm and gossip. As a foreigner, what is more, from the same neck of the woods as Cain – born west of Nod with a whiff of forbidden Eden in his nostrils – he is more than usually on the watch for that form of high Shinarite disdain which goes by the name (the name *he* has given it) of anti-Edenitism. And as a performer in his own right he is insulted that Naaman hasn't recognized him, or estimates him so lowly that he does not see any necessity to practise discretion in his presence.

This third objection is not unconnected to the second: it being proof-positive of what Preplen means by anti-Edenitism that those who exhibit it do so without discretion. But then all of Preplen's objections – and in the course of a single day he broods over and raises many – are blood-related. Here is another reason why his spine is swivelled and each part of him casts a shadow over every other.

The moment Naaman's group leaves, Preplen cranks his neck back so that he can look up, makes certain there are no birds in the sky to unsettle him – for the poet is uneasy in the company of anything that can attack him from above – and begins to move his lips. His voice normally is guttural and confidential, like gargling. But on this occasion, perhaps because he does not want to lessen the virulence of his male-diction, he emits no sound. Or at least no more sound than a person gifted with preternatural hearing would need in order to understand him. 'Cursed shalt thou be in the city,' he appears to be mouthing, 'and cursed shalt thou be in the field. Cursed shall be thy basket and thy store. Cursed shall be the fruit of thy body, and the fruit of thy land. Cursed be the man that trusteth in man. Cursed be the man that trusteth in woman. Cursed shalt thou be when thou comest in, and cursed shalt thou be when thou goest out. Cursed . . .'

But whether the object of his curse is Naaman, some other citizen of Babel, or himself; whether his words are a promise of suffering to come or a reiteration of deprivation already undergone; and by what means he has succeeded in extinguishing all light both to and from his person – not even Sisobk the Scryer, who has been watching Preplen watching Naaman, and who, as chance would have it, just happens to be gifted with preternatural hearing, is able to tell.

In fact, Sisobk the Scryer – who answers, when he answers at all, also to the names Imdugud the Insightful, and Enki the Enlightener, and Talmai the Tipster, and Ningursu the Nobody, according to how he feels about himself – has not been watching what he seems to have been watching. His attention, in so far as he can be said to possess anything so steadfast, is taken up with what is present only in the hereafter, using that word strictly in its secular sense. He is not, though, entranced or stupefied. His eyes do not roll. His limbs do not tremble. There is no fowl lying eviscerated on his table. Unlike most professional prognosticators, who are stolid by temperament and look to artificial stimulants to prick their powers of foreboding into action, Sisobk the Scryer is suggestible stone-cold sober. A single feather, dropped by the smallest of those birds from which the poet Preplen flinches, is enough to send his fancy scudding into unborn time. Were he able to nail his imagination to a bench, or bury his mind under a flagstone in the here and now, Sisobk thinks he would willingly sacrifice all he knows of the forever. But his senses are as slippery as fish. Sounds wriggle from his hearing. Smells side-step him like mud-crabs. Thought squirts through the fingers of his reasoning the moment he tries to clamp his mind around it. And nothing will stay still once it has occurred to him.

This includes Cain, whose unheralded arrival Sisobk had of course been expecting, but whose lack of curiosity as to the long-term prospects for his name, his progeny, his reputation – prospects which Sisobk is peculiarly well-positioned to vouch-safe – is surprising, even to a man who has answered, in his time, to the name Urirenptah the Unsurprisable.

Surprising and, it should be said, dispiriting. Dispiriting and, it should be said, insulting.

Darius the Dispirited. Imhotep the Insulted. Shmuel the Slighted.

What it amounts to is this. The prophet has been endeavour-ing for some weeks now to secure the fratricide's friendship, or at least his interest, or failing that, his notice; but so far he has received nothing for his pains but curt rebuffs.

No, Cain is not desirous of learning, thank you, what has become of the children he has not sired yet, nor of their children, nor of their children's children, nor of their children's children's children.

No, Cain is not remotely tempted to hear how he is spoken of by men, waiting in the womb of time, who have so imperiously mastered science that they are capable of destroying a thousand strangers in a single act of faceless aggression, and not merely one frail and unarmed younger brother, nose to nose.

No – absolutely no – Cain is not somewhere in his heart gratified to foreknow that there are sects grown up, rebellious blasphemers and murderers-in-the-mind who take their name from him, calling themselves Cainites and believing him, their patron-saint, to be the seed, not of his father with a little *f* and not of his Father with a big one, but of a still greater and more potent force whose will it was that he should be the inaugurator of killing.

Well, be surprised then, but there it is – Cain is not curious or grateful.

A word about these Cainites.

Long before Byron and Baudelaire adopted Cain as a hero of romantic, anti-bourgeois *méchanceté*, giving him, as it were, a gammy leg and an inclination to opiates, others saw the cultic possibilities in a figure who, it could be argued, was the victim and not the initiator of the first act of violent irrationality between man and God, and who was therefore the murderer not so much of a brother as of a falsehood.

'These Cainites,' according to the heresiologist Iraneus, 'declare that Cain derived his being from the Superior Power' – that is to say from the true God whom the Judaic Jehovah dispossessed – 'together with Esau, Korah and the Sodomites. All such persons they declare as being of their kindred.'

'Woe unto them!' was Jude's timely rebuke, 'for they have gone in the way of Cain, and ran greedily after the error of Balaam for reward, and perished in the gainsaying of Core.'

For Core read Korah. For running greedily read Sodomy. For Cain read Cain.

And for gone in the way of . . . read Cain's reluctance to see his reflection in the eyes of the future. It was never his intention to be an exemplar or a fugleman. He had never meant to show anyone the way. Least of all the way to brother-murder – he who had been the very model of brother-love. Except that it was never his ambition to lead the way in love either.

As for the theory propounded, the theory that *would* be propounded, by the sect that took, that *would* take, his name – to wit, that he had raised his hand only against an impostor-god, that it was the Lie he smote, and not a flesh-and-blood brother at all – he knew better than to let such flattering unction near his heart. Or he *would* have known better had he been aware that such a theory existed. Hence his refusal to attend to Sisobk the Scryer's prognostications: he knew better than to find out.

Sisobk himself, meanwhile, reads and rereads the Cainite bible in scraps that flutter round the feet of cup-bearers and their customers, in vapours that rise from the plumbing concealed beneath the hissing flagstones, in passing faces whose suggestiveness spills light that stings like vinegar on a wound. Whatever moves has words on it. He reads a page in a fraction of a second, an entire gospel in a fraction of a minute. He does not consume their meaning, their meaning consumes him. This Korah, this Esau (he skips the Sodomites, turns a seer's blind eye to them, selectivizes sin) – but this Korah, this Esau . . . what fatherers of murmuring and lawlessness they are, what saints of discontent! It is inconceivable to him that Cain, a fatherer of murmuring and lawlessness himself – no, the fatherer of fatherers, the patron saint of saints – does not care to know of them. Inconceivable and, well . . . quite frankly . . . intolerable. Sisobk the Scryer is growing increasingly moralistic about this. A man, he believes, owes a responsibility to his future, is ethically obliged to confront his consequences.

What does Cain suppose? That a life simply stops? That it is over when you reach your hundredth birthday? When you reach your five-hundredth, your nine-hundredth? When you have been a thousand years in the grave? Sisobk has something to tell Cain – it never stops. Don't strike if you want an everlasting oblivion. Don't raise your hand. Don't hate your brother. Don't love your brother . . .

There is, no doubt, an element of vengefulness here. If Sisobk has to endure what is waiting for the name of Cain, he cannot see why Cain should not endure it too. Share the weight of prescience, since the future is a universal obligation that should not fall only on the shoulders of those who arbitrarily possess the power to perceive it. But this is a small part of what motivates him to wait upon the first son of Adam before and after every public recital, meaning to woo him with soft words – murder, lawlessness, blasphemy, the children of his children's children. Mainly, all Sisobk is looking for is the opportunity to express his admiration, to prefer his offices, to be in some way of use and consolation. Korah and Esau (he skips the Sodomites) he may only read about in vapours. Cain he might actually and in body serve.

If he were to roll up all he wanted in a single sentence, Sisobk the Scryer would say he wanted to hold Cain's hand. The hand Cain smote with? Not necessarily. Sisobk isn't particular. It's the warm vein he wants to feel. Either hand will do.

Sisobk the Sentimental.

IV

The doubters had been right about the colour. The city was not that blinding white which imagination, helped by hearsay, had painted it. On the hardest of summer mornings, after the wettest of summer nights, it was possible to fancy Babel as seething in its own milk; a creamy opalescent mist rose from the roof tops, a pearl haze hung upon the towers, the temples mounted as though on marble feet, like flights of spotless cranes ascending. None the less, the overwhelming impression was of a place more silvery than white, more burnished than translucent. Cain did not object to this. Given that silver seemed to him the colour of artifice, he considered the effect to be, if anything, an improvement on expectation.

As for the people, the many-headed hydra that strode smiling always smiling between the ziggurats, they were as yellow as report painted them. Sometimes, coming upon them in numbers with sleep still in his eyes, he felt their brightness to be a trouble to him. Here was a burnish that put a strain even on his love of false lustres. It wasn't always a joy to him to be pierced by their mineral blue-green eyes, to be irradiated by the gold-filled tusks they showed in laughter always laughter, to be dazzled by the electric frizz of orange hair which many of them left uncovered, no matter how hot the day, as a sort of challenge to the sun.

They were brilliant, they were stellar, they were a moving mosaic of light, but they were not beautiful. Not if beauty was as he understood it, a grandeur of feature, a weight of expression, an extravagance of facial swoops and circumflexions. Their faces were too indistinct to bear any of those primary passions he considered it the first duty of a face to suggest. Why, they barely hinted at any differentiation of sex, let alone of age or temperament or faith or presiding terror.

From the moment he had seen himself mirrored cruelly in stagnant water he had hated the fresh thumbprints of God, the rough stabs and gouges which he shared, a common disfigurement, with his father; but better by far to look as he did – prototypical and jagged – than to have a countenance that was a careless smudge, a discourteous and half-hearted dab administered without attention to contrast or volume, to chiaroscuro or perspective, by an assistant hireling creator, working for no one in particular.

Their faces were without anteriority, that was what it came to, because they were turned to no single divinity who could remind them of the exact hour of their communal birth. There was no past in their eyes. No precursory notation on their brows. Provision had simply not been made for those slopes and planes on which memory – the memory of mud – likes to etch her lines.

Hard as it was for someone whose bones had been actuated by a god – Godhandled – to reach such a conclusion, Cain eventually came to see that the Shinarites had built their own faces. Adam had woken up one morning, prodded at his skin to discover what he was made of, and invented a character for himself on the basis of what he'd found. In Babel the process had been reversed. Here, configuration was a consequence of personality. Here, flesh had modelled itself on spirit. If features in Babel bore no imprint of a past, that was because their owners had no concept of a past. What did they remember? A sequence of scuffles with cereal gods who came and went according to the weather; an occasional scare at the hands of some double-headed keeper of an abyss. But never a moment when they lay bellied in the slime, knowing the time had come when they had to behold the One – the One and Only – and face Him down.

Hence they looked forward and they looked up – their dreamy blue gaze following the direction of temples whose function had been forgotten – but they did not look back. They felt the pull of nostalgia and antiquarianism and spookery, but nostalgia and antiquarianism and spookery are merely the playthings of the forgetful: harmless shells from which all the deadly poisons of the past have been removed. Any further curiosity as to origins was satisfied by the itinerant romancers and mythologists who collected in Babel like eagles smelling blood.

Unless it was they who were the blood, and the Shinarites the eagles.

Either way, each swarmed around the other.

The people of Babel prided themselves on their love of stories. They gathered wherever one was being told, their high shoulders tensed, their hazy mouths hanging open, their usually swimming turquoise eyes fixed as though in a hypnotic trance. Was this not proof of the generosity of their minds, the receptivity of their intelligences, the breadth and scope of their sympathies? There was not another city in the known world that welcomed such a dissonance of voices. Anyone could speak. Anyone could auspicate or historify. And everybody listened. How then could a single native of Babel be charged with awelessness in relation to then, now, or later? Or irreverence towards that which was here, there, or somewhere else?

Cain scratched his head. Close to where his horns ought to have been. He had heard the rumours. He would not have minded sprouting a pair. Their surprise revelation in the midst of his narrative – sharp, twisted, and perhaps a little bloody at the ends – might have shaken the complacency of his audience. For there was the problem. They listened like children; they gulped, they started, they wept, they cheered, they pressed their fists to their cheeks and stuffed their sleeves into their mouths – but they did not believe a word of what they heard. It was all extravagance, exaggeration, a distortion of what was *actually* the case. What was actually the case being what they knew about and saw with their own eyes in Babel.

Of course things happened in distant places and remote times that would not be tolerated in Babel, but the actors must have felt there and then as they in Babel felt here and now. They must have measured their emotions and circumstances by Babel emotions and circumstances, and if they lacked knowledge of the real Babel as a standard, they must

have erected an ideal Babel of the mind. Babel was thus ultimately the centre of every story, the haven to which all exiles
dreamed of returning, the goal of every traveller, the reward
for every virtue, the pattern for every striving, the paradise by
whose loss every sinner calculated his deprivation and every
criminal his fall. Thereafter, there was only trespass on credulity. And if these foreigners gifted with tongues could only
fantasticate and falsify, then what did that show but the merit
of having been born in Babel, and how much more honourable
it was to listen to a story than to tell one.

Cain reaches for his horns once more, and scratches. Knowing what he knows about the Shinarites does not remove their
seduction: the glamour of their city, the white light they enjoy,
their appreciative perturbation when he walks amongst them,
the ardency of their gaze upon him when he addresses them,
their siren-whisper flattering him with the notion that *he* will
be the one to find a way through their complacency at last.

A delicious consciousness of treason against himself ac-
companies him now whenever he speaks in public. Is he harder
on his history than there is any justification for him to be; is
he harder on those who shared it with him; does he express a
greater antagonism to the laws and customs of his country
than in truth he feels, simply in order to keep the unspoken
compact with his Shinarite audiences – namely, that he will
not show excessive loyalty to his past, that he will confirm the
esteem in which they hold their present, provided they . . .

Provided they what?

Agree to love him, he fears.

V

She clinks into his room on spiced feet, bearing balms and
ointments. Her eyes are greyer than is common, and more

serious. Notwithstanding the ringing of her jewellery and the diaphanousness of her dress, she could be taken, such a picture of womanly solicitude does she present, for a nurse.

'I am a present to you,' she says, 'from Naaman.'

He has not as yet tried any of the fabled temple shuris of Babel. The comprehensiveness of their service dismays him because it does not appear to include whatever it is he would seek, were he seeking anything. In the cities of Shinar a shuri is assumed to be capable of discharging the simultaneous duties of daughter, sister, mother, companion, interpreter of dreams, reader of palms and minds and foreheads, laundress, seamstress, manicurist, pedicurist, defiled virgin, chaste harlot, contortionist, singer, dancer, looker, listener, linguist, mute, physician for all ailments of body or of soul. And still there was nothing there for him.

'No, it isn't necessary,' he protests, as, to the accompaniment of a tabret, she begins to imitate the pelican of the wilderness, reviving her young ones with her blood.

He holds up a hand to stop her.

She reads it.

He turns his head.

She reads that.

'No,' he says.

'My name is Silili,' she tells him, kneeling upon his chest in the shape of an egret and anointing his eye-lids with attar of roses. Her lips are fragrant with wild honey which she has collected from locusts. She parts her mouth so that he can collect from her.

'I am not ill,' he says. 'I am not in need of resuscitation.'

'My name is Silili,' she tells him.

She sings to him, a low crooning, a high wailing, enfolding the soles of his feet in her bosom as though they are the doves his father conjured with – sings of cedar forests upon which the rain falls odorous with spikenard and saffron; sings of abundant vales of sycamore watered by the hundred rivers flowing underground through caverns studded with amethysts and rubies and the sacred droppings of ambrosial bats. She dances for him, her arms the necks of swans, the precious bells through which her hair is braided tinkling like distant goats, heard by shepherds on icy mountain nights. She feeds him root of mandrake, ground with ambergris in lotus essence, spooned from a golden bowl. She drips saliva into his navel, agitates the pond with her lashes, blows it into a storm, takes the vegetation that grows around its banks stem by stem between her teeth. She trails her tongue the length of his rigid spine, then down the insides of his thighs, leaving silver tracks upon his skin, so that it looks as though a multitude of snails has glided over him. 'That was the Winter Migration of the Snake,' she hisses. 'And now,' she growls, 'the Ravening of the Lion . . .'

'No,' he says, 'it really is not required of you.'

'My name is Silili,' she tells him.

'It is not what I want, Silili,' he says.

It is as if he has inadvertently pressed a hidden button, or uttered by accident a password. She rises from him, jingling her bells, clanging the copper rings that spin like moons around her wrists and heels, and, pulling back her hair, gives him her ear. He sees, for the first time, that it is artificially enlarged, the lobe distended, weighed down by a hanging ball of lead, the porch to the cavity itself gaping obscenely with the promise of infinite attention, infinite indulgence, infinite receptivity.

There is a moment of silence between them, the first unmusical interlude since she came tinkling into his room. The ear gapes and waits and listens.

'What would you have me do?' he asks.

The ear drinks in his words. Pulsates. Flowers. Advances upon him.

'What would you have me put into your ear?' he asks.

She is distressed that he needs her to tell him. 'Anything,' she says, 'and everything. Your life story. Your laughter. Your terrors. Your seed.'

He thinks about it. 'Why would you want to hear my seed?'

'It is not a matter,' she says, 'of what *I* want.'

Wants. Wants. He looks without interest into the unshapen swirls of skin and membrane. 'What pleasure or comfort can it be to *me*,' he asks, 'to confuse an organ of perception with an organ of generation?'

She turns her rejected ear from him, letting her hair once again conceal it. 'In Babel,' she says, 'there is a saying that there can never be too many openings to a woman's body.'

'I cannot decide,' he replies, 'whether that is an expression of extraordinary refinement of mind or extraordinary literalness.'

She meets his glance, in which there is not the faintest play of mirth, and without warning revolves her eyes so as to make her pupils and irises quite vanish, in their place only the terrible unflickering milky screens of unsightedness. As he does not care for openings, she can just as soon close down every ingress of sensation. 'Behold, I am blind for you,' her action says, except that she would have him know that she can be mute for him too.

He feels giddy, and would take to a couch were he not already stretched out on one. He cannot look into the shocking lactescence of her unseeing stare. It reminds him of how his father, to entertain or frighten him, would put blanched pebbles into the sockets of his eyes; but more, of how his mother turned up her eyes in shy, self-effacing supplication to the All Seeing. Blind, blind, every woman in the hour of her adoration. Blind to reason. Blind to refusal. Blind to herself. As if any man, even the most epicurean in cruelty, could count this annihilation into chalky blankness a gift worth the receiving. For his part, he is unable to conceive of a single satisfaction to be found in the company of women – mothers, nurses, shuri, call them what you like – which does not insist, as a prerequisite to pleasure, on their appalled but unswerving stare. What a woman does not see him suffer keenly, he does not relish keenly. And, could he be certain of sensibility and squeamishness leaving his fingers – as once before, fighting blindness in his brother, he had felt them desert his whole body – he would reach under Sililî's unresisting lids, quivering like moths, and forcibly right her eyeballs.

Instead, imagining blood, he says, 'Look at me.'

She sways, holding on to him with her long, spicy fingers. Entranced.

'Come,' he says, gently. 'Come, Sililî. Look at me.'

She finds her smile first, her Shinarite phosphorescence – ambiguous but not, of course, ironic – then her balance, and last of all, her sight.

'There is nothing I cannot demand of you, then?' he says.

'Nothing.' She is already half-blind again.

'And nothing I cannot demand that you demand of me?'

She takes longer over this. But, 'Nothing,' is what she finally agrees.

'In which case, look at me,' he says. 'You have seen a goat tethered to a stake?'

She nods, hesitantly, trying to remember what she knows. 'I am skilled in the seven positions after the fashion of the ram,' she says. 'Is the goat similar?'

'No, look at me,' he says. He would like her to forget what she is skilled in. 'Look at *me*. You have seen a tethered goat. You have about your waist a sash which will serve well as a tether. I am to be the goat. The bed-post can be the stake.'

She shakes her head, a slow shamed disbelieving movement, causing the little bells in her hair to ring funereally. 'Is there some illness in you?' she asks.

'Didn't they warn you about my horns and tail?'

She shakes another tinkling death-march out of her hair. 'I have felt for your tail with my tongue,' she says reproachfully –

42

for her tongue has not stirred him – 'and I know that you do not have one. But there is illness in you.'

'And do you not cure illness?'

'Not in the way you would have me cure it. I can be an empress for you. I can be a temple priestess or a goddess fashioned according to the theology of your choice. But I cannot be a farm-girl. In Babel, men who wish to enjoy the favours of a farm-girl visit a farm.'

'I do not ask you to be a farm-girl. Only that you assist me to be a farm-animal.'

She leaps from him, retreating until her back is up against the furthest wall. She means to cover any unexpected direction, it seems, from which his words might penetrate her. She puts a hand to her distended ear and compresses her lips until her mouth is narrower than a key-hole. He fancies he can hear all her openings of pleasure – and he is sure he has not come close to discovering how many she possesses – shutting against him, one by one.

'You are not a man,' she says. 'You do not take pride in a man's prowess.'

He sighs. He has not asked for any of this. An hour before, he was alone, with only his thoughts to trouble him.

'Why should pride in one's prowess as a man,' he says, taking care to excise all mockery from his voice, 'exclude a desire, just once in a while, to suffer indignity as a beast? I mean no disrespect to the hospitality your city has shown me, but I do fear that you are slaves, here in Babel, to a most narrow interpretation of sensuality. Find access to a woman's body in as many unexpected places as you like, empiercing – you will forgive me, Silili – is still empiercing. Introduce repetition into delight, and like any chore, it will weary. A city as grand and as various as this one ought to be better able to enjoy itself. But fixation on pleasure is hampering you. If you would permit me to import the altogether more subtle dissatisfactions of unpleasure, I wager you would find . . .'

But Silili does not wait to learn what she would find. With one last carillon of precious bells, and a pitiless jangle of copper moons, she flies from his presence, leaving behind her tabret, her set of golden mixing bowls and spatulas, her little jewel encrusted casket of unguents, balms and washing powders, her rosewood sewing box inlaid with ivory of walrus, her sacred promise never to abandon a male stranger to the excruciations of unappeased cravings, but not, alas, the silken sash with which, by tethering him to a bed-post, she might have helped a man who had raised his hand against his brother find respite from his humanity in the attitude of a stinking, ruminating goat.

Not wanting to betray her personal distress, nor, at this very witching hour, to be seen out of an occupation, Silili glides as soundlessly as is compatible with the instrumentalization of her tailoring across the darkened, sleeping streets. Only Zilpah, brooding in the shadows of rearing temples, observes her leave.

3. Cain Encourages His Father
in a Blasphemy

You will recall that our modest family had grown.

Not counting Our (Supranatural) Father, who is infinite and indivisible and therefore never to be subject to enumeration, we were now four. Three plus one. Two plus me plus him. Her minus me plus them squared. However you do the sum you arrive at the same answer; which proves the inadequacy, to any job not merely mechanical, of mathematics. For we had grown by far more than the small addition we were increased by, and the entire architecture of our commonweal had been shaken and defaced to an extent that made a mockery of the paltry arithmetical difference between three and four.

As if the second fruit she bore had been the sun, my mother narrowed her eyes into two milky slits and became earth mystical, a sow-goddess sprouting udders (paps, teats, dugs – I named them all) sufficient to feed a tribe of Abels.

Divinity, I must allow, had been invoked at my birth too. *I have gotten a man from the Lord*, my mother had sung out, to the consternation of my father and the Lord both.

It turned out to be a masterstroke of diplomacy, reminding the Latter, at a time when He was thinking hard about washing His hands of us, of His complicity in our natures and His instrumentality in our continuance. It flattered His powers and tickled His sense of occasion.

But it was a masterstroke of irony also, taking into account the circumstances of her getting, of her *be*getting, at the instigation, so she'd been led to believe, of Satan who, it was even hinted, was still in there, still in my mother where he'd entered, and would not be dispelled again except by prayers and promises. 'Me? Oh no, you can leave Me out of it; you have gotten a man from the very Devil,' was the reply she dared Him to come back at her with, knowing what havoc that would have played with the politics of the cosmos, and the principle of there being only One (infinite and indivisible) Creator.

There was scant irony now, though, about the awe in which she held her own fertility. She squatted, round-shouldered and double-chinned, wherever she found mud, or mud found her, milk streaming from her, the smell of black earth coming off her skin like gasses from a compost heap, her expression drowsy with the voluptuousness of maternal knowledge, her lips swollen and pendulous, caked with clay, cracked from kissing the sun. The clay only quickened the kissing. The more her infant rolled in it, the hungrier she got for him. It seemed she could not stuff enough of herself into his mouth, nor enough of him into hers. And when the ravening stopped – not from surfeit but from exhaustion – a rapt contemplation took over. For hours without end she would stare at him, stunned upon her breast or howling in his faeces, as though every movement he made was essential to the unravelling of a riddle, as though he were a godling of the chthonic mysteries and she, so long as her devotions never wavered, his high priestess.

If the Only True God saw the beginnings of apostasy in this, He kept His counsel. He could not have been unaware of what advantages flowed His way from it. He took a long view of things. And in the short term, too, the benefits outweighed the unorthodoxy. For while my mother's attentions were consumed by each infinitesimal spasm of my brother's person, she forgot my existence altogether; and so long as her thoughts dwelt on dark sources and germination, on slime and seepage and renewal, there was nothing she could discuss profitably with my father who wanted to be a conjuror. As a votary of loamy secrets there was only certain company she could respectably keep. And He – the Certain Company in question – not needing to be asked so much as twice, not needing, if the truth is told, to be asked so much as once, popped in between a dirt-born husband and his single recompense, between a solitary son and his assuagement. She was not to be available to make it better for either of us. 'Thou shalt not lie with her, nor touch her, nor touch any thing upon which she sitteth.' The All Prohibiting One had spoken. 'No, not even with the tips of thy fingers. For she has conceived seed, and born a man child, and is unclean.'

So much for seed. So much for me who came from seed.

My father wanted to know how long she would be unclean for.

'According to the days of the separation for her impurity.'

And . . . how long would that be?

My father's incautiousness, or absent-mindedness, or inability simply to feign knowledge when he lacked it, always astonished and terrified me. Of all subjects, my mother's impurity was the very one not to have suddenly gone vague about. Were we not forcibly enjoined, just as regularly as the blood issued from her, never to forget those swarming haemophobic stipulations?

Every bed whereon she lieth all the days of her issue shall be unto her as the bed of her separation; and whatsoever she sitteth upon shall be unclean . . . and whosoever toucheth those things shall be unclean, and shall wash his clothes, and bathe himself in water, and purify himself in fire, and boil himself in oil, and graze himself upon rocks that he might rend his flesh and remove therefrom every spherule and atom of uncleanness, and, still finding a speck or droplet, be it no more conspicuous than a mote, shall run howling into the howling wilderness and there deliver himself, as an abomination thrice abominated, unto the jaws of wolves . . .

If my father was still looking for guidance as to specifics – *When you say whatsoever she sitteth upon, O Lord, am I to understand that you truly do mean whatsoever?* – what did that signify except that thus far he had not been obeying God's injunctions to the letter?

I waited for the thunderbolt to strike him, or the whirlwind to carry him away. *How long are the days of her separation? Longer than thou shalt live to see!* But the Voice that finally replied to him was temperate, you could even say jovial. 'She shall be unclean seven days,' It said. 'But unto you' – what fun It had shrinking my poor father into that worthless *you*, what a good time It was giving Itself reducing back to dust what It had once, with a single syllable, enlarged from dust – 'but unto y-you' – It could barely get it out now for amusement – 'but unto you she shall be unclean . . . *twenty*-seven.'

This time, at least, my father knew better than to quibble. But when the twenty-eighth day came round and my mother waved him away with a nod in the direction of the Source Of All Taboos – nothing to do with her, ask Him; her mind, and come to that, her body, was engaged on other things, mud, milch, manure – he sought further clarification.

And was told: 'Unto you she shall be unclean twenty-seven days.'

But had he not already . . .?

'*Another* twenty-seven days.'

Again he accepted the ruling, again he waited, again he appealed, and again he was put off a month. This procedure was repeated, four, five, six times, until my father, afraid of spending the second half of one year as uncomforted as he had spent the first, cried out, What then am I to do? Go in to my own cattle?

'Whosoever lieth with a beast,' the Lord reminded him, 'shall surely be put to death. Defile not yourself therewith; it is confusion.'

But I thought that He did not put His accustomed feeling into this warning, and that for all He cared my father could defile himself with who, or even what, he pleased, so long as it was not my mother.

From this one hundred and sixty-eighth day of my father's expropriation can be dated the growth of a new, though largely undeclared and wordless, friendship between us. I should take back growth. It is too organic a term to describe anything that could possibly have occurred between two such determinedly *in*organic people – we had inanimate longings on us, my father and I; we yearned after brute matter – and it gives an impression of slow and purposeful development quite inappropriate to our circumstances. Growth? If we are to be accurate about these first probationary years of creation, nothing *grew*. Things just appeared. We woke up one morning and where thorn and thistle, bramble and briar, had not been, there thorn and thistle, bramble and briar, were. This was a consequence, partly, of nature being compelled to serve a vindictive function. When we erred in the eyes of the Lord, it was nature He visited upon us, cursing us with the very ground we trod on. With every new transgression, a new prickle to madden us. A word spoken in irritation, a show of less than abject gratitude, and bugs never before seen or imagined, lice without ancestor or precedent, came to nip us in the night. But even leaving aside these vegetable or verminous chastisements, the ground hourly threw up surprises and anomalies out of no other motive than confusion. The seasons had not settled yet; our zone was simultaneously temperate and torrid; we lived at one and the same time in jungle and in desert. *Grow*? Why should anything bother with the tedious process of *growing* when it could fling itself out of marsh or sand-bowl on its own say-so, because no one had ever told it it couldn't?

And so it was with the new friendship between my father and me. We made no arrangements and did not allude to causes, but every morning, after we had hacked our separate ways through whatever murderous thicket had multiplied itself while we slept, we met, as if by accident, at the foot of a bare granite pinnacle whose ascent was attended with many difficulties but whose summit, once attained, gave us respite from the sloshings of my mother's milk, and a sort of deliverance, an illusion of freedom from all things fructifying and earthy.

Nothing lives here, I said, during our inaugural climb, unable to keep the exultation out of my voice.

My father's eyes met mine. Little fires danced in his pupils. And nothing ever will, he exulted back.

Nothing lived there. Nothing could live there. No sap rose; no spongy breeding soil yielded to our tread; nothing stirred or whispered from the depths, because there were no depths – only rock supporting rock. We walked on stone, mounting higher and still higher until we stood among the clouds like angels, pure intelligential substances who were thus far and no further corporal: we loved to breathe in thin air and feel flint, uncreated and uncreating, beneath our feet.

At first, lizards, geckos, salamanders – frogs ambitious to resemble alligators – would follow our ascent, looking lidlessly at us, estimating how much of a gulp it would take to pass us through their gullets; but we became so adept at stoning them – my father, especially, throwing with great accuracy and malice, as though he owed them an injury – that soon we had the entire tumble of silent boulders to ourselves. Once in a while, in order to draw breath against the fierce heat the sun slung down at them, the rocks would spit and explode, leaving a rip like a frightened mouth to deface their impassivity. But no eager organism sprang fully formed from the scissure, as happened down below; no hippogriff or amphisbaena groaned itself into being in the breach, sniffing the air and rubbing clay from its burning eye, both front and rear.

We barely spoke. Discussion distressed my father. He believed it disadvantaged him. On the few occasions he did bring up the subject of his God-inveigled wife, islanded in her marsh of sacred pollutions, he referred to her as *your mother*, as though she were my fault, and quickly became too uncomfortable to proceed. In the matter of possessive priorities we were without guidance; we none of us knew whose, first and foremost, any of us were. And in the matter of her physiology he was, anyway, more reserved, which is to say at once more delicate and less fastidious, than the Deity whose invention that physiology was. Rivers of unclean blood did not course through his conversation. Uncovered fountains did not spray their infection on his thoughts. Neither her body nor his own served him as a storehouse of invective. This had to do partly, I freely grant, with the poverty of his vocabulary. You have to be verbal to be disgusted. But it is not utterly out of the question that he kept himself short of words precisely in order not to give offence. Words are power, and power has no truck with sensibilities.

Anyhow, he would say, as though someone had to bring this interminable conversation to an end, we haven't come up here to discuss your mother. And he would at once engross himself in his hands, which were the size of pole-axes, which had been given him so that he might tear down trees and smite wild animals, but which he wished to employ only as instruments of innocent subterfuge, and therefore, by implication, as proofs of his essential probity.

Behold! Empty! An honest man!

God is not here, I said to him once, after I had caught him in an attitude suspiciously like that of supplication, attempting to separate his tuber-like fingers in the sight of heaven. God is not on this mountain, I promised him. He is not watching. As we both very well know, He is with my mother, talking plenitude and foison. So there isn't any use in your showing Him how clean your palms are.

He followed me through some of this, moving his lips in accompaniment to my words. But I lost him before I'd finished. As usual, my fluency startled him, pleased him and bored him, all at once. He allowed a decent interval of speechlessness to elapse before showing me that he held a large bay leaf between his thumb and first finger, and that he intended to do something surprising with it. You'll like this, he said.

There was no basis for that presumption. I had never liked anything he did with his hands. But I was more concerned with where he had found the leaf. I hope you didn't get that round here, I said.

From the look he threw me you would have thought our roles had suddenly been reversed, and I was the slow one. Round here? Had I forgotten that nothing grew round here? Had I forgotten that that was why we came here?

I eyed him suspiciously. I might not have believed in his magic, but I was still too young to believe completely in my disbelief. What if, after all, he could make the barren rocks bloom? Strike vegetation out of stone?

So where did you get it?

He inverted the thumb that wasn't busy with the leaf. It was a sign we both used to designate, with a minimum of reference, the place we fled from: the fertile valley, our teeming cradle, omphalos, hell, home.

You brought it up here with you?

I've been bringing it to practise with, he said, for days. It shows how little you notice. Are you ready now?

You aren't going to turn it back into a tree?

He laughed. The thing he did best. Good humour spilling like gum arabic down his chest. I'm not as good as that . . . yet. What I am going to do, though, is turn it back into air. Are you ready?

I said that if he was going to turn it back into air I was certainly ready.

He cleared his throat. He always had to begin from the beginning. In the beginning . . . He required silence and attention, formlessness and void, to remember how it all went . . . is the leaf. You may check it if you wish. Satisfied? Good. Now watch carefully. Let there be . . .

He made an abrupt downward movement of the hand, as if trying to throw off something that was sticking to it, followed by a still more abrupt upward movement, as if something else were sticking to it even harder.

. . . AIR!

And so it came to pass. And it was good.

He showed me his palm, held open in the shape he made shadows and reflections of animals with on rock and water. Empty. Then, without altering its profile, he showed me the back of his hand. Empty also. Or at least empty*ish*. Empty if you discount the green fibres that were just visible between his fingers.

Well? He was impatient for my verdict. Well?

I nodded. Miser that I was.

Effective?

Very effective.

I did not add that if he meant to unmake creation, a leaf at a time would be slow going.

He insisted on explaining how it was done. Ungodlike of him.

The leaf is held between the thumb and the first finger. The thumb relaxes – that's important – allowing the leaf to droop against the backs of the first, second and third fingers. The little finger grips the edge of the leaf between itself and the third finger; the first finger falls away so that the thumb is now gripping the opposite edge of the leaf between itself and the second finger. Now, how does it go? . . . Yes . . . the first finger slips down the edge of the leaf and replaces the thumb

in gripping the edge of the leaf against the . . . which is it? . . .
the third, no, the second finger . . . the second finger, that's
right . . . which permits the thumb to move away, leaving the
leaf firmly gripped, like . . . like . . . so, between the first and
the second, and the little and the third. Extend and straighten
the fingers and, watch! – are you watching this? – the palm of
the hand is empty! Now, in order to transfer the leaf from the
back of the hand to the front, close the fingers of the palm,
grip the . . .

I held up my own empty palm – empty of leaf, empty of
pity – and stopped him. Enough, I said. Don't spoil the
mystery.

All animation fled his face. Light died in his eyes. His
shoulders dropped. His hands fell open, inelastic, bleeding
green, like discarded vegetable matter.

Right, he said, turning from me. Right.

As he walked away, I thought he didn't just look defeated,
but shabby as well. Run down. Neglected. More the orphan
than me.

I knew I shouldn't have interrupted him. An interruption
when you are in full flow is like a blow to the heart. In
Adam's case a blow to the heart and to the soul, a stab in the
back, a poisoning of the central nervous system, a torture to
the mind, a suffocation and a braining and a garrotting – so
dependent was he, for definition and dignity, for the main-
tenance of the illusion of freedom and authority, for life itself,
on this fatuous enthusiasm of his. Stop him in the tracks of his
magic and he fell back at once into those craters of original
Chaos that were always opening behind him.

It is crueller to be a son than to be a father. A son sees into
his father's terrors. Sits like a bucket under a fractured pipe
and catches the drip, drip, drip, of all his shameful secrets.
You should look away, if you are a son. You should turn your
back and stop your ears. You should up-end your bucket
every night, slop out, before the drip, drip, dripping begins

again in the morning. At the last there is only one virtue a son must practise, and that is charity.

So where was mine?

Forgive me, ladies and gentlemen, but there is also such a thing as charity to oneself. There were my own feelings to consider, my own illusion of definition and dignity to maintain. And the spectacle of my father – the only father with a small *f* that I had – expending his time, his energies, his love, his small capacity for conversation and his prodigious allotment of nerve and muscle on the juggling of a bay leaf did nothing to ease the conviction of worthlessness – worthlessness in the very blood – which my mother's rejection of us both had started in me.

Small wonder she preferred the company of God, who could tell the stars in their infinity and reckon the dust of the earth and count the number of the beast, to my poor father, who considered he did well to number his ten fingers. And small wonder, if in some essential and irrefragable way I was like him, that she turned her breast from me and gave it, with all its spouting papillae . . .

Stop. This is not an accurate description of what I felt. I must not invent an enmity I never did, and still do not, acknowledge. I did not hate my brother. I am not even certain I got as far as resenting him. If I say that I experienced a clear sensation of opposition and rivalry to him, what have I said that is not true of the relation of all things to all things, whether they be living creatures or inert matter? Opposition is the beginning and the end of us. Out of division – the rivalry order enjoyed with chaos, light with darkness, form with void – we passed from idea to actuality. *Blessed art thou, O Lord, King of the Universe, Who hast made a separation between what is holy and profane; between the upper waters and the lower; between an elder brother and a younger* . . . Strife is not merely in our bones, it *made* our bones. Allow a little for the possibility of unequal contest, the arrogance of victory on one side, the slow seeping dejection of failure on the other, and you have envy. Introduce a third party and you have jealousy.

Undoubtedly I was envious of my brother; undoubtedly I was jealous that what had once been mine had gone to him. But here too, don't forget, I was in harmony with first causes. A jealous God. A murmuring Satan. Injunctions at every turn against our daring to trespass on privileges never intended for our appropriation. If I cried out against my brother's putting forth his hand, and taking fruit that was not his to take, and living for all time therefrom in the knowledge of unbroken happiness, the model for my possessiveness was the Lord.

It is not my intention, far from home, to mitigate or apologize. Least of all for covetousness, which is as instinctual to us as thirst. The truth of the matter is not that I wished to deny my brother but that I feared for my own provision. If creation itself had been more generous, then so might I. But wherever I looked about me I saw reason to believe I might go hungry. Not for mere bread. And not for honey to spread on it. But for notice. For valuation. For esteem. I could not be convinced that there was praise enough to go round; that compliment and favour would not suddenly run out. The teeming land sent up more monsters in an afternoon than I could have catalogued in a year, but its store of validating commendation was exhaustible, finite, dwindling.

You are great lovers of growing things, you Shinarites. You plant gardens inside your houses. You festoon your rooms with flowers. You therefore know I am not exaggerating when I say that there can sometimes be a conflict between you and your inhaling foliage. Sleep in a confined space with a plant close to your pillow and the night is witness to a deadly respiratory struggle. Take this figure to be an analogy to my relations with my brother. I believed Abel was breathing my air.

Not fancifully. Actually. Because it was air itself to me to receive my mother's plaudits for my cleverness, to be congratulated on every antic, worshipped for every word, kissed after every new coinage, as though I were not like any other, truly exceptional – the one and only child upon the planet.

Which is exactly what I had been.

And yes, I will admit it, since I see the accusation in your eyes – which is exactly what I would be still.

We were a sorry pair, my father and I, the unloved magician and his unpraised son, sitting back to back on the highest hardest rock within our compass, putting as much distance as we could arrange between ourselves and the earth which had unaccountably disgorged and then disprized us. We ought to have been more of a consolation to each other. One should have danced and the other should have clapped. There was no one watching who might have jeered. No One. We were sole lords of the silentness.

At the very least I ought not to have discouraged him from explaining how you uncreate a bay leaf, and stopped the only flow of which he was capable.

We sat. Sullen. Mismatched. Staring into nothing.

The sun was hot, but somehow not hot for *us*. Whatever took place in the sky was not for our benefit. We were incidental. The interest – the human interest – was elsewhere.

Suddenly, my father spoke to me. I've been thinking, he said.

I was grateful for the opportunity to make amends. I hadn't expected to hear from him again for a fortnight. I've been thinking too, I said. I'm sorry about before.

Before?

With the leaf. Do you want to show me again how you did it?

He waved away my false filiality. Thereby making me feel more false still. Ought I to have thrown myself in his arms? Would everything have been all right after that . . . for everyone?

No. We were meant to be disharmonious. It was how we'd been designed.

I've been thinking about what you were saying, he said. His voice tailed off. Maybe it didn't matter.

About?

About your mother and . . . His voice tailed off again. He scanned what clouds were in the sky, not entirely convinced by my claim that they'd been vacated. He dropped into a whisper, just to be on the safe side. About your mother and . . . Y-H-W-H, he breathed.

Had I not been under the sway of tender new compunctions I might have tackled him on this question of linguistic primitivism. I hated the way he left vowels out, or pronounced some words as though they were possessed of eyes and could penetrate his every secret, or would not dare to put his tongue to others until he had turned round three times, spat upon the ground, and lifted the hem of his robe to his lips. A word itself has no properties you need fear, I wanted to tell him. You're confusing the slave with the master. They become powerful only under your command. It's you who – But kindliness was to be the keynote. Temperateness the tune. Yes, I said, my mother and Him. (Temperate or not, I refused absolutely to say H-m.) My mother and Him. What is it you have been thinking?

He looked uncomfortable. Already this was, by his standards, a searching and protracted conversation.

You're the clever one, he said.

I waited.

You're the clever one – so you tell me . . .

What?

He sighed. All these demands! You were the one, he reminded me, who said they were down there talking.

I couldn't deny it. Well?

I had stolen his question. Well? he echoed, angrily. *Well?*

As I had to find another word, I resorted to 'What?' again.

Well what, he almost shouted, are they down there talking *about*?

After the pains it had cost him finally to get it out, I could hardly declare myself shocked by him. I was in no position to affect the air of one superior to low curiosity, or to try arguing that he had forced his confidences on me. But I was shaken to hear the question put so bluntly, and that must have made some difference to the quality of my answer.

What were they talking *about*? How was I to know! The weather? Soil? Babies?

Anybody listening – not that there was anybody listening – would have supposed I was the one who was against conversation.

My father shook his head. Now that the subject was in the open, it was plain he had been thinking about it from all angles. I don't believe those are the sorts of talks they have, he said.

They'll be addressing weightier issues, you imagine?

He took his time to answer, screwing up one eye to aid concentration. His eyebrows were overgrown, making it difficult for him to see. I remembered that my mother used to trim them for him, laughing about how hairy he had become, and what would happen if the flake of flint she was wielding missed its mark. *Ouch!* he used to say, the joke being that that was the noise she would make, not he.

The thing is, he finally replied, I can't imagine them talking to each other at all. When I think of your mother talking, I hear her talking only to me.

I looked away. And was proud of myself for not saying, And when I think of my mother talking I hear her talking only to *me*.

What about when you think of Him? I asked instead.

That's just it, he said, tapping that corner of his skull wherein all this epic conceptualizing, or all this epic failure to conceptualize, was taking place – that's just it, I can't. Threats and promises are all I can hear. Threats and promises and then off, in a black grumbling cloud, before there's time for a reply.

Not easy company, certainly, I said.

He suddenly saw the funny side, clapping me about the shoulders and laughing his sizzling resin laugh. I could just see your mother taking that from me, he said.

I can't see her taking it from Him, I returned. In which case you've got nothing to worry about. They probably don't converse at all.

But you said –

I made a gesture disowning responsibility for idle chatter. It was just a manner of speaking, I explained.

But he was not as satisfied by this as I'd expected. Then in that case, he said –

I waited.

He stared up into the sun as if noticing it for the first time. A cloud in the shape of a hand passed across it. I think it's time we went down, he said.

Then in that case what? I insisted.

If they don't talk, then in that case, he retorted – and it really was a retort; truly he recoiled on me – what *do* they do?

That was the moment that taught me how much worse, that's to say how much better, his condition was than mine; how many more were the compensations of jealousy fuelled by passion compared to those of envy fuelled by greed. I was fundamentally only covetous – forget the teat, I wanted primarily to be the miracle of recency my brother was – and covetousness lies cold, like your own corpse, beside you. My father, as I now perceived, was aflame with jealousy – he saw what did not happen, coined gruesome fictions out of the furnace of his brain; but what was that, if not a sort of increase? The jealous propagate. The envious suffer only slow depletion.

Jealous of his jealousy, I would willingly have leapt with

him into the fires. Do? – I encouraged him. Do? What can they do?

You must mean, he said recklessly, what *can't* they!

We were at a desperate pass: that moment of stasis when only cowards go back and only lunatics go on. We sat very still. For a time – this time – not at all mismatched. Although the sun was clouded and declining, the mountain seemed to be ablaze. We both had too much colour in our cheeks and we were both branded red around the eyes. The red that comes, not from weeping, but from fire-gazing.

That, I said slowly, would be an abomination. *It is confusion*, I reminded him.

He wanted me to be right. But of course he also wanted me to be wrong. Who can go on dining on the gruel of fact once they have tasted the rich meats of uncertainty?

By what law? he asked.

Is He not your Father, I said, and is she not your wife! *And if a man lie with his daughter-in-law, both of them shall surely be put to death: they have wrought confusion; their blood shall be upon them.*

Except, he reminded me, that He – Our Father – is not a man.

Did I dare? I dared. *And if a woman approacheth unto any beast, and lie down thereto, thou shalt kill the woman, and the beast: they shall surely be put to death; their blood shall be upon them.*

I held back from appending my own commentary to the text. Narrowly, narrowly, I stopped myself adding, Kill the beast! Kill the beast!

Just as well. We all have to kill our own. It is a private matter. And as it was, fearing retribution for loose talk, my father had raised the hem of his robe to his lips, almost devouring it in fright. Y-H-W-H, he said, in a voice as low as he could make it, dropping vowels as though they were hot coals, Y-H-W-H m-st n-v-r b- c-ll-d b--st.

In that case, I said, if He is neither man nor beast, I do not see how, as man or beast, He can have wronged you.

He thought about it. All this took time. We had been given no guidance. Only a jumble of prohibitions. And you cannot construct much of a cosmology out of those.

Unless, I went on, you would argue that a wife can betray her husband with an Immanence?

How were we to know that that is what wives do all the time? Our terrors, in those days, were all tangible. We feared first and foremost through our eyes. So it made my father feel immediately better to see his Rival losing clarity, dismantling even as he watched. The more God receded to the realm of pure idea, the more my father saw himself reassembling into solid fact. For the first time since he had initiated the conversation his fists had become unclenched – one, two, three, four fingers and a thumb visible on one hand, and, yes, one, two, three, four fingers and a thumb visible on the other. Soon he would be making what was not himself vanish again.

But he was still red around the eyes. He had had a bad time of it, imagining God's feet touching the ground, God's arms . . .

And he was still without a wife. He said: Do you know what puzzles me now?

I tried to guess. What you were ever doing worrying about it?

No, he said. What she sees in Him since He can't be seen.

I could have replied: It's a puzzle what my mother sees in anyone! But I didn't want to fan my resentments into life, just as we were putting out my father's. Maybe she is impressed by what He can do, I ventured. Maybe He shows off His powers. Floods rivers for her. Drains bogs. Splits tamarisks with lightning. Invents wart-hogs. Changes the earth's colour. Shaves slices off the moon and then makes it whole again.

My father's eyes opened like moons themselves. Tricks! he said. What you're saying is that He does tricks for her!

I laughed. Yes, I said. He does tricks. What else do you expect a God to do?

He didn't reply. Suddenly he wanted to be alone with his thoughts again. We sat a little longer, watching the granite beneath our feet change from grey to purple to red to brown, then we made our way down the mountain in silence.

From time to time I thought I heard strange noises coming from the rocks, and once actually ran off in pursuit of a sound that put me in mind of a new disgusting creature that He had visited on us – a creeping, hobbling half dog, half cat-like thing that secreted sticky fluids as it moved, seemed to be of both sexes simultaneously, and preferred offal to all other foods. Another of God's tricks to please my mother? I had given it the name hyena, in imitation of its laughter, and it was a hyena which I thought I heard. But I was wrong. When I reached the place from which derision had seemed to emanate, it was empty. When I put my ear to the stones that had seemed to sing and whistle, they were mute.

The moment we reached level ground it began to rain. A brief sporadic pitter-pattering at first, followed by a heavier, more rhythmic fusillade, like the galloping of horses. Mysteriously, though, this was rain that was not wet. I looked up at the sky; a few courtier clouds, billowing pink, attended the dying of the sun. Immediately above us it was clear, in preparation for the ritual entrance of the stars. My hair was dry. The ground I trod on was dry. Yet rain hissed around me, squelched underfoot, gurgled among the rocks we had quit, parched just a few minutes earlier.

I turned to remark on this strange phenomenon to my father, who was dawdling behind me, too preoccupied, I supposed, to have registered with his own faculties that we were caught in an invisible downpour. He was smiling broadly, with his tongue out, pretending that he couldn't get it back in again – a piece of nonsense that had a history between us, taking me back to my first childhood and our earliest collusion in mischief. Bleh! bleh! bleh! he used to say to me when he had scored some minor triumph over adversity or had got himself in and out of trouble with my mother. And I, lacking words, used to tongue it back: Bleh! bleh! bleh!

After all this time, and in the light of what we had been mulling over on the mountain, it was odd seeing him standing there with his eyebrows wild and his hands hanging and his tongue adrift, saying bleh! at me once more.

You're looking pleased with yourself, I noted.

So I should be, he said. I fooled you, and you're the clever one.

For a moment I wondered whether he meant that he'd been having me on all afternoon and was no more a jealous husband than he was a philosopher.

He watched me not understanding him. That gave him pleasure, too.

The rain, he said.

I said, there is no rain.

The rain you can hear, he said.

I listened. It's stopped, I said.

He was more than pleased with himself; he was out of his skin with excitement. That's because *I've* stopped, he said.

What do you have to do with the rain?

He came up close to me, dropped his tongue out and pointed to it. All in the mouth, he said. All in here. Tongue, teeth and air – that's all you need. Do you want to hear thunder? Listen . . .

And sure enough, rumbling in from the very direction in which we were heading, from where the smell of holy excreta and gushing milk was already reaching us, I now could hear thunder.

Well? What do you think?

I said I thought it remarkable.

So much for weather, he said. Nothing to it. Tricks? I'll show him tricks!

And before we were home he had done a cloudburst, a river in full flood, a gale howling unimpeded across the waste howling wilderness, a thin oozing thistle wind, the bark unpeeling from a Tabor oak, locusts in flight, duck fat spitting in a fire, a crocodile devouring our new enemy the hyena, and, in his lowest voice, for just the two of us, the Lord God making up to Eve on a quivering breeze.

But it was not until the next day, when I saw him fashioning a clay doll, a puppet, a marionette, a dummy, a *golem* in the image of himself, which it was his intention to sit upon his knee and animate – actually produce sound and personality and opinion and, who could say, maybe even rebellion from – that I realized my father's campaign to win back my mother in fair and open combat had begun in earnest.

4. HAIRLESS IN KADESH

I

Now Korah, the son of Izhar, the son of Kohath, the son of Levi, the son of Jacob . . .

Jacob?

Sisobk the Scryer pounds his temples with the heels of his little hands. He has been reading the Old Testament in his room all morning, descrying scripture in the steam that rises from the jorum of frothing water he grips between his knees, but he cannot get to Korah for the knot of roots, the rotting bark and dead wood, that chokes Korah's ancestral tree. Jacob? What is Jacob, the ankle-grabber, the thief of his brother Esau's birthright, doing here? Sisobk knows Korah's story better than he knows his own, and never until now has the name of Jacob figured in it.

The future is not something Sisobk is prepared to play fast and loose with. You can't have people slipping in and out of it at will. Hence his resorting to that unnatural expedient, that *aide-mémoire* of second-rate diviners – steam. He means to clear the blockage in his faculties.

A thin moustache trails across his lip like a lost platoon of ants. This he traces with two fingers, as though its presence is a surprise, or perhaps a disappointment, to him. Then he pinches his nostrils, compresses his tiny eyes until they squelch like raisins, lowers his red perspiring head into the fumes,

66

and tries once more to turn the pages of the Book of Numbers.

NOW *Korah* . . .

His mind lurches, slides, stumbles, scalds – so much ash wheezed up from the bronchitic chest of a volcano. Korah to Levi, Levi back to Izhar, Izhar on to Kohath, from Kohath back to . . . But it's no use. Again it all unravels with the unauthorized intrusion of Jacob, the smooth one.

Sisobk the Scryer changes his names to Iykhernofret the Ineffective, and wishes it were as easy to change Jacob's. It is not only that his prophet's pride is hurt. He is also thwarted as a reader. He has been looking forward all week to spending the day with Korah, steeling himself in *his* steel, rebelling in *his* rebellion; but he cannot proceed with the narrative when a name that decidedly isn't on the page refuses to dislodge itself from his brain. 'Nothing ever sticks in my mind,' he complains, 'so why suddenly should Jacob?'

Let us intervene here and help Sisobk out.

It's true we do not possess his gifts of prescience, but do we need them? We have scholarship on our side, hindsight, carbon-dating, computers, universities. Poor Sisobk is hardly a match for us, with just cuneiform and inspiration to call on. And as for the parcels of papyrus he wears tied around his feet instead of sandals, the as yet uninscribed codices and still-to-be erased palimpsests he shuffles along the streets in like a vagabond – why, a single pin-head of technology is sufficient space for us to store those and the entire intellectual footwear of the ancient world besides.

Let's put Sisobk out of his misery, then, and tell him some of the things that we know. As for example that Jacob was indeed the great-great-grandfather of Korah, but chose to absent himself from the catalogue, as protection against the disrepute into which his great-great-grandson would bring the family name. Smelling the fruit – for he too was a breather-in of steam, this Jacob, he too was a hot-mountain slitherer and soothsayer – he sought to sever the branch. This is the meaning of the curse he delivered on his death-bed to his sons Simeon and Levi: '*O my soul, come not thou into their secret; unto their assembly, mine honour, be not thou united.*'

Sisobk could have uncovered this instance of family squeamishness himself had he been as dedicated a student of Genesis as he was of Numbers. Or had he been aware of Rashi – Rabbi Shelomoh Yitschaki – the worried Talmudical scholar in a skull-cap whose interpretation of Jacob's precautionary curse we have unapologetically borrowed. Alternatively, he could have searched his own psychology to find the reasons for his mind's retention of Jacob, and recalled that he too – even Sisobk the Scryer – was the cursed son of a son-cursing father, and the cursed grandson of a grandson-cursing grandfather before that.

'There is some fatality in us,' Sisobk's male ancestors had taken it in turn to predict. 'Not a one of us is born to escape a premature and violent death. It is written. Pass it on.'

In receipt of this message from a father who fell on to the tusks of wild pigs in his thirty-fifth year, the young Sisobk took up celibacy to spite succession, and scrying in the hope that absorption in other people's futures would preserve him from his own.

The wonder is not that he pre-remembered Jacob, the caster of long shadows, the prophet of all that would befall his sons, but that he ever pre-forgot him.

Sisobk the Scryer, of course, now knows of our intervention in his difficulty and thanks us for it. We have freed him to get on with his steam-reading.

NOW Korah, the son of Izhar, the son of Kohath, the son of Levi, (no son of Jacob); *and Dathan and Abiram, the sons of Eliab and On, the son of Peleth, sons of Reuben, took men:*

And they rose up before Moses, with certain of the children of Israel, two hundred and fifty princes of the assembly, famous in the congregation, men of renown:

And they gathered themselves together against Moses and against Aaron, and said unto them, Ye take too much upon you . . .

The smell of insurrection floats deliciously into Sisobk's nostrils.

II

So, now that we've extricated one prophet from the story, and thereby made another happy, who does that leave us with?

Let's deal with the small-fry first.

On On, the son of Peleth, we need not for the moment dwell. He found himself enlisted in a mutiny by wills stronger than his own, before being safely hauled out of it again by a will stronger even than theirs. Like many before and since, he owed his survival more to a spouse than to a father, and ought to have been known as On, the husband of his wife.

Dathan and Abiram, on the other hand, had been agitating in alley-ways for years. In Alush they had broken the Sabbath. In Pihahiroth they had infuriated the Lord by suddenly waxing lyrical about the comforts of the country from whose servitude they had just been led. In Egypt itself they had carried stories to the Pharaoh – 'We have this minute seen Moses smite a citizen, Highest' – and gave further notice of their sullenness the time Moses caught them fighting over brick and mortar, and tried to step between them – 'Who made thee a prince and a judge over us? Intendest thou to kill us as thou didst the Egyptian?'

It was hardly unexpected, therefore, when the muttering began at Kadesh-Barnea, in the waste Wilderness of Zin, that the voices of Dathan and Abiram should be heard louder than almost all the others, and that their disgruntlement should be as wind to fire.

Korah, however, *was* the fire. Intelligent, articulate, vain of his looks, of his influence, of his gift for satire, Korah had been treasurer to the Pharaohs, in which capacity he had stumbled on one of the three great hoards amassed by Joseph as a precaution against Egypt's unstable economy, and had helped himself thereto. It was said of his wealth that it was so great, three hundred mules were needed to carry the keys to it alone. In order to arrive at a just estimate of his importance you have to imagine the Lord holding apart the waters of the Red Sea long enough not only for the Children of Israel but also for each of those three hundred mules to pass safely through.

There is an argument that says Moses should have been more careful of Korah. Should have and could have. It doesn't, after all, take much to alleviate the dangerous sadness of the immoderately wealthy: a kind word or a title, a ribbon here, a garland there. Yet when the time came to hand out the chieftainships of the families, Moses passed over Korah in favour of his cousin, Elizaphan. As son of Izhar, who was the second son of Kohath, Korah had a far stronger claim to head the house of the Kohathites than did Elizaphan, whose father, Uzziel, was Kohath's last and least born. A slight or an oversight? Surely not the latter. The Children of Israel were able to remember who had begotten whom, and in what order, since Adam begat Cain; they cannot lightly be accused of inattentiveness to the niceties of family precedence. So what did Moses intend by his rudeness to Korah?

Korah had his own theories. One of them relating to his, Korah's, wife.

A word of caution here. Korah was careful and courteous, as well as shrewd, sad and rich. He knew better than to lay about him with charges of sexual covetousness. A man can look foolish, even in a desert, always suspecting others of wanting to crawl through the flap of his pavilion. And he had no actual proof that Moses lusted after his or, come to that, any other man's wife, even in his heart.

There was a rumour in circulation that Moses had long since ceased lusting after his own. In a rare but very public falling-out with their brother, Miriam and Aaron had taken the side of their sister-in-law, the Cushite woman, and accused Moses of neglecting his conjugal duties to her under cover of piety. What was *he* doing, they wanted to know, separating himself from flesh as if that was what the Lord expected of him? 'Hath the Lord indeed spoken only by Moses? Hath he not spoken also by us?' *They*, his sister and brother – not exactly deficient in holiness themselves – were not aware of any new prohibition against lawful lying together, no, not even if the wife of God's chosen prophet did happen to be as black as night. It looked liked spiritual pride to them; sanctity over and above what was necessary.

Nor was Zipporah the first of Moses's wives to have complained of his aloofness, or to have remarked on his propensity for withdrawal, for quickly upping his tent and pitching it in some other place.

Accounts varied as to how long, after he had fled from the consequences of slaying an Egyptian, Moses spent in Ethiopia; but two reports consistently recurred. The first told that he had attained great military distinction there and eventually won the hand of Adoniah, the dusky Queen of Ethiopia herself. The second intimated that in no time at all the Queen had grown disillusioned with his performance as a husband and more or less given up on him as any sort of usefully functioning consort or companion. It appears that after some initial enthusiasm he had bethought himself of Isaac's words to Jacob (we whisper that name so as not to discompose Sisobk the Scryer who is still reading) – '*Thou shalt not take a wife from the daughters of Canaan*' – and on that pretext never laid a finger on her again.

Moses liked his wives to be dark, foreign and forbidden – or at least borderline forbidden – that much can be said, and after that he liked not to have to suffer their proximity.

That such a pathological compulsion to make women disgusted with themselves should have assumed the guise of a religious imperative was no surprise to Korah, who had a secular intelligence, suspected all impulses to mysticism, and was himself sufficiently at ease in his virility not to mind being under the sway of a wife. It is not out of the question that Moses, too, had an inkling that what made him grow as a mountaineer and law-maker shrunk him as a mere terrestrial man, for he fell unusually quiet – unusually quiet for a person of quick temper – whenever he was challenged in this weak spot in his probity. Miriam's and Aaron's opposition called out meekness in him, not rage; confronted, later, by Korah's rebellion – *Ye take too much upon you* – he dropped upon his face; and later still, when Zimri would challenge him with the Midianite woman, Cozbi, and taunt him with the inconsistency of his disapproval of her –

Zimri: Is this woman permitted me in concubinage or no?
Moses: She is forbidden thee.
Zimri: By whose proscription?
Moses: By the Torah's.
Zimri: Then where, as a faithful exponent of the Torah, does that leave you? Is not your wife a Midianite? And what is more, is she not the daughter of an idolatrous priest?

Moses would be at a loss to find any response other than tears.

Sisobk the Scryer gleefully scrolls and re-scrolls the scene on the runny walls of his steaming room:

Zimri: Well, Moses, what sayest thou to this?
Moses: Boo-hoo.

Moses could have argued that he had met and married

Zipporah long before God's revelation to him of the Torah. But he did not. He could have shown that, however idolatrous her father, Zip had become as pious and pernickety a proselyte to Hebrew ways as any in the camp. But he did not. Instead he brought his hands up to his eyes, and wept.

It is sometimes said that it was because of this faint-heartedness that God buried Moses where no man knoweth of his sepulchre and no seer seeth his boo-hooing, unto this day. Alternatively, it is argued that to be granted such a ringing obscurity is the highest proof of God's favour.

Who would dare adjudicate between two such liberties taken with the name and justice-mechanism of the Almighty? The truth is – whatever HE thought – that Moses's courage failed him, time and again, and always at the same extremity: that critical push when his accusers charged him with sanctimoni-ousness and hypocrisy in sexual matters. He could not look them in the face. He could not defy them to say their worst. He stuttered and knew he was not in the clear. He had wished to be impeccable, and with that very wish – for why should a man be impeccable? – he had muddied his home waters. That much Korah knew about him too. And it was enough to persuade him that Moses was no more incapable than less exalted men of begrudging others their domestic happiness, their physical content, and every bit as prepared, on that account, to do them mischief.

Such as appointing Elizaphan to a position of authority above their heads.

Korah was helped towards this radical mistrust of Mosaic motives, it goes without saying, by the very person on behalf of whose sex he had agreed to smell a rat. On his own he would not have thought to enter sympathetically into the feelings of poor Zipporah, left to swallow sand and shudder without company each night, imagining what it was in her, what it was *about* her, that appalled her husband. On his own he would not have noticed – would not have had a motive for noticing – that Moses averted his gaze whenever a woman, *any* woman, passed by him, thereby investing her, whoever she was, with the most libidinous and inflammatory properties, as though her look alone, had Moses been mad enough to meet it, would have cast him into hell. Only someone who had herself been made to feel she carried this potentiality for destruction in her glance could have conveyed the idea of it to Korah, and made him see how little it contained of flattery or compliment. For this knowledge, as for so much else, Korah was indebted to his wife. 'The mind of your prophet,' she told him, 'is a stables. He must assume that you are all in the identical mental condition, you men. There can be no other explanation for the stream of stipulations which every day issues from him anew, in relation to the bolting of the doors.'

'The doors, my dear?'

'The stable doors.'

He levelled an innocent's finger at his temples, at his mind. 'I hope you are not implying, my love . . .'

She turned her face from him, depriving him of its fine points of light. She might have been sheathing a dagger. 'If yours is clean,' she said, 'that is only because you have me to sweep it.'

More than most, a rich man needs a clever wife. Without her, his complacency would blind him to the thousand upon thousand tiny insults to which his merit is continuously subjected. Korah did not himself think, while it was happening, for example, that being shorn by Moses of every hair on his body was any particular affront, or at all too high a price to pay for the privilege – the *simcha shel mitzvah* – of priestly consecration. But when Korah's wife beheld him pushing a path through a throng of astonished onlookers, bald from head to toe, napless, exfoliated, tonsured – he whose raven hair had hung as comely as the ten curtains of the tabernacle and been a source of pride to him almost as great as his three hundred bow-legged mules – she let out a gasp which told him at once he had yet again submitted himself unwittingly to ridicule.

'Who did this to you?' she cried – the woman's wail, the terrible female lamentation which all men, rich or poor, await with dread. The last inordinate expression of outrage, for which only women have the vocal chords.

'My love . . .'

'Who did this?'

He smiled a sheep's smile, though he could see in the reflection of her dagger eyes that it was pig she saw, the pink flesh of forbidden porker.

'My own,' he pleaded, 'anyone would think I'd been assaulted.'

'You have. Tell me who was your assailant.'

She knew, but she would make him say it.

'Assailant?' He laughed an ass's laugh.

'Tell me.'

He hung his head. In the circumstances, a bad idea. 'Moses,' he said. 'King Moses.'

'You allowed *him* to take your hair!'

It had gone further than she yet grasped. Korah wasn't sure how best to break it to her. Should he remove his clothing and then recite the ordinance, or should he recite the ordinance and then remove his clothing? He decided to remove his clothing *while* reciting the ordinance.

'*Take the Levites from among the Children of Israel,*' he chanted, loosening his sandals, '*and cleanse them. And thus shalt thou do unto them, to cleanse them: Sprinkle water of purifying upon them, and let them*' – he reached for the hem of his gown and drew the garment slowly, slowly up his trunk – '*and let them shave . . . all*' – the truth was before her

75

now, any moment, any moment now – *'and let them ...
shave ... ALL ... their ... flesh.'*

It seemed to Korah that his wife took an eternity – as long
as it would have taken him to count the keys to his treasure –
to examine the shame that had been brought upon them both.
She turned him around, touching his hallowed and inflamed
skin only with the tips of her unsanctified fingers. Where was
it all? The dense fleece that had covered his neck and shoulders
like a burnous, and whose texture had reminded her, miles
from water, of black seaweed – where was it? The odd, unruly
straggle of finer hair that sprung up where his spine ended,
where the first murderer was reputed to have grown a tail,
and which spread up his lower back like vine – where was it?
Gone, gone. Gone too – sheared with microscopical attention –
the sleek thistledown that had matted his buttocks and his
thighs. Barbered, his legs appeared thin and girlish, too insubstantial to bear his importance. But worst of all, when she
turned him about once more, to look a second time, like a
horse-dealer, like a stock-breeder – worst of all, his privates:
loose and defenceless, absurd, a boy's privates, a children's
joke, a secret not worth the keeping.

Raw meat.

'And Moses did all this,' she finally asked, 'with his own
hands?'

There was a particularity in her question which Korah could
not meet with his eyes. He merely nodded.

'Even though the ordinance has it that you should do it to
yourselves?'

'It is considered a greater honour – altogether more of a
koved – to receive purification from Moses personally,' Korah
said.

He felt that in her concern for what had been taken from
him, his wife had missed what had been given.

But no sooner did he hear himself speak than he remembered
how Moses had held him by the hands and feet, and lifted him

bodily, although he was much heavier than the prophet, proclaiming, 'Now, Korah, art thou clean!' An honour indeed, but he could not deny he had disliked the sensation of being raised, of being carried and cleansed and sprinkled by Moses, as if he were an infant or a ram, and all his material substance counted for nothing.

'Besides,' he went on, for the purpose of pacifying himself no less than his wife, 'Moses purified his own flesh likewise, and that of his sons.'

'A small price to pay, had he shaved every man in the house of his father, for making a fool of you. What hair worth speaking of does he have to lose? Or his sons, who must squint their eyes against the sun, their lashes are so thin? But even had they been a quarter as lustrous as you are – as you *were* – do you suppose he would have cared how far they were debased so long as he could debase you with them? You are a fool if you still do not know how much you gall him.'

Because Korah's intelligence was secular, that does not mean it was free of superstition, untouched by the protocol of priestly ambition, or given over completely to his wife's. 'What I do know,' he said, 'is that you cannot call a man debased who has been sanctified – and what is more has been singled out for sanctification – according to the law.'

'The law! Do not go on making an ass of yourself, Korah. Enough for one day!'

He forbore to argue. Shirtless, shoeless, hoodless, hairless, bare as a rat, he was uncertain what dignity was left to him to stand on.

He smiled, showing the gold in his teeth. Had his mouth been big enough to house three hundred teeth he would have crowned each one of them with gold. But even then he could not have flashed her a more sumptuous smile than he did now. At the last, his smile said, there is only one law I choose to obey.

She, though, his law-giver, was still arguing with him in her head. She stooped, gathered up his clothes, and held them out for him to see. Evidence of his barbering, needles of hair, nap, clusters of curls that might have been a child's, still clung to his white linen.

'What proof have we,' she demanded that he tell her, except that she would not suffer him to tell her anything, 'what proof have we that this Torah we hear so much about is not Moses's invention? Do you never suspect its authenticity and origination? Are you not surprised that a God who roars out of the throat of a fiery mountain should bother, for our small behoof, to proliferate such trivialities – every day a new inanity, and every new inanity spawning every day a dozen more? Take this latest vagary into which your high priest has fallen: blue fringes. Blue fringes! Upon these garments of yours, which you are lucky I do not burn, I am to sew a tassel, and then upon the tassel I am to put a riband of blue. Tell me, Korah, why my seamstressing is a matter of importance to a busy God.'

All that is gold glisters in Korah's mouth. 'Angel, fringes ribanded with blue are to remind us, every time we look upon them, of the commandments of the Lord.'

'You call this reasoning? Were I then to sew scorpions into your shirts and tell you that the Lord commanded them, would they too not bend your thoughts to heaven? And what is there in particular about the colour blue – and do not say, the sky – that lends it this magical property of a memorandum? If there is a virtue in blue wool, then let blue wool be brought out and we will clothe the congregation in it forthwith, and not be worrying ourselves with knots.'

III

For this, the rabbis of the Gemara would remember Korah's wife.

'Thus it is written,' they would say, comparing her with the wife of On (the Husband of His Wife): 'Every wise woman buildeth her house; but the foolish plucketh it down.'

Woe to her, and to hers, who speaketh against the fringe!

IV

On her husband too, as of course on Sisobk the Scryer, her words made a strong impression.

The very next day Korah sought an audience with Moses. Two hundred and fifty of his followers accompanied him, among them – allowing that one who comes before in time is not disqualified from following in spirit – Sisobk. Garmented in *tekhelet* – vestments of forget-me-not blue that covered them from neck to ankle – Korah's men flapped like a banner of insurrection outside God's chosen prophet's tabernacle.

Korah himself, though, a study in humming sapphire and sea-sick turquoise, began his questioning with exaggerated courtesy.

Korah: We have come to you to learn your ruling, Moses. To these garments is it required of us – on pain of our iniquity becoming a byword among nations – that we attach fringes?
Moses: That is the commandment.
Korah: A blue fringe?
Moses: Yes, blue.
Korah: It must be blue?
Moses: Blue to recall to you the sea, which will in turn recall to you the firmament, which will at last put you in mind of the Throne of Glory. Where sits He who brought you out of bondage to be your God. Yes – blue.

Korah: But if a single fringe of blue suffices to fulfil the commandment when the garment is white all over, or all over some other colour (which might equally, by the by, remind us of the firmament), then should not a garment which is *already* blue all over meet the conditions of the commandment more satisfactorily still? If we were to learn that the Lord preferred an offering of goat to an offering of a lamb, we would send out for goat, not cut Him up a lamb and stick whiskers to it.

Moses: The commandment specifies a fringe of blue. That is my ruling, as I interpret the intentions of the God of Israel.

It did not take at all long for the word to get about that, bald as he had become, the rich Levite, Korah, had made a fool of Moses.

Sisobk the Scryer hears about it centuries before it happened. Remarkable, even though he was there to verify it in person.

The following day Korah turned up with his company again, to request another ruling.

Korah: King Moses, if upon a man's skin there be a white rising, or a bright spot, white and somewhat reddish, in size no bigger than a bean, is that man clean or unclean?

Moses: He is unclean.

Korah: And if the white rising or bright spot spreads and covers all his skin, is that man clean or unclean?

Moses: He is clean.

Korah: (*turning to his company and, forgetting he no longer owns an eyebrow, arching that part of his face where an eyebrow once had been*) One wonders whether such irrationality can have its origins in God. But I have another question. This *mezuzah*, which contains twenty-two lines of the Torah, and which you would have us affix at the entrance to our abodes . . .

Moses: Not I. It is the Lord God who has said, 'And thou shalt write them upon the doorposts of thine house and upon thy gates.'

Korah: It will relieve us all to hear that the Lord God who has brought us out of bondage into this wilderness intends that we should one day live in houses. We had thought sand was become our natural habitat. (*from Korah's company murmurings, mirth, hollow as idols to the ears of Moses*) But be that as it may, tell me, Moses: if this *mezuzah* is to serve as a symbolic reminder, at our very portals, of His law – a foretaste, so to speak, before we enter – then presumably it is not necessary to have one on the doorposts of a house which already contains the sacred scrolls from which these twenty-two lines have been extracted.

Moses: A *mezuzah* is to be affixed at the entrance to every dwelling.

Korah: Without exception?

Moses: Without exception.

Korah: What you are saying, then, is that three hundred and seventy-eight portions of the Torah will not suffice to meet God's prescription, whereas a mere twenty-two lines will do the job perfectly?

Moses: There must be a *mezuzah* upon the doorposts of every habitation.

Korah: Must?

Moses: Must.

The pungent smell of a rival's dicomfiture, sweet like the

meat offering to the Lord, spiked with stacte and salted just so, reaches Sisobk's nostrils at the very moment it reaches Korah's. As a mere reader, Sisobk can enjoy only a sedentary, second-hand exultation; as an actor, albeit one who recites lines written for him by his wife, Korah is able to point a long, jewelled finger at the first expounder of Mosaic law, and cry, 'I do not hear the word of God in any of these absurdities.' And to show that he has some idea how a real God thinks and speaks, he thunders now – 'The Torah that thou dost teach Israel cannot be the Lord's and therefore must be thine. Thine and thy brother Aaron's, whom thou dresseth like a bridegroom and calleth High Priest. But he is a High Priest, Moses, in the service of no one but himself and thee!'

And that, for one day, was as far as Korah was prepared to take it. He needed to speak further to his wife, repeat his performance for her, watch the dagger flashing in her glance. He needed to test the resolve of Dathan and Abiram, to say nothing of other grumbling Reubenites camped close by him. And he needed to ponder tactics, to regroup his intellectual, no less than his military, forces.

He could not, without damage to his cause, go on dismantling the Torah, law by law. Moses was capable of inventing new ones quicker than he could ever hope to discredit them. Besides, he did not want his campaign to degenerate into merely rote rejection, gainsaying without discrimination. He knew the limited life of an appeal to the people based on irony and denigration. He was not a rich man for nothing: he understood that the common mind tires quickly of criticism, suspects the motives of those who practise it, and always gives its vote at last to the state of things as it is, to the dead weight of incumbency. Possessed of envy in the ratio of at least a hundred to one above all other emotions, the mass of mankind naturally holds envy to be the mainspring of action, and so lives in awe of that inert power of prior possession which, because it already has everything, cannot be suspected of wanting anything more.

'If I were a democrat I would despair,' he told his wife.

'If you were a democrat,' she answered him, 'you would not be my husband.'

He put it to himself that he had no hope of toppling Moses until he could learn to leaven ridicule with sentiment. The people liked sentiment almost as much as they liked authority.

'What brings a tear most quickly to your eye?' he asked his wife.

'Desert wind,' she told him.

She was the wrong person to try. If it was affectibility he was after, Dathan and Abiram – petty agitators and hoodlums, keepers of low company, confidants of the poor – were his men.

'Widows,' Dathan said.

'And orphans,' added Abiram.

'Widows of anyone in particular?' Korah was curious to hear. 'Merchants's widows? Treasurers' widows?'

'Just poor widows,' said Dathan.

'And hungry orphans,' added Abiram.

Korah fingered his rings, thanked them, and went away to think. Among the many things he thought about were his shaven body, his wife's opprobriousness, and the part Moses had played in both.

The next afternoon he was once more outside Moses's tent. But this time, instead of calling on him and asking for a ruling, he assembled a multitude to whom he related a story which had been told to him, he swore, and not by some filthy dreamer or parabolist either, that very morning. Inapposite as many of his audience would doubtless find the agrarian content of his narrative – cruelly, bitterly inapposite to speak of fields and farming here, amid the scant wells of Kadesh-Barnea – he trusted they would none the less recognize the injustice and the sophistry to which each of them was hourly subjected by Moses and Aaron in the name of their phantasmagorical Torah.

'There was a destitute widow,' he began, 'a pauper's relict, mother of two starving daughters, orphans . . .'

V

Sisobk the Scryer, follower of Cain, is already overcome with grief.

5. Cain Expatiates on the Strange Resemblance that Devotion Bears to Envy

Now that my father was occupied modelling effigies out of clay and whistling thunderstorms through his teeth, I was once again thrown back on my own company. This meant that I could resume spying on the progress of my mother's amours. Her muddy infatuation with my indolent baby brother. And her more stately meeting of minds with the Ethereal.

I was of course lying when I told my father that I had no information to impart relating to this second matter. How could I possibly have been ignorant of what was taking place? What kind of a son would I have been to my mother had I not seized every opportunity to observe her in her finest hour, captor and mistress of her Creator's heart? Regardless of all other family considerations, I believed that the sight of at least one of us exultant was owing to me. I had named fear in all its shades, shame and shrinking in all their fine gradations; if there was self-congratulation going, I wanted to name that.

As for not being straight with my father, I considered myself above reproach. I had not seen anything that would have satisfied his jealousy. Had I been able to deliver him a foolishly besotted Jehovah, wooing my milk-filled mother with shy looks and flowers, His hair slicked down like a water rat's, His beard combed and smelling of aloes, I would not have hesitated. Ridicule is the jealous man's salvation, the breath of all our being; and could I have conjured my poor perplexed father some, I would have. But this was not how the Lord came courting. He knew better than to put in a personal appearance. That is unless one considers the shekinah – His glow, His aura, His glorious refulgence – to be personal.

It is a rare thing to be hidden in a tree watching one's mother making up to a golden cloud. Though not as strange as it would have been, I maintain – thinking of those stories of love between mortals and divinities which I have heard since I came among you – had I been hidden in the selfsame tree watching my mother presenting her hindquarters to a gander. I am speaking of degrees of strangeness only. Strangeness to *me*. It would be a poor return of your famous Shinarite hospitality, and a waste of all my wanderings, were I to entertain preferences for one god's way of attending to his needs over another's. Some deities are compunctious when it comes to employing their versatility to satisfy their lusts, and some are not; that is all there is to it. Yahweh happened to be one of those who didn't hold with irresponsible metamorphosis. It's as likely to be a question of stomach as morality. He – Yahweh – just felt more comfortable keeping His own shape.

And so He philandered with my mother through the medium of pure light. I employ no figure of speech when I say that He took a shine to her. Irradiated her. Lit her up from without and within, while He Himself throbbed above her in the sky like a flaming sunset, or flowed molten like a river ablaze with stars.

For my part I was not overly impressed. Display, when all is said and done, is only display. Coruscations of the heavens only management and timing. Who knows, He might have cut a more awesome figure after all, had He come down snorting and pawing the ground, with a brass ring through His nose and His pizzle bristling.

That, anyway, was how it struck me at the time. Reflection has since taught me that He knew to a nicety what He was about. He kept His distance and lit fireworks not only because that was what He was best at, or all that His fastidiousness would allow Him, but because it enabled Him to creep the long way round the back of carnality. Much of the harm that sex had done to His original scheme – conjoining what He had intended to be separate, fusing what He had meant to keep distinct – He now saw His opportunity to undo. He would reactivate the allure of the inaccessible. Restore hopeless yearning to the central position in human affairs He had always wanted for it.

To this end He painted the sky with colours that made my mother ache to set free her soul from its vegetable clothing. He played her heavenly music – divine melodies – which reminded her of where she had never been and woke her to anticipations of where she would never go. He whispered pastoral poetry in her ear, transforming her familiar mundane geography into enamell'd ground, watering her irriguous valley with fuming rills, protecting her complexion 'neath blissful bowers or in the shelter of umbrageous grots. He beguiled her into a pathetic fallacy, perpetuating the delusion in her that at His bidding the whole of nature would bend to her every feminine want, reverse the seasons rather than let her shiver, dapple her in sunlit gaiety before she should so much as think of letting go a sigh of sadness. 'Where-e'er you walk,' He sang, 'cool gales shall fan the Glade. Trees where you sit,' He promised, 'shall crowd into a Shade.' When had my father ever given her guarantees of that kind? Or last lisped the sweets of devotion as insubstantial as air –

> I did but see her passing by,
> And yet I love her till I die.

Everything that is mawkish in art, in other words, the All Trembling loosed upon the world in pursuance – in pursuance of the principle of the futility of pursuance – of my mother.

And she?

Well, naturally she had always been weak before the power of art. What woman is not? Which of them is proof against a little culture laced with compliment? A song, a dance, a pretty turn of wit, for which she might conceivably be credited with the inspiration?

It was my mother who had encouraged me, in the face of my father's obdurate tonguelessness . . . dysphonia . . . muteness . . . recalcitrance . . . obmutescence . . . to coin words.

If I by chance stumbled on a rhyme in conversation – I am talking about my golden age now, my piping time, my fabled years before my Abel'd years – she showered praises on me, calling me her wonder boy, her prodigy, her little demi-god of language, all the while planting kisses on my head, as though to cool the forge that was my brain.

When I drew pictures in the soil she cried out in amazement at their lifelikeness, sometimes frightening my father who came running, fearing she'd been savaged by wild animals, and who was then asked to erect a fence around my work to keep those same wild animals from defacing it with their art-hating hoofs. As for my singing . . . there were times when I worried for her health, so direct a path did my trilling voice find into her heart, so violently did she roll her head to keep time with me.

Slim chance she had, then, against Someone who had put in more millennia daubing skies and harmonizing spheres than her little demi-god had given minutes to scratching sandscapes with a pointed stick. Her capitulation, when it was demanded, was all but complete. She made mawkish art herself – made mawkish art *of* herself – sitting like a virgin with a baby at her breast and her eyes cast heavenwards, averted from the source of generation, modest, impregnable, fixed upon idea, not matter.

And yet there were moments, as I hung hidden in my tree, when I could have sworn those eyes drooped heavily again towards my muddy brother, and the old look of insentience in slime once more took possession of her features. I cannot say for certain there was a struggle going on. As a supporter of neither side I wasn't on the look-out for signs of swerving loyalties. But it might have ended in a tussle had another god decided to try his luck in a more personable form. Who knows whether a snorting bull, making no bones about his intentions, may not after all have won the day, so many traces of the cow-in-heat did my mother still retain, so much steam still rose from her humid flanks, so full were her udders, even though Abel was fast approaching his first birthday, and divine melodies filled the air.

But there was no bull preparing to make a charge, and no notice served that any other god was willing to take up the challenge.

Unless you count my father, secretly perfecting his magic.

Leaving aside all the bodily disadvantages – cramps, stiffness, muscular spasms and seizures of the joints – it is not a good idea to spend as much time in a tree, spying on your family, as I did.

It is not a good idea *emotionally*.

You start to see your own absence, to notice how little your not being there is remarked on, how well others not only get by without you, but actually appear to thrive on your inexistence. To say that it is like observing your own death is altogether too grandiose. And too pleasing to yourself. You must suppose that you would in some measure be the hero of your own death, the reason why of whatever obsequies, and that at the very least you would be acknowledged sometimes as having been. What *I* saw, through leaves and fronds whose first function and principle of growth was to close around me, whose every breath seemed like a threat to mine, was more like my ... cancellation. I was lodged in no memory because I had been expunged from the almanac. Eclipsed. Occulted. The consoling illusion that however blurred you become to yourself, you enjoy a clear outline in the minds and affections of those who love you – the child's delirious supposition that at every waking moment a phantom of himself haunts the consciousness of his parents – came away in my aching fingers like stripped bark. I did not exist as an abstraction outside myself; I was not served and perpetuated by an army of impersonating spectres. If I had being anywhere, I had it in the tree; but, as my days in the tree were a sort of suspense of animation, I was as good as gone.

This condition is known to all, but not exclusively to all, who embark on espionage of the feelings. It is also the experience of the envious. For what else makes envy the most excruciating of the passions if not the dread of discovering your utter redundancy to the world's business? If the envious man could be made to believe that those whose good fortune he covets, those whose successful instrumentality he lusts after, actually think about *him* sometimes, take him into their consideration, out of love or hate, for a minute or two each day, for a day or two each year, and in this way intertwine him with their happiness or their riches, above all with their operativeness, he would instantly lose his envy. It is not their well-being that he cannot tolerate, but his unnecessity to it; not their prosperity, but whatever shows prosperity itself prospering excellently without him.

I see a Babel-suspiciousness on your faces. You find me too sophistical in this matter? You would have a spade called a spade and greed and grudging given their proper names? Your prerogative. Your city. But you will not understand the metaphysics of envy, you will not even understand why anyone should envy *you*, so long as you suppose that mere thwarted materialism is the goad that pricks the envious.

When God smelled the smoke of Abel's sacrifice, spread wide His nostrils to accommodate every pungent wisp and curl of it, do you think I fretted over the bounty He was sure to extend my brother in return? Do you think there were any cubits of inhospitable crawling scrub or homers of rotting straw to be handed over, that I could not bear to be without? There was nothing I wanted. Nothing I begrudged my poor obedient industrious younger brother. My feet slipped on the turning earth, failed to hold their ground against a force which seemed to blow me about the universe impalpably, like spores from a puff-ball – my ears roared, my skull collapsed inwards – not because I was greedy but because I was slighted.

Sleighted.

Palmed clean out of consideration and contention. Made superfluous in proportion as Abel was made to feel favoured, made supererogatory precisely *to* that favouritism.

Had the Architect of our emotions thought to come down and whisper in my ear, 'Let us together, you and I, give something to that lovely boy, Abel; let us confer, we who want nothing, as to what that gift should be,' all could have been saved. I would gladly have joined Him in His deliberations. Urged Him on to wilder and wilder extravagance. Give my brother everything, I would have said. Roll up fields for him like carpets. Gather him forests like bouquets. Keep not a stone from him. Keep not a worm. And my heart would have burst with love then, as it bursts now, imagining my munificence.

This, though, I will grant you:

I was not hanging hour after hour in an inimical tree, watching, weightless, my mother presenting her profile to one voracious lover and her nipple to another, because I was made to. Nobody forced me; I had alternatives.

The mountain, for example, was still amenable to unspoken sociability even if my father was not. And I did miss the mountain for the cold comfort its rocks gave me when I could bear fecundity no longer. There were more naming expeditions to go on, rare root and tuber hunts of my own devising – for truffles, yams, rhizomata, artichokes (by which I mean the fibres of the sun-loving turnsole, not the thirsty audi shauki which you in Babel use to spoon up oil and vinegar, the same way you slop up stories). There were rivers to navigate, unentitled rills and runnels to follow into whatever caverns of the earth they emptied. I could have been gone half a year – longer – before anyone noticed I was missing, and in that time have become a mighty hunter, a wayfarer of genius, a surveyor of the soul and spirit with his sights set on himself. Oceans might have borne my name, the lavic slopes of volcanoes the impression of my sandals. Who knows? – it is not beyond the bounds of credibility that an avenue of this very city might have celebrated me – CAINSWAY – and been tramped on in my honour for perpetuity . . .

Had I only leapt, swung and leapt, light as a boy, from those hypnotic branches.

But there was never a chance of that. Never. The tree held me enthralled, as rooted as itself. It was from the tree that I could view without distraction the drama of my existlessness made flesh, and no salt water voyage, no truffle hunt or pilgrimage to find and pocket the last opalescent bead of the river Pison, was as interesting a pastime to me as that. Once you have seen yourself not there you cannot cease from looking.

The sub-plot also – mere illustrative stage-business as it was – had begun to engross me. I sensed a crisis, heaven huddling into conference, a reappraisal of tactics, a decision, by no means lightly taken, to underprop the shekinah with something more tactile. To bolster it up. To flesh it out. It was becoming apparent that my mother's attention could not always be held by streaked skies and throbbing dawns. Pink gave way to silver. Blue to white. Sometimes, in a sort of inspired desperation, God the Painter would let go a great puff of flaming breath and seem to canopy her with the ribbed sands of the shore itself. But the likelihood that she was watching was diminishing. She lacked celestial patience. The chip of Adam's bone from which she had been taken still determined her disposition; she was brittle, obstinate, unadaptable, impervious; she was not content passively to expend aeons marvelling at light. If He was to keep her thoughts raised from the earth and fixed perpetually on Him, the Creator of Everything That Is Garish had to come up with fruitier, meatier inducements. He had to compete, in other words, with His own Adam.

Descending in Person remained out of the question. Pride kept Him invisible. A conviction that things would have come to a pretty pass indeed the day our reverence for Him became contingent on His possessing a body. As if we had the right to insist that our Maker be fashioned in the likeness of ourselves. Such a scruple did not preclude, however, as it had not precluded in the past, the employment of mediators, giant go-betweens that partook of His divinity but were, in appearance anyway, prepared to meet us halfway.

One of them, moved by my father's fervent prayers, had dropped to earth, my mother said, to soothe her while she cried giving birth – she who had never given birth before, and never been born herself – to me. He had stroked her face, her shoulder, touched her breast, seeming to console her even against the white-hot indifference (*that* time) of the Master he served.

A diaphanous man stood by you, she told me, at the moment you came into the world.

I had no memory of him, but it troubled me that he had stroked her face, her shoulder, touched her breast.

Had my mother changed the verbs, I wondered, after the wonderful event.

Another diaphanous man, of whom I also had no memory, breathed day and night upon the flames that licked up from his sword, barring us for eternity, so I was told, from a place that my parents, frankly, found too abstract and conceptual, sown with too many exclusions and symbolic interdictions, ever to miss.

Nephilim. Angels. God's single compromise between matter and non-matter. And just the beings to entrust with the delicate task of turning Eve's turning thoughts away again from things sublunary.

'Go to her,' I imagine He must have instructed them, 'go to her and brush her lightly with your wings so that her skin may have knowledge of the feather touch of heaven. But in your hearts let love unlibidinous reign.'

I am certain in my own mind that He had always known it was a poor idea to breach hierarchical etiquette, that nothing good would ever come of commerce between the sons of God and the daughters of men. But He too was a compulsive spectator, He too hung in a poison tree, and narrative curiosity must have got the better of Him; *morbid* narrative curiosity – an inclination to see how it would turn out precisely *because* it was bound to turn out badly.

This may look to you, who have lived for some time now without a Single God to trouble your equilibrium, like wanton cruelty on His part, the idle malice of a well-fed cat toying with whatever squeaks. In fact He meant harm primarily to Himself. Like all creative forces He was bent on apocalypse and ruin – the grand destruction of His grand design. The Lord giveth and the Lord taketh away? No, no – He is not so whimsical. The Lord giveth *in order that* the Lord may take away.

A thousand times a thousand years before He made the world He must have itched to flood it. Destruction was such a powerful impulse in Him it is a miracle – perhaps the miracle of all miracles – that He was ever able to stay His hand long enough to fashion something *to* destroy. *And God looked upon the earth, and, behold, it was corrupt.* Behold! Did I not know it! Did I not tell thee!

Ah, the bliss of it! Vindication! Ah, the joy of it!

And this His own handiwork. Was there ever artist who hated his own artistry so feverishly? Or lover so intent on proving himself betrayed?

A thousand times a thousand years before He made the world He itched to flood it, burn whatever in it was flammable, flatten whatever in it was round. And there is no reason not to believe that He laid plans as far back as then to drop the angels Azael and Semyaza before my mother on a day so hot it was necessary to close one's eyes against the unendurable harshness of colour, on a day so moist it seemed as though rain had forgotten gravity and was falling upwards, from earth to heaven.

They landed soundlessly, showing every consideration for her afflicted senses, fanning the air about her cool with their pinions, their breath winnowing her hair, a soft soothing tinkling, flatter than the sound of ice-cold water playing over stones, more like wind rattling a banana plant, coming from the jewellery Azael wore – it seemed to me defiantly, as a reproach – around his wrist and throat.

It was an age before my mother became aware that they were there. When she raised her head, she found herself held by Semyaza's insistent gaze. So it would be wherever they went, whomsoever they called on: Semyaza demanding first notice, his stare bold, unwavering, his plumage high and tense, and Azael to one side, crestfallen and peevish, fingering his ornaments.

Semyaza folded his feathers and bent low over my mother. 'Better?' he inquired, his voice as naked as his face. 'Is that better for you?' She was to understand that he was the one who had watched over her, he was the one who had blown her cool.

She nodded, screwing up her eyes as though to shield them, as though to shield herself and her credulity, from the dazzling irradiation of the angel. I recognized the expression. She had used it on me when I had impressed her with a sentence; on my father when his great boyishness had softened her heart; on Abel when he blew bubbles in the mud. Deities, the expression said, Everywhere I look I see deities; who shall protect me from Their Glory?

Where would gods be without the devotion of women? Here is why my father had been put into a deep sleep and a help meet extracted from his side. It was not Adam's welfare the Lord of Creation had been concerned for. The one craving love and companionship, homage and adoration, was Him. H-M.

Semyaza, too, was greedy for a woman's regard. From the steep planes of his unguarded and unshadowed face his thirsty spirit looked out, on watch for any movement or response that could be construed as admiration. At the moment of positive identification – such as now, when my mother screwed up her eyes against his splendour – his very bones shone; but should nothing be returned to him, his features offered no hiding place and bitter disappointment burned on his countenance like fever.

He was larger than any angel that had been sent to us before, half as tall again as Azael, with a wing span surely double that of his companion's and with a more profuse feathering at his waist and heels. He was not resplendent, though – neither of them was resplendent – despite my mother's impersonation of a mere mortal woman entirely overcome. There was something soiled about them both, as if they had journeyed too far without refreshment, or had decided to travel in borrowed plumage. This was an effect partly, as had been noticed on earlier visitations, of a fault in their engineering. Advantageous as it must have been for them, in matters relating to survival, to have arms unencumbered by feathers, in addition to wings, the drawback was an over-elaboration of musculature that impeded ordinary terrestrial movement. Sometimes the wings got in the way of the arms, sometimes the arms interfered with the functioning of the wings. They were not always certain which part of themselves to employ. They walked awkwardly. They toppled easily. The extra load told on the shoulders and the spine, creating problems of posture and any number of dermatological complications. I never once saw an angel who was not round-shouldered and stiff-necked, or whose skin was not chafed and frayed by the weight and irritation of his feathers. And this is to say nothing of lice and ring-worm and all the other consequences of careless grooming.

Even from where I was hidden, a bowshot away, I could see that Azael's flesh was broken wherever that section of him that was bird joined that section of him that was man; and that Semyaza had only to begin to stretch a wing or scratch a scapular for a small snowstorm of snapped quills and ruined skin to fill the air around him. You invariably knew where an angel had been from the droppings of down and covert, plume and flesh, he left behind him.

Although it was not her function to notice imperfections in men or gods or angels, my mother was not able to pretend for long that she was unaware of how seriously her visitors itched and flaked. What would later become a ritual, a service expected and fought over by Semyaza and Azael, began as an act of common charity. Why don't you let me, she said, when for the hundredth time Semyaza stood on one leg, reached behind him, and tried to rip his back apart.

'Let you?'

Yes, she said. Adding – inconsequentially, it seemed to me – I have sons of my own.

Semyaza knelt before her, bent his neck and drew in his wings. It was a motion intended to suggest a willing submission either to execution or to pleasure – she might choose; a gesture as winning as a pet parrot's; but from behind, as I saw him, he appeared hooded and predatory, a tattered carrion crow the colour of a dirty pigeon.

I think you need more than a scratch, my mother said when she saw how badly he was damaged. Be still. Be still, I will try not to hurt you.

'You cannot hurt me,' the angel told her.

She had her baby balms by her. Her Abel remedies. Her salves and balsams for sucklings and angels. Using an ointment made from crushed camomile, she bathed Semyaza's chaps and ulcerations. Then she dusted them, as she once dusted mine, in a powder of mica and talcum.

And now you, she said to Azael.

The whole time she attended to Azael, whose shoulders were like rotten fruit, the entire rind ready to fall away in her fingers, Semyaza stood where she had to see him and be aware of his relentless attention. His eyes would not leave hers. It didn't matter if she looked away or stared only into Azael's sores, Semyaza was always there, claiming her thoughts.

'I'm extremely persistent,' he said to her. 'That's one of the reasons I enjoy so much trust.'

He didn't suppose she needed to be told *whose* trust.

She made no reply, treating him instead to her blurred and blinded look. I had never much cared for it, even in the days before I had a brother and it was mainly I who had blinded her; but ever since she had sat down in the mud and become careless of her weight I had not thought it suited her to be bedazzled. Her jowls had grown too heavy to be tipped up in blithe innocence of all meaning; her cheeks too rounded to risk a girl's tremor.

'I have a stronger will than is good for me,' Semyaza went on, still not releasing her from his gaze. 'It's important to me to win. I warn you of this so that you will not be surprised by what you see when you know me better. I hope my perseverance hasn't distressed you. If it has, I am sorry. But perseverance is of my essence.'

It was the first of many boasts and the first of many apologies. What he wished to force on her was not only his presence but also the idea that he was somehow or other ambiguous. The tarnish I had seen upon his grandeur had not got there by accident, nor was it a blemish he was in any way anxious to conceal. If a fragrance less than celestial blew from his plumes, he wanted my mother to smell it; if the drama of his moral life revolved around the issue of whether it was his destiny to inspire trust or betray it, he wanted her to sit in on the struggle. Some men seek to hide the thing in their nature that perverts their goodness; others, and these may include angels, are happy only when their soul's corruption is made public.

'Hail, Mother of Mankind,' Semyaza had said unto Eve after the opening pleasantries – an angel of the Lord remembering himself. 'Hail, Eve, whose fruitful womb . . .' (I closed my ears to this.) 'Hail, first and best of women. Blessings we bring thee from the Most High.' He had used his full height, showing, in his divine lineaments, how recently he had brushed majesty. Truly, the sun had reddened in his countenance, the seven thunders had rolled in his chest, and his feet had been as pillars of fire. Yet I could have sworn he had put an alternative gloss on his mission – appended a derisive footnote – daring my mother to detect it and thereby be the cause of his defection. What I am doing for Him, I would rather be doing for myself, he seemed to be saying, and he was saying it on the strength of the briefest acquaintance, a handful of sentences, a minute or two of beating his wings on a hot afternoon.

I wondered if the afternoon itself had anything to do with it, so sudden and violent did I find Semyaza's willingness to pull down the very heavens, let my mother only wink him to it. It was a day for extraordinary event. Beneath a sun hotter than we had ever yet been punished with, a molten fire-spitting sun, the earth fainted. Birds dropped from the sky. Mosquitoes browned, like dead leaves, in stolen gore. Tusked, probosci-formed creatures crawled out of the forests on their bellies, unable to separate their tongues from the dried-up gullies of their mouths. Had my father thought of doing his rain impressions, wherever my father was, he could have called all nature to him. Bleh! bleh! bleh!

It was a perverse, tormenting heat, baking rivers into rocks and melting rocks back into rivers. Plants that had not been there in the morning grew to the height of angels, flowered the colour of blood and fell apart. Irrigated by my perspiration, the tree I hid in rose six cubits every hour, with me in it. Why then should not a seraph stand with his wings open between my mother and that great ball of flame, look shamelessly on her muddy breasts, and chance Hell on a kiss? It was just the day.

Naïve of me. The sun plays no part in incinerations of the kind Semyaza sought. And neither, strictly speaking, did my mother. Semyaza's nature was treacherous, and treachery stokes its own fires. It needs no circumstances or pretexts or motives. Motivelessness is the very thing it thrives on. Ask any recreant – the slighter the precipitating agent, the sweeter the treason. Semyaza had it in him to whistle off his allegiance to the Lord God of Hosts just to pass the time of day. And of course the Lord God of Hosts had it in *Him* to watch Semyaza do it.

Azael's disgruntlement – for all I knew as long standing as Semyaza's perfidy, and for all I knew they both had been what they were now ever since they'd been bred or hatched from spirit – was, by comparison, mere stripling sullenness. He had been passed over in some way, demoted, valued under his deserts, made an envoy instead of an ambassador – this seemed to be the sum of his grievance. His jaw trembled in remembrance of it, he picked his skin and wore his reddish hair in curls beneath a coronet, presumably out of self-spite, in order to resemble a half-fallen cherub, but he did not look capable of plotting serious rebellion. He did not have the verve or the ambition to go the way of Satan. If there was venery in heaven, a hankering for matter where matter was not meant to be, Azael would certainly have been among those whispering on its behalf. It was easy to imagine him waving a silver sword and turning that pettish, slightly second-hand look of his into a prizeable commodity where languor was in short supply. But futility was his object; failure and oppression the only outcome he looked forward to.

And he was decidedly not interested in my mother.

The moment Semyaza began one of his charged interrogations – 'Tell me about yourself, Eve. What is it like being a mother? Do you have to make conscious adjustments to the way you think when you go from husband to son? Are you a different woman when you are a wife than when you are with your children? Does your body feel the same to you in both contexts? Whose touch do you prefer?' – Azael would rattle his hackle-feathers and take off on a short, dipping walk, until his wings became entangled in vegetation, or the spontaneous eruption of fungi beneath his feet made him nauseous, and he was forced to return.

To my surprise – because I thought he might have liked the composition of virgin and child – Azael was not interested in my brother either. It's possible he did not want a baby pulling at his ravaged flesh, or that he thought two cherubic urchins in such restricted company was one cherubic urchin too many. Whatever his reasons, he would back away, with something between disgust and terror in his eyes, whenever Abel crawled towards him; and sometimes, when the crying started, he would lie belly down in the guggling mud and pull his wings over his ears and head, like a bat, so that everything around him would be black and silent.

Semyaza, though, could not put Abel down. He searched his fat little body for the buds of wings, threw him high into the air to see what sort of flier he would make, swung him across his shoulders, rubbed him between the palms of his hands as though mystified by the substance he was made of. 'What do you feel when you see him?' he asked my mother.

'What do you feel when you see him with *me*? Do you mind my playing with him like this? Do you fear for his safety? Is that what it is to be a mother – to be continuously anxious? Forgive me for asking, but does love for one child supplant love for another? Do you have to remind yourself not to let such a thing happen, or is maternal love too blinding to be controlled? Can you point to the place where you feel this love? Does it have a specific location in your body, or is it diffused and spirituous as it is with us? Please don't answer if you would rather not, but it is all fascinating to me.'

All? My mother did not flinch when she said this.

Nor did Semyaza. '*All* – you, your children, your husband.'

Fascinating though we were to him, Semyaza never once inquired as to my father's whereabouts, or mine.

Later, on a third or fourth visit, while Azael was off limping through the undergrowth, Semyaza for no apparent reason scooped Abel up in a single hand and began to squeeze him. Very slowly, very purposefully, with his fingers supporting Abel's back and his angelic thumb pressed into his middle, he made as if to close his hand. The baby's screams kept Azael out of the way. Semyaza held my mother, as surely as he held Abel, at the end of an unfaltering stare. In proportion as he increased the pressure of his thumb did he intensify the coercion in his eye. All three of them were joined in a perfect equipoise of tension; whatever thrill of fear ran through one, ran through them all. Ran through me too, to the degree that I thought I would have to give my game away and come running from the tree, calling for Semyaza to stop, crying blue murder, and shouting for my father to do something useful with his own hands, just this once, and wrestle down an angel.

Then, just as suddenly and unaccountably as he had begun, Semyaza left off. Still without lowering his stare or making any gesture to shadow his naked and unprotected face, he handed back Abel, a spray of crushed flowers, to my mother's care.

'I am sorry,' he said. 'I had to do that. It was a test of my will-power over yours. I did warn you to expect this. It is very important to me to win. You were aware, of course, that it was you I was squeezing.'

She put her baby to her breast. A protective gesture all round. But she was no longer striking poses.

I don't care what you are testing in yourself, she said. But I would like to know what you are testing in me.

He angled his head, this way and that, so that she should see how unconcealed he was. His brow, his nose, the great sweep of his jaw, as bare as a clump of boulders. Then he smiled, an angel's smile, irradiating them all. 'You were created good,' he said. 'You have not, however, always stayed that way. We are sent, by a God who loves you, to report on your progress and to remind you of the benefits of perseverance in virtue. Consider the squeeze to be both a token from me, whose essence is perseverance, and a memento from Him, whose essence, as you know, is love.'

He ordered you to hurt a baby?

I am still able to recall the exact tone in which my mother asked that astonished question. Perhaps because I have heard it so many times since, and will go on hearing it as long as there are mothers. *Hurt a baby?* Can there be those who would wish malice on *a baby?* Astonishing that they should be so astonished, when all along it is the clamour of young, helpless, demanding life that is most likely to turn us savage, and makes murderers even out of mothers themselves.

'We enjoy a degree of latitude,' Semyaza told her, opening and closing his wings and fluttering in his own draught, 'as to how we interpret His will. Else we would be slaves, not angels. But now, I think, is as propitious an hour as any to the application of camomile and talcum.' He lowered his head, like an itching macaw. 'Remember – I feel no pain.'

When he next essayed the strength of his grip and will-power it was on her in person. A cooler day, no perturbations of the heavens, his descent all unannounced, not a rip or ruffle of a single feather to tell her he had landed. He was behind her before she could let out a cry, a hand on each breast, tightening.

This time I did come down from the tree.

Does it surprise you that I could feel concern for my brother's safety, when it was I who at the very hour of his birth had passed a death sentence on him?

It shouldn't.

Who can you possibly care more for than a person whose continuing existence depends largely on yourself?

I loved Abel. Considering how little contact I had with him as a baby, how infrequently we played together, how few were the occasions when his rubbery belly was given me to blow on or paddle in, I loved him to excess. Let him not die, I prayed, lying sleepless under the too-bright stars. I will not allow him to die, I promised. I will not allow a hair of his head to be harmed. If he dies before me I shall not be able to support my grief.

Does this mean that I had lifted his death-sentence? Far from it. I simply took upon myself his protection because I knew better than anybody the extent of the danger he had to be protected from.

I see incipient amusement watering the corners of an eye or two among you. Our old difficulty. Or rather, *your* old difficulty. Babel-levity. Shinarite-scepticism. Evidently you are uncomfortable with the robustness of my definitions of devotion. This is a pity. A man who has slain his brother has the right to feel he should be listened to on the subject of love. Especially in this city where, if you will forgive me, you hold to the sentimental, parochial view that the affections are not to be confused with the disaffections — at least in discourse.

Which is tantamount to taking a vow of silence on the matter, and a consequence, as you don't need me to point out, of every deity having fled the glaring sunlight of your streets.

I put it to you anyway, whether or not your smiles go off like crackers on your faces, that we never have more to fear than when we are loved extravagantly. Not because extravagant love turns to extravagant hate, but because extravagant love already *is* extravagant hate. Only the impulse to murderousness, known here – no, here! here! – in every heart, can explain the irrationality of the thing we call adoration. Only murderousness would ever look to hide in such a place. It is common for lovers to set out on their acquaintance as enemies. It is regarded as quaint, touching even, that they should have misread each other quite so badly in the beginning. They did not. They fell in love – yes, even under the shadows of your immaculate rational ziggurats they fell in love – precisely so as not to fall, each to each, in bloody combat. What we call infatuation is nothing other than being mesmerized by the realization that we can juggle violence.

And I did infatuate myself with Abel. With the idea of his well-being. With the very principle of his life. I mean, quite unfancifully, that I assumed responsibility for the beating of his heart. I listened out for it. I watched over it. I monitored its regularity. In the dead of night, once I could be sure that my mother was asleep, and my father – at that distance stipulated by the laws of pollution, from where he could not inadvertently roll over and uncover the fountain of my mother's blood – was on his back and whimpering in his dreams, I crept along the ground like the unmentionable serpent, silently, invisibly, my trunk slithering in sand or sucked downwards in the mud, until I reached the hollowed bark, the hallowed boat beached in a desert oasis, where Abel lay unconscious alike of enemy or protector. Sometimes I would be content to sit with my back against his crib, looking up into the stars and listening for his breathing. I did not especially want to see him. Or touch him. Mine was not a love of that kind. It was sufficient to know he was alive. If the smell of new-grown hair and new-formed bone blew from his skull into my nostrils, well and good. But I did not need to grasp him through my senses: the idea I had of him did not want for vividness, and besides, the odour of new creation was of all odours the one I would most happily have gone without.

There were nights, though, when his breathing was so quiet that I could not be certain it was there at all. And it was on these nights that love became indistinguishable from panic – an obstruction the size of a mountain blocking up *my* breathing – and I would crouch over him, a black shadow obliterating the moon, and lay my ear to his silent heart. Hours on end I would stay like that, not daring to withdraw for fear that I might choose the very moment to leave that his heart chose to stop.

It is a fearful burden, to be one's brother's keeper. The vigil breeds its own impositions; the precautions turn on themselves and become hazards.

What if my listening was itself a pressure on his chest?

What if the weight of my head was the very thing that would make his heart give up?

What if he should sense my alarm through his sleep and die of my dread that he would die?

Or suppose he should suddenly wake and find me looming above his cot, a beast preparing to devour him with its ear – what then? Would that not have been enough to stop a heart twice the size of his?

The darkness gave me no respite. Once I had staked my peace on his pulse I could not leave until the first sickly glimmerings of dawn. Make no mistake: I knew that that too was arbitrary. That Abel might just as soon pick that minute to spite me with his extinction, might just as plausibly stop living in the light as in the dark. But all obsessional behaviour this side of madness must make a concession to normality somewhere, and light was the determining factor in where I made mine.

I had to avoid being caught hanging over him. I did not want it to be known how immoderately I feared for his life. I shrank from being exposed for what I was – a brother lover.

Is that not normalcy? A resistance to the whole world's knowing that I doted on my sibling? Even if the whole world only did comprise the four of us. Two plus me plus him. Her minus me plus them squared.

Roughly coincident with my immoderately loved brother's first birthday (I kept a tally of the days of my desolation, just as my father did his), two events occurred, independent of each other but combining to produce a result the majority of us (Abel not counting) thought desirable: the resumption of family relations and the phased withdrawal of the supranatural to Its proper sphere.

The first of these events, to which I have already alluded briefly, was Semyaza's abrupt avolation – call it decampment, or desertion, or simply resignation – from the ranks of the heavenly choir, where I suppose him to have grown weary singing the praises of Somebody Else, and his unheralded appearance on earth, sans Azael, sans ceremony, his feathers scorched from the velocity of his descent, hell-bent on rape . . .

But I cannot be convinced you have earned the right to hear of that tonight. A man does not speak to strangers of a rape upon his mother by an archangel unless he can be certain of their seriousness . . .

6. OPENINGS

I

'There was a destitute widow,' Korah began, 'a pauper's relict, mother of two starving daughters, orphans . . .'

. . . left to shift for herself and her little ones after her husband had been stoned to death by enthusiasts for gathering sticks on the Sabbath. Gathering sticks, my friends, in order to build a fire by which his wife and daughters might have warmed their shivering hands.

In the Torah this is adjudged a sin.

Now I must tell you that these maids were fair before their father's murder, and that their mother had been comely. But now the three of them were bent like hags, their bones as dry as the firewood they'd been denied.

Despairing of change, the widow prayed for death. And death would surely have answered, had not a relative of one of the murderers, middlingly touched by guilt, offered her a corner of his least productive field. You and I, my friends, would not have attempted to grow a turnip in this wretched paddock; but any expectation is better than none, and thus, trusting to the God of Moses – the same God who has delivered us from the honey-pots of Egypt into the dry wells of Kadesh-Barnea – the widow put her wasted shoulder to the plough.

And had no sooner hitched her team than she was espied by Moses himself, out walking among his people early. 'Thou shalt not plough,' he told her, 'with an ox and ass together.'

Obeying this statute, for she was as fearful as she was pious (a conjunction, gentlemen, upon which our leaders do not hesitate to prey), she set about sowing. Once again Moses happened to be taking the air. 'Thou shalt not sow thy field with mingled seed,' he reminded her.

The widow sowed as she was bid. On the appearance of the first juiceless fruits of her stunted field she raised her eyes from labour and saw . . .

Moses!

He was carrying an empty basket. 'For you,' he said, meekly.

Mistaking this meekness for magnanimity, as many of us have done since, the poor woman felt her face suffuse with gratitude. 'For me?' she cried. She could not remember how many years it had been since she had last received a gift.

'For you, yes,' said Moses, 'in order that thou shalt not omit to take the first of the fruit of the earth, that the Lord thy God hath given thee, and shalt go unto the priest, and shalt give unto the priest . . .'

She did as she was told to do. Even had her piety deserted her, she would have obeyed; for she had seen what punishment is meted out to the impious.

When harvest time approached, she was dismayed but not surprised to find Moses, knee-high in grasses, in the field before her. 'I came to see thee reap,' he said, plucking slugs from his fringes, 'for thou shalt not make clean riddance of the corners of thy field when thou reapest.'

'But this field is itself a corner,' she pleaded.

He closed his eyes, a man of God unwilling to behold the speciousness of the ungodly. 'Neither shalt thou,' he went on, 'gather any gleanings of thy harvest. Those shalt thou leave unto the poor, and to the stranger.'

The distraught woman bowed her head, and did not say, 'But Moses, I *am* the poor!' Or, 'Who is stranger, Moses, to good fortune, than my children?'

Her head was always bowed now. Her back permanently curved, like the crick in Aaron's priestly rod.

As she prepared to thresh the grain, she knew by the creeping of the hairs upon her neck that Moses stood behind her with another statute.

'And of the grain that thou separatest, thou shalt give unto –'

But she did not this time wait to be told unto whom. 'No,' she said. 'I will not give a portion – I will give all. I am bled dry. You cannot squeeze more out of me. Tomorrow, if I can find a buyer, will I sell my field.'

With the little she received she bought a single ram – more miserable than herself. And to go with it, a single ewe – scrawnier even than her daughters. No sooner was the firstling of her sheep born than Aaron called on her in all the finery of his ephod – woven work around its collar, and upon the hem pomegranates of blue and purple and scarlet alternating with golden bells – a proper bridegroom, come to claim the flesh that was his due.

The moment she began to shear he was there again, his sacerdotal hand outstretched. 'The first of your fleece,' he demanded. And upon learning that the widow had decided she could do no better than slaughter her little flock, Aaron raced across the pastures to her, as fast as his ephod would permit him. 'Mine, all mine . . . the shoulder, the two cheeks, and the maw.'

'Since you persist,' the woman cried, 'I consecrate all that is left to the Lord.'

'In which event,' said Aaron through his sinuses, practising that high-toned nasality which has served him well in his capacity as holy spokesman for his slow-tongued brother, 'the whole of the flesh of thy flock belongs to me.

Everything devoted in Israel is mine. It shall then *all* be mine.'

And so saying – so *intuning* – he departed, bearing off with him, in strict accordance with Torah, the entirety of the poor widow's meat, leaving her and her ailing orphans unprovided for, to forage or to perish as they pleased . . .

'For these things, my brethren, I weep,' wept Korah. 'Mine eye, mine eye runneth with water to see that such things are, and are allowed to be, even now, even here in our deliverance, in the name of the God of Moses and his brother Aaron.'

II

'On song,' says Naaman approvingly. 'On song tonight.'

Cain nods and thanks him. He finds talking to Naaman difficult, and accepting praise from him, if praise is the appropriate word, impossible.

Whatever the delicious joke is, the after- or foretaste of which always sits like a winking pearl of dew on Naaman's womanly lips, Cain knows that he is doomed never to get it. Sometimes the joke he doesn't get is attributed to himself, as when Naaman says, 'I think you may have been a little dry, perhaps a little *too* tart, even for me, this evening.' Or, 'Wicked, quite wicked of you. I had to chew on my sleeve to silence my guffaws.' And then Cain is left to puzzle over his narrative, wondering which grave episode this time has struck the senior dignitary's funny-bone.

Tonight, Naaman would have addressed himself at length to 'those two quite delicious angels . . . a species of being

never witnessed, I believe, though much spoken of, in Babel . . .
what names did you give to them again?' – but the weight
of his daughter on his arm shortens his appreciation. 'I do not
know,' he says instead, 'whether you have met my . . .'

Cain inclines his head. He has not met Zilpah, but he has
been observing her observing him in public places, in parks,
on the streets, around theatres, ever since his arrival in the
city. It could almost be said that although he hasn't met her he
has talked to her, for she regularly, no, she *religiously* attends
his recitals, and so startles him by the solemnity of her concentration, that many of the things he says have her, so to speak,
as their object. She would appear to wish to see further into
his soul than he sees himself; so he is at pains to show that he
has nothing to conceal, that he is built of hollow tubes through
which anyone may peer.

Given his usual complaint against audiences in Babel –
that they are embarrassed into laughter by whatever is not
moderate – you would think Cain would be grateful for
Zilpah's sorrowing demeanour. But he doesn't like her. Although he hasn't met her, he knows he doesn't like her. It
may be a fact that her omnipresence has been troublesome
enough to interest him, but her appearance is definitely not
interesting enough to trouble him. She is too unprotected
for his taste, her face too exposed, her skeleton somehow
too deducible. When she turns from him he can count her
vertebrae like buttons through her gown. When she sits listening to him talk, following his vision as though the iris
that floats in the humour of his eye is floating in the fluid
of hers too, he believes he can see the fibrous cords and
papillary muscles of her heart.

They see into each other; she with pity threatening to be
love, he with disinclination determined to be hate.

The one item of intriguing artifice about her person is the
meticulously braided plait that hangs like a second spine down
her back. This is the only part of Zilpah that Cain is able to

envisage when Zilpah is not in front of him, and so comprehensively disgusts him that he can imagine forgiving all her other lesser failings for its sake. If ever he lays a hand on the assortment of pumping valves and easily splintered bones that is Naaman's daughter – and he does not expect to – her fanatic plait will be the only reason.

The only reason other than her father, that is.

'But we must leave you to your refreshment,' Naaman remembers. 'You must be dry. Can I have anything sent to you? A jug . . . a pitcher . . . a ewer . . . a gallipot . . . a jeroboam of wine?'

The grudging Cain allows a little light to flicker from his face. They are standing in a public place and members of his audience are still passing, still trying to secure him with their smiles. He has the use of a room in the bowels of the theatre and is suddenly impatient to be in it. He would like to lie down for a while. Rest his feet. Close his eyes. And try not to imagine all the ways in which he has inadvertently amused Naaman. To say nothing of inadvertently unamusing Naaman's daughter.

'Yes, wine,' he says. 'Yes. Thank you. A jeroboam should just do it.'

He watches Naaman and Zilpah depart, the father tall and loping, the more frightening for never being quite serious, the daughter barely held together by the twenty-four buttons that run down her spine, her plait rising and falling of its own will, capricious like the tail of a tree-monkey.

III

He does not, after all, repair immediately to the artist's rest room, but takes a turn instead through the courtyard at the rear of the building, a fragrant, galleried garden built of stone, from which he can enjoy a view of the great white-tiered amphitheatre that climbs the marble mountain and loses itself in a smoking haze of dying sun and burnished cloud and olive trees.

Like everyone else in the talking business he sometimes imagines himself performing there, addressing a multitude so vast that those in the uppermost tiers, those sitting where the gods should have been, appear as nothing but iridescences of pigment in the marble. But the amphitheatre is reserved for mere games – bull-baiting, dog-fighting, horse-races – and for popular entertainments such as circuses and epic dramas set to sickly music, celebrating, as best as can be remembered, the engineering of Babel.

It is not in use tonight. It is too warm for sport. But like a sea-shell it retains its roar, although its only population now is bats and lizards.

The other outdoor venues – the market squares where the prophets and the pranksters gather, the parks and river banks that are popular with acrobats and near-sighted poetesses, the temple steps favoured by the little brown fairy-tellers from beyond the Indus – have not proved suitable to his purposes either. The competing voices jangle his nerves; the sight of a crowd half-listening to him and half-attending to a plate-spinner who can also imitate the roars of fabled monsters makes him lose his place in his story; and the atmosphere of rude commerce, one skill jostling for notice with another, men selling their experiences as though they were camel-bells or carpets, does not seem to him to be conducive to that deliberation of delivery, that covering up of tracks and thwarting of expectation, which is for him the sole justification for telling anything.

It was Naaman who found him an intimate indoor lecture theatre, assuring him that his natural audience, the city's elite – teachers, civil servants, wives of men of action, the lame, the lost, the lonely – actually preferred to take their entertainment in the dark, off the ground, in small numbers, and far from sunlight.

'Now if we had somewhere in one of our towers,' Naaman had twinkled, 'that would be absolutely perfect.'

Cain had watched him carefully. What did Naaman know about him and towers? Was he waiting for Cain to say, 'Well, it's strange that you should mention that because I mean in the end to erect a tower of my own'?

In fact the theatre was ideal. Cain, too, favoured elevation and the dark. And his audience was exactly as Naaman had predicted it . . . with the exception – that's to say, with the inclusion – of Naaman's own daughter.

Cain wishes he were as comfortable with the audience as with the theatre. He cannot describe his ideal congregation, but he knows what it isn't. And what it isn't is always what it is. 'Why am I drawn to clerks and tutors and curators?' he wonders. 'And why are only those who squint and rub their foreheads drawn to me? I relate the blackest secrets of the heart; I discourse on disobedience, faithlessness, blasphemy and crime – yet when did a blasphemer or a criminal last come to hear me talk?'

He is not revolving these particular questions in his mind as he returns inside, although they are never distant from his thoughts. But a note which is waiting for him on the door of his rest room instantly revives them. The message is from the satiric poet, Preplen, whom Cain has encountered briefly on his promenades through the city, but has in the main chosen to ignore on the grounds that he, Preplen, appears to be after a connection, whereas he, Cain, is after whatever is the opposite.

A *dis*connection? No. That implies a prior tie, and prior ties are precisely what's at issue between them.

The note is addressed, freely, to *Cain the Edenite!?!?*, and says:

Fratricidal greetings!

(Or do I mean, fraternal?)

Peace, anyway.

I see that you are still working at getting the barbarians to like you. When will you be satisfied that they like you *enough*? Ignore that question . . . I dread the duration of your answer.

Tell me this, instead. What do you see when you look into a mirror. Yourself? You take my breath away. You'll tell me next that a reflection cannot lie. Do you know what the average citizen of Babel sees when he looks into a mirror? He sees a saffron-skinned giant disappearing into silver cloud. Your father, against whom I will not hear a word, saw a magician. Your mother, against whom also I will not hear a word, saw the handmaiden of archangels. YHWH, against Whom I will not hear a vowel, has no reflection, but if He had It would be LAW.

Whatever takes your eye in the glass, Cain, you do not see the thing your barbarous Babel friends see. I have watched them looking at you. I know what form an Edenite assumes in their sight. Not pretty. Not pretty. And to think of your concern to dispel horn rumours, tail rumours, lest any offence to their refined aesthetic come between you and their liking – why, it would be tragic were it not ludicrous. Horns and a tail? Let me advise you, Cain, like a brother . . . all right, like a friend: horns and a tail would be an improvement, horns and a tail would be beauty itself, compared to what they *think* they behold when you walk among them.

It's not my intention to upset you. Only to remind you what you are supposed to be here for. We do not flit in and out of other men's houses, we Edenites, we do not settle on other men's land and drink other men's wine and water, merely in order that they should like us. We are meant to be demonstrating the transportability of our faith. Look: we do not convey statues, but we carry a voice.

Have you forgotten why you were sent from the presence of Your Creator? It wasn't in order to be decorative, Cain. It wasn't to show Shinarites that your skin was smoother than theirs. You were sent to be a goad. To prick with the tenacity of your remorse and His love. And to shame those who have never heard of either.

Call yourself a murderer!

You have forgone your fearsomeness, Cain. Your iniquity doesn't shock them any more. Your naked greed doesn't shock them any more. A word from the wise: your naked arse wouldn't shock them any more!

So what am I asking you to do? Oh, why are you always bothering me with questions? Just this: show them out of what terrible disharmony of soul Edenites like you and I achieve our final unity. Make them choke on our sins. Make them vomit on our farts. After all . . .

. . . THEY ALREADY DO.

I enclose a number of my recent pieces which may, or may not, interest you. *Please return* any not.

> Fratricidally,
> (No, I don't mean, fraternally,)
> Preplen, poet

IV

In reply to that unctuous fiction, as in reply to Korah's previous offensives against the Word (we speak softly in order to spare Sisobk), Moses could not muster the eloquence that a modern might.

Chronology and culture were against him.

Even in the desert, when you would have expected travelling light to be their first consideration, the bedouin Israelites trusted too much in the material proof of God's election for Moses to be able to sway them against riches. Or against the falsehoods which of necessity issue from a rich man's mouth.

At best, he might have got away with,

Hear me, O Israel, the rich man is wise in his own conceit

or,

Let not the wise man glory in his wisdom, neither let the rich man glory in his wealth

– these being only perfunctory musings on vanity in general, and not any particular singling out of wealth for censure.

As for,

Go to now, ye rich men, weep and howl for your miseries that shall come upon you ... Your gold and silver is cankered; and the rust of them shall be a witness against you, and shall eat your flesh as it were fire

– no such dehortation against materialism was conceivable, because no such passion against it existed. It would be some while yet before men attached a higher value to what was absent from their eyes than what was present; and if the word for that is spirituality, it must not be forgotten that the spirit is what is sought at the end of a national dream, not at its beginning. With everything before it and a promise of spectacular conquest and well-being to realize – houses full of all good things, which it filled not; vineyards and olive trees, which it planted not – Israel was hardly in the temper to dissociate plenty from holiness.

Despair drives men to believe that riches and salvation are

incompatible; and so, sometimes, does repletion. But seldom hope; and never hope in its infancy.

So Korah was safe, in the thirteenth century before Christ, from the charge of champagne insurrectionism. His three hundred mules count against him only in the modern mind. But there was another accusation, quite apart from his possessions, that Moses could have levelled at him. He could have expressed surprise, ecclesiastic to ecclesiastic, at Korah's naïvety. 'How little you appear to have grasped, Korah,' he might have said, 'of the real significance of those rituals and commandments which, in truth, any fool can parody.'

Had Moses been an early Freud – as Freud surely was, for the purposes of another sort of Jewish deliverance, a later Moses – he would have wasted no time explaining to Korah what Korah, as a member of a priestly family, ought strictly speaking to have known for himself, namely . . .

'. . . namely, that the elaboration of those Mosaic edicts at which you scoff, Korah, serve the function of satisfying a guilt which is inevitable when a people make the journey from sorcery and magic – *Zauberei* and *Magie* – to a *Monotheistische* religion, and thus, by worshipping a father, duplicate communally the individual experience of family.

'Having made religion personal, a matter of covenants and reciprocities, and therefore (you're a family man, you know) treacheries and betrayals, you Israelites – you *children* of Israel – can justify God's lapses of love and attention only by blaming yourselves; suppressing your hostility or disappointment in a ritualized performance of duties obsessional in character – *Zwangsneurose . . . verstehen?* – which serves at one and the same time the surreptitious ends of self-aggrandizement and self-abasement. In short, masochism. The voluptuous expectation of unpleasure. Literally the prevention, the forestalling of catastrophe by anticipation of its terrors, and by an acceptance, before the event, that whatever befalls you, you have brought upon yourselves.

'I suggest that you consider your baldness in this light, Korah. Recalling – if you have the courage – *everything* you felt when you swung helpless as a baby in Moses's paternal arms, and allowed him to take a blade to your genitals.

'Thus, to return to the matter in hand, by setting yourselves ethical standards more and more impossible to observe, and on account of whose non-observance God-your-father has no alternative but to chastise you, the self-proving logic by which you understand yourselves to be chosen is assured. What your enemy/father Moses is effecting every time he returns from the mountain with another adjunct to the Torah, is nothing less than the perpetuation of your people's faith. Only bind them in this complex of convenance and rupture, of arrogance and guilt, and no disaster can ever shake them. The more terrible their fate, the more conclusive the evidence of their election.

'*Nicht wahr*, Korah?'

This was the process – still wet from the mould, still at an early and precarious stage of evolution – into which Korah, fired by individual rather than national ambitions, and excluded by his too-great wealth from the devious pleasures of asceticism, blundered.

And this was why Moses, who on many another occasion had pleaded with God for the life of a sinner, this time made it a condition of his and the Torah's veracity that the gain-sayers should not die the common death of all men, but should perish in a manner that would prove once and for all who was speaking through whom.

It wasn't just punishment he was after. In order to strike a rebellion of this magnitude at its heart, Moses requisitioned spectacle. And went so far as to specify the precise spectacle which alone seemed to him commensurate with the danger his people faced:

Let God do what God had never done before, he said. Let Him make a NEW THING. Let Him cause the earth to open and swallow up the wicked men and all that appertain to them. Let them go down quickly into the pit. Into Gehenna itself. Let the earth's crust close over them. And *then* let them say that Moses and his Torah are false!

Show them, LORD, that who provoketh me, provoketh THEE.

Even as requests to God go, this was a big one.

The God of Moses may have pulled a trick or two in Egypt, but essentially he disapproved of magic. He was not disposed to unlock the earth on the say-so of a prophet.

One of the explanations for the Jewish imagination never being much stimulated by the idea of a subterranean hell – another, of course, has to do with the adequacy of its experience of horrors above ground – is Yahweh's cosmic scrupulousness, His reluctance to confuse morality with geology. Too random a policy of open sesame, too much rattling of the gates of heaven and hell whenever the issue of reward or punishment arose, and He would have been as liable to the charge of cultic backsliding as those recidivists among His chosen people whose feet tapped the moment there was mention of a golden calf.

An eschatology rooted in a palpable terrain invariably led back to animism and the legions of warring gods of agriculture. The future He had mapped out for the Israelites lay in a spiritual indifference to topography, a virtual disregard for the visible face of nature, let alone her rumoured cellars and underpasses.

None the less, what Moses asked for was not unprecedented. The earth had opened its mouth once before. And that was . . .

*

The pleats in Sisobk the Scryer's neck unrumple like a squeeze-box. His head snaps back. Precognition has about-turned without ceremony and lurched in the direction of pre-occurrence.

He has no more stomach for digesting the past than he has neck for discovering what's behind him, but sometimes it rears on all sides like a mountainous wave, swamping the bobbing future. Or opens like the earth . . .

And that was . . .

And that was . . .

. . . to receive the blood of Abel, beloved only brother and companion of Cain.

V

It is only when he has finished reading Preplen's letter that Cain recognizes someone has been standing at his shoulder, reading with him.

He turns his head and is not irrecoverably vexed to see that it is Naaman's daughter, Zilpah, the plaited girl, bearing his jeroboam of wine, handmaiden fashion, on what would have been her hip had she had one.

He notices that she is raw-eyed, that her lashes are wet at the very tips, as though she has dipped them infinitesimally, like two bathing birds, in emotion.

'You should not read in the dark,' he tells her.

It is open to her to say something simple, such as, 'I know I should not' or 'In truth I did not'; but she is drawn to deviousness. 'I followed the characters,' is what she decides to say, 'but I did not make out their meaning.'

'Then why are you distressed?'

'You suppose me to be distressed on your behalf?'

He only stares at her.

'By a private letter?'

'So, you made out it was private?'

She adjusts, steadies the jeroboam of wine. 'You can tell when writing is sad,' she says, 'just by the marks on the parchment.'

He pushes at the door of the rest room, gesturing her to go inside and take the weight of the wine off herself. Directly the door closes on them he can smell her. Neither sweet nor sour; neither fresh nor stale; but ticklish on the nose . . . peppery.

'It wasn't sad,' he tells her. 'It was imbecilic.'

'Then it's sad that something imbecilic should have such a powerful effect on you.'

He wants to say it hasn't, but he knows that she is bound to find that even sadder. And he isn't sure anyway how Preplen's words have affected him.

He falls vacant, wondering what she has read and what she hasn't; what she will have made of the poet's needling dissection of his faint heart, his apostasy (for that was the charge, wasn't it? – disloyalty, defection); whether Preplen's rant against Babel will have offended her as a citizen; whether the vomit and the farts will have scandalized her as a woman.

A *woman*. The word is invariably grotesque to him now – overblown, foolish, laughable. Except that he doesn't laugh. *Woman*. It sits like a stone on his tongue. *Woman*. Too much was demanded of the word from the very beginning. Too much was invested in it by his father . . . *she shall be called Woman*. Too much was feared from it by Yahweh. And too much was expected of it by him. Poor Eve! It wasn't her fault. No one – no *woman* – could have lived up to that fanfare of pre-publicity.

There are other words that adequately meet Cain's experience. Wife, daughter, nurse, girl, widow, hag. He has no need of *woman*.

Naaman's daughter, the girl Zilpah, pours him wine, wiping the goblet before handing it to him. Maidservant.

They sit opposite each other, in low gossip chairs. Or rather, he sits and she floats – a cushion of ecstatic temerity, bold fear of him and bold fear for him, keeping her a quivering hair's breadth above the rattan.

'So,' he says, 'do *you* think I am unnecessarily sensitive about my horns?'

She drops a fine film between them, a watery mist, like sea-spray. Behind this she shakes her head and enacts a hurt incomprehension.

He flaps the air with the letter which he still holds, folded, in his right hand.

'I told you,' she says, 'I did not read it.'

'Ah yes,' he says, 'you only saw the sadness of the characters.'

A flinch from her. A misty tremor that lightly sprinkles him.

'But you would like to feel the place, anyway,' he goes on, 'from which I proliferate my ivory? You would like to finger the bumps? Perhaps you will be able to read them, at least. I'm told the science of phrenology is far advanced in Babel.'

She closes her eyes. Shuts her sight down, the way he has seen another Shinarite man-pleaser do.

'You are not as strange to us as you fear,' she says, not looking at him, 'or as you hope. We are used to foreigners.'

'With tails?'

'They all have stories.'

'I said *tails*.'

She has a tail of her own, a plaited pendulum which counts the beats of her humourlessness against her spine.

'Your only oddity,' she says, 'is in your thinking you're an oddity.'

'You would do well telling that to the unicorn.'

'It's too late for the unicorn.'

She dares him. She opens her eyes and dares him. Go on, go on – say, 'It's too late for me, too.'

He wants to co-operate. Every instinct in his body is civil. If he thought he could see comedy in her, contempt in her, cruelty in her, he would set no bounds to his preposterousness. 'Me, too. For me, too, it is too late.' But the only greed he can find in her face is the greed for commiseration. It's his dying fall she is after, and that she can't have. A letter from a mad poet, the marks of God's disfavour on one's brow – these belong to one order of secrecy and good taste; but a dying fall is in another category altogether.

'You are not drinking wine?' he inquires, belatedly.

She waves the offer away, with her hand and with her plait. 'I never drink,' she says.

'Even though the wine in Babel is so good?'

'I didn't know it was.'

He nods, raises his goblet like a torch, toasts her, toasts the unicorn.

'I'm glad you find something to admire in our city,' she says.

'I find many things.'

'We wouldn't guess that from what you say about us.'

'It isn't what one says.'

'What, then? What one does? By every account all you are doing is planning to build your own city somewhere else.'

'I could hardly plan to build it here.'

'So it is true?'

'About the city, no. I intend – that's too grand a verb – I think, only of a tower.'

'A temple?'

'Just a tower.'

'As a memorial to your brother?'

She has moved closer to him. He can distinguish the smell of her hair from the rest of her, and it reminds him of the smell of Abel's scalp, when Abel was more fragile than an egg, a veined transparent oval of warm blood and sour milk – a new thing.

She notices a dark flicker in his eyes, like the memory of

grief, or worse, the memory of the memory of grief. Sadden me, her own eyes plead. Sadden me until I cannot bear it.

'As a memorial to myself,' he says.

'You are a vain man?'

He shrugs. 'No more than the common. But I must have somewhere to be buried.'

She is not sure that she follows. 'Why would you choose to be buried in a tower? In the hope that your soul will ascend more quickly to a god?'

'I am not thinking of my soul. I care only about my body.'

'You wish to be conspicuous in death?'

'No. Merely comfortable.'

'And the earth will not do for that?'

Very well, he decides, you have worked hard enough for this – I will sadden you. He takes a sip of wine, religiously, showing her a spotless hand; then draws a spotless sleeve across his mouth. He is a paid performer: he knows how startling the effect is, of fine linen on an ancient face.

'I have a terror of death,' he says, 'which is equalled only by the revulsion I feel for earth – actual earth, the crumbling substance, the stone-deaf clod itself. It is likely that the first of these impieties is a consequence of the second. Clearly, whoever loves silence must love soil. But as there is nothing I can do – nothing I *will* do – to reconcile my noisy thoughts to the unechoing quiet of unpeopled nature, to the certain prospect that mud will muffle them, that a mulch of droppings and manure, blind seeds and the broken legs of spiders, will swallow the last leakings of my blood, soundlessly, without a gulp, as it swallowed my brother's, then I must at least shuffle my alarms, try to separate what I dread of death from what I know of slime. Better to be walled up in a high cold tower – for it is not freezing that I fear; it is only incubating heat that makes a worm of me. Better to be imprisoned for all time in a swaying ziggurat of icy stone, with the din of the city below, and not a slug to leave its trail across my throat . . .'

Sadden *her*? He has so comprehensively saddened himself that he is already mourning his passing, and has not the wherewithal to resist the girl when she puts her face closer still to his, stays the agitation of her plait, and presses her lips to the very ground along which the obscene slugs have slid their silver.

VI

On the top floor of the House of Hearsay and Hermeneutics, meanwhile, where Sisobk the Scryer keeps an antique room (though he would much rather, from the point of view of personal management, keep an antique face, like Cain's), the prophet Moses has persuaded Yahweh to shake open the gates to hell.

The prophet Sisobk knows what happens next, is familiar with every smoking fissure in the earth, but he is not the less frightened or incensed for that. He climbs the table, puts his little fingers in his ears, beholds Korah's shaven shadow advancing down his wall, watches Korah's laden mules troop across his floor, but cannot, will not, hear the cries as the carpet opens wide its weave beneath their feet, devouring Korah and Korah's wife and all who appertain to them, yea, even unto their shirt-buttons.

A terrible thing.

A New Thing.

A Newish Thing . . .

Sisobk the Scryer has Cain-longings on him and can scarcely wait for the sulphurous earth to close over again so that he can quit the table and prepare himself to go out.

This is not as strenuous a procedure for Sisobk as it is for some. He dries the perspiration underneath his arms with a scrap of papyrus torn from his feet, and picks at any crusts of foam which are still left around his mouth from the previous night's fit. That completes his toilet.

It isn't necessary for him to shave. For all that he has a bullock's shoulders and an old bear's stoop, it is a boy's fluff that covers his face, a stripling's moustache that stains his lip. In Babel, where they like a prophet to sprout a forest on his chin, because that's how prophets are described in stories, Sisobk's sparseness goes against him. Despite the voices that issue from his body, speaking tongues hitherto unheard; despite the parchment bandages he walks in instead of sandals; despite ecstasies and epiphanies in the course of which he has been known to fall down the twenty-two hundred steps of the ziggurat to the God Whose Name Has Been Mislaid, without splintering a single bone; despite such overwhelming testimony to the conscientiousness with which he pursues his calling, Sisobk the Scryer cannot command an audience in excess of ten when he guesses birthdays in the park, so inflexible are the Shinarites in the matter of prophets having beards.

One way of circumventing this prejudice, you would think, would be for him to change his job description. Sisobk has already thought of this himself – or at least he has anticipated our thinking it – hence his current choice of Scryer, which is of course inaccurate in as much as Scryers meet the promise of the what-will-be in the wall-eye of a crystal ball, an object which Sisobk neither owns nor craves. But it is not his experience that Shinarites care about the niceties of prognostication: in Babel you can tell fortunes or you can't. Nor is he confident, anyway, that any description adequate to his genius can be found. He is not a seer – seers specialize in spiritual insights, sniff the sacred. Mystics implicate themselves in mysteries. Visionaries are addicted to extravagant fancies, spend weeks in bed, hungry, willing on fevered dreams. Pyromancers risk serious damage to their hands. And prophets – do not prophets speak for deities? The only deity Sisobk cares to speak for at present is Cain – a deity in the sense that he has stood up to a deity – but how do you convincingly speak for someone who won't let you so much as speak *to* him?

Sisobk shuffles out, on paper feet, into the street. He would not be much of a visionary or a seer, he would be a poor mystic and an even poorer prophet, if he did not know where Cain was. He does not bother to say: 'I see a theatre.' He knows the theatre well. He has suffered many a rebuff outside its doors. The whereabouts of the dressing rooms, the suspiciousness of cleaners and janitors, present somewhat more of a problem, but nothing serious. The advantage of a repulsive appearance, however little it fits the prophetic category, is that while men may call at you, few will want to put out a hand to apprehend you.

He decides against knocking. Cain will only ask who is that, Sisobk will only reply Sisobk, and Cain will only say go away.

Instead, he arranges his face into what he takes to be the lineaments of adoration, extends his arms, kicks open the door, declaims, 'My joy, my strength, my crown, my tower...'

... and sees his hero, the fratricide, the fugitive, the father of all Cainites, the God-crosser, lying with his head in a girl's lap, rather stiffly, Sisobk notices, his eyes closed, his fists clenched, while the girl pecks at him like a raven, raising her lips and putting them again to the place where horns would grow, were Cain to have horns.

Not for the first time today the earth opens up beneath Sisobk the Scryer's parcelled feet.

7. Cain Beholds His Mother Fall to Earth

. . . hell-bent on rape.

Wasn't that where we were? A-quiver with the falling angel, Semyaza.

Hitherto, angelic visitations had always been courteous and considerate. It was understood that as a mortal, and more to the point, as a woman – a *woman* – my mother needed to be given notice, time to prepare herself for company, chance at least to bathe her eyes in collyrium and apply tincture of antimony to their weepy corners, liberty to paint her mouth with beeswax, spread the cooling paste of henna between her raging thighs, and remove Abel – pop! – from her nipple.

A rather drawn-out and unsubtly choreographed spectacle-sequence usually warned of the imminent arrival of spirit: shafts of light, yellowed as though from ageing in a drawer; refraction of the sun's rays in rain; glorious windowings of the sky through which it was shamelessly easy to imagine one could hear hosannas, brass trumpets tuning up, the sounds of orchestral angels moistening their ruby lips. In addition, Semyaza and Azael had taken as their motif, their seal of descent, the fierce heat from which they'd saved my mother on their first appearance: thus, the spontaneous combustion of shrubs and trees was now the signal they were coming, some of the incendiarism so closely threatening the tree I hid in that I wondered whether my position hadn't all along been known.

They came in fire, these carriers of messages from the Heart, and they left in smoke, and it was always *they*.

Semyaza *and* Azael.

Not as now, Semyaza *sans* Azael.

Azael's role was never clear. Apart from the camomile and talcum he fought Semyaza over, there did not appear to be any reason – though I have thought of one since – for him to have come among us. As a representative of the Divine he made a poor impression, and as a proxy suitor to my mother he was ineffective – a go-between whose jaw quivered like the pistil of a lily. He brought her gifts sometimes, it's true, airy trumperies of fine-spun glass and gilded tracery, for which she had no earthly use. And he would unexpectedly touch her cheek, or draw back her hair to admire the ornaments in her ears. But these actions, although marks of sincere affection I believed, were meant to demonstrate how far he was from registering my mother's power, how little she agitated and therefore interested him.

He was on a mission he had no regard for, so much can be safely said, and that mission could only have been the chaperoning of Semyaza. 'Watch that one scrupulously; don't let him out of your sight for a single minute,' God must have directed him, knowing what evil follows when two creatures not of the same sex – man and beast, bee and flower, angel and mortal (species makes no difference) – are left alone together; but knowing just as well how unsuited Azael was to do His bidding. Having entrusted the progress of His affairs to an angel He could not trust, the All Anticipating confided His compunctions to a second angel in whom He had no confidence.

Once again this may look to you like callousness, but see it from His point of view: what else is a First Cause to do to spice up the tedium of predestined effect? Looked at from *their* point of view, of course, it is small wonder, with so much of their future already, as it were, in the past, that Azael chafed and fingered his bangles, and that Semyaza singed his very eyelashes in a furious plummet to perdition.

Inefficient as Azael had been as a restraining influence on

his fellow intermediary, it was his not being there at all that told me this time Semyaza meant harm, that the suddenness of his landing and the impetuosity of his grab for my mother were expressions of more than merely enthusiastic attachment. I heard my mother call – one long noooooo – and the sound of Semyaza starting to beat his wings, a flapping like frightened geese, and then I was out of my tree and running. I reached them just as they were airborne, and might have been able to hold on, perhaps even to add the ballast that kept them grounded, but the downdraught from Semyaza's wings knocked me over, and when I was on my feet again they had risen level with the tops of the trees, not secure in their ascent by any means, but circling in a death struggle of feathers and flesh, Semyaza's shoulders pumping frantically, my mother writhing in his grip and tearing at him where she had once rubbed lenitives and where she knew he could eventually be clawed apart. Hearing Abel howling, I ran to him and gathered him up in my arms, pressing his heart to my ear, in case the shock of seeing his mother flying should stop its beat.

To this day I am unable to say whether Semyaza intended to make off with my mother, to fly her to some far-flung corner of this or another planet, for the purpose – and why not? – of starting a brand new race, half-human, half-divine, half-pedestrian, half-pinioned, or whether he was prepared to risk all on possessing her just this one afternoon, just once in full flight, before dropping her cruelly and carelessly to earth. Nor am I able to say for certain, should that single hour of glorious rapacity have been his objective, whether or not he achieved it. Ferociously as my mother fought, they were in the air long enough for an angel of Semyaza's strength, whose lust had been brimming over for millennia, to have had his way with her as many times as the Lord God Almighty had surely warned him, at the cost of his virgin sempiternity, not to. But I believe, on the evidence of her cries – on the evidence of *both* their cries – that she eluded him. I was a student of wails and screams. I had named every gasp and groan, every sob and sigh my mother emitted in pursuance of pleasure or sufferance of pain. I had listened to Abel mewl and my father yammer and the angel Semyaza bleat and crow. I knew what triumph was, and submission. And I heard neither. Only lamentation. Even as their aerial engagement grew in desperation – no quarter called for, no quarter given – only a low threnody like mourning, a melancholy expression of shame, each for the other and, more inconsolably still, each for himself. Semyaza, because the hour for payment was at hand, prize or no prize, but priz*eless* he would have no weapons to ward off bitterness throughout the long night of his headlong fall. My mother, because below her she could see, foreshortened, her two sons locked together, looking up in terror and astonishment, their faces and their bodies, like the ground around them, spattered with blood and tears and feathers and the semen – colourless and thin like the distillation of pure spirit – of a balked angel.

It ended in a way that no one, unless perhaps Semyaza himself, could have anticipated. I had not given my mother up. I felt sure she had the beating of her abductor, if only because he was not constructed efficiently to bear his own weight let alone another's. But I feared his coming apart too suddenly, at too high an altitude, and the distance my mother, who was not constructed for flight at all, might have to fall. I listened for that loathsome rip, the sound of his wings being torn finally from his back; I willed the event on, but I dreaded it too. And when I saw them at last begin to tumble, unmistakably to lose control and height, I felt the weight of terror drop upon my shoulders and I buried Abel's face in my neck.

But Semyaza had not come apart; he was still entire, whole but shrinking, losing form and outline, collapsing in on himself like a carcass that was host to maggots, as though, at a silent word from Whoever had loaned him substance, his materiality had instantaneously been called in, and there was now nothing to prevent his liquefaction. Slowly, slowly, as in one of my father's recurring nightmares, Semyaza dissolved, his corporeality trickling into the very mud from which he had swept my mother, and to which she was now returned, until even his plumage – every quill and barb and vané of it – had oozed away, and he was once again intangible, ideal, a thingless thing of irreducible spirituality, just another bad idea of God's.

He left no trace, no magical discoloration of the earth, no holy pool which would fill up unaccountably on his anniversary and from which no animal would dare drink. He did not leave so much as a puddle or a stain. And there was no mark of his passing signalled in the heavens either, not a pillar of light for his soul to ascend by, not a single forgiving golden aperture in the clouds. Unless it was precisely by the refusal of all magniloquent effect – the leaden sky itself, the repossession of radiance and light, our sublunary sphere seemingly evacuated – that I Am Who I Am expressed His feelings.

A slime the texture of quicksilver, covering my mother's flesh and making her burn and shiver all at once, was the only souvenir of her adventure. Months later she would still be trying to wash it off, discovering beads of it, as tenacious as lice, in her hair, upon her belly, between her thighs. And I too kept finding it on me, mercurial proof – of which I was inordinately proud – that she had taken me in her arms the moment she was safe, and that she and I and Abel had held one another in silence for as long, it seemed, as we had previously not held one another at all. Until darkness dropped with a sudden thud, like a coconut, and my mother put her finger first to her own, then to my lips, and said:

What do you think? Not a word of this to your father?

And I put my finger first to my own, then to her lips, and said nothing, because there is no sensation more exquisite for a son than to be conscious of conspiring with his mother against his father, and I was so moved I could not speak.

*

Could not, and – when I recall that devilish, masterly, motherly inflection – still cannot . . .

What do you *think*?

What *do* you think?

What do *you* think?

Who would not have Adam near his conscience if he could be italicized by Eve?

Meanwhile, in another clearing in the forest, which the day before had been a desert, and the day before that a flood-plain, and tomorrow could be a swamp or sand-dune, the Adam in question, the father to whom *not a word, not a word* . . . was putting the finishing touches to a bold campaign. Not knowing that his wife had been decisively returned to him as a temptation too hot for divine essences to handle, he was just seconds from launching his strategy to win her back.

It is a moot point whether we would have been in time to stop him, even supposing we'd been free to speak; and it is another whether he would have thanked us for it had we tried. Months of planning had gone into this. Months of practice and memorization and workmanship and – it goes without saying – anticipation of success.

I had not seen much of him for some time. He was up early and worked late, and I was up my tree, working even later. But when I did run into him I thought he had never looked more conformable to himself. It suited him to be purposeful, to have a definite objective, spiced with vengeance, to aim at, and to have all his faculties expectant, in a state of perpetual rehearsal. He appeared less confused about what his hands were for. He was not subject to those implosions of temper whose source was a mystery to him. He was not regularly to be found hanging from the short rope of his own patience. Although he had not completely stopped crying in the night, I fancied I could deduce from those cries that he was sleeping better, dreaming dreams in which he was not *always* stamped back into the earth, reduced to those original granules who were his only ancestors. I might have been mistaken, but there were some nights when I thought he actually laughed in his sleep, rejoiced and exulted like a man who was at last the author of violence, and not just its bewildered victim.

But he remembered his manners when the time came. We heard him from a distance, my mother and I (oh, and Abel too), while we were still in a slithery seaweed embrace – the viscous memory of the angel between us yet – and we exchanged glances of approval, raised a combined eyebrow, surprised that without us Adam had found words and resolution.

O Lord, our Lord, he extolled, Whose name in all the earth is excellent, chastise me not for what I am to ask, but be merciful unto me, and say: How many more will be the days of my wife's separation?

I trembled for him. He did not know what a bad hour he had chosen to sue for mercy or to speak of wives.

The heavens remained mute. Gave no intimation that they had heard him, let alone were considering Their reply.

Then my father spoke again. O mighty God, Who shaketh the wilderness with great winds, and maketh the sun to shine upon us, and taketh our fear from our hearts, give ear unto my prayer. How much longer is my rightful wife to be kept from me?

And just as he had amended his tone, from entreaty to vexation, so did he appear to have amended himself, vanishing from where he had first preferred his appeal, some thirty angel-lengths (taking Semyaza as a standard) to the east of us, and materializing again in the west, no more than nine or ten prone Azaels away.

Still the heavens shut Their ears against him.

O Lord of Hosts, my King and God, he began again, only this time his voice was fainter, seemed to have desert in it and to be borne in upon dry winds from afar – O Lord of Hosts,

Who out of the horrible nothing of miry clay brought me up and breathed into my nostrils, and stuck arrows in my side, and planted the thorn in my right foot and the thistle in my left, and cut me off from Thy presence and from the presence of she whom Thou, in Thy everlasting bounty, provided for me, and cast me back into the lowest pit of darkness; O King, wilt Thou now cause Thine anger towards me to cease, and tell me to the homer, to the ephah, yea, even to the hin, how much more uncleanness one wife can have in her?

But before this sandy psalm had been completed another was in progress, and then another, and then another still. All at once my father's voice was everywhere around us, echoing rarefied and flinty from the arduous heights of our lifeless mountain, issuing muffled and sappy from inside the barks of the very trees that shaded us, welling up waterlogged and spluttering – P-l-l-lo-lo-lentiful as ar-r-r-re Thy blo-blo-blessings, O-lo-lo Lorrrd my Godle-oddle – from the pebble-ebbled beds of cold running rivers. The whole of nature seemed to have rallied to his cause. Impervious stones stood up for him, toothless worms became eloquent on his behalf. Every blade of grass, every splinter of stone, every unfeeling atom, had been Adamized, and spoke as he spoke.

Because we – his astonished family – were unsighted, we missed the best of it. We caught the sound effects but lost out on the animation. It was only later that we discovered the extent of my father's ingenuity, that he had not thrown his voice indiscriminately – remarkable achievement though that was, to make the mountains and the desert talk – but had aimed his words at specific targets, assigned them to the mouths of complainants fashioned in the image of himself, *by* himself, and stationed high and low where God the Jealous Potter was bound to see them the moment He looked down: a hundred Adams modelled out of clay or cut from rock or carved in wood, with heads made from potatoes, melons, cabbages, and each wanting to know how much longer, how much longer, the days of his wife's separation.

For years Abel and I went on finding remains of these effigies, some of which bore a striking, though most no more than an approximate, resemblance to our father. Those made out of vegetable or fruit were, of course, rotten and fly-blown, the home of termites and leucous-bellied grubs, the sanctuary of snails and slugs by the time we came across them, and of use to us only in a philosophic sense. But the stone ones weathered well, losing only beards and noses, and otherwise retaining so much of their life-likeness that Abel kept a couple which he played with as toy brothers, setting them against each other in imaginary conflicts. To this day I have an especially fine example in my belongings, and although I never attended sufficiently to my father to learn the art of ventriloquism, I do sometimes try to make it speak, to make it say, *Bleh! bleh! bleh!* and *Very good* and *Right* and *I have spoken*, and to get it to agree to forgive me for what I did.

Whether God ever forgave my father his usurpation of the Creative Urge, whether in fact He did not choose finally to punish him with *me* – I am not the one to say. But His wrath was indubitably kindled when at last, driven to near distraction by the universal complaint my father had orchestrated, He drew back the curtains of the skies and beheld the full extent of the blasphemy:

Whole hillsides peopled with puppets . . . with their mouths open . . . and their fists raised . . . and mutiny on their lips.

'Ye shall make you no idols nor graven image,' He said – spake rather, for truly this was SPEAKING. 'Neither –'

Said the puppets: We are not idols.

'Neither rear you up a standing image, neither shall ye set up any image of stone, to bow down unto it –'

Said the dummies: We are not bowed down unto.

'Thou shalt not make unto thee any likeness of any thing that is in heaven above, or that is in the earth beneath, or that is under –'

Said the dolls: We are rough, inferior likenesses. We speak only with the single tongue You gave us, and express the frustrations only of the single heart You made.

Perhaps this sounded a little too like sympathetic magic for the One True Voice-thrower's taste; or perhaps my father's new command of language smacked suspiciously of necromancy; whatever the reason, the charge was suddenly no longer idolatry but occultism.

'There shall not be found among you any one that maketh his son or his daughter to rise in a lying position, or that useth his hands to conceal, or that casteth his voice to deceive. For all that do these things are an abomination to the Lord. A man that is a charmer shall surely be put to death; he shall be stoned with stones; his voice shall be cast back into his throat; the rod that he conjureth with shall be as a sword upon him.'

There followed a dread period of silence. The Mirthless One had spoken. As always, after one of His pronouncements, I could smell blood in the wind.

The old weariness descended on me, and on my mother, and, I do not think it would be fanciful to say, on Abel. The old suffocating storm-cloud oppression of the Universal Mind closing, closing, closing . . .

Moral entities we may be, but there is only so much morality we can suffer at the end of a bludgeon. If the Devil addresses us in honeyed words, no wonder we listen to everything he has to say. Let hell gape, we leap joyfully down when the heavens boom and threaten.

We bent our necks and waited, hoping that my father, wherever he was, *which*ever he was – for we had not so far distinguished him from his marionettes – knew to bend his neck and wait quietly too. It would not have been a good idea for him to have continued playful – Adam of the thousand voices – under these lowering skies.

But then he had not put himself to all this trouble, had not stationed copies of himself wherever he could get them to stand, only to capitulate at the first reprimand. He was not a thinking man but he must have anticipated resistance. He must have planned what he would say to God once he had secured His attention in this novel manner and stood revealed in the perfect light of His blame.

The silence stretched dreadfully on. The Universal Mind, which had been closing for more years than there were numbers to name them, closed still more. We did not hear the ancient gates creaking on their hinges, the dragging of rusted chains – but it was as if a lid were being slowly lowered over us, taking away the air we breathed, the illusion of height, space, choice.

I counted the beats of my mother's heart, and Abel's, until they were indistinguishable from mine. Somewhere out there, biding its time, was my father's resolution. I believed I could follow its pauses and detect its rhythms. Soon, soon, it would have to seize its moment.

And then it spoke – truly, as though it were a god itself, it *spake*:

Lord (and that word was enough to cause the hairs to rise like Babel's towers on the three bowed heads of his little family) –

Lord (so proud of him were we) –

Lord (and so fearful for him were we) –

Lord (and so sure was I that he'd already used up all the language in him) –

Lord . . . unto Thee do I give thanks. Thou broughtest me out of the miry clay and gavest me the power to bring out from the same nothingness an hundred others like unto me. Behold, I can make their mouths to open, and I can lift up my voice in their voices, and I can bind their purposes to my purpose. See, how they wait upon my will, as I, O Lord, wait upon Thine. See, how I dandle them on the end of a cord, as Thou, on the end of Thy cord, dost dandle me . . .

(Was this *my* father?)

But my likenesses, Lord, are without spirit, and without soul, and without heart. They will perish in the sun and rain. And they will not know their passing. Therefore am I a poor manufacturer compared to Thee, and a sorry wizard. I was not there when Thou laidest the foundations of the earth, and the cornerstone thereof. I do not know where is the way where light dwelleth, by what way it is parted and joined again. I cannot compel the unicorn to serve me, or clothe the horse's neck with thunder, or draw out leviathan with an hook. Wherefore I am weak, Lord, and abhor myself, and in my frailty and solitude miss the comfort of a wife.

How much longer, then, I pray Thee, the days of her separation?

More than once had I listened to God listen, felt the earth tremble like a tuning-fork to the vibrations of His mighty auscultation, actually heard the hairspring of His hearing whirr and click like the drumming of a monstrous cicada. But never before, to *my* ear, had His attentiveness been so audible. It hummed, it buzzed, it rubbed its legs together; before my father had finished it even droned, sending everything in nature that had the skill to bore scuttling into its holes, scattering the birds off the trees, driving the fish deeper into their waters, and forcing us to screw up our faces and clasp our hands around our heads.

There was no mistaking the meaning of the sound.

Divine approval.

Divinity liking what It heard and wondering how soon It would be able to appropriate and use it as Its own.

The spirit of Ineffable Plagiarism, in other words, rejoicing in Its right to repossess whatever took Its fancy, droit de Seigneur – for all things must be rendered unto Him who originally rendered all things – and enjoying in advance another grand effect, one more killing refutation of one more detractor waiting undisclosed (but not undisclosed to *Him*) in the corridors of time.

Knowst *thou* what way light is parted . . .?

Then abide in shadows.

Canst *thou* clothe the horse's neck with thunder . . .?

Then clothe thyself with silence!

As with mortals, so with gods: we lose ourselves in ill-definition and crave elucidation – heroic elucidation if we can find it – of who we are. Hence the prodigious success of flattery. To look into another's words and see there a reflection not only distinct but resplendent, magnificent and immutable – ah, that truly is the best we ever know of happiness. Found! found! – the errant self. And with not a hair out of place. If love sometimes obliges similarly that is because love, too, sends out search parties. But love is supererogatory, a luxury, expendable so long as there are courtiers and choirs, knee-benders and kneelers, to do the job. He Whose Name Is Praise gave up on my mother – as it was eternally written that He would – in the instant that my father sprang up here, there and everywhere, in a multiplicity of crudely fashioned guises, and returned from every one the sort of godlike reflection that no god can resist. Why bother landing mere flesh and blood woman in One's net when One can whistle out leviathan? He had always known what He was capable of whistling, of course, but knowing One's own strength is not the same, is nothing like the same, as hearing it attested by a choir of voices.

Greedy for praise, thirsting for offerings and anthems, the heavens stretched the membrane of their hearing. Nothing could escape it. Not so much as the forethought of an unformed prayer. Not so much as an orison in the conscience of a flea.

The whole canopied firmament, all ears.

And then, all smiles, the skies opened and poured down shafts of rosy light; beams, in every sense of the word – great grinning girders of lambency in whose brilliant refractions the merest specks of dirt shone magnified like jewels hung around one gorgeous universal neck. The earth jolted, rocked once, then fell still upon its axle. Stopped in its tracks, the engorged sun bounced as weightless as a bubble, pricking its circumference against mountains, leaking redness. So pleased with itself was Creation that it seemed to consider reversing its motions and doing it all again, starting from Chaos and finishing with *this*.

Afloat on His radiant complacency, the Lord spoke:

'Blessed be the fruit of thy body, Adam, and the fruit of thy ground.' (In other moods He had cursed both, promising only sorrow and thistles. Today He had seen His bounty in a glass, and so was bountiful.) 'Now set aside thy necromancy, which is an abomination unto me, and take thy wife. To her shalt thou cleave, for she has washed for thee thirteen times twenty-seven days. Therefore I say to thee, Take her, for she is thy lawful wife, and has borne thee two sons, and has kept her apart from thee thirteen times twenty-seven days according to my commandment, and now is clean unto thee.'

He was prolix, but He was clear. This time, though, it would be my father's turn to show particularity.

Clean?

Let the All Surrendering, in His discretion, only turn His back and retire to the chaste hosannas of His angels, and we would see about clean.

I have a theory to explain my father's failure to accept victory with good grace. It can be blamed, I maintain, on the mischievous intervention of a third party. I have no hard evidence to support such a conviction other than the foreignness to my father's nature of what he was about to do, and the foreignness to his capacities of what he already had done. The ventriloquism presented no challenges to likelihood; that was his, right enough. Similarly the cumbersome device of the look-alike statuary. That whole side of the project bore the unmistakable marks of his childish wastefulness – an expenditure of time and ingenuity and concentration out of all proportion to any foreseeable result. That the outcome was, after all, such a resounding success for him had nothing to do with crepitation of the abdomen or puppeteering or impersonation. Words were what won him the day, not magic; a linguistic persuasiveness which he could not possibly have found in himself, which he assuredly did not come to me for, and which must therefore, by simple elimination, have been lent him by someone else. And the someone else in question – the someone else I do not hesitate to *put* in question – had just the temperament, and just the conviction of aggrievedness, and, not to beat about the bush, just the inwrought misogyny (how many thousand thousand years singing of seedlessness does it take?) to concoct the little ordeal to which my father – quite uncharacteristically, I repeat – was soon to submit his wife.

But before the criminal, the crime . . .

It should have been an occasion for rapturous emotions, their first night together after so protracted a quarantine. They should have burned the skin off their fingertips just touching. They should have drowned in each other's tears; twined eyebeams until they did not know whose gaze was whose – just as I, put to bed betimes but lying listening with my thumb to Abel's pulse, willingly mistook the evenness of his breathing for my own. It should have been a night for sweetness and ebullience; after the crushed petals and the music of the flesh and the dancing beneath the moon, a night of subdued riot. They were still in their infancy, remember; sent finished, fully formed into this breathing world, they had scarcely more experience of it than I had. It should have been a night of escapades and monkey-tricks and hot pursuit.

And for an hour or two it was. For a brief atheistic interlude, they gave themselves over to reckless horse-play. Reckless and wordless horse-play – for there had been words enough today – the mad abandon of the mute.

They ran, they chased, they shinned up coco-palms, they

fought for fruit, they swung, they fell.

As soon as they had gained their breath, they began again. Shaking nuts out of the trees, pressing dates into each other's mouths, throwing sand, lassoing each other with loops of vine, piling leaves, like pyres, over their glinting bodies.

Lying on his back, panting, with a moon in each eye, and his legs braced to support her, my father invited his reclaimed wife to climb aboard him, her feet secure in his magician's hands, her fingers suckered to his knees like clams, so that when he rose and she fell their positions were reversed, whereupon she rose and he fell, and he rose and she fell, and she rose . . .

They made so much noise, rising and falling, that they woke Abel. I was never far from him at night. How could I be? His heart was still beating for the two of us. I was over him before he could begin to cry, pinching his collapsing lips together. Unable to come out at his mouth, fear spurted from his eyes.

I gathered him up and hoisted him on to my shoulder. Look, I said, pushing aside fronds for him, snatching him a brief clearing in nature. Look, do you know what that is?

He looked. I looked. Brothers in astonishment, we peered out of foliage at our noble progenitors, far gone in hilarity and quite indistinguishable one from the other – a single beast with a circular spine, able to move only by tumbling over and over itself – cartwheeling crazily between the palms, crashing through undergrowth, bringing down figs and pomegranates, threatening to spin off into the night, a permanent revolution, laughing from both ends, lit by a million incurious stars.

Look, I said, our father and mother.

Only when they were bruised and exhausted and had come apart with a sound like the breaking of suction, did my father venture to speak. And only because she was bruised and exhausted did my mother not venture to stop him.

Let's play at supposing, he said.

My mother said nothing. The first rule of supposing is that silence on either side denotes an unwillingness to play.

I assume this rule applies in Babel too. Unless in Babel you are never unwilling to play at supposing.

In which case you will approve of my father's persistence.

Let's suppose a man's wife go aside, he said. And . . .

He was having difficulty breathing. They were both having difficulty breathing. And words were as much the reason as the cartwheel.

. . . and commits a trespass against him . . .

Still nothing, still no playing, from my mother.

. . . and a man lie with her carnally . . . and it be hid from the eyes of her husband . . . and be kept close . . .

You use too many ands, my mother said. You sound like God. *And* I do not know what you are talking about.

. . . and . . . AND . . . she be defiled . . .

(*Defiled*? Hidden in leaves, frightened, I rolled Abel's putty fingers into a little fist and crammed it into my mouth.)

All right, my mother said, let us suppose. But first what am I to suppose is the purpose of this supposition?

My father looked alarmed. Having done all the supposing so far, he was not prepared to be on the receiving end of my mother's. He put his hands out to stop her. There seemed to be a precise incantatory order, a due sequence of supposings, which he was anxious not to break.

And, he said, and . . . and the spirit of jealousy come upon him, and he be jealous of his wife, and she be defiled; or . . . or if the spirit of jealousy come upon him, and he be jealous of his wife, and she be not defiled . . .

A laugh without laughter from my mother. A laugh with ice and distance in it, like a sea-bird's cry.

I see the termination of all your ands, she said. And . . . and . . . and . . . what is to be done to soothe this husband's jealousy? How to know if it is founded or unfounded? By what means is it to be released from the torment of its uncertainty?

Exactly, said my father.

It isn't, said my mother.

Now it was his turn to be at a loss. It isn't *what*?

It isn't to be released. Not ever. Jealousy is a broken wing. No flight is possible thereafter.

(*Flight!* I stuffed Abel's fingers further down my throat. Was it wise of her to speak of *flight*?)

Wrong, my father said. And he made the word resonate like the gong it rhymed with. Wrong! – you set free the jealousy by proving or disproving the cause.

Another wintry sea-bird laugh from Eve. So this is where we're leading, she said. You have a system for getting proof.

Or disproof.

She pondered it, then said: You have been busy lately.

He took less time over his reply. So have you, he said.

I still count the minutes of the silence between them, and wish it had been longer, even though, in truth, it was long enough for a man's wife to have gone aside, and to have committed trespass against him, and all the rest of it . . .

Abel was the lucky one, the shrewd one. He fell asleep on my back, and so missed the ignominy of what ensued, unless you call the ignominy of what ensued the next twenty years.

Particularly, though, he missed our father with a little *f* – with an *f* so little it was barely there this night – descending from his earlier victory over our word-mad Maker into a slush of mouldering ritual: oaths, curses, potions, bitter brews of dust and water which would make the belly of a bad wife swell, and a guilty woman's thigh rot like a fluke-infested sheep and fall away like a broken branch. For in the measure that we measure is it meted out to us, he said. Thy transgression began with thy thigh and proceeded to thy womb; therefore shalt thou be punished, like to like.

This was not our language or our thinking; it was not our spirit or our procedure. How it could be that some things seemed obsolescent to us, although we were the first family, I cannot say. But it was so. And here is another reason I suspect an alien instrumentality: we were primal, but we were not *that* primal.

Nor was my mother *that* deaf to abrupt changes in my father's use of the personal pronoun. At first it had been *her* belly and *her* thigh – the transgressive parts of the suppositional wife of the hypothetically jealous husband. Now it was *thy* womb – which meant that all supposing and hypothesizing had stopped.

Before we talk about me, my mother said, can we clear up the identity of this man?

This man?

The original defiler. The reason for the punishment. The excuse to have a woman swallow dust.

Not dust, my father corrected her, just bitter water. And it is a trial, not a punishment. If the woman is innocent –

Yes, yes, my mother understood, her thigh stays on. But this man . . . this man not my husband . . . who would that be? What man not my husband has the breeding earth bred for me?

If my father heard a double reproach in this – refutation of his slander *and* regret that the thing of which she stood accused could not be true – he was meant to. In that hour he learned what a fierce weapon you hand the blameless when you charge them with unchastity. 'Where was my opportunity?' is a protest with a thousand blades. And jealous flesh cuts easily.

That might have been why he seemed to want to retreat. When I say man, he said . . .

You don't necessarily mean man? I see. What about when you say defiled?

He grunted. He was sitting with his back against a tree, pulling absently at bark that fell around him like shredded rags. My mother was sitting opposite him, her hands folded in her lap. They were close enough to touch toes.

She took his grunt to mean that when he said defiled he meant defiled.

Yes, but by whom? she asked. Then, remembering that when he said man he did not necessarily mean man, she added: Or by *what*?

I was relieved that in moving so quickly from the idea of man to the idea of thing we had bypassed silently the idea of boy. Throughout the exchange of hostilities concerning the existence or not of a creature man enough to commit trespass with my mother, I had held my breath, conscious that a stray missile could easily hit me. *I* was man enough. Man enough to think I was man enough anyway. And to be wondering what other provision, if not this one, Great Creating Nature had made for the end of my boyhood.

Good to be off whos and on to whats, then; except that here too there were dangers. Would my father be rash enough to risk the wrath he had stilled only a few hours earlier, and point an accusing finger at the What of whats? Had he somehow (and I will tell you how) got to know of Semyaza? Did he have a list of abominations to go through that even I knew nothing of?

There is a way out of this, I was relieved to hear my father say. All you have to do is suffer the trial.

(Suffer it! I whispered. Suffer it for all our sakes!)

You want me to swallow dust?

It is only clouded water, he reminded her.

You want my thigh to rot?

Only if you are guilty.

You should not want it even if I were guilty.

I do not want it, my father said. I tremble for it. But if you are innocent you have nothing to fear.

But much to resent.

He had stopped listening to her. He was on his feet, looking for a vessel, looking for water, scooping up dust.

Here, he said. Drink.

She put her hand out. Will there be an end of this if I do?

There will, he said. But I detected the trembling he spoke of in his voice.

And do you accept that though these waters of bitterness may have no effect on my belly or my thigh, they will leave an acid deposit around my heart?

If you have not misconducted yourself the waters shall pass cleanly through you.

You do not know the meaning of your own trial, my mother said.

And because she would be sour of soul, because there was no other man for her to go aside with but my father and yet she was still accused, because the angel Semyaza had come in light and gone in paraffin, she drank.

And her belly did not swell and her thigh did not rot, but she never again – Azael had seen to that – cartwheeled with my father in the moonlight.

Azael?

Who else? I have no proof. Angels leave no proof. But only a member of the all-male choir invisible could have devised such a stratagem for the withering of a woman's body, could have anticipated the distension and disfiguration with so much zest, and found such torment for the conventionally unclean minds of husbands – yes, all right, and sons – to boot.

A two-headed cruelty, punishing both human sexes equally.

Whether Azael was acting solely on his own initiative, or settling an account for Semyaza, or in some way settling a score *with* Semyaza, or whether he had been on an undeviating mission all along, carrying out the express instructions of the Great Choirmaster Himself, I cannot pretend to know. Nor can I do any better with such practical questions as when Azael approached my father, what manner of address he employed, what form he chose – whispering conscience or diaphanous visitant or merely flaking bird.

None of this matters. Just trust me when I tell you that there is no more remorseless or retaliative envy in the universe than the envy matter excites in spirit.

Though what good I do saying that in Babel, I can't think.

8. SKIRTING SODOM

I

He has taken to bathing and barbering to excess.

Four baths at the hands of refugees from Anatolia in a single afternoon. Three shaves in the chairs of journeymen from Sodom in a single morning.

'I cannot get the mildew off myself,' Cain complains.

Seeing him coming, the barbers talk among themselves. The consensus is that a clean chin is not really what's he after – he wants a clean slate.

He thinks he can come in old, they say, and go out new.

A new thing.

He knows he is becoming an object of broad amusement. The Anatolians slap him harder on each visit, assuming this is the reason he returns. The shavers of Sodom bury him under hot towels and make faces.

But the mildew still grows on him.

He is cobwebbed, too. Primordial. Stagnant. In Yiddish – though of course Cain has no Yiddish – *farshtinkener, farfoylt*.

Mouldy.

And senses that everything is conspiring to make him mouldier.

His last session in the recital room hasn't helped. His last session in the recital room never helps. Like all obsessive autobiographers, on a public stage or in a private diary, he feels even more ill when he has disgorged himself than when he hasn't, and he feels ill enough when he hasn't. The reason for this is to be explained by another Yiddish word – *kishkas*. Entrails. Obsessive autobiographers suffer from a psychological ailment centred on their *kishkas*. They cannot bear to leave them in and they cannot bear to drag them out. The first – containment – results in an unacceptable sensation of costiveness and obstruction; the second – extrusion, unravelling – is nothing short of cannibalism of the self.

You are going to feel queasy either way.

But this is a general complaint, routinely incident to Cain's calling, and is not a specific cause of the fungi which he believes to be gaining on him no matter how frequently he bathes. So what is?

First and foremost, he blames his past. The past will grow like mould, of course, in the mind of any man who keeps his memory warm and damp enough. But in Cain's case, the chamber where he cultivates remembrances of his childhood, of his parents, of his native mud, can be likened to a hothouse. He acknowledges his own hand, his own architecture, in this. He doesn't have to grow such gorged, primeval blooms. Take as an example the story he has just told about his father's dust-and-water paste, the bitter potion that reacts adversely to unchastity: there is another way he could relate it. He could wipe the dirt of ages off it; hold it to the light; show the shrewd humanity of a ritual capable of calming the mental fears of husbands without doing physical damage to the wives. 'Don't you see,' he could tell his bewildered Babel audiences, 'no thigh is going to rot whatever the woman's done. The thing works precisely because it doesn't. You may wonder whether you have as subtle a method for solving martial differences in your scimitar.'

Similarly, it isn't necessary for him to be so hard on his

mother's flight into spiritual darkness. There is something to be said for inhabiting the gloomy corners of yourself; there are surprises to be gleaned there, jewels of the soul that only those willing to mine underground will ever find. The sun is not the only source of light. In Babel especially, where there is a craze for incandescence, it should be just the sort of mission Cain likes, to press the claims of night.

But he is in Babel as a vagabond, not as a proselytizer. He is in love with his own vagrancy. *Would* be in love with his own vagrancy. Which means that he must wash his hands of home. If he is truly to be a new thing, with a new head for Babel's heights, and new lungs to breathe in Babel's thin clear air, he has to obfuscate his past. And here's the catch: the more he obfuscates his past, the more it grows on him like moss.

'Serves you right,' the poet Preplen scoffs at him. 'What are *you* doing hoping to be moss-free, you who grew out of the bogs of Eden? Where's your patriotism?'

Preplen is another agent in Cain's mouldering. Preplen's letter, with its queer claims of consanguinity, another putrescence he would like the Anatolians to wash off him. Preplen's denunciation of his treason and triviality, accusing him of caring only how spruce he looks in the eyes of Shinarites, still more reason for Cain to care how spruce he looks in the eyes of Shinarites.

And then there is the mad prophet, trailing after him on rotten feet, muttering about heroic lawlessness, bursting in on his philandering (itself a sort of mould of the affections) and turning up at his recitals with eyes wetter than a dog's.

Let's leave everything else aside. On his own, Sisobk the Scryer is enough to keep Cain confined to the barber's chair, blasted with antiquity, eating towels.

He isn't a cause of Cain's spongy fungoid blight – he *is* Cain's spongy fungoid blight.

Sisobk the Stale. Omar the Obsolete. Marduk the Mildewed.

II

Barring exceptional circumstances, there are only two reasons why a man of marriageable age remains a bachelor: either he doesn't love women at all, or he loves them too much.

Our maligned friend the Scryer is a bachelor of the second category. He esteems women so highly, has such a pure regard for them in the abstract – as *woman* – that any thought of taking one for himself would be killed at birth, as a mis-creation. Instead, he holds torches for them, lights candles to them, prophesies happy futures for them where he can, and even tries to keep his mind still while they're talking to him.

Among the women he lights candles to are his great-great-grandmothers and great-great-great-aunts, the widows of all those morbid ancestors of his who couldn't wait for their fatality to ripen but had to hurl themselves, before their time, into the jaws of anything with teeth. He sits them, in their weeds, on mourning stools – a long row of identical faces protruding from each end of his unlocked imagination – and agitates them into every known attitude of womanly distress. They weep, they wail, they keen, they pull their hair, they gouge their flesh, they rend their garments – especially they rend their garments – they call for salts, for opiates, for death itself. Sisobk the Scryer loves women so much that they cannot be too deranged, too distraught or too delirious for his taste.

Or too damaged.

Those he holds a torch for are seldom in one piece. When he isn't chasing Cain or second-sighting scripture, he visits homes for invalids, hospices, asylums, where there are frag-ments of forgotten women to be comforted. Babel mislays its old and its imperfect as cheerfully as it lets slip its past, so there is no shortage of infirmaries for Sisobk to haunt. He isn't the ideal person to have tramping wards and sitting on the edge of sick-beds: he isn't ideally clean; he isn't – with his bear's shoulders, and his circular boy's face, and his trickle of a moustache, and his squashed sultana eyes – ideally encouraging. But it is surprising how many decomposing women with a hand left to hold will let anybody hold it, not excluding Sisobk the Scryer.

He loves women too much to tell them he loves them, even though that may be the last sentence they ever hear. Yet he has many a time left a death-bed convinced in his heart that a promise of bliss has just been snatched from him, which he didn't know existed an hour before.

Small wonder, then, if his first sight of Zilpah, pecking at Cain's brain, made a strong impression on him. To Cain's eye the girl might have been a mere transparency – a row of buttons, a spinal column and a braid; by Sisobk's standards she was blooming.

He didn't love her. He didn't, that's to say, *discretely* love her. He beheld her in her individual woman's glory, which confirmed the high esteem in which he held the species, the subgenus – that was all. But he loved Cain for loving her. Saw it as a vindication of his idolatry, and also as an additional bond between them, that Cain loved women as much as he did. 'Just let me hold your hand,' he had pleaded,' 'just let me hold *both* your hands,' as Cain was kicking him out.

At least on this occasion he didn't take Cain's lukewarm hospitality personally. Of course the first-murderer wanted to be alone with the woman. Of course he didn't want acolytes and apostles barging in on him while he was drying tears, offering words of comfort, lighting candles and otherwise prosecuting his amours. Sisobk understood all this. And smiles to himself whenever he thinks about it. That Cain! Incorrigible! He still wishes he'd been allowed to hold the fratricide's hand for a second – *both* their hands – but he understands, he understands. That Cain!

Had he known what Cain was actually thinking throughout the girl Zilpah's woodpecker ministrations, Sisobk would doubtless have been horrified. Killing a brother is one thing; not loving women – not loving *woman* is quite another.

III

Although he doesn't attach a high value, while it is happening, to being beaten by Anatolians, Cain rather enjoys the sensation afterwards of steam wisping and weeping over his broken skin.

It isn't only mould that brings him to the baths. Water remains a luxury to wanderers long after they've stopped wandering, and Cain cannot immerse himself too often. He loves the superstructure of bathing, too: the hissing pipes, the furnace chimneys, the high windowless walls, the tiles, the stacks of laundered towels. Hard to believe, here, that water was first divided from water by God. And that's another argument for coming to the Anatolian bathhouse: it persuades you that water is a substance made by men.

He sits on a slatted bench and gives his thoughts up to the vapours. He sits, vapid, for too long. A steam room is not the place to clear the mind of mildew. One more minute, he promises himself, and I will shower cold. And then he perceives he is not steaming alone.

'Thought I might catch you here,' a voice like gargling announces.

Cain wonders if he might get away with not looking up, not noticing he is being spoken to, pretending to be occupied, deaf, dead. But he feels the bench sag under the weight of another body, and registers that a foot identical to his foot, but *not* his foot, has entered his field of vision.

He is relieved at least that the foot is naked, and therefore isn't likely to be the prophet's. In which case he is just about prepared to meet civility halfway. I'll talk if I have to, he agrees, but only to the foot.

'That's twice so far I've seen your lips move,' the voice says. 'But since you obviously weren't addressing me, dare I hope that you were communicating with God?'

And now Cain knows to whom the toes identical to his toes belong. They belong to Preplen, and are being shown as evidence – that's horribly apparent now – of their common Edenite inheritance. Look – we even cut our toe-nails the same!

'You can hope what you like,' Cain says. 'But God is the last person I come here to find.'

'Whatever you say. I don't know about "person", but whatever you say. Get my note?'

'I got your note.'

'Read it?'

'I read it.'

'Like it?'

'*Like* it!'

'The writing.'

'Was I meant to?'

'No . . . yes. When a poet pens a little something to you . . .'

'It wasn't in verse.'

'Verse! Verse! Who's to say what's verse? Anyway, the enclosures were.'

'Ah, yes – those.'

'Ah, yes – those! Can I have them back, then?'

Cain gestures to his nakedness, establishing that he has none of Preplen's poems about his person.

'Of course, had I known you were going to be here . . .' he says.

'. . . you would have been prepared to look at me.'

'I'm looking at you.'

'You're looking at my foot.'

'Isn't that enough?'

'Is it enough for you?'

'It's plenty for me.'

'Do you like what you see.'

'A foot's a foot.'

'Ha! A foot's a foot, is it? It's easy to see you're no poet. Shall I tell you what a foot is? And we can take yours if you're not impressed with mine, although there's hardly any ... I'll tell you what a foot is – it's God and the Devil ... it's air and lead ... it's your wherewithal to soar above the earth and the reason you don't ... it's a star and a stone ... it's a ladder and a shovel ... it's a cloud and a boat ... The one thing it isn't is a foot!'

'In my case,' Cain says, more lead than air, more stone than star, 'the *only* thing it is is a foot. You forget how much walking I've done.'

'Forget! Me! How could I forget? Who knows the distances you've travelled better than I do? Do you want me to tell you how many paces it is, heel to toe, from here to Eden?'

And he is up before Cain can answer, measuring like a mad thing, as if he intends to pace it out, foot over foot, the long journey Cain has made from something Preplen thinks was worthy to something Preplen thinks is not.

Cain looks at him for the first time, vanishing and appearing again through the steam, a naked twisted gnome with a bad neck and hollow buttocks and Cain's feet. And Cain wonders, is this an old man or a young man?

This is not idle musing. Or vanity. Cain is not comparing bodies. For Preplen's age has serious bearing on his claim that he and Cain were once near-neighboured. If he is an old man, if he is Cain's senior, then where was he in the days when Cain still had a brother? Why hadn't Cain heard of him? If he is a young man, whose issue is he?

The question *Is this an old man or a young man?* therefore means *Is this man family?*

Encouraged by the steam, more fungus grows on Cain.

IV

As bright and as nervous as budgerigars, the barbers flutter about the entrance to the shop, mystified by the non-appearance of their best customer. They look up and down the street. They toss their heads back and regard the sun, estimating its angle. Almost evening. Then where is he? He has been in three times today – twice in the morning for shaves, once at lunchtime for towels. But that last visit is now four . . . five hours ago.

'Well, I'm not touching him if he doesn't come soon,' says one, a junior washer and latherer with eyes as dark and beautiful as wounds. 'Can you imagine the state he'll be in.'

They try to imagine.

'Egregious.'

'Flagrant.'

'Gross.'

'In need of fumigation.'

'In need of despumation.'

'In need of defoliation.'

Much merriment from the budgerigars, great excitement occasioned by the similarity of this word to another.

Laughter rises, but dies quickly. An atmosphere of desuetude descends upon the shop. You would think the barbers hadn't worked for centuries. They stare at curls of hair lying unswept around their feet as though they have never before seen such things and hesitate to approach them in case they're dangerous. They examine combs minutely. They look into mirrors and make circles of their mouths. They push their sleeves up, then roll them down again, and make similar adjustments to their pantaloons. Just so much skin, and no more, must be visible. Just so much as will implant the suggestion, but not quicken the thought, that barbers are vulnerable to pain.

Faced with this fever of inactivity, Sisobk the Scryer suspects he has come to the wrong place. He has had his head around the door a full five minutes before anyone notices he's there, and even then no one is in any hurry to attend to him.

He is looking for Cain, has Cain on his mind, and so does what he thinks Cain would do. Coughs.

Affronted, the barbers, one by one, look up.

'Closed,' they say.

'Too late.'

'Too busy.'

'Too particular.'

'Unless,' says one, 'you would like us to see what we can achieve with your moustache.'

'Assuming we can find it,' says another.

'And that we don't accidentally blow it off,' puts in a third.

'Like . . . so!' they say, huffing together.

Sisobk the Scryer doesn't like it here, but he was sure he was going to find Cain tilted back in a chair, perhaps under towels, perhaps with a razor at his throat, but in any event ill-placed to offer resistance – and now he doesn't know how to fill the tickling hollow in his expectation. 'Can I wait for him?' he asks.

'Not in the shop,' they tell him.

'Not at this hour.'

'Not when we're so busy.'

And anyway, they want to know, who is this *him* he's waiting for?

Sisobk is astonished they need to ask. Does anyone else come here? In his mind's eye he has always seen it as a place given over wholly to the cleansing of Cain. 'The murderer,' he says.

The barbers make little round mouths at one another. Of course, the murderer. Aha, the murderer. Incontestably and without a doubt and how could they have been so stupid as to have forgotten, the murderer.

'Can I leave a message, then?' the prophet asks.

'Verbal,' says a barber, 'or will you be writing it on your foot?'

'Will you tell him,' Sisobk persists, 'that I've located the fissure.'

'Just so we can be sure about it,' inquires a barber, 'which fissure exactly is this?'

Not having been here for defoliation, Sisobk is unprepared for the success of fissure.

'Where the God of Israel unzipped the desert,' he explains, 'and swallowed all Korah's followers but On.'

'*But on* what . . .?' a barber would be told.

'I think he means *but one*,' another ventures.

'On – On!' Sisobk tells them. '*On* – the husband of his wife. And that's someone else I want to talk to him about.'

'On?'

'On's wife.'

'Careful,' they warn him, 'we'll have no wife talk in this shop.'

'Unless it's bloody,' says one.

'Oh, it's bloody,' says Sisobk.

'And hair-raising.'

'Oh, it's hair-raising,' says Sisobk.

'And barbaric.'

'Oh, it couldn't be more barbaric,' says Sisobk.

'In that case,' they all say together, 'and seeing as we've nothing much else to do, why don't you tell us about her?'

Which is how Sisobk the Scryer comes to be sitting on the floor of Cain's barber-shop, with possibly as pretty and excitable but certainly as numerous a gathering around him as he has ever mustered, spinning stories from the Cainite bible, the Haggadah, and his head.

'There was a wife,' he says, 'a brave, beautiful, suffering *woman . . .*'

But we'll tell it our way, before he has the budgerigars

falling off their perches and a cage of psittacosis on his conscience.

V

It is night in the desert.

Soon, very soon now, the earth's crust will crack and a gash like the shadow of forked lightning will open in the sand.

There is little movement about the camp. There are no more meetings. No more mutterings. Now is the time for waiting. Only Moses and Aaron are out, muffled against the coming chill, fringed against temptation, bejewelled against impertinence, wound, in gorgeous linen and phylacteries, against the night-flying infection of scepticism. Only Moses and his brother Aaron visiting the tabernacles of the unrighteous, making one final appeal to the spirit of God within them.

'I have said my say,' Korah declares. 'Be gone.'

Ditto Dathan.

Ditto Abiram.

And On? He is asleep in his tent when Moses and Aaron come by. Asleep, snoring and drunk. He has his wife to thank for this condition. 'Sit here, drink this, say nothing, and I will save thee,' she has told him, knowing how unfitted he is to save himself sober.

He has been a no one, a no On, a *nebbish*, all his life. 'What matters it to thee who runs this hell-hole?' she asked him, when he returned puffed with the rhetoric of conspiracy from his first secret meeting with Korah. 'Thou art but a disciple, whoever rules.'

He rubbed his hand over his face, frustrated because a hand was not a sponge. He gets hot when his wife asks questions of him. 'I don't have a choice in the matter any longer,' he protested. 'I have participated in their counsels and they have sworn me to be with them.'

'You have a choice,' she told him. 'Sit here, drink this, and shut up.'

He obeyed. Why not? Trouble in the tent, trouble out of the tent . . . a man's only friend is his wineskin.

He snoozed through the rebellion, through Korah's twitting of Moses, through the gainsaying of the Law, and he snoozes now through the last errand of mercy that Moses and Aaron make to his tabernacle.

Or at least to the environs of his tabernacle. What stops them getting any closer than the length of a dozen donkeys, lined up nose to rump, is the sight of On's wife sitting at the entrance to her tent, her hair unloosed. They see the tumble of black curls with moonlight in them, reaching almost to the sand, and they retreat. It is not seemly for a man to look upon the unloosed hair of a woman not his wife. More to the point, it is not safe. It distracts a scholar from his studies and a prophet from his tablets. It inflames . . .

Sisobk the Scryer makes a meal of this, of course, to put before the barbers. But we must assume a smaller proportion of hairdressers among our readership. Besides, it's common knowledge what a single strand of hair inflames in already hot places . . .

Suffice to say that rather than risk a fire in their natures, with the earth about to open any minute, the brothers feel for their fringes, turn on their heels and consider On to have relented.

On's wife sits on her seat and watches them go: Moses, affecting the stoop of unappreciated beneficence, of gentle-heartedness misunderstood; Aaron, stiffer in his gait, the golden bells on the hem of his ephod and the onyx stones on his shoulders flickering like fireflies in the darkness. The desert has turned quickly cold, the sand between her toes sharp and icy suddenly, like broken shells. She shudders. Inside the tent

On is snoring loudly, as helplessly given over to unconsciousness tonight as he was yesterday the slave of Korah's eloquence. There is nothing and no one that cannot sway him. He bends before the gentlest breeze. She can keep him safe only so long as she can keep him drunk. But safe for what?

On's wife is not as far gone in despair as many women in the camp. She does not succumb to the wilderness hysteria that keeps some wives hidden inside their tents, screaming and laughing, sometimes unable or unwilling to move a limb, frightened of sun, sand, scorpions, convinced they have been led into a habitation fit only for ostriches and dragons. The terrain of her disquiet is emotional not vegetal, crossed not by wolves and jackals but by wild yearnings and savage disillusionments. She is a rare gift that no one is worthy to receive. She is an unseen flower (we are handing back to Sisobk for this) – an unsung poem, a golden goblet of untasted wine upset in a desert at midday.

In short – a *woman*.

She sits, without a shawl, waiting for the fireflies that flicker around Aaron to go out. A light wind has got up, bringing with it the smell of spices and sea and rotting jungle from afar. It lifts her hair, separating the tresses as loving fingers might. Without warning, the wind turns around. She can hear voices on it now. Altercation. Defiance. Scorn. The peevishness that would surely be finding a path to On's small spirit had she not closed its ears.

Then all words are engulfed by a terrible sound, as of the earth tearing. She does not see the rip. She only feels the ground give way, heave like the deck of a ship, slump like the back of a grudging camel, then subside altogether, as though a mole of enormous size has begun mining beneath her. A hand reaches up from the underworld and claims the stool on which she is sitting. Something tugs at her skirt. And then she sees the tent begin to lurch.

Inside, although the ground is not yet broken, a great whirlwind has been raised. Vessels heavy with wine and oil take to the air and rain down their contents. Rugs which had once belonged to Pharaohs, inducements from Korah, are thrown about like leaves. *Mezuzahs* and phylacteries unscroll themselves, scattering scripture. Everything is in violent and fastidious motion, impelled by an urgency of separation. In these final moments all things wish to be inviolably themselves. Including On's bed, which shakes and rolls, seeing its way of being rid of On at last.

But On is oblivious, oiled in his own sweat, too pliant, too slippery, too comfortable, to be thrown from his mattress. No matter how steeply it rears, it cannot toss him. Resolved not to be denied, the bed gives up its convulsions, makes for the opening in the tent, and proceeds at an even but determined pace towards . . . towards what?

Now she sees it! The fissure, the hole, the nothingness, the unseamed desert smoking crimson like Gehenna, another Red Sea awash this time with Israel's children, not Egypt's. But brought up short at her threshold, stopped dead at her feet – a lake of bodies lapping at her shore.

And – oh God! – On in his bed on his back, heading for the lake.

She thought she had saved him already with her unloosed hair. But Sisobk has a taste for placing women in exaggerated attitudes of devotion. And a hell-fire pit with a hog's-bristle mattress hanging over it is too good an opportunity to let pass. He streams her beautiful black hair in the evil wind that blows from the chasm, hurls her on the teetering bed, and clasps her arms around its sodden cargo.

The barbers grow restive, wondering whether this is the best the fellow with no hair on his face is going to be able to do for them.

'Hang on,' Sisobk says, 'I haven't finished yet.'

*

The first light of morning sees the bed and its occupants still poised above the precipice, half off the cliff, half on it, and only the weight of a pin holding the balance between deliverance and damnation.

The cries of Korah's company have not yet died away. Nor the screams of their animals. Nor the reverberations of their every last pot and pan as they rattle down to hell.

It may be these sounds which wake On to his new surroundings. He rubs his eyes – wishing as always that his hands were wet sponges – looks around him, spits, and beholds his wife clinging piteously to his legs, her own legs streaming out behind her in space, like coat-tails.

'I'm not telling you again,' he says. 'You know the rule. No gazing at me with love first thing in the morning.'

And he kicks out . . .

The barbers look up from their finger-nails.

'Men!' they say.

'And when do you reckon all this happened?' they ask him.

'About a thousand years from now,' Sisobk says.

This is Babel and these are barbers. Prophets are nothing new in this shop.

'If you can tell the future, tell ours,' they say.

They are still listless, still sitting on the floor amid the clippings like broken dolls, still raising and lowering the hems of their pantaloons.

'Go on,' they say, 'tell ours.'

Sisobk explains that it isn't quite so easy. 'First I have to know more about you. What your names are. How old you are. Where you come from.'

'We come from Sodom,' they tell him. 'Heard of it?'

Veins break in Sisobk's face. His little eyes wrinkle like dried fruit.

'Never,' he says. 'But I'm sure your future will be a long and happy one.' And he is off, out of the shop, down the street and round a corner, before the men of Sodom can make their little mouths at one another.

VI

'Do we have to sit outside?' Preplen asks.

'I need a sherbet,' Cain says. 'And I need breeze.'

They are in an open square, enclosed on all sides by white-stepped temples, the vast expanses of stone relieved by orange trees and fluttering pavilions of striped cloth.

'What I like about it here,' Cain says, 'is that we could almost be by the sea.'

Preplen shudders.

Splintered by leaves, an early evening light the colour of honey patterns their arms. Preplen starts, fearing that his skin has erupted in impetigo. Then he searches the sky. 'To be frank with you,' he says, 'I'm frightened of birds.'

'Frightened of them as portents or frightened they'll attack you?'

He pulls his head down into his shoulders. 'Why split hairs?'

'Are you frightened of any in particular?'

'What do you mean, *in particular*? A bird's a bird isn't it – just as a foot's a foot.'

Cain looks up. A solitary pelican glides above them on currents of warm air. It circles aimlessly, the same colour as the ziggurats, offering its belly deliciously to whoever will look at it. He thinks of Semyaza. 'No,' he says. 'There are birds and birds.'

Preplen darkens his face. 'You haven't turned into some sort of nature lover or seasonalist since you left home, have you?' he asks. 'You aren't telling me you've picked up a fertility thing and spend your time bowing down to vines and cereals.'

'I don't bow down to anything,' Cain says. 'Not even partridges.'

Preplen looks alarmed. 'What's a partridge?' he wants to know.

'A bird.'

'So why would anybody bow down to a bird?'

Cain lets his eyes wander from temple to temple. 'You're asking the wrong person,' he says. 'But those who are smitten with the partridge claim great versatility for it. They say, for example, that a cock-partridge can impregnate a hen-partridge with just the sound of his voice. He can skirl his seed into her – skIE R R R R R Rek!'

Preplen covers his mouth. 'Birds!' he says. He looks as though he might easily retch. 'Birds!'

'Nor does its versatility end there. Those who are smitten maintain that cock-partridges console themselves with a round of sodomy while their womenfolk are on the eggs.'

This time, just to be on the safe side, Preplen leaves the table and takes a turn, hobbling like an old man, around the sherbet cart. He is careful to keep his head down. He returns only when he thinks he's strong enough to be told precisely what kind of holiness, what species of numen, these Partridgists divine in their divinity.

'I fear there's something you've not grasped about the zoomorphic imagination,' Cain tells him. 'Holiness hardly enters into it. What the lascivious partridge provides for its congregation is, firstly, a good dinner – easy to catch you see, while it's skierrrrreking and sodomizing – and thereafter an excuse for a riotously imitative dance.'

'Imitative of the partridge?'

'What else?'

'And they call this religion?'

'What else?'

'Listen,' Preplen says suddenly, propelling himself across the table and taking Cain's wrists, 'why don't you leave this place? Why don't you go home?'

Cain makes no attempt to free himself. He looks at the hands that hold him. Old hands? Young hands? He doesn't know. But they are yellow, unhealthy hands.

A flock of cranes passes overhead. There are men in Babel who faint at the beauty of cranes in flight. They faint professionally. To please audiences. It occurs to Cain that they might be out there dropping on the river banks this very moment. Their fall cushioned by soft mosses, their colour coming and going, a breathing waxen, like Abel's. For Abel, too, was a fainter.

But for Preplen the cranes' high honking triangular flight is an abomination, a danger to him personally, an affront to the single Godhead, and worst of all, an obstacle to the unfolding of his opinions.

'This is no place for you,' he continues. 'I know you . . . you won't fight. You won't stand up for yourself. You don't want them to see how extreme you are. You want to smooth it all out for them, make it shapely, make it elegant, conceal what is the truth: that you strove extremely and then fell out extremely with an extreme God . . .'

Cain interrupts him, pointing to the cranes. 'Oughtn't you, as a poet —?'

'Oughtn't I to be writing odes to fowl?' Preplen's head has sunk into his shoulders again, as though that is its preferred and natural way of growing, a flower without a stalk. 'No. I'm not that sort of poet. I leave that to your friends. Your blue-blood worshippers of the Holy Goat. Those Partridgists I wish you'd never told me about. I do something else. I curse. I course. I run around the object of my contempt. I copy him. I mimic him. I confound him. And by these means I bring him down.'

'This is poetry?'

'This is satire. The highest and most healthful form of play. I blow away malign influences. I curse out demons. I do what you should be doing.'

'I'm not a satirist,' Cain says.

Preplen looks at him. And withdraws the light from both their faces. 'No, you're not, are you,' he says. 'Too much like your father, I suppose. Not enough of your mother in you.'

VII

It is late when he gets back to his room. Already he can smell the morning on the night. He pushes open his door and resolves not to light a candle. There is nothing he needs to see. He slips out of his clothes, hanging them carefully, sleeves always out, pockets always emptied, and gropes towards the bed. His hands touch hair and flesh. He flinches from the contact, fearing that a stray dog may have crept under his blanket, or a stray prophet, or a stray relative from Eden. But what he touches next tells him that this is neither a scryer nor a satirist lying on its back on his bed, with its lips parted and its breath held and its small breast heaving.

'Zilpah?'

The lean, abrasive arms reach up to clasp him. Once again his first thought is that she is too thin.

Girls without flesh are a delicacy in Babel. Like quail, they are valued because they can be consumed in a single mouthful. But Cain lacks the epicurean's lightness of temperament. He is grave and seeks gravity. A slight woman confirms all his

worst fears about existence. A slight woman proves the nuga-
toriness of things. A slight woman proves there is no hereafter.
When you penetrate her you enter nothing.

She hangs from his neck, as weightless as a locket. With her
mouth she seeks the lines and furrows of his suffering. She
must taste every crime he has committed and every punishment
that's been visited on him. Of her own free will she must
drink of the waters of bitterness. *His* bitterness.

He unlocks her fingers from behind his head.

'What do you need?' she asks him. She has a little voice,
such as a mouse might have, to match her little body. But in a
low register, as though the mouse behind the draughty wains-
cot has caught a little cold.

He shakes his head, vainly, in the dark. What does he need?
Would she know what he meant if he said he needed scraping?

There is silence in the bed for a while. Nothing moves. He
wonders if she has crept out without his hearing, nibbled
through the mattress and escaped under the space beneath his
door. Then suddenly the blanket is thrown off and she is up
on all fours, whimpering like the stray dog he had at first
taken her for.

'This is what you need . . .' the cur within her cries.

She presents her narrow, shadowed hindquarters to him,
spreading herself open so that he may have complete and
unobstructed access to the little puckered flower that grows in
the very eye of her rump –

– What he needs.

The odour of her offering, her floral tribute, is rich and
sour, suggestive of what is arable; its recipient at the mercy of
just such impulses as must have riven his father in the days
prior to Eve, when only a field of bullocks stood between all
he knew of frustration and all he imagined of felicity.

He sighs, his father's son. Old Adam's boy. A vexed sigh. A
sigh of this and that.

Then he takes hold of the fanatic plait.

'This is what you need isn't it . . .' she growls, reaching between her thighs to make herself more available to him yet, a skinny hand on each furred and skinny hemisphere, '. . . a brother.'

Farshtinkener, farfoylt, farshimmelt.
    Cain has the sensations, whether or not he has the Yiddish. But he still doesn't let go of the plait.

9. Cain Loses Himself in Pathos

He grew into a beautiful boy.

Does that sound like the language a connoisseur of catamites might use? *A beautiful boy?* It is meant to. His beauty was of *that* sort. Golden. Fragile. Petulant. Pliable. Fleeting. Cruel. Had Yahweh been a God given to enjoying good wine, He would not have needed to look beyond Abel for his cup-bearer. But Yahweh did not drink. Had we been more populous and there been older men, other than his father and his brother, to gaze upon him, they would have trembled for their chastity. His beauty was of that sort. You saw him once and you wanted to sail away with him to some enchanted surf-fringed isle, just the two of you, free of all distractions, so that you might torment yourself exclusively with the impermanence of love and loyalty and flesh.

His eyes were a pale wandering blue. His lips were full and moist, not quite together, not quite resolute, not quite a pair. His neck was long and luminous, a milky chrysaline white, the colour and transparency of pupae. You could see the blood pumping below his skin. His hair hung in yellow hoops that turned half-circles on his shoulders when he ran. He ran like a fawn in the afternoon. None of it could last.

Such precious perishability is wasted on mere family. You wonder why your brother doesn't have a healthier appetite, why he is looking quite so translucent, then you go about your business. You have to be a perfect stranger to appreciate it perfectly. It was Abel's bad luck to have been born before there were strangers.

We all suffered to some degree from this misfortune. Each one of us secretly imagined foreigners, impartial witnesses, angels on no particular errand – unrelated company to whom we could show off what we took to be our qualities, or express what we knew to be our grievances.

The gift of pleasing lay rotting in my father's heart. For want of guests his instinct for hospitality turned inward, and every night he welcomed new terrors into his dreams.

Unconfided vexation massed like gallstones in my mother's gut.

I . . .

But leave me out of it. This hour is consecrated to my brother. And our self-sufficiency, our entirety unto ourselves, was crueller to him than to any of us. For what good is a genius for unattainability when there is nobody out there to try attaining you?

In the absence of a god who hankered after boyish company, or older men who would cradle youth only that they might see it spill from their embraces like golden sand, Abel's beauty found the adoration it couldn't do without – in my mother. She fed on it, drank from it, following it everywhere with her eyes, repairing every accidental bruising to it with slow suppliant idolatrous fingers. She sat him on her lap. She pressed his head between her breasts. She blew on his neck and shoulders, to cool him when he was hot, to warm him when he was cold – a climatic system all his own. She stroked his chest. She kissed his navel.

Nothing maternally untoward in that? Then let me tell you she was still bathing him when he was eighteen, and would have been drying him when he was twenty . . .

There had been no pacifying Eve. Her anger was fed from invisible sources, was nourished by a root system so complex that had Adam hacked at it for a thousand years he would have diminished her supply not a trickle.

From the moment he saw that the bitter waters had left his wife's belly flat and thigh intact, but had begun to seep instead into her affections, my father threw himself into a frenzy of expiation. Elaborate apologies were not his way. You could say he was without grace. Without, too, any of that capacity for transferred anguish which later men, men not muddy in their origins, would employ as a means of righting wrong: 'You think *you* are hurt by what I've done? Look at how it has affected *me*!' He was unsubtle, in other words, and sought to make amends the only way he knew how – manually.

He hewed for her. He drew for her. He chopped and axed and chipped and carved and sliced and scythed and smoothed for her. He bevelled bowls for her. Whittled ladles. Cut down palms to shape her bowers, bound lianas to make her hammocks, bent bamboo and plaited rushes so that she should have simultaneous shade against the sun and shelter from the cold.

You rejoice in moderation here in Babel. I ask you to remember that for us the seasons were still unsorted. The Six-day Miracle notwithstanding, it was still possible to sweat and shiver at the same time, to feel the sun frizzle on our shoulders while our feet crunched snails iced up in their shells. The earth did not know what the air was thinking; the sea enjoyed no commerce with the shore – the thing we call amphibiousness came later, when co-operation between the elements could be counted on. In our time there was no relying on a single medium to co-operate even with itself.

As it happened, we never did wake to find the sky lower than the earth, or fire flowing like fog through river beds, but that might have had as much to do with Divine Luck as Divine Judgement.

Such uncertainty, anyway, meant that my father could not take any particulars of my mother's comfort for granted. He could be fashioning her a punkah out of palmyra one minute and be expected to lash a raft together to save her from the freezing floods the next.

I say expected, but all consciousness of obligation was on his side. For her part my mother asked for nothing beyond simple produce – cereal, root vegetables, an orange that she could pick at with her nails, the occasional small bird – and showed no gratitude for the ingenious presents he showered on her. She didn't want another bowl. She didn't need another ladle. She ate standing up and with her back to him, and since she had no one to entertain, could find no use for a table that sat twenty.

But indifference wasn't the beginning and the end of what she felt. There was a design problem between them, too. She detested the look of every article he made.

In retrospect I take no sides, except to say that what the objects of my father's hands lacked in elegance they made up for generously in size.

She passed no comments about his carpentry to his face. A complaint could have been mistaken for an acknowledgement, and you cannot acknowledge where you are determined not to notice. She kept her head turned from him and all his works: when he called to her from the heights of a tree he was lopping, she looked down; when he hallooed from under-ground, where he was mining coloured stones for inlay work – he loved the test that marquetry set his banana fingers – she looked up; when he approached her with his mouth full of wooden nails and his flesh flayed by scalding resin, she looked away. If circumstances forced a conversation, she curtained her eyes and addressed an incorporeality – an idea of him, so to speak, as notional as a ghost and located in some even more theoretical dimension. But when he wasn't in her vicinity, before her or behind her, above her or below her, waiting against all experience and likelihood for his reward, wondering whether he hadn't this time stretched the parasol or gummed the trinket box that would melt all her resistance to him, once and for all – then, *then* she would let her opinion of his handicraft show.

Whatever was throwable she threw, whatever was breakable she broke. Sometimes she filled the air with flying lumber, made monstrous birds of his monstrous bowls, dispatching them with an aggression so pointed and individual that they might have been pieces of my father himself. But if the object of offence happened to be some edificial shebang he had taken it into his head to knock together – some summer-hut or wind-break or cold-cupboard or tree-house or canary-cage or bee-hive or rabbit-trap or vegetable-store or wood-shed or sheep-fold or pig-pen or lean-to – she went for it as though it were a mausoleum containing the relics of her enemy entire. She shook it until her shoulders ached, and punched it until her knuckles bled, and hammered at it with her forehead until the pain behind her eyes was greater than the ugliness before them.

We looked on, Abel and I, at a loss to understand the violence my father's woodwork inspired in her. We did not know about the destructiveness of woman. That the circumstances of her creation had been such that she would never be happy until she had undone all making and seen the globe itself beaten back to its original flatness. We were in no position to try generalities. There was only one woman for us to go on. We could see she was upset and embittered, but we could not know that she was thereby expressing her fundamentally anarchic and vengeful nature – set upon an unswerving course to pay back Divinity for having conceived her only on another's prompting, sequentially, function first.

This is the reason you never meet true religious faith in women, not even here in Babel, where you can pick and choose among discarded deities, but only a hysterical inversion of hate parading as devotion, a sort of mockery of reverence, as like as not accompanied by high temperatures and trembling of the flesh. Since all gods must of necessity be champions of order – even godlings of chaos insist on organized ritual – and since order was woman's undoing, how can relations between them ever be anything but ironic? Think of the little domestic world of lord and servant you all know: was there ever a wife yet that did not discharge her offices sardonically?

I mean at best. Doubly, trebly incensed, our mother did not discharge her offices at all. She turned her back on her husband's person and smote the offerings of his hand.

You'll never destroy them, I once said to her, they are too well made.

She stopped what she was doing – what she was *un*doing – let the adzes and axes with which she'd been laying about her fall to the ground, and shook her head at me. A slow, sad shake. Not becoming in a woman who had put on too much weight, whose jowls rattled and whose cheeks flapped. And not flattering to me either, because it implied there was much I didn't grasp and probably never would.

She repeated what I'd said. Too well made. If you mean by that, made to last for ever, she said, then I couldn't agree with you more. Look at the brute permanence of the things. Have you ever seen anything more monstrous? Look!

We were a demonstrative family. *Look*! (Look at him, your baby brother . . . *Look!*)

I looked.

Over a narrow shallow stream that we could wade across in three strides my father had thrown – no, had erected – a bridge wide enough to accommodate a whole legion of marching angels. The trunks of at least a dozen trees – Tabor oaks, carobs, pines, pistachios (all named by me and therefore mine) – were lashed together with braided bine and ivy sufficient to crochet a ladder up to God and back. Although there was not the remotest possibility of their moving, a pile of boulders secured the logs on each bank. And then more felled trees boxed in the boulders to secure *them*. Anyone passing – any of those strangers who secretly peopled our imaginations – would have supposed he had come upon the fortified dwellings of a pair of infuriated dinosaurs waging war across a rivulet.

I could see that it would not be easy to argue for my father's bridge, using beauty as a criterion. The difficulty of crossing, because of all the timber and masonry in the way, steered me off the issue of utility as well.

It looks extremely safe, I said.

My mother shook her head again, more in anger than in sadness this time. And at the bridge rather than at me. It will be here in another thousand years, she said. Here for a thousand years and no doubt another thousand after that. Without beauty, without use, just . . . just here.

I had thought she was going to say, just . . . just like him.

A man can't win, I confided to Abel when we were alone. If he made things that fell apart in a day she would still complain.

I got no answer from him. And didn't expect one. From something like his second year to something like his seventh (while his beauty was maturing), Abel put himself into a trance, ignoring all quarrels and contention, and gave over his every waking minute to sitting in the dust, spinning shells. Nothing could distract him from this. Not hunger, not thirst, not fatigue. Sometimes he would have as many as a hundred shells of all sizes spinning together. He followed their revolutions minutely, relating the length of time they kept going to their shape and weight, to their degree of transparency and concavity, to their colour and crustation, crying at last with dizziness and exhaustion, but screaming if anyone attempted to stop him.

It didn't matter how hard a skin his fingers grew, by the end of each day they were bleeding from the friction. He was covered in cuts and dirt, calcareous splinters having embedded themselves beneath his nails, in his ears, in his nostrils, in his scalp, in places unknown even to my mother. By nightfall the joints of his body were locked in a position from which they had not moved since morning.

My mother's custom of bathing him began from this time,

when he had to be carried, bawling and bloody, from his shells. Only her hands, lovingly lathering, could quieten him and make him flexible again and send him to sleep. But I could tell from the movement of his eyelids as I crouched over him, that he was still spinning in his dreams; and when I awoke in the morning, there he would be, up before any of us, already in the dirt, already rigid, already crying, with his carapaces whirring.

Had he been able to sustain this preoccupation beyond early childhood it might have been better for all of us. There was safety in his spinning. But although he was to remain withdrawn in temperament, capable at any time not just of feigning deafness but actually of becoming deaf when things were said which he preferred not to hear, Eve's appreciation of his appearance awoke him at last to himself.

She had never been sparing in her praises of him. Even on those early bath nights when she gathered him up, kicking and giddy, there was always some preliminary rhetorical marvelling over his loveliness. Look – isn't he beautiful! she would sing. Look how his skin shines. You can almost see yourself in him! Look how he sparkles in the dark, like a star. My little star!

He had resisted it all then. Fought against the coddling and the exhibiting. Not a good idea to be held up and shown like this, a sound instinct warned him, especially in the presence of a father whose labours went unappreciated and a brother who ... sat up at night listening to heart-beats. But as he grew older he began to give in to the delicious sensation of exciting compliment. When my mother drew attention to the slender bow of his neck, or to the wheels of yellow hair that appeared to complete circles whenever he moved his head, it was as though she lit fires beneath his transparent skin. He didn't flush; never once, not even in moments of crisis, did I see my brother, living, stained red. There was always white in his colouring, always something ghostly in his pigmentation; but you could see the flickering of warm lights, and you could smell distant burning, like sweetmeats roasting, the centres of self-esteem – the heart, the stomach – turning nicely on their spit.

What a lovely boy you are, my mother said to him, kissing him behind the ears or rubbing her nose into that place between the shoulder blades where, had he been an angel, he would have itched unbearably. I could eat you, she would say. I could eat you all up for my supper.

He no longer squirmed on her lap. He had lost his embarrassment with his milk teeth. He gazed up at her, older than his years, playing younger than his years. All of me? Even my nails?

She put them to her lips, one by one. Ten little fingers. Ten little toes. Every bit of you, she assured him. Even your nails.

His smile was furtive. He had only one smile and it was always furtive. My mother's was the same. And mine too. No matter how much we meant to smile, no matter how little concealment we intended, we all betrayed some sneaking satisfaction, some minuscule and unworthy triumph, over and above. As though, like a well-treated slave or a pickpocket come into an inheritance, we had to take, even where we had been freely given. It was a gracelessness passed on down the family through the female line. A mark of our plebeian origins. Errand boy's lip. Help meet's mouth.

Only my father was free of it. The first and worst of architects, engineer of constructions whose uncouthness and deformity defy description almost as successfully as they defied decay, he at least possessed a smile – that's when he smiled at all these days – that was harmonious. It went with what occasioned it. It went with what he felt. It went with himself.

He was lucky. It is not pretty to be disfigured by the one sign all men take to denote pleasure. And to my eye, Abel was never less pretty than when he was pleased.

My mother neither.

Rather than smile like that – rather than smile like us – it is better not to smile at all.

*

But let me tell you, if you can bear it, how she bathed him.
All right, let me tell you if *I* can bear it . . .

FIRST, smoking ashes packed around the scalloped rock wherein we washed, to take the chill, whether there was chill or not, out of the circumambient air.

SECOND, water drawn from a stream in a jar (or an amphora or a pitcher or a ewer or a gallipot or a jeroboam.) But *drawn*, not syphoned – educed, liberated, water delivered out of servitude .

THIRD, frangipani and jasmine and queen of the night and clove gillyflower crushed in a mortar and sprinkled into the pool. Lotus petals floating on the surface. And the wings of butterflies who had had their day and chose to expire here, so that their last memories should be their best, at this nightly festival to beauty.

FOURTH, Abel presented. Passive. Furtive. Hands held straight above his head for the removal of his shift. A pea podded.

FIFTH, exclamations instructional. Careful. Steady. Stand still. Keep straight. That's it. Head up. There we are. Ah . . . there we are.

SIXTH, hands on. My mother folded, her haunches on her heels, her neck bulging like an eel, her hair streaming in the water like algae. Starting from Abel's feet, in a slow repetitive circular motion, the first application of salts and soap.

SEVENTH, the ascent. Each blue-white shank traced, as if to corroborate a pattern in the memory. The scars on Abel's knees (where he had knelt, unknowing and engrossed, on broken shell) anointed in a manner perfected while tending the flaky shoulders of angels.

EIGHTH, exhalations rhapsodical. Oh! Ah! There? There! How your skin trembles! How your blood pumps! Oh! Ah! So still on the outside, so much activity within. So red on the inside, so white without.

NINTH, no civility shown to my father, who arrives to mock a thing he hates. *Still rubbing? Do you mean to rub the boy away?* No civility shown. No answer given. Her eyes closed like curtains on all communication. But washing giving way to towelling, and the trance broken until the next night, unless . . .

Abel comes up so prettily under the friction, so startled-pink in all the dents and caverns of his body, that TENTH, my mother cannot refuse herself the indulgence – there, below his ear, or there, in the golden valley of his throat, or there and there, where she has pasted henna around his paps – of a kiss.

When this happens, the stifled smile on my brother's lips, of shame and victory commingled, is impossible to bear. And

ELEVENTH, I turn my back on him, and on her, and repair to the garden I have been cultivating as an act of vengeance on myself, and plunge my arms elbow-deep into the soil, into the mud, into the slime, whether there is a moon to show me what horrors I may be touching, or whether there is not.

But I continue to watch over Abel in his sleep. I continue to plant my ear into his powdered chest and listen to his henna'd heart beat. My fear that something may happen to him, that he will simply stop living in the night, has not diminished. I still consider it my responsibility to guard against this eventuation, to monitor the evenness of his breathing, and there is no doubt in my mind that the engine for this vigilance is love.

A great protective passion for him overwhelms me when I see him sleeping. It is so strong that I am sometimes taken by the thought that it will be me whose heart goes. It will give out, or burst, with the exertions of worrying over his.

I do not believe it is his beauty that inspires this heaving love in me. That imposes this heavy love *on* me. I am proof against beauty, and cut down the loveliest flowers in my garden in order that there should be no lingering certainties around that question. I am untouched by beauty.

Fragility cannot be it either, by the same reasoning. Nothing fragile prospers in my garden.

So what do I see when I hang over him and count the rhythmic valvular openings and closings of his body's whimsical flirtation with life?

Can it be that I see only my own intentions? Can it be that love is nothing other than a mirror held up betimes to hate? A warning, a precautionary palpitation, a pang of remorse in advance of the event? If that is so, and my care for my brother is in direct proportion to the harm I bear him, then he has much to fear from me, because the tenderness I feel scalds my eyes, and my sorrow for him hammers at my ribs.

The other view I take is that he upsets me because he is a version of myself. An idealized version. Me unspoiled by intimate, inside acquaintance. Me as I might look to him. But observed without that coldness which always mars a younger brother's regard. Me sweet. Me pretty. Me bathed in water scented with frangipani and narcissi.

Me wordless.

Upset is a better word for it – since we are back to words – than love. Upset more accurately denotes who is doing what to whom. It is not that *I* love *him*. *He* upsets *me*.

Let us be clear who is the instigator and who – *whom* – the victim. I didn't ask him to come and lie by me in the life-expunging darkness, or sleep defencelessly on his back with his neck exposed and his pale shoulders pulsing, like a starfish on a moony beach. I never laid it down as a condition of our brotherliness that he should absent himself for the better part of his boyhood, spinning mollusc shells in preference to naming them, and thereby causing me to upset myself over him some more. He *chose* a fragile nature. It was *given* to me – an older brother's obligation – to safeguard it.

Thus do the meek inveigle the brave and snaffle the earth.

*   *   *

He stops, Cain the inveigled, and raises a perfect sleeve to those seams and scissures of the face from which feeling is expected to leak. They do not need to be dried but he dries them anyway.

A dramatic gesture. He has told this story before and knows its pauses. But is there not a danger, even in godless and ingenuous Babel, that his ruse will be rumbled? That someone will say to him, 'You affect emotion so studiedly that you must mean us to believe you are emotionless; but why would you bother to do that unless it too is a study to conceal how emotional you really are'?

Of course. 'Drama does not at some point cease to be drama,' he is always ready to reply. 'You should never suppose you have seen to the bottom of a dramaturgist's intention. Why stop at one stratagem concealing another? Why should not a stratagem hide a stratagem hide a stratagem hide a stratagem hide a stratagem . . .?'

A serious man talks to no one but himself. The only person Cain is keeping guessing is Cain. In truth he did not know how dry he was going to find the corners of his eyes and mouth until he dabbed them.

It is for his own benefit, not for Babel's, that he pauses.

'Give me a minute,' he says.

10. A MINUTE CHAPTER

What can you do in a minute?

You can look around a room and see that all the people you are anxious to avoid are in it.

The girl is to be expected. She would be here, hanging on to his every sorrow, even had he not been hanging on to her pigtail, in a brotherly way, for the last week.

Her father shouldn't be here, but is. Naaman is famous for his quick, discreet visits to performances staged under his patronage. You notice him at the beginning and you notice him at the end – what you don't expect is to notice him in between, bent backwards over his seat, just waiting to get the next joke, he would have you believe, but actually locked into a figure which gymnasts on the temple steps refer to as The Crab and would rather not perform.

Cain does not have to be acute to see that Naaman is not relaxed.

What does Naaman want?

What does Sisobk the Scryer want, mouthing to him, whenever there is a pause in the narrative, 'D-i-d t-h-e-y g-i-v-e y-o-u m-y m-e-s-s-a-g-e?'

What does Preplen poet want, what does he *mean* by bringing along a staring woman in an ill-fitting wig – presumably his wife – and five children – presumably his children, although they all look older even than their father – and sitting them in a ringleted row right under Cain the Family Desecrator's nose?

A Minute Chapter

These are rhetorical questions. Cain knows what they want.
They want him. And all of a sudden he doesn't mind.

Hence his request for a minute's pause. He would like to
accustom himself to this untoward and somewhat sickly sensation of calm.

Is that what it signifies, then, to have mould growing freely
on your person – that you are permitting others to write your
history for you? Is that what mildew is – the body's abrogation
of its own rule?

He doesn't know. His minute's up.

11. Cain Forgets a Birthday

I had begun to garden. I must have known more about my future disinheritance than I knew I knew. In a spirit of pure mockery – don't ask me whom I was mocking: it is always everyone and no one – I had paced out an allotment, put a fence around it (a fence of which my father would have been proud, had he bothered to notice), and cleared it of the disorderly mess that grew there. When it came to design, there was little to choose (which is hardly surprising) between my father and the God who had fashioned him. They both favoured grand effects, overreached themselves, grew tired, and ended up throwing everything they had at a project and insisting that the jumble was intentional.

Life, they called it.

The principle of life that operated in my garden, prior to me, was parasitic, commensal, strangulative and noisy. Nothing had enough room or wanted the particular room it had. Nothing was calm. Nothing was patient. Nothing was generous. Nothing had any sense of decorum, or shame, or . . . humour.

It is no good your eyeing me whimsically. I mean what I say. Talk to any of those sensitive gardeners you boast in Babel, men who are on confidential speaking terms with their plants, and see if you can find one in possession of a single humorous anecdote told to him by a marrow. Screams are all they hear. Shrieks from the battlefield. The first great act of creation lacked drollery, and every smaller germination since has been solemn likewise. The more a thing grows, the smaller its capacity to amuse itself. The tallest animals are the saddest. The highest mountains the most contemplative. This is a truism which can be extended no less reliably to our own species. Only stunted men are funny.

So this was my test: to plant comedy in my garden. Always remembering that by comedy I mean something less frivolous than you do.

I wanted the plants I grew to be in rows and I wanted them red – not just red in flower, but red in stem, red in leaf, red in petiole and pedicel, red in bract and bud. If I could achieve a perfect row, I thought, a regimentation of height and spacing and efflorescence, accurate to the nicest measurement, I would be imposing my will on luxuriance and clamour. And if I could grow red greenery only I would be striking a blow for perverseness. Although the earth frequently did throw up crimsons and scarlets and maroons, it did so grudgingly, it seemed to me, its instinct for random plenty at war with its preference for verdancy. I wanted a contrary, cross-patch garden. I would have planted it to grow downwards, had I known how. I would have seeded it to decrease. Whenever I pondered the challenge of an entirely red tree, I wasn't thinking of proliferation – far from it – I was thinking of the offence it would give to God.

He -HE – had not bothered us for some time. Perhaps we had at last learnt how to behave, stumbled upon the domestic arrangement He had always intended for us: wife at a Godly distance from husband, nursing a sainted grievance, turning a cold back; brothers divided by the burnished sandalwood sheen that sat on the skin of one and not the other. Or perhaps we had become plain and uninteresting to Him: no births; no magic; no more fleshly goads to celestial celibacy; now that my mother had lost *her* sheen, no more siren songs to spirit.

Whatever He was up to, it is arguable that my motive was

metaphysical mischief; that I fenced off my vegetable patch and shoved my hands into the humus I hated essentially for the purpose of worming a response out of Him. It's disconcerting, suddenly to be left in peace by a hectoring tyrant. You are not sure you know what to do with the freedom. You are not sure you like it. You begin to take the transformation personally. You wonder what you may have said or done. You become aggrieved, moody, jealous. If you go on being left alone, you have to face the possibility that you have been forgotten and that there is now Someone Else he enjoys tyrannizing more. So it's not out of the question, given that I was as jealous as my neighbour (supposing I'd had a neighbour), that the reason I started to play around with genetics was to see whether I could lure Him back.

Not for myself. You cannot have come this far with me without observing that He and I never enjoyed particularly close relations at any time. My sense of being circumscribed and shepherded by Him came through my parents. They were the harried lambs. So far, He had never dealt directly with me. I suppose I was too young. I figured, in a general way, in His poetry – *Out of the mouth of babes and sucklings ... Ye are the children of the Lord your God ... And the leopard shall lie down with the kid, and a little child shall lead them* – that sort of thing; but as a flesh and blood fact, as an entity rather than a metaphor, I didn't hold much interest for Him. Abel, on the other hand – but we've been through that. The Immanent Grandpapa. Which also turned out to be a notion more lenitive to the ears of heaven than practicable here on earth. When it came to the point, He did not poke His great finger through the clouds to play piggy with the baby Abel's toes. Let's be more charitable to Him than He ever was to us, and ascribe His failure ever to father us with a little *f* to a general awkwardness around small things. Whatever wisdom flowed between burps and bubbles from the mouths of sucklings, He communicated His own thoughts more comfortably to the grown-ups. And so I say it was for them, my poor warring mother and father, that I set about enticing His voice to come walking among us once more. If they had His heavy tread to resent, they might just start remembering why they once found each other lightsome.

My father was sleeping badly again. Perhaps it was his bed and not Abel's that I should have been visiting in the night. But my father was bearded and Abel wasn't. And a beard on the chin of a sleeping man forbids approach. I can still picture its sometimes grave, sometimes jaunty rise and fall, its tipped-up bravado, the air of dignity but also helplessness it lent his face. A man – a father – is never more a law unto himself than when he lies on his back and points his snoring beard to the skies; but he is never more unprotected either. I shunned my father with his whiskers in the air both because I feared him and feared for him.

His cries alarmed me too. A cry can be coaxed out of a child's body as smoothly as milk massaged out of a cow. From a grown man, though – from a grown bearded man – it is wrenched as cruelly as testes from an ox. He was in too much distress for his size. Like a fallen elephant he changed all one knew of the scale of pain. And I didn't have the courage to go near.

He was dreaming new dreams.

On warm nights little monkey-men came for him. They were covered in hair but very pink between their toes and fingers and in their private parts. He believed he knew their faces and could trust them. Even when they flicked him with their tails and took bites out of his sides and laughed at him among themselves he saw no reason not to trust and follow them. They were company after all. They absorbed the loneliness around him.

They led him to a place where everything moved backwards.

The cattle retreated in their grazing, regurgitating grass. Trees groaned, bent double with the stitch of descending sap. Water flowed uphill. Air whistled back into the throats of shrinking singing birds.

He was laid out, beard up, upon a slab of marble, cold beneath his back but glowing and running molten at the corners, where his feet and wrists were bound. Are you comfortable? his monkey friends asked him. Are you relaxed? He told them he had never been more comfortable in his life. They laughed at that. Unless they wept. He wasn't certain what their tears denoted. He lay on his back not looking at them, just staring at the sky which was neither light nor dark, neither a day sky nor a night sky, merely matter without coloration, from which both the sun and moon had receded.

They began to play on him, using tiny wooden hammers, as though they knew there were hidden harmonies in his body and sought only to release them. At first, he liked the sensation of being played. He heard the tune his ribs made and sang along with it. It was as familiar to him as the faces of the players, though as with them he couldn't locate the memory. Only gradually did it dawn on him that they were playing the tune backwards and that it was hurting him.

The hurt had laughter in it initially. It was like tickling. And it was like desire too. When the hammers found the inside of his thighs he called out to them to stop but in reality wanted them to strike him with more precision, *there* and *there* and *there*, and to beat out a rhythm more concordant with his own. Then he saw that what he wanted had nothing at all to do with it, that the orchestra was playing for itself. There was no longer pleasure in the pain. His skin began to blister and fall away. Underneath, his flesh was brown and crusted, like burnt meat. Elegantly, dexterously, always in time with one another, the monkey-men hammered it from the bone.

He realized that his skeleton had all along been their objective. In order truly to make music they had to have unimpeded access to his vertebrae, to his sternum, to the phalanges of his toes and fingers, to every minute ossicle hidden behind his hearing and his sight. Only now, stripped of whatever might muffle sound or impair precision, had he become the perfect instrument.

Alert in every faculty, sentient in every bone, my father watched his companions raise their hammers for their cadenza. Victim of the most terrible desolation, a sadness that was the greater for its unsurprisingness, he listened to himself being beaten back into powder.

Then there was Lilith. The night-hag. My father's first wife.

In his waking hours he was not aware that there had been anyone before my mother, but when he slept he called grievously for his first love, begging her to return to him, promising that he was sorry, that he had changed, that in respect to every one of her complaints he would be the husband in the future he had failed to be in the past.

She had left him in displeasure at the manner of their intercourse. He had lacked sensitivity and politeness. Was without feeling for the etiquette of conjugality. Although they had been created equally, at the same time, Satanael vomiting uncleanness into their mouths simultaneously, my father had insisted on precedence, demanding that she cook and otherwise attend to him, and assume the inferior position during congress. This last compliance, he argued, was owing to him because of the sharp verrucose scales that covered her body. If he wasn't to be pierced in a thousand places, or otherwise fouled and nauseated, it had to fall to him to choose the time and the method of approaching her.

They had also fallen out over theology. Their souls, he maintained, were composed of millions of particles of light, stolen from the original Realm of Light and imprisoned in their bodies by the Demons of Darkness. Eventually these particles would be gathered back to their natural source and they, Adam and Lilith – Lilith and Adam, if that was how she preferred it – would no longer feel strangers in creation.

Gibberish, was her opinion of this theory. Their souls were nothing other than toads and worms, put there by Satan, who was good, to remind them that life itself was the invention of God, who was bad. She would ask him to remember this when he satisfied his lust for debauchery upon her with his serpent's tail, and initiated a seminal process that was bound to end unhappily. Do not expect me, she warned him, to look kindly on any infants born to us in perpetuation of this evil.

It was not a marriage made in heaven. Even before she left him he was searching his desires for alternatives, and practising how to ask God for Eve. A smooth skin, was his first stipulation. A gentle disposition. Calm eyes. A strong maternal instinct.

But now, in his dreams, he was missing the abrasion of Lilith's badness. Her fiery stare. Her stables-stench. The nettle-sting of her embraces, which a man might simulate only by taking the head of a wart-hog or an enormous pineapple into his arms.

He cried out for her. Lilith! Lilith! But she was out on the night with the vultures and the screech owls, hunting for new-born babies – the abode of toads and worms – to strangle and devour.

He fared no better with his twin.

You could say, because there was no name, because the first and last of his nightmare was a hopeless search to find the name, that he fared worse.

Hence his grief. He was one half of a whole, he had once shared a completeness, complemented a reflection, but he could not remember with whom.

He had loved someone dearly but he could not quite – no, he could not at all – recall the face. He could recall only the last recollection of a recollection. And that was featureless.

He could not hear the voice either. Or make out the shape. Or guess the sex. Or be certain of the species.

He was beholden, he acknowledged debt, he rejoiced in obligation and fantasies of requital, but his gratitude hung disregarded in the black waters of his memory, like an unbaited hook.

He went wandering high and low, hoping for a trace, an intimation in some passing countenance. But no one passed. Not a single person.

He began to search the faces of animals. Horses, pigs, jackals, cattle, ostriches, bears. Except for the ostriches, who took his curiosity to be an impertinence and ran from him in rage, all the animals were good about it, showing him their profiles, right and left, and letting him peer long into their molten eyes until he was satisfied they were not who he was looking for. The bears were especially sympathetic, and laid saddened paws on his shoulders, as though they had gone twin hunting themselves in earlier days and understood its anguish.

But it was with cats that he came nearest. In them he saw a misincarceration as tragic as his own, a confused isolation, a companionlessness that stretched every second between eating and sleeping into a futile eternity. If ever a creature was an incomplete half of an idea, a cat was. He tried to engage them in conversation on this topic but they professed not to know what he was talking about. If ever a creature was sufficient to itself, they told him, a cat was. He told them, in his turn, that they were bound to say that. They reminded him that he was the one who had stopped to talk. He said it wasn't his intention to challenge, only to condole with them. They thanked him but wished him to be assured that they didn't need his condolences. He thanked them but explained that he badly needed

theirs. They said they were not in the business of commiseration. He offered it as his opinion, though they might take it or
leave it, that that was because their alienation from the other
half of themselves had led to a hardening of their hearts. They
said they would leave it. He said they had chosen badly. They
asked who he thought he was to know what was best for
them. He asked who they thought they were to know what
was best for themselves, when half of themselves was missing.
Thereafter it always ended with his getting scratched.

On these nights the cries that were torn from his chest were
not so terrible as when the monkey-men had him, or Lilith
was out on the wind. They were more like yelps or whinnies,
the sounds of merely routine animal excruciation. But that
didn't mean there wasn't torment in the dream and bitterness
in the aftermath; it simply meant that it was the missing twin
who suffered it.

I don't know whether I could have been of any help or comfort
to him, even if I'd had the courage to go near. Ours was not a
touching family. We didn't give embraces easily – my brother's
bath-time was hardly evidence of *ease* – and we didn't receive
them comfortably. We could be rough and ready with one
another, we could cuff and clip and buffet, provided that
every blow was glancing and there was no lingering in looks
or clinches. Had my hand rested on my father's skin for any
longer than it takes a lizard to lick up a fly, I believe it would
have burst into flames. To this day I carry no knowledge of
what his flesh felt like – which is in accordance, I suspect,
with how the Lord wanted it – and only guess that it was
clammy: oily and rubbery but cold, like octopus.

I can't imagine on what basis he'd be able to offer any more
detailed a description of mine.

Modesty – I mean modesty in the sense of bashfulness not
inexpectancy: pure bodily unwillingness and shame – had been

his trouble from the start. Often, when Abel had fallen asleep coiled like a kitten in my mother's lap, and hot nights and bitterness had salted and loosened her tongue, I learnt things about my father I would never have heard from his own lips. Such as, that at the very moment of his creation, when the clay was still wet and the outline of the pattern still indistinct, he had sought the means to cover himself; that his functions were a horror to him, impossible to perform in the sight of an earthworm let alone an All Seeing Creator; that, solitary and unpaired upon the planet, without the sensibilities of another of his kind to consider, he nevertheless put a smothering hand to his mouth every time he belched or hiccoughed, and suffered agonies rather than audibly, in the hearing of no one, No One, break wind; that he had been fashioned with more ingenuity than forethought, to propagate his species out of his single self (small wonder he invented a Lilith) – by fission rather than by fire, like an amoeba rather than a phoenix – but had demanded a wife for companionship and pleasure because he could not approach, could not contemplate, could not without abhorrence envisage, the alternative.

I take it that by the alternative, I asked, you mean celibacy?

She laughed. From low, low in her chest one of those ashen, acrid, mother's laughs that make a God-hater and father-killer out of every son. I mean, she said, his pigs.

His *pigs*? Wasn't that . . .? Isn't that . . .?

I wanted to be sure I had this right. We had all heard with our own ears – and frequently enough to be in no doubt that He expected to be obeyed – the Vowelless One pronounce against confusion: the familial confusion which is wrought when a man uncovers the nakedness of his father's wife, or lies with mankind as he lies with a woman; and the still greater confusion of the fields – confusion worse confounded – the defilement of man and, oh God, beast! '*Surely the man shall be put to death,*' He had warned. How could I forget that? I had discussed the self-same topic with my father on the eve of his taking up ventriloquism. And how could I forget what came next? '*And ye shall slay the beast!*' It seemed so tough on the poor beast, who might just have been ruminating in a field, jaws going, without a lubricious thought in its head.

Could it be, then, that against the very crime from which He so vehemently and particularly swore us, He had originally made no adequate provision? Had left it entirely to the fancy of my father whether he had the stomach for it or not?

My mother laughed again. Low, low. The Eve-laugh, derisive of everything. Almost everything. Her fingers tracing the circles of my brother's hair. It only became a sin, she said, never mind an unpardonable crime, on the day that I, the afterthought and antidote, was given existence. Until then, until *me*, there were few distinctions made between one kind of brute behaviour and another. The Lord God, blessed be He, did not concern Himself greatly where your father put his body. But He did concern Himself – as I recall He concerned Himself every minute of every hour – where I put mine.

On the grounds that you might breed monsters?

On the grounds that I might *approach* monsters.

Rising like a river mist, my mother's bitterness wreathed around us in the night air, creating an illusion of safe intimacy, encouraging a sort of camaraderie in extremity, the swooning desperation of drunkenness.

So the Law originates, I began, in the Lord's fear . . .

Precisely, she said . . . of a woman's incontinence.

And morality resides . . .

Precisely, she said . . . in the pizzle of a pig.

We should have taken it as a sign, an anti-covenant, that we were not at that instant smitten with madness, blindness and astonishment of heart. He was not listening – that was the one certain conclusion we could draw from the stars not immediately going out in the heavens. He was not at home, else our lives should have hung in doubt before us. He was off, absent, otherwise engaged. I don't know, now, why it took us so long to work out He was moonlighting, had found Himself another set of nostrils to blow into – but that was the obvious explanation. We had cousins out there and He wasn't telling us their names.

So I consider I did well, getting His voice to come walking in my garden in the cool of the day, given what other calls there were on His time. But I had to sweat for it. In an element I abhorred.

Of the success or failure I enjoyed, cultivating what nature had never intended to be seen, controlling what nature had always intended should be free, I cannot, in this company, summon the effrontery to speak. The gardens and gardeners of Babel are justly famous. It is no surprise to me, now that I have seen them for myself, that men travel vast distances for the privilege of admiring the smoothness of your lawns and inhaling the perfumes of your rockeries. There can be few sights better calculated to soothe the temper of inhabitants of a blistered land and make them aspire to a green and watery hereafter, than the husbandmen of Babel up early on the seventh day, cutting back their grass, falling upon enthusiastic growth – chickweed, thistle, twitch – and otherwise waging war on that garish propagation which is the combined wish of a hot sun and well-dug wells.

Back! Back!

That so confirmed an enmity to growth should be a prerequisite in all those who call themselves growers would be a puzzle to me were it not for my own experience of husbandry. I have this in common with you, gentlemen and gentlewomen cultivators of Babel: we are each of us convinced that we can improve at every turn on what is natural. Beyond that, I would not dare to press the similarity. Your aim is a quiet beauty, an expression of vegetal serenity that will serve as an example in the moral sphere. And the success of your faith may be judged by the number of your citizens who actually resemble gardens. I, on the other hand, lopped and pruned lustily, as I have already hinted, for purposes that were pre-eminently political. I did not require that the soil should, merely to soothe the jagged nerves of growers or to harmonize with secular hymn-singing, be more temperate in its yield; rather I wished to educate it in the science of self-dislike. Perverseness, if you prefer. I saw no reason why it shouldn't feel as odd about itself as I did. I mean as odd as I did about myself. But I suppose I also mean as odd as I did about it.

It was thus that I discovered something disgusting about nature. You cannot be too cruel to it. Short, that is, of wiping it out altogether, there is nothing you can do to it that it doesn't in some way find provocative, stimulating, a challenge to its ingenuity. An incision is as encouraging as a caress. An amputation a positive incitement. Set fire to it and you can see its gratitude putting forth tender shoots of green appreciation, naked as wounds, almost before the smoke has cleared.

I had observed the same phenomenon in stray animals that took up residence with us, hoping to be adopted, yearning for domestication, greedy, in a way that shamed me personally, for love. Abel made a better fist of giving it than I did. He had a rabbit that would let him stroke it. An ass that would rub noses with him. A rat that walked across his head from one shoulder to another. And Enosh, a miserable pariah-dog of low intelligence who wanted nothing out of life except to curl up in Abel's lap while Abel lay curled up in my mother's. How large my menagerie might have been I never found out because I quickly sent packing whatever had expectations of me which I knew I would be unable to fulfil. It is a frightful thing to be looked at by a helpless creature that wishes you to know your power over it, that wishes you to exercise that power, this side of Lilith-like strangulation, in return for a devotion only a sick man could value in his heart.

But what was true of the pain lust of a stook of corn, and

true of a retarded mongrel's hunger for humiliation, was no less true of us, made in the image of a God that hourly rehearsed feelings of rejection. My father soaked up punishment from my mother as though he were a dried-up river bed and my mother's coolness to him, rain. I sat myself on the ground and observed the nightly soaping of my brother's blue-white limbs for all the world as if I'd been frozen in that attitude, mesmerized, pinioned to a tree trunk from which I could not hope to move, when all along I was at liberty to take a quiet stroll in any direction I fancied. My mother visited cruelties on herself, pumping bile around her body; envious, though there was no other woman in our world for her to envy; reclusive, though there was no one for her to hide from; ill-prepared to face a day until she could taste the poison of her own nature in her mouth. And Abel – ah, Abel – never once thought about practising a retreat in preparation for the day when I would begin striking him in earnest.

He visited me occasionally in my garden, once he had grown too big for spinning shells. We didn't speak much. He had a capacity for enduring long spells of inactivity and silence in my company which I took to be a compliment to me and a proof of our affection. It was not like my father's taciturnity, which had something to do with finding me uncanny, but more an affirmation of mutual confidence: we didn't need to talk because we were sure of each other's esteem. Words are invariably aggressive, belligerent in intention no matter how defensively one pretends to deploy them. The fact that we scarcely used any must have meant that we were essentially at peace.

Mustn't it.

I hoard my memories of those long mute afternoons. There is never a time when I am not turning them over. They have a burnish on them. A yellow light. Reminiscent of those pulsing sunsets with which the Word once wooed the idea of woman in my mother, when the sky crinkled and curled and swallowed flame, like a leaf swept on to a gardener's fire in its last second before cremation.

He is aflame himself, my brother, in all of them. There is so much fire around him that I cannot make out the expression in his eyes. Only his mouth is distinct. Lacking colour. Not quite steady. The lips a little apart so that he can show his teeth. A flicker of amusement upon them . . . not the smirk of plebeian triumph, no, not that, but something the smallest bit like mockery, as if it's all just too droll, too droll even to talk about, I on my knees mixing blood and bone, stirring mulch, grafting poppies on to convolvulus so that we can have scarlet wound around every post and tree trunk, so that we can have an incarnadined backdrop to our conversationlessness, and he pacing up and down, as mute as his own shadow, wasting his beauty on thin air.

It is partly the idea of brotherhood, of brotherliness, of blood relation, that keeps us so reserved with each other. I believe we both recoil from something demeaning in the connection. It isn't personal. We wouldn't rather have *other* brothers. Or sisters, come to that. We have no quarrel with the particulars; it is the principle that makes us uneasy. The business of having to be blood-related to anybody at all. What, at the last, is there to say to a brother, when what lies at the bottom of your connection is a labyrinth of pipes and tubes, eggs, sperm, smegma, phlegm?

My father cried out in the night for brothers. The fragments of refracted light that were his soul lay iced up in his chest. He feared he had not been adequately animated. He had missed the experience of birth. But I sometimes envied him his pristine origins, his unrelatedness, his clean start.

I was luckier than Abel. I named things to make them mine. By naming them I took a hand in their origination and commanded them to begin again in my mind. In this way I was at least associated with a sort of purity and could new-create the objects of my observation, even if I couldn't new-create myself.

I also possessed the other invaluable advantage of being able to vent my spleen. I attacked the earth. I drove weapons into the soil. I hacked at limbs and branches. I changed the colour and disposition of the vegetation. I warped its character. I broke its spirit. I made it bleed.

My brother did not have it in him to cleanse his way. He never thought to seek redress. He absented himself, tried not to notice – that was enough. But you start noticing, willy-nilly, the moment you begin to speak. Words have ears. They have a past life, a keen retentive memory. So he kept quiet. He learnt to make music out of grass, and came to enjoy the company of sheep.

He went for long walks with them, not looking where he was going, as though he half meant to walk himself off the earth altogether. Later, the Lord would come to regard this as reverence. Quietude has this effect on gods. They mistake it for worship, whereas nine times out of ten it is actually horror.

It was my theory that our distaste for what bonded us physically ended up bonding us spiritually. We were as one, I thought, in our abhorrence of what made us one. I took this to include, not our parents exactly – for they too leapt from what was incontrovertibly fleshly and familial – but anything overtly referential: birthdays, anniversaries, festive proclamations of our periodicity and connectedness. So I was surprised when he came to my garden in his eleventh year or thereabouts – I am not saying that I was unaware of time, only that I didn't intend to mark it – and asked me to gather him a nosegay.

I wondered what his reason was. Had he fallen in love with one of his sheep?

He raised his eyes, let me see their wandering light, then lowered them. He presented his throat. Flashed me a smile. Made much of his teeth. Quite a show. Told me he loved all his sheep equally and wouldn't dream of upsetting the others by singling out one.

Banter. Brotherly banter.

I have always been convinced that I amused him. That I
could make him laugh, or at least smile, almost at will. I
prided myself on this while he was alive, and even afterwards
found consolation in the thought that I had at least lightened
life for him, cheered him out of his silences, invigorated him
and ... and thereby earned his love. Only recently has it
occurred to me that he might not have found me in the least
funny. Might not have congratulated himself on his good
fortune in having a brother who was so diverting. Might not
have loved me for my probes and sallies. Might not have
thought I was clever. Might not have wanted to be me as
often as I wanted to be him. Might not have been smiling in
all the instances when I took it for granted he was smiling.
But might have been snarling instead. Showing me his teeth in
the way a wild and frightened animal shows his teeth, not in
the way I fancied that a doting younger brother does.

Maybe that wasn't a joke, then, his rejoinder to my joke.
And maybe he was right and my joke wasn't a joke either.

But now is now and then was then. I told him I could put
together a bouquet big enough to please his entire flock.
Provided they liked the colour red.

He thanked me – it *looked* like a smile; I close my eyes and
I still *see* a smile – but no, no, my generosity would be wasted.
He knew his sheep, and all they would do with my flowers
was eat them.

Probably just as well, I said – keeping it up, keeping it up –
given the condition of the blooms I was meaning to off-load.

And now perhaps I *do* see rings of tiredness round his eyes.
And the colour vanishing from his face, as it used to do when
I pinched him hard, surreptitiously, and would not release
him, or fired a fusillade of punches on him, one blow succeed-
ing another, one punch becoming weightier than the last, first
on this shoulder, then on that, then on his chest, an endless
battery of flat punches, like someone hammering at a door

that wouldn't open ... And he would sway, and the light would go out in him, his beauty would die there and then before me, and were I not to hold him, to take his dead weight, to put my arms around him, he would fall ...

Was this not a strange reaction to a joke? *A joke?*

He was a fainter, my brother. Not a holy fainter of the kind that is preserved as a national treasure in your country, one who espies the godhead in artefacts and buckles before their radiance, a passer-out on aesthetic principle, a collapser in the service of the sublime. Abel's susceptibilities were less specifically targeted. It was life itself he was sensitive to. And any sudden strong experience of it could be sufficient to lay him out.

Your brother is exquisitely attuned, my mother once said to me. It is your job to watch over him.

Because I am *not* exquisitely attuned?

Because you have more resources.

You make that sound like a disparagement. Are resources things to be ashamed of?

Yes, if you do not properly employ them.

In the service of my brother?

In the protection of your brother.

I didn't say I felt so protective towards him that I sometimes feared for the balance of my mind. I didn't refer to the black nights I watched pale into sickly dawn, counting time by the ticking of his heart, my ear moth-fluttering above his chest. I didn't mention that it was enough merely to see him, some days, in an attitude of abstraction, or deep in concentration on a matter of small moment – his lips compressed, his brow taut – for a scouring terror to descend on me, a purgative melancholy such as I had never known (outside what I knew of it in relation to him), whose mission was not completed until it had hollowed me even unto my bones. I didn't say anything. Why argue? Against charges which are so savagely unfair you do not bother to defend yourself. It is only the

The Very Model of a Man

small injustices you go to war over. The grand misrepresentations you fight in your heart.

But what did my fainting baby brother want those flowers for?

A gift.

I must have looked up from what I was doing – cross-pollinating, as I remember; double-cross-pollinating – because I know that I registered his hands. Which ever so slightly were trembling. And which ever so slightly were dirty, from the fleece of sheep.

I weep today, for those fleece-stained hands.

A gift? Flowers? A gift of flowers, I asked, for whom?

For my mother.

(He called her *my* mother. I called her *my* mother. Never once did we think of using the word our. Or dropping the possessive altogether.)

Why did he want flowers for my mother?

I always give my mother flowers on this day.

This day? How was *this* day any different from all the others?

He let out a little laugh – no, he let out a little air. It's the day my mother . . .

He couldn't find the words for it. . . . met my father? . . . married my father? . . . did the deed of knowingness with my father . . .was chosen to be a help meet to my father? . . . was extracted from the glop and gristle of my father's innards? . . . was, to leave my father out of it, to all intents and purposes *born*? Single out one anniversary for my mother and you singled out them all. If this was *the* day, then it certainly put forward claims to noteworthiness. Unless you argued it put forward even stronger claims to be forgotten.

But I didn't turn my mind to this. Or to the accuracy of his time-keeping. My curiosity had narrowed to something smaller, hairier, stickier than the seeds of common groundsel I carried, for the purpose of yellowing out a family of purple loosestrife,

206

in my fist. How long, was all I wanted to be told, had he been indulging this sentimentality.

I had already been told. Always. That's to say, for as many years as he could remember.

Without me? Without asking me if I'd like to join him in the commemorative gesture? Two brothers, one bunch?

But you don't believe in such things, he reminded me. You have always scoffed at such ... festive proclamations of periodicity and connectedness.

I didn't believe in them? I thought we *all* didn't believe in them.

He shook his head. His nimbus of curls spiralling like golden worms. An expression of closure, of not wanting to air or raise any difference of opinion between us, dimming his features. I could see he was ready to be somewhere else now, away spinning shells, off with his sheep, unconscious on his back in a dead stupor of exquisite over-attunement. It saddened him too much, saddening me – was how I understood it.

So they'd kept up this ritual of giving and taking just between the two of them?

Yes.

And my mother would be expecting him to keep it up today?

Yes. But I can gather flowers for my mother by myself.

I wouldn't, of course, hear of it. What, let my brother chance the fairness of his skin on murderous thorn or nettle? Risk him fainting from the smell of primrose or the delicate configuration of freesia? No. I would not have been able to live with myself. I scattered my seeds and took him by the wrist – not meaning to pinch hard – and led him to the buttercups I had bred red, and the cornflowers I had empurpled, and the bearded speedwell I had crimsoned by a method of chromosome interference so drastic that I knew what it was to be a god.

Here, I said, gathering him armfuls of my favourite mutations. Here. Here.

I loaded him up until he looked like a sport of nature himself.

Will that do? I asked.

I couldn't see his face, but his voice rang clear through all the vermilion foliation. Absolutely, he said. Let's just hope my mother likes the colour.

You see: he *did* enjoy a joke.

Is there any distinction to be drawn between love and sorrow?

Everything about my brother broke my heart. The slightness of his stature. The passivity of his temperament. The pale incision that was his mouth. The flicker of grey agitation in his eyes. Above all, his back. Not specifically its slenderness and tensed expectancy – as though it knew the direction from which trouble would finally come; but just the sight of it receding. I hated seeing him go. No wonder turning one's back on a king is counted a rudeness. The action has a finality which is too suggestive for the fraught nerves of monarchs. Whenever Abel turned on his blue-veined heels and left me, I thought I was seeing him for the last time. He will vanish from my sight, I thought, and that will be the end of him.

As though it were my sight, and my sight only, that gave him existence.

Whether this small confidence I had in his viability was first and foremost a sorrow for him, or a sorrow for me, I cannot say. But if I feared it was only my sight that gave him physical life, it's possible I was also afraid that the idea of him was alive only in my sorrow. The moment he no longer broke my heart was the moment he would no longer be there.

I cannot determine, although I coined the word, whether this is solipsism or not; only that everything around me that was human saddened me. Abel closing my picket gate behind him, bearing a bouquet of unnaturalness bigger than he was, distressed me unendurably. Because of him the gate was sad.

The flowers were sad. Growth was sad. The idea of a small person carrying a large bundle was sad. Giving was sad. Getting was sad.

Mothers, of course, are always sad. The tears you are bound to shed for them come to you in their milk. But my mother's milk had curdled now, and any other child she bore would cry from the sourness. And this made me sorrier for her still.

I climbed into my old tree, sick in my stomach that after all these years I had not overcome the desire to inflict pain on myself by observing what I was not meant to see, by sitting in on the drama of my exclusion. The signs of my erstwhile frequenting were gone. The branches were no longer shaved of their bark, no longer smoothed and polished from my restive vigil. I couldn't see where I had been. But the tree knew me, creaked more in pity than in welcome, and parted its leaves so that I could watch.

Watch Abel make his presentation to my mother. Watch my mother receive it from him, the only person who remembered her.

Ah! she said. Not as in surprise, but as in grief.

She had taken to saying Ah! frequently now – her own expression of the dolefulness of things. Eventually she would pronounce an Ah! over my father and his unwieldy carpentry, which he would have to accept as the nearest he would ever again come to being loved.

Meanwhile I matched her with an Ah! in my own heart. Perhaps I outmatched her. Out-Ah'd her. For although this pageant of filial devotion was touching to behold, pitiable because transient, because inessential, because contingent, because it didn't have me in it, what was truly distressing was that neither of them could do better, each was all the other had to mark a ceremonial, to people a procession – she him, he her.

Whereas she, who had once been beloved of the Lord and as near as matters abducted by an angel, and he, my poor Abel, shaped to be a cup-bearer to a more sexually curious god than Ours ever was, should both have been garlanded by celestial courtiers, fanfared by bugles, swept up in the arms of those soft-bearded strangers we all languished for, whose raiments would be of gold and whose admiration for our mortal beauty and accomplishments would be unbounded.

Ah!

We weren't enough for our ambitions, that's why I was so sorry for us. Or maybe we weren't enough for mine.

Either way, we were too much or too many for God's.

He dropped into my garden at last, in plenipotential disguise, and as good as told me so.

12. YETZER AND YOTZER

I

'Until pain entered the universe,' he tells her, 'there could be no sensuality worth speaking of.'

'That's so sad,' she says, shaking her head.

This is how they spend their evenings now – he cogitating, she whimpering. The philosopher and his dog.

His words have sent a shock of electricity through her hair, and fine strands of it break from the careful containment of her pigtail and incline towards him like needles as he speaks.

Were he to reach out and pat her he would bleed.

'There are sadder things,' he says, wondering if she intends ever to go. She has adopted an attitude on his bed that has a worrying permanence about it, her knees drawn up sculpturally to her chin, her buttoned back occupying the junction of his two walls so naturally that she appears to have grown there, like crystal out of rock.

'Such as what?' (Tell her, tell her sadder and sadder things.)

'Such as inurement to pain. Which puts paid to all species of expectancy, the expectation of sensuous gratification being merely one.'

They have arrived at this topic because she has heard gossip – not from him, not from him – of his parents' earlier garden life, and she is curious to know whether it was indeed as paradisal as people say. What he wishes her to understand is that, companionableness aside, his father desired his wife only from the moment he became jealous of her, and that his mother stopped desiring her husband at more or less the same time. Thereafter, their desires went on enjoying this perfect inverse of synchronicity. 'Paradise,' he explains.

'That's so sad,' she says.

He doesn't know what to do about her.

She makes him anxious. She seems to think it is possible to dodge the wheels of careering fate. She thinks he is telling her a bad-luck story. As if, under different circumstances, his father and mother might have torn at each other's bodies in an ecstasy of unknowing, unprovoked, unperjured cohabitation. Such as they might – she and he. Even though she knows his flesh creeps, and owes the stimulation of her own flesh to that certain knowledge, she is still holding out for a happy ending. Smooth lawns. Birdsong. Grazing deer. Plump fruit. Fangless serpents. Stately oak trees. Gurgling fountains. Moonshine.

Moonshine. He cannot dim it. It is the same wherever he stays long enough to drum up an acquaintance. They request the story of the paradisal garden from him, only they want it told the way they want it believed. They have their own little clearings of paradisal verdancy front and back, and any assault upon the First Garden is implicitly a rudeness to theirs. They either show him their doors or their shrubberies. If it isn't rejection it's reform. Zilpah is of the reforming party. She has climbed the walls of her garden in pursuit of the rotting stink that rises from his; but now she would like to take him back with her, over the wall, through the gate, down the path, under the arbour, to where the air is sweet.

Moonshine.

It seems to be her intention to move in with him by stealth.

She leaves hairpins behind. Brushes. Brooches. Bags. Shawls. Eventually she will leave herself.

Whatever she mislays he finds and returns to her. Formally. He doesn't like there being bits of woman lying around his room. He is as particular about his floor as he is about his appearance. Traveller's scruples. Fugitive's fastidiousness. He defies the God who punished him with vagrancy to mistake him for a nomad. He has oiled fingers and well-swept rugs. He shines like a permanent man moving in his proper sphere.

He is surprised how little of this particularity Zilpah has perceived. Not only is she careless with her possessions, she thinks she can win him by slothful habits – intimacies, he assumes they are meant to be – in respect of her person.

She is by nature and upbringing particular herself. One look at her bacillophobic braid had told Cain that. Her clothes are expensive and fussily precise. Her undergarments are made of the best cottons and decorated with beautiful needlework. Where they have ribbons or straps, these are always well-pressed, daintily stitched, and as narrow as the shoulders and waist for which they have been designed. If there is one thing about Zilpah that Cain finds even more repugnant than her plait, it is the fineness of the straps of her undergarments. It is a puzzle to him why he feels this way. Strictly and logically, her haberdashery meets every one of his usual objections. The material is not coarse. The dimensions are not gross. Seams are not frayed, colours are not garish, and there has been no let up in the laundering. So how has Zilpah erred? Cain puts it to himself like this: there is indelicacy in excessive delicacy; there is grossness in too determined a denial, too pretty a denial, of what is gross. That helps him to explain half of his disgust, but gets him nowhere when Zilpah throws all prettiness and delicacy to the wind, scatters her fine embroidery across his floor, refuses the consideration owing to a lady's toilet, riots in forgetfulness and indolence, and otherwise shows that she has mistaken dereliction of hygiene for abandonment of inhibition.

'You use your mind for *that*,' he explains to her. 'You should treat your body with more respect. It connects you to the business of life. Please pick up your clothes.'

He cherishes a wild hope that she will be offended by this, gather her disregarded dainties, and go. But she wants him to see that she cannot be offended by anything he says, because in his company, in his time, in his . . . *presence* – she searches for the god-like word – she does not consider herself violable. She is without shame and without entitlements – when is he adequately going to grasp this? He can do as he chooses with her. How he uses her is entirely his affair. She does not even want to be consulted on the matter. Should he choose to dishonour her, he, Cain, the great dishonourer of the family, should he raise a hand to her as he raised a hand to his dear brother, why, she will esteem herself privileged, exalted . . .

It goes – he knows it goes – with the exquisite lace bodices and the eye-ruining needlepoint. It goes with the creaking cotton. The creaseless ribbons. The perfect symmetry of her lacing. The fanatic plait.

It goes with the bows.

But how does it go? And, more to the point, how does *she* go?

Every discourtesy rebounds on him. Every rudeness is a favour. He orders her out of his room. He remarks on her shapelessness, the protrusion of her bones, the flatness of her thighs and buttocks. He forces her to acknowledge the poor condition of her skin, its greasiness, its inelasticity, rolling collops of it between his thumb and forefinger, like a merchant appraising burlap. He spends whole evenings with his back to her, not uttering a word. He disappears without any explanation, returning in the early hours with common prostitutes – not shuris, but women compared to whom shuris are as unspotted as Eve on the twenty-seventh day – and forces Zilpah to lie beneath the bed among her hairpins while he simulates common sex with them. He threatens to have her removed by the authorities (some joke: she is the daughter of authorities) as a thief or a madwoman or a prostitute herself. One night he sets fire to her. On another he douses her with fouled water. 'Yes, yes, do that!' she cries, opening her mouth, extruding her bottom lip to catch the swill, showing him her glistening tongue. 'Yes, yes, don't stop!' she pleads, as flames lick the soft soles of feet she will no longer use or wash. 'Make me your sacrifice, make me the offering you wouldn't give your God!'

And then in the morning she wants to promenade with him through the scented gardens – his sweetheart.

He doesn't know what to do about her.

II

Sisobk the Soppy does.

Build a temple to her, that would be his advice.

Tear out your heart for her.

Transcribe her utterances on to parchment and wear them on your feet.

Sit her on a little stool and include her in that line of noble matronage that protrudes from both ends of every man's imagination.

Revere the *woman* in her.

Hold her to you as you sway together above the precipice.

Don't kick out.

Sisobk's own reverence for *woman* has been boosted by his brush with the barbers. Those . . . those . . . boys! Those . . . those . . . beauticians! He never thought he would see the day when he was grateful to have no beard in need of barbering, but that day has arrived.

He fingers his ants'-trail moustache with satisfaction. He
rubs a pleased plump hand over the smooth globule of Anatolian delight that is his chin. Those . . . those . . . Sodomitical
sods!

He is gratified to discern a consistency in his prejudices. He
has always skipped the Sodomites whenever their unruly city
has figured in the Cainite gospel. He doesn't know why. They
just never felt right. Not even their name – who wants to get
his tongue around Sodomites? They seemed there only to
swell the Cainite numbers. To pull in whole cities no less than
errant individuals. And although there were women in Sodom
deserving of Cainite commendation – women who one day
disported with strangers shamelessly, and the next refused
them so much as a crumb of hospitality, and the day after
that, to keep strangers always guessing about a Sodom welcome, pulled out whichever of their limbs declined to fit into a
doll-size bed – they none of them quite touched Sisobk's soft
centre. They didn't have the wife of On's devotion, or the
wife of Korah's audaciousness. There were women in Sodom,
in other words, but there was no *woman*.

The more he thinks about it, while tramping the wards of
terminal infirmaries, closing eyes from which all light but the
light of womanhood has fled, holding wasted hands which are
still and always will be women's hands, the more convinced
Sisobk becomes that Cainite heroes are nothing without Cainite heroines. Take Esau . . . Or rather, take Rebekah, Esau's
mother . . .

A look of faraway fondness passes across Sisobk's face. A
delicious nostalgia for what has not yet been. A happy remembrance of things to come. Ah, Esau! . . . pity about all the
red hair, but . . . ah, Esau! And ah, Rebekah! He is sitting on
the corner of a hospital truckle-bed, wheeled out to ease the
final hours of someone's forgotten mother. He can hear the
soul's wings whirring, clumsily, unaccustomedly, like a game
bird's. So much effort to depart. So much effort to have

stayed. So much effort to have conceived and carried and given birth. Without exerting any pressure he holds on to what is left of the woman's ankle, his fingers meeting in a circle no bigger than a baby's or a barber's mouth. And suddenly he is not where he is . . . he has slipped, slid, sidled out of the hospital and himself . . . and is somewhere else, somewhere the same but somewhere else . . . for behold! – he is in the womb of Rebekah . . . no . . . no . . . he *is* the womb of Rebekah.

Rebekah is famous for her womb. Was it sealed, the way a maiden's is supposed to be, when she left Padan-Aram to be the wife of Isaac? Or had she, as the rabbis like to speculate, been 'fingered' by her father, or her brother, or Abraham's messenger, Eliezer? There are those who affirm that when Isaac 'fingered' her and found her faulty, she explained she had hit a stumpy bush after falling off her camel in surprise at seeing him, Isaac, walking towards her on his hands. A man should not be so novel when he first greets a wife that others have found for him.

But Rebekah's womb was going to be famous however she came off that camel. 'Be thou the mother of thousands of millions,' it was said of her; 'and let thy seed possess the gate of those which hate them.'

Sisobk the Seminal is not conscious of quite such a press of numbers, but he is full, the bearer not of one embryo but of two, and already the nest of rivalry and dissension. Afloat in the same fluid, the twins agree on nothing. They fight for elbow room. They jostle for pole position. Whenever Rebekah, proud in her striding, goes past a temple erected to the worship of idols, the red twin, the strong twin, rejoices at the lewdness and the merriment he hears; but when she passes a synagogue, the slighter, lighter brother struggles to break free, impatient to join the mournful sanctifying. And so they kick together, one eager for the joy of life, the other for its lamentation.

Speaking with the best interests of her womb in mind,

wouldn't Rebekah do well to stay at home, passing neither synagogue nor temple? No. She welcomes the conflict in her belly, relishes the war being fought without words within her, because she knows it will end up a war for her love.

Weary of the buffeting – so much effort, the conceiving and the carrying and the giving birth – Sisobk becomes the buffeter. Esau, bristling with more hair at forty weeks than Sisobk himself has managed to grow in forty years. Sisobk doesn't like the prickles. His gums ache from prodigious teething. His expanding bones knock against his skin. His finger-nails pierce the soft pouches of his little clenched fists. Time to leave, time to head for the light. But, as he winds his shoulders for the great leap of life, he feels a hand tugging at his ankle. The hairless one, holding him back, determined that he will either come out first himself or keep them both in, drown his brother with him in the black sea of maternity. Feeling her boys twist inside her, Rebekah shivers with pleasure. Sisobk summons up Esau's strength, draws on a desire to be alive he never knew he had, and . . . jumps! . . . dragging them both into the world, himself first, bloody and triumphant, the other, the brother – conserving energy, intent on marring his twin's victory, and because he cannot find it in his tiny embryonic soul to concede precedence – still clinging to his heel.

Isn't it the whole point of twins that you cannot be one without being the other? Thinking he is Esau, Sisobk is startled to hear a faint cry from the truckle-bed, and to see that, Jacob-like, he still has hold of the dying woman's ankle, and that her foot is blue.

He looks into her worn-out eyes. 'I am the puller and the pulled,' he tells her, orphically. 'I am hairy and I am smooth. I am a cunning hunter and a plain man. I dwell in fields and I dwell in tents.'

He pats her hand, closes her eyes, and covers her up. At the far end of the ward another one is being wheeled in. There is so little of her that even from this distance Sisobk can count her ribs and see the lilac dye of death beneath her skin. He shuffles over and sits himself on the corner of her bed. 'If you gave birth to twins,' he asks her, 'one too feeble to come out of the womb under his own steam, and the other with such an excess of life in him he landed fully grown between your legs, red all over like a shaggy carpet, which would you prefer?'

She has less hair herself than the baby Jacob had. And lacks force to hold on to anybody's ankle. She makes a faint sound from the back of her throat, like a page turning.

Sisobk inclines an ear. 'Just what I think too,' he says. 'Neither of them.'

His theory is this.

If *Isaac loved Esau, because he did eat of his venison; but Rebekah loved Jacob* – then clearly she loved him only to spite Isaac, who had 'fingered' her near Hebron, made her the mother of thousands of millions, the first two of whom were such as no mother could bear to look upon, and now passed his days and nights blind in his tent sampling game.

On his own, Jacob had little to recommend him to a mother of spirit. While Esau flew through the fields, a red flash, spearing supper for his father, Jacob stayed quietly indoors and sod pottage. The ruse whereby Rebekah got the lesser of her two sons to steal the greater of her husband's blessings – disguising him in goatskins and teaching him to lower his voice – served a psychological and a practical purpose. She could see her favourite looking manly for an hour, and then, by warning him of Esau's wrath, remove him from her sight for a period considerably longer.

Sisobk the Scryer closes another set of eyes and leaves the infirmary. These women! He had wanted to persuade Cain to accompany him to that fissure in the desert, that divide which never cooled or closed, and through which, if you listened carefully and knew what to listen for, you could hear the cries of Korah and his company, browning for all time, like meat in a casserole. But now he would like Cain to go with him to the well at Padan-Aram where Rebekah is waiting to be spotted by Abraham's servant, carrying her pitcher – a damsel very fair to look upon, a virgin whom no man had ever known.

Just like Zilpah.

III

He doesn't know what to do about her.

He thinks about boring her with affection. 'Perhaps we can try face-to-face congress,' he suggests one night.

It takes her a little time to turn over. First of all she has to unwind him from her plait. 'What?' she says. 'You mean use me like a woman?'

Already it is going further than he intended. But he is at his wit's end. A desperate man. 'Not *use* at all,' he says, he whispers. 'Do you not think there is too much *using* in this room already? Is it not time I showed you some consideration?'

'Consideration?'

He wonders if her question is a weapon, and if it's loaded. But the expression on her face is neutral. She seems genuinely to be curious about what he means by consideration.

As if he knows! 'Things like calling you by your name,' he says. 'And . . . talking. And . . .'

'Kissing?'

'Yes, kissing.'

'Stroking?'

'Yes, yes, definitely stroking.'

'Looking?'

'Indeed – looking would be marvellous.'

'Well, if that's what you'd like . . .' she begins.

'It is not a question of what I'd like.'

'You want to hear me say that *I*'d like it?'

'Only if it's the truth.'

'Truth is to be part of this as well?'

'Only if you'd like it to be.'

She thinks about it. 'All right,' she says, 'I'd like it to be. I'd like it if you treated me as a woman tonight.'

But before he can mount her, face-to-face, she places two prohibiting hands on his chest. 'Well?' she asks.

He doesn't follow. 'Well what?'

'You were going to show consideration.'

He goes very cold. Icy fingers paddle in his heart. He wonders if he could get away, now, with turning her back on to her belly.

'You were going to call me by my name,' she reminds him.

'Ah, yes . . . Zilpah.'

'And you were going to stroke me.'

'Yes, I was.'

'And kiss me.'

'Yes, that's right, I was.'

'But considerately.'

'Ah, yes.'

'And remembering to use my name.'

'Ah, yes . . . Zilpah, Zilpah.' He murmurs it considerately, considerately stroking her, considerately kissing her, lowering himself considerately upon her. And again, 'Zilpah,' using her – no, no, *treating* her – for the first time as a woman.

Considerately.

It is, as he has counted on, an awful experience for them both.

'I do not work well in concert,' he tells her, looking up into the darkness, keeping satisfaction out of his voice as best he can. 'I fear I am disjunct.'

She touches his shoulder. 'It isn't important,' she assures him. Her face is washed in the dew of forgiveness. He can see it out of the corner of his eye, an oval of moist early-morning light. She squints at him, near-sighted as a saint. It has all along been her habit to follow his every changing expression with her stare, but now her night-time seeing seems to be plaited with his, bound with an invisible ribbon of devotion.

He rises from the bed and goes to stand by the window. At this hour the temple stones appear to be alive; not a ziggurat is still, not a flight of steps is where it was a second earlier. They move, in a stately grey-shadowed priestly dance, not backwards and forwards, and not up and down, but with a looming motion that tilts the night.

'I'm not suited to it,' he says. 'I'm not rhythmic.'

He can hear her sniffing – not crying, just gathering her forces for a tremendous feat of understanding that will require the armed support of patience, selflessness, forgiveness, and may even result – who knows? – in lasting cure. He fears her patience most. It ticks in his ear like a promise of eternal life, like the interminable scratching of insects that used to keep him awake under the stars when he lay revolving love and murder in his heart.

'You have to work at harmony,' she says.

Tsk . . . tsk . . . tsk . . .

'When I say I am disjunct,' he answers, 'I am describing an immanence, what is bred in the bone, not a learner's hesitancy for which practice is the remedy. I am unable to make a rhythm with anybody. I have no choice in the matter. My nature is dissonant. I have no co-operative instincts. I cannot dance, for the same reason. I cannot sing in tune or unison. You must have noticed that when we walk together I do not keep in step with you. The very idea of harmonious conjunction with another person, with another body, with another *thing*, is alien to me; it incommodes me, it embarrasses me, and, to be truthful with you, it appals me. To and by are words I was moulded to accept; blame my Creator, but I fear I fall foul of with.'

Tsk . . . tsk . . . tsk . . .

It is so audible, her patience, that he mistakes it for an interruption.

'No, you must let me finish. Small as they are, these prepositions determine the courses our lives take. I was not made to be included in another's orchestration. I am not a fit partner or companion. You must find someone else, someone more agreeable, to be your accompanist.'

He hears her slip from the bed, and in a second she is kneeling at his feet. 'What have they done to you?' she says softly, softly as a prayer, pulling at him so that he will join her, make a harmony, find a rhythm, both of them, together, at his feet.

He holds back, keeping what little he knows of balance by staring fixedly at the temples looming in the tilted night. But her pressure is irresistible. 'What have they done to you?' she repeats. 'How have they damaged you so badly, my poor brotherless boy?'

Damage? Has he been describing *damage*? And who is she to speak of *they*? But before he can repudiate her terminology, she is on all fours again, turning a blind eye to his disjuncture, like the beasts his father had declined, and is once more ready to compensate him for his loss.

This time he does not rein in the indecorous pigtail.

IV

Where would we be without coincidence and word-play? At the very moment that Sisobk the Scryer is departing the infirmary, reluctant to leave behind the smell of dying woman,

Cain the murderer of his brother is running from his apartment to escape the smell of living girl, and Asmar the potter is sitting at his wheel, settling in for a night of sniffing clay.

In a moment we will bring all three of them together, by the nose.

And the word-play? *Yetzer* and *yotzer*.

Yetzer is Hebrew for purpose or inclination, inclination one way or the other but usually the wrong way. If you follow your *yetzer* you are likely to end up doing evil. *Yotzer* is a potter. It is impossible to forecast what you will end up doing if you follow a *yotzer*, the outcome being dependent on the *yotzer*'s *yetzer*. But it should be clear already what opportunities for moral equivocation lie coiled like paradisal garden snakes in these two words' seeming sameness. Why fault the pot when you can blame the potter? 'We are the clay, and thou our *yotzer*,' Isaiah reminds the Lord, at the conclusion of sixty verses itemizing the ways in which we leak.

Not that there is anything leaky about what Asmar makes, unless we number among his productions his son, whom we shall also introduce coincidentally in a moment.

The sight of Asmar potting in the night is not an unusual one. It is the great ceramist's boast that he can knock out three hundred amphorae identical in shape and size and glaze in the interval other men squander, between dinner and bed; and in order to keep up with this record he must sometimes be bound upon a wheel of clay until morning. 'But that's cheating,' Naaman has been known to tease him. 'That is extending the interval unfairly.' 'Not so,' squeaks Asmar; 'some men do not go to bed until it is light. I know that from the number who come to my window before the dawn to watch me.'

Asmar loves to have an audience when he is *yotzing*, and finds it hard to understand how any Shinarite who has seen him at his wheel with his fingers wet and flying could ever derive satisfaction from watching anything else. He wears a smock which he has designed himself, a loose, billowing garment that leaves his arms, his legs, and most of his chest free. Asmar would not be surprised were anyone to tell him that his appearance – or whatever the word is that encompasses his dress, demeanour, skill and confidence around clay – has an inflammatory effect on the women of Babel. He has seen three wives into their graves so far, and can conceive of no obstacle to his seeing another dozen. Women are drawn to him, flimsy as he is in stature and squeaky as he is in voice. It is not up to him to decide why, but he assumes it is a combination of well-shaped limbs, engaging manner, free morality (as advertised by his single ear-ring) and familiarity with the first material – the earth itself.

'They smell something primal on me,' he explains. 'They would know, even if they were blind, what I've been doing with my hands.'

The chief recipient of such explanations is Asmar's eldest son, Esay. Asmar is having trouble convincing Esay of the plain and functional let alone the venereous properties of grey earth mixed with a little water. He has the ambition of passing on to his son a successful business and a name loaded with honours, but Esay, though he holds with the wearing of a single ring in his ear, pictures himself in a more verbal profession – perhaps story-telling – earning the admiration of women because of what comes out of his mouth, not what sticks to his fingers. The activity of *yotzing* itself, by which he means the way it is necessary to sit and the shapes he must make with his hands, is inimical to his idea of creative freedom. 'I hate having to bear in upon the clay,' he counter-explains to his father. 'The pot expresses its true nature by trying to escape from the wheel, by swelling upwards and outwards, by returning to its original plastic matter. But the potter must prevent this. He must be a sort of gaoler to the pot.'

If you would see a *yotzer* beside himself, Asmar is the man to watch. He flattens whatever is rising from his wheel. He overturns trays of frit and feldspar, sends flying jars of bat-wash, slurry, bowls of blood-red water for moistening his sponges. 'A gaoler to the pot! What sort of talk is this? Show me the bars! Show me the keys!' He attacks his boy with biscuit-bats and whirlers, he corners him with cutting-tools, he threatens to lock him in the kiln – he'll show him gaol! – and not let him out until he's stone.

'I just don't have the right temperament for it, father,' says Esay, backing off. ('I don't have the *yetzer* for it,' he might have said.) 'I'll only end up setting all my pots free.'

Tonight, as Cain approaches from one direction, and Sisobk shuffles from another, this is exactly what Esay is doing. He is liberating every pot he can lay his hands on – pitchers, ewers, gallipots, amphorae still wet from the wheel – by throwing them at his father. And Asmar, because he is holed up in the production and not the display section of his *yotzery*, and because he would not damage anyway a *yot* he has turned with love and exactitude himself – Asmar is retaliating with the only weapon he has by him, which is clay.

What Cain sees when he pauses at the brilliantly lit window – Asmar's stage – is two men, covered from head to foot in slub the colour of rats, each with a little hoop of gold protruding, and each groping in his primal blindness for something more to plaster on to his assailant.

What Sisobk sees is Cain.

His heart leaps, lurches, begins beating on the right side of his chest. 'Come with me to Padan-Aram!' he cries, but then holds back, for the father of nay-sayers, the lover of Zilpah, is in difficulty, is having trouble breathing, can barely stand, must squat right there, right now, in the public street and clasp his legs and drop his head below his knees.

Is this my moment, Sisobk wonders, is this the hour when it is given to me to hold his hand?

For his part, Cain is unaware of Sisobk's presence. Asmar's

window holds all his attention, fills him with a repugnance which won't let him look and won't let him leave. Any other man would find the slime-fight funny. He wishes he could find something droll in it himself. But he is disabled by the spectacle of fisticuffs, cannot see one man raising his hand against another, no matter how farcically, no matter how feebly, no matter how playfully, without tears squeezing into the corners of his eyes, without tight bands of pain encircling his head and chest like hoops around a barrel.

And there is a second reason why the pantomime in Asmar's studio compels him to stop and bend his back and allow his breath the time to find itself again. Babylonian bitumen. Jew's pitch. Aluminium silicate and water. Clay. Mud.

The sight of Asmar and Esay stripped of skin and bone, returned to their own prototype, two slithering maquettes of potter's paste, without vision or balance, rhyme or reason, reminds Cain of what he never saw but always sees – his father's 'birth', the terrible moment when he rose grey and dripping from a bog, and had to shield his face against the light.

What does his father look like now? What did his father look like *then*, when in a single minute he went from having two sons to having none? Cain cannot grieve for Adam without grieving for himself. It isn't personal. All fathers have this effect on all sons – they recall to you, if only by brute association, the sad, sickening, insulting inadequacy of beginnings.

Tsk . . . tsk . . . tsk . . .

The next he knows, a prophet with a round face is bending over him, stroking his hand. He is not too surprised or put out by this, although the heat from the prophet's face, and the odour from the prophet's parchment feet – an odour of drains and dead leaves – persuade him he should get up off the ground.

'Thank you,' Cain says. 'I think I will walk.'

Sisobk still does not release his hand. 'Master, I will follow thee,' he says, 'whithersoever thou goest.'

Cain shrugs. And allows the prophet to keep the part of him he wants. It seems a small enough favour. One sweet, well-oiled, well-manicured hand. A hand you wouldn't expect to find engaged in fisticuffs. Or clay-making. More of a *yetzer*'s than a *yotzer*'s hand. A not particularly serviceable hand. And anyway, he means to walk off the person patting it well before light reveals them to the populace of Babel as a pair.

He takes his accustomed route, as though he were alone, avoiding the parks and river banks where even at this hour there may be poetesses out, refusing the suburbs famous for their avenues of cedars and hillsides sorted prettily into small-holdings. As a general rule of travel he turns his back on those places where populousness peters out, fearing the encroaching quiet of the last dwellings, where stone surrenders finally to grass and the din of commerce expires in whistling thorn. But in Babel especially, where the streets are elevated and paved, where the hoofs of horses and the shoes of men ring like copper pans, and the cries of chiropodists and curators, administrators and acrobats, close on the ear as though they were voices in your own scullery, the prospect of desert or bramble is unthinkable. He loves the commotion. If there were riot without fisticuffs he would love that. Other men's carousal soothes his spirits. Let other men have it. Let other men do it. To stand (unaccompanied and unfollowed) on cobbled paving, to lean between ceramic cones in the shadow of a stuccoed wall, to listen in by a window to voices made mellifluous by wine, softened by drapery and cushions, free of earth, free of silica and alumina, free of a germinating God – what more can a vagrant who would be in love with his vagrancy ask for?

He does not shake off the prophet. Nor chill his ardour. Nor put a stop to his marvelling, his gratitude, his solicitations, his hand-patting. By morning, Cain has agreed that a man is

the author of his consequences and the owner of his future, that
he has an obligation to be curious about his children's children,
and his children's children's children, that he in particular, as
opposed to man in general, owes a more implacable commit-
ment to the Cainite cause, must not be satisfied with touching the
hem of disobedience, but must raise its skirt for everyone
in Babel to see, unless he would argue that he has come to town
only as a tourist. Moreover, he has promised to cherish the
woman in Zilpah, promised to visit Sisobk at the House of Hearsay and Hermeneutics, and promised to accompany him in the
very near future on a pilgrimage to a watering hole outside
Padan-Aram, where a damsel destined to be the mother of
warring millions will one day slake the thirst of Eliezer's camels
from a narrow-necked earthenware pitcher. More pots.

'Your solemn oath?'

Cain fiddles with the hem of honesty. 'Solemn!'

But he is so concerned now, in sight of his lodgings, to have
his hand returned, yet so unwilling to go back to his room and
find the woman in Zilpah waiting for him, rump-ready, that
when a ringleted, stiff-necked, ancient infant, with a face
hidden in its own shadows, thrusts a note up at him, saying

YOUR LIFE IS IN
DANGER
FOLLOW
ME

he makes no bones about following.

V

'Welcome,' says Preplen, 'to my home. Fratricidal greetings.
Or do I mean fraternal?'

'From whom?'

'What do you mean from whom? From me! Come inside and I will fix you greetings from the rest of the family.'

'From whom am I in danger?'

Preplen scans the skies. 'From whom *aren't* you in danger in this place?'

He gathers up the ancient infant as though it were milk left on his doorstep, and waits for Cain to cross the threshold. There is no urgency about his movements. Whatever is going to happen to Cain, it isn't going to happen to him here. By the calm conviction with which he shuts and bolts his door, he means his guest further to deduce that this is probably the *only* house in Babel where he can be sure of that.

'Meet the family.'

Cain already has, or at least has met their eyes, boring into his from the front row of the theatre, in search of whatever resemblance Preplen has talked to them about. Looking at them lolling uncomfortably on cushions, shipwrecked in their own home, it suddenly occurs to him that he may have been brought here for no other purpose but to compare feet.

'My wife Nanshe – goddess of springs and waterways. Nice, eh? Her real name's Naomi, but we thought that would be a bit of a give-away. And these are Tiras, Talmai, Talmon, Tekel and Telem – otherwise Jabal, Jubal, Tubal, Gether and Mash. You can't be too careful. Girls . . .'

Cain cannot conceal surprise.

'Thought they were boys? Good. Good. You're meant to. Girls, kiss your Uncle Cain.'

'I'm not your uncle,' Cain says. He thinks of adding, 'I am no one's uncle,' but does not know how to empty the statement of an anguish he doesn't choose to feel.

His coldness may be one reason they do not, as he feared, swarm over him like cockroaches; but the furniture is another. They cannot get up from it, they cannot rise without falling, certainly they cannot manage anything as simultaneous as a swarm. Cain takes the opportunity of their confusion to extend a hand to Nanshe. She too is sunk in sumptuousness, so well-sprung that in stretching to meet him she slithers sideways down the sofa and comes to rest in a chasm between two feathery squabs.

Because he does not want to see what is happening to Nanshe's wig in the course of this manoeuvre, Cain commands his gaze to travel round the room. Not since God the Great Draper recurtained the heavens to impress his lactating mother has he been witness to such excited festoonery. Burgundy chiffon billows from the ceiling. Organzine the colour of peach-blossom swathes every window, sighing like a young girl's chest whenever there is a breeze. Not a wall is bare. Not a chair lacks covers for its covers. Not a doorway is without hanging tassels of gauze, twined in a riot of hot transparency.

'It wasn't like this when we got it,' Preplen explains. 'You know how the Shinarites live.'

Cain does. 'Heathenish?'

Preplen pulls a face and rights his wife. 'Worse than heathen-ish. Primitive. Since you told me about partridges, I am better able to guess what went on here.'

Cain is sympathetic. 'You didn't find feathers?'

'Feathers . . . bones . . .' Preplen can barely bring himself to remember. '. . . sticks . . .'

'Sticks?'

'Don't ask me to be specific. I don't want to know what they did.'

And doesn't want his family to know either. He makes this plain by lowering his voice and turning his profile into even more shadow than it normally enjoys.

Cain thinks of the lustrous, high-shouldered Shinarites on the streets of Babel and is at a loss to imagine what employ-ment they might have found, other than in the garden, for *sticks.* Far more barbaric mysteries reside, to his eye, in the fringes and tassels that canopy the poet's tabernacular shrine to family. Nowhere in Babel – not in a face, not in a shuttered room, not in the night sky – has he seen anything so black as the coals that gleam under Nanshe's skew wig. Nothing in Babel – whose marshes have been cleared, whose rivers are fragrant – recalls more vividly to him the first slitherings of life in slime than Nanshe's brood, five baby crocodiles with their mouths open, losing their balance on the muddy banks.

'Why did you tell your daughters I am their uncle?' he asks, out of the blue.

'Daughters? You think they're girls? Good. Good.'

'Why?'

'It's just a manner of speaking. Family is as family does.'

'And how,' asks Cain, 'does this family do?'

He doesn't mean it to be rude. Just shapely. But syntactical shape is not always the best friend of easy conversation.

All his years of sleeping on three or four pillows too many tell on Preplen. His neck clicks twice, sinks a couple of notches into his shoulders, and locks. If Cain wants to see his lips move, he has to walk around him, lower his own head and look up. Two parrots. Preplen's message is clear, though, wherever one stands. 'We are children of the same God,' he says. 'We are planted in the house of the same Lord. My children are as saplings that grow straight. How straight do you grow, Cain?'

'It is a little late for me to be worrying about that,' Cain reminds him.

'I see. I see. Having committed one sin you are now free to commit all the others.'

'I don't know about *all*.'

'Having broken your parents' hearts once by taking from them a beloved son, you will break them a second time by taking to yourself a heathens' whore.'

Cain looks from the wreck of shadows which is Preplen to

the tropical plantation which is his family. Is this fit language, he wonders, for the ears of saplings? But they show no signs of having heard anything amiss. They still wallow in up-holstery. And through Nanshe, too, the word whore seems to have passed like a speeding missile, leaving no trace of its trajectory. She smiles, blacker than beetles.

Whatever the proprieties in this greenhouse, Cain knows better than to bother defending a woman's reputation. 'I see no reason why my private life should travel so far abroad,' he simply says. 'It has already gone far enough.'

'"Ye shall do my statutes," the Lord said. He didn't say, "Ye shall worship partridge semen in the company of harlots."'

'I don't know how to reply to that,' Cain admits.

'You reply by promising that thou shalt love the Lord thy God with all thine heart, and with all thy soul, and with all thy might. And by acknowledging that when the One True Intelligible God demanded such devotion, it was a historical injunction and not a botanical one. He didn't mean, I am a farmer's seed and will come up for you if you bow down to Me.'

'He meant . . .?'

'He meant what He meant.'

'You have to do better than that.'

'I don't have to do anything. Neither does He. *That's* what He means. He doesn't have to *do*. He doesn't have to give. He doesn't have to notice. He doesn't have to reward. Ours is a religion, Cain, a faith, not a system of bartering.'

'*Ours?* You have forgotten that I fell out a long time ago with your One True Intelligible God.'

'So you fell out! So you had a little disagreement! What's that? He likes a little disagreement. It proves you're listening. It proves you're taking an interest. Why do you think He likes blasphemers so much? As long as you keep talking, Cain, as long as you keep talking . . .'

'Will you forgive me if I stop just for today? I have not slept. And I followed your –'

233

'Tiras.'

'Tiras –'

'Real name, Jubal.'

'I followed Jubal –'

'Ssh . . . not here. Walls have ears.'

'– I came in answer to your note. Am I to assume that the danger you alluded to is more moral than actual?'

Preplen cranks his head up from his chest and, at the risk of splintering, turns his face to Cain. 'A whore is a deep ditch,' he gargles, brewing in his throat all the perils of lechery and apostasy.

'And a strange woman,' says Nanshe, speaking from the corner of her mouth, and for the first time from anywhere in Cain's company, 'is a narrow pit.'

But the unexpectedness of her intrusion proves too much for the plumped-up cushions, and the whole family slides softly from the sofa to the floor.

VI

Somewhere between Preplen's hatchery and his own lodgings – he is not paying any attention to where his feet are leading him – he stumbles into the girl. He does not see her approach but is aware of an unwelcome radiance, such as one experiences when waking from a doze under a hot sun, and then feels her touch on his arm. A light fingering, exerting no more pressure than a moth might, but adhesive, like the feet of spiders.

'Zilpah,' he says. 'Go back home. Go back to *your* home.'

He does not think she is a deep ditch or a narrow pit. If he had to choose a metaphor from excavation for her, he would say she is a shallow grave.

But he would rather not call her anything, not even to himself. He is too scrupulous to allow Preplen's words to have any bearing on his feelings. He is a grown man. He has, without promptings, committed grown man's crimes. Without promptings he will rid himself of Zilpah. But he is, of course, furious that an attempt has been made to turn him against someone he has already turned against of his own accord. Will Preplen see this as a victory for him, for Nanshe, for Tubal and Jubal and Tekel and Mash? Damn Preplen! And damn the girl!

Thus does every third-party slander work its poison. The intermediary, the bearer of the ear, cannot forgive slander's object for being slander's cause.

She falls back from him without ceding a handsbreadth of ground: a wonderful, ecstatic twist of the torso, a sort of unhinging of the trunk that leaves her throat horizontal and her eyes retrograded beneath their lids. The blind whites of a person's eyes invariably call out murderous impulses in Cain. He sees the raised arm of God in them, the reflection of Creation the moment before It etches another signature on the blank screen of personality. To put out those blind screens would be to extinguish the idea of submission itself.

But he does not strike her. He has been too generous to her, too giving of himself, already. He does not care for her enough to shame her utterly in a public place. Nor does he care enough for Preplen to want word of such a scene to reach him.

In an honourable life there are so many people not to please.

He will not raise a hand to her. Instead, he patiently unsticks himself from her feelers. Plucks her from him, palp by palp.

'Go home,' he says to her again. And scores it as a mark alongside his integrity, his independence, that he does not add, 'You heathens' whore!'

Were he to look back, once he has left her, he would see

that she has gone down on the symmetrical, lozenge-shaped flagstones exactly as his brother Abel went down in his dusty field. She had insisted on knowing how Abel fell, and he had told her. And now she has his attitude to a T. Abel, for all the world – were he to turn and look – Abel ruined at his altar. Very still. Very flat. Only the legs a trifle crooked, the ankles almost crossed, as though a mere trip has been the occasion for the fall. The eyes open. Quite white. The skin dispirited, inelastic, irresolute, but broken only in one place, where it had been peppered with small stones. How she has learned to simulate the symptoms of lapidation without so much as a pebble being thrown at her, he would be unable to say, even were he to look.

But *were* he to look, he would comment on how much less beauty she possesses in ecstasy than his brother took with him into death.

VII

Somewhere between Cain's lodgings and Preplen's hatchery, hunger seizes Sisobk. He is careless about such things as eating at the best of times, but it has been a long night and threatens to be a still longer morning. His stomach growls, prophesying want.

He has followed Cain, following the child, because there are further arrangements to be made – dates, maps, manner of transportation and so on – relating to the pilgrimage to Padan-Aram. Sisobk knows that if you don't get all this settled early, plans tend to evaporate. He sits, rumbling, on a bench from which he will see Cain when he emerges. And falls into a food trance.

'Woof!'

He starts. The barking seems to be proceeding from the fricassee which his beloved son, the wild and woolly Esau, has that very moment prepared and set before him. Aiiee, this boy's venison! Not only does he hunt it, find it, shoot it, he cooks it in a sauce that is so succulent the old man is almost able to forget what a nobody and a disappointment the other son is, standing stirring lentils in the kitchen.

'Woof!'

Becoming blind now, from old age and good living, Isaac brings his fork up to his face and peers at what is yelping on its prongs. A terrible fear grips him. What if this is wolf, or hound, or hyena, and the Lord is warning him against transgression?

Here is a dilemma of no small portion for poor Isaac, who had nearly once been meat himself, who rejoices in his obedience to pre-Levitical dietary laws, but rejoices no less in his appetite. Does he question the contents of his bowl further and risk forgoing one of the finest fricassees of his life, or does he put the barking down to extraneous desert noises, order the meat to 'Sit!' and carry on consuming it?

'Woof! Woof!' says his supper.

It is Rebekah, repairing from her dressing room, who decides the issue. 'You evil little swine!' she shouts at Esau, sitting sheepish in the corner of the tent. 'Is your father one of your Canaanite women, that you'd feed him dog?'

'Funny,' says Esau, rubbing a hairy orange hand over his hairy orange face, 'I *thought* that was a small and unaccountably bad tempered hind while I was chasing it.'

'Does that mean I'm on pottage tonight?' Isaac piteously wonders.

Hearing the word pottage, Sisobk's stomach lurches. 'Funny,' thinks Sisobk, coming round, that a cook as inventive as Esau should arrive home tired from the fields one morning and swap his birthright for a platter of his brother's gruel. Sisobk gets home tired himself some mornings, and he wouldn't know a fricassee from a flambé – but there's always an egg!

Sisobk listens to more commotion in his stomach, then discovers it isn't his stomach but his prophetic soul. Something is wrong. He has missed Cain. Let him go by while thinking about food. He tightens the strings around his parchment footwear, winds his robes around himself as though for flying, and pads off in the direction of Cain's lodgings. Shortly before arriving at which he finds Zilpah lying motionless, legs a trifle crooked, eyes open, skin irresolute, a bundle of narrow bones not so much discarded as disposed.

Walking away from her, back pitilessly turned, is Cain. Sisobk calls after him, cries, shouts, appeals, but gets no reply.

He kneels, sure that all the kneeling he has done in life has been but a dream of this. He takes her hand. Puts a thumb on the blue tracery of her narrow wrist. He has never said it before, but he will say it now. 'I love you,' he says. 'I love you more than all the world – the world that was, the world that is, and the world to come.'

His eyes crumple and ooze, like raisins that have been trodden on. A tear trickles down his cheek. Others follow, brown and gummy. They stain his face, gather like dewdrops in his smear of a moustache, and at last fall on to the forehead of the stricken woman.

That about does it for Zilpah. 'Do you know who I am?' she says, uncrooking her legs, gathering her things, and rising. 'Do you know who you've been addressing? You clown!'

Sisobk falls where she'd fallen, like a man stoned.

13. Cain Refuses Dominion over the Kingdom of Sin

I have said that I missed admiration. That I mourned the passing of praise. That I longed to be marvelled at again. I now repudiate these charges against myself. What I needed was a fight.

There weren't enough of us. You cannot locate an enemy, raise an army *and* appoint an adjudicator when there are only five of you – four, once God went moonlighting and left us unattended. And there was no dispensing with an adjudicator. When I say I needed to fight, I mean I needed to win; and when I say I needed to win, I mean I needed to be seen to win.

So perhaps it comes back to being marvelled at, after all.

My father was violent but had no fight in him. He still from time to time recalled the old thunderous scaremongering filched from on high – *I have spoken.* But it ended, as always, with his sitting sulking underneath a tree. If he no longer closed his hands to illustrate a frightful finality, that was because they had become too bruised in the service of carpentry to close. He was an impatient man. If the tool was not near, by means of which he wished to drive home a dowel or a rivet, he used his fist.

You would have thought, in that case, that I might have been able to coax a contest out of him. But the fist was precisely the problem. He either employed it or he didn't. He either promptly won or promptly lost. He had no instinct for sparring. For strategy. For attrition. For guerrilla tactics. For satisfying, in short, the frictional necessitudes of a growing boy for whom no provisions as to marriage or fornication had been made. He had no aptitude for friendship either, which would have served as well.

Not bad, he said when I showed him the mischief I was hatching in my garden. Very nice.

Not bad? I had been experimenting with parasitic fungi and cankers. I was enjoying spectacular success with carnation rust, getting those insipid pastels to yellow and then brown. Let the gentlest wind blow and the air in my garden was thick with copper-coloured spores. Leaf by leaf, I was rotting nature. Very nice?

All right, he said, when I drew his attention to the precise character of my ambitions – all right, he said, then not very nice.

He couldn't have been easier about it.

He was too much of a boy himself to be a father. I don't mean that he looked young. The bitter battle with my mother had dulled the shine that once sat on his skin. You no longer looked at him and wondered how he could ever have been modelled out of base materials. Now you could see their traces – the peat, the particles, the salts, the mineral striations, the clouded water. He might live for another thousand years but he had rounded that corner from youth to age; he wasn't a gleaming apparition any more, he did not seem to have been dropped here from another planet, he resembled the earth he trod on. But he was a boy in this way: he was still hoping for something for himself; he needed to be marvelled at as much as I did. He could not do for me what had not been done for him. And he could not be a father because he had not finished – let us be fair about this: he had never even begun – being a son.

I could see, as he walked among my strangulated blooms, that he had no eyes for what was around him. They were not his. *He* had not made them. *He* could not be praised for them. I did not then, and I do not now, call this selfishness or egoism. It was more a sort of hysterical blindness, occasioned by loneliness and sensations of shame. What did not proceed from his hands or his desires simply was not visible to him. The necessity he felt to be the cause of pleasure used up all his senses. He strained his hearing, he wore out his sight, he put a permanent twist in his neck, expecting appreciation. And like the rest of us, he was disappointed. For him, too, there were not enough of us. We were too few. And because we all wanted, we were none of us – except my mother at Abel's bath time – free to give.

A more revelatory, less obfuscated God might have made his life easier. A man needs a Father he can see. Whether they enjoy cordial relations is not the point. The important thing is palpability. There are other views on this matter. Some argue that incorporeality is of the essence. I speak only of what I saw in my father's case. His bad, unassisted dreams. The melancholy that never left him, not even when he was busy building penfolds, or tearing down forests to erect bridges over rivers we could paddle across. The heartbreaking prayers he had once or twice tried to lead us in but now practised in solitude, great sobbing psalms lamenting One Who Wasn't There, Who Never Answered, Who Never Would Be There, Who Never Would Answer – the certainty of failure at last becoming an end in itself, a vindication, so that the music swelled into a triumphancy of despair. Rejoice, we are ruined!

A tin god would have served him better. A tumble of roughly carved rocks, with sticks for arms, that he could at least have kissed.

Do you have no feelings about it, I asked him, one way or the other? Meaning, my garden. Meaning, whether what I was doing in it was nice or not nice. Meaning, whether *I* was nice or not nice.

Should I have?

Yes, I said. I think you should. I think it would be good for me to know your opinion.

My opinion? (He laughed.) I can't see you taking any notice of that. (I was wayward – we were all wayward – that was his explanation, his excuse, for leaving us to our own devices. No prizes for guessing from Whose example he learnt this disingenuous stratagem.)

I might take notice of it, I said. And I might not. What matters is that there should be something I can make that choice about. It's possible I have to know what you think precisely so that I can oppose it.

He looked around. It was infinitely touching to see him really trying to use his eyes. To discover what I was up to. To discover who I was. I could feel how hard it was for him. How much it hurt his brain. I could see the pain, starting from his temples, like a bone that had suddenly become dislodged. If I'd been a better son, I wouldn't have put him through this. Good sons don't ask anything of their fathers. Not even the time of day.

He was standing beside a reddened fig tree, which I'd observed and then perversely encouraged in an act of parasitism quite breathtaking in its beauty. It climbed the trunk of whichever helpless unsuspecting host tree took its fancy, attained the summit, and from there sent down its own roots, a curtain of shimmering foliage which was at once a deed of suffocation and the veil behind which the deed was concealed. A murder and its alibi. A theft – for murder is only theft – in the guise of a gift.

I explained its principles to Adam. I got him to feel the tenacity of the fig's grip. I made him put his ear to its branches, to hear the hectic unrhythmic breath of voracity. I walked him through the ensanguined curtain so that he should enjoy its leafiness and behold the victim, blanched and hapless, without expectancy, without vitality, without worth, within. Thus does the stronger, I said, eclipse the weaker, in will, in splendour, in elation, in vigour, and in promise.

I did not believe everything I said. If you care to hear the truth from me, I did not believe any of it. But it was my intention, my hope, to inspire my father to disgust. I looked forward to his reprimand. I welcomed with an anticipation that was almost sensual, that was certainly of the body, the idea that he would so far take cognizance of me as to find my words shameful.

He screwed up his eyes. He rubbed the back of his neck. He ran his hands across the fibrous curtain as though every whip contained a note and he might make music out of them. He looked me up and down with great indecision. He put his ear back to the parasite. Then he stuck out his tongue, and said, Bleh!

Bleh?

He was smiling at me, I think smiling at me, and panting like a dog. Bleh! Bleh!

He wanted us to play together. To roll around in the warm dirt like a couple of bears.

I didn't move. I didn't extend a paw. So there's no point in looking to you for an example then? I said. The only word you have for me is Bleh!

He withdrew his tongue and allowed all the muscles in his face to slacken. It was a punitive collapse. Look how old you have made me, his face said. But there were no actual words exchanged. We stood looking at each other in reproachful silence. The only sounds to be heard in my garden were vegetable-vindictive: the groans of throttled plants, the viscous dripping of my euphorbias, the ticking of voodoo lilies, and the slow predacious rattle of my favourite epiphytic tillandsia opening its fans. Otherwise nothing. The primordial dejection of fathers makes no sound. Nor the primordial hard-heartedness of sons.

Why do you want an example? he asked at last.

So that I can resent it, I said.

He turned to go. Awkwardly. I mean physically awkwardly. He had been so badly made that he could barely swivel without falling.

Resent someone else, he said. His parting word.

He made it sound mysterious, a riddle infinitely tormenting. But in truth I did not have that many choices.

Is it possible that He – HE – had been listening to this conversation? Or was it nothing but mere chance that directed an angel of the Lord into my garden a mere fifteen minutes after my father – father with a little *f* – had left it?

It's a tricky business, balancing fortuitousness with design, especially when He whose design is in question is also the One who sets up the mechanism whereby chance operates. Ascribing motives is trickier still. An Unseen Hand is on the wheel; It might or might not have turned it; It might or might not have meant to; in these circumstances it takes an eternity just to decide what we mean by Whim.

Nevertheless, an angel landed. Which means that he'd been sent. Which means there was intention somewhere down the line. And behind intention, reasoning. And behind reasoning, promptings viewless as air.

I have had time – not eternity, but time enough – to consider what they might have been.

HE was sentimentally attached, like all truants, to the impression He imagined He had left on the hearts of those He had deserted. It was time to gaze with fondness upon this idealized image of Himself again.

HE had been rebuffed elsewhere and wanted confirmation of affection. (This would explain the lengths the angel was to go, explaining the protocol of oblation.)

HE had observed that my parents were no longer keeping company at night and that there was therefore no imminent prospect of further offspring – no sisters, that is, for Abel or for me to mate with (supposing such coupling to be allowable, exceptionally, for the purposes of pro-creation). If we weren't to die out as promptly as we'd sprung up, some intervention, some initiative for change, was necessary.

HE disliked the aromas rising from my garden.

HE was bored with Divine Vacancy. An appetite for drama is incident to whoever comprehends time, and we were His theatre.

HE had begun to notice Abel's beauty.

I do not offer this as an exhaustive list. They are the motives I most favour, that is all. I am aware, therefore, that they might say more about the complexion of my mind than they do about the Tetragrammaton's. Especially in the case of the last motive – no, I must return to my original word: the last *prompting* – I have attributed to Him.

It is certainly a delicate matter. And full of contradictions. Have I not already stated that this God was no gatherer-in of grapes or grape-boys? Yet something has to explain why, as soon as Abel reached his thirteenth birthday, the Lord,

Suddenly made the removal of the prepuce – a superfluity of skin for which He alone had originally been responsible – an issue of the first importance in relations between man and God . . .

Suddenly expressed a desire to taste the best of my brother's flock . . .

Suddenly demanded a comparable tribute from me, at which He promptly turned up His nose . . .

Suddenly put the idea of holiness into my brother's head, and the words with which to express it into my brother's mouth . . .

Suddenly sent down an angel, one of whose functions, whatever else he had dropped to earth for, was to make my brother more than ever aware that he was fair, and found grace in the eyes of whosoever beheld him . . .

Suddenly decided it was time to make it known to me, by that same angel, that I wasn't, and that I didn't . . .

Suddenly had all of us, in short, imbuing my brother's penis with piety, and Abel himself, stripped down to his shirt, dancing between his sheep, lighting fires, and perspiring prettily.

The angel's name was Saraqael, but we had to force that information out of him. Unlike Semyaza, he was unforthcoming about himself; though unlike Azael, he was not surly in his reserve. We had to *guess* him – that's what it came to. He was an angel of the personal enigma, and we had to work him out.

This did not apply to the new regimen of rituals and duties he had been sent to institute. In every instance this was punctilious and undeviating: a specific code of regulations governing cuts of meat, precise frying times, just this amount of seasoning and no more. Aside from metaphysical questions – the wheretos and the wherefores of all this ceremonial circumcision and cookery – his instructions were unambiguous. Here's the blade, there's the spirit; there's the ox, here's the skillet. Which might be why he made such a puzzle of himself. Men who practise the routine, pedantic professions – keepers of rolls and registers, collectors of duties, temple functionaries and monitors – frequently like to drape gaudy veils and gauzes around *their* wheretos and wherefores. And officiant angels are presumably no different.

But guessing him was only the half of it. Once we'd guessed him – that's to say, guessed close – we had to please him. And this was a tougher proposition still. For he was an austerely melancholy angel, with a blazing black stubble on his chin, and blazing black eyes that held the memory of tears but the promise of reproof, and a strange coronal of blazing black hair, cut severely, as though to suggest abstemiousness, but worn somehow with dash, with a consciousness of styling and design, as though also to appease whatever vanities (and there, perhaps, abstemiousness *is* a vanity) obtained in the celestial courts. As for his wings, these he carried high and inflexibly, gathered into his sides like a cloak. And they too were the colour of a raven. To bring relief to that solemn countenance, to coax the light of laughter or approval out of those funebral eyes, at the very least to send a flutter through his rigid feathers, became, for each of us, our first and sometimes our only concern. We lined up to lighten him. We competed for the privilege. And when we failed – and we failed more often than we succeeded – we took our failure to heart and thought the worse of ourselves as a consequence.

In this way do the heavy in spirits wreak their terrible revenge on the light.

It is a law as immutable as gravity. And it was devised by the same Heavy Hand. Whatever is dark draws brightness into it. Wherever the lugubrious gather, there you will find the frivolous dancing their hearts out for a sign of favour. I am a jealous God, said the Lord, and what I am above all jealous of is your gaiety. You will therefore expend the lightness of your hearts in My heavy service.

So it was; so Saraqael dropped like a stone to remind us it should be; so it still is.

Light? Us?

These things are relative. Had you seen my father skipping to the high places with buckets of dung and slush slung over his shoulders, the wherewithal to build altars to the exact specifications laid down by Saraqael, you would have said, There goes an alacrious man.

Had you seen my mother sifting flour and beating oil – a tenth deal of one for every quarter hin of the other – you might have thought, Now that is a willing woman.

And had you seen my little brother sorting through his flock, separating those without spot from those with spot, divorcing those with blemish from those without blemish, inclining his golden head to be certain he understood the angel's words. – 'Then shalt thou kill the ram, and take of his blood, and put it upon the tip of thy right ear, and upon the thumb of thy right hand, and upon the great toe of thy right foot'; had you beheld the concentration in his wandering eyes as he took the fat that covereth the inwards, and the caul that is above the liver, and the two kidneys, and the fat that is upon them; had you watched the slow, sensuous movement of his fingers, the caressing of the carcass, the obedient washing and cutting and sprinkling round about, that family look of low triumph disfiguring his lips, parting them so that the white of his teeth might do something to touch the heart or tickle open the pinions of Saraqael; had you taken in the sudden starts of astonishment he managed, the seizures of amazed fleshly disquiet, whenever he caught the gaze of the blazing black angel fixed upon him, the blazing blond boy; had you beheld his shivering suspense, his tantalizing trepidation, his compliant palpitating passivity, promising everything, everything, even unto hell – then, then might you have taken a stone to him yourself, long before I did.

And this is to say nothing on the subject of the commotion he raised when it came time for circumcision. Perhaps I *should* say nothing. I am mindful that I am addressing an audience – at least that part of which is male – renowned for the erectness of its carriage and for wearing its foreskins with a pride bordering on fervour. I have not forgotten I am in Babel. I have my own feelings to consider. I will not willingly expose myself to ridicule. Suffice it to say that when the moment came and I found myself unable to budge the angel from his appointed course, I took the sharpened flint from him, bundled the medicaments in a pouch, refused the good wishes of my parents who not only approved this barbarism but actually seemed to be exhilarated by it, and set out for the consoling privacy of my garden where, attending promptly to my own amputation, I was able to bleed in peace, and I like to think with dignity, among my flaming amaryllids.

My brother, on the other hand, was unwilling to settle for anything less than a universal assistance – I use the word in its double sense of both attendance and instrumentality. We all had to be there and we all had to help. I except, as I then excepted, myself. What need of me when there was an angel of the Lord to give instructions, and the first of all fathers to wield the blade, and the first of all mothers to whisper comfort?

He howled for all that. Then he fainted. Then he howled again. Then my mother fainted. Then my father howled. Then even the blazing angel changed colour.

Stimulated by the spectacle, the Lord Himself spake – the first words He had spoken unto us since my father had stepped between Him and my mother. 'This day,' He said, 'have I rolled away from you the reproach of –'

But amidst all the fainting and the howling it was impossible to hear Him. And to this hour I do not know what reproach was rolled from me along with my prepuce.

A third thing went as a consequence of Saraqael's visit. The regard in which I held my family.

I do not say love. Love, I suspect, cannot go. It might suffer adulteration with baser passions, might shrink or warp or seek concealment, but, like a birthmark, like a stone that crystallizes in the bladder that hoards bile, like bile itself, it never leaves your body.

Regard, though, survives only by the grace of judgement. It

is contingent and temporary. A mark awarded for performance. And in its dealings with Saraqael, the angel of the personal enigma, my family performed poorly.

For a start, we – I mean they, but accept collective responsibility – *we* set too great a store by his name. We couldn't stop using it. *Saraqael* – it wound around our tongues and wouldn't let us speak without it.

Saraqael, my mother said, has just informed me – haven't you, Saraqael? – that he will not be with us many more days. I've told Saraqael I don't know how we'll manage without him.

Him? I said. Who's *him*?

Saraqael.

It hadn't been so with Semyaza. Then my mother was the one sought, not the one seeking. She was younger. Mud clung to her breasts. She had not drunk of the waters of bitterness. Was not using an angel's name to settle scores with a mortal. And Semyaza himself had not been a guessing game. Throwing himself away – that had been his idea of fulfilment. Falling out of the sky. Coming apart in your hands. I don't know how these things are judged in heaven – erroneously, though, you can be sure – but in my opinion this makes, this made, Semyaza the better angel. Self-hoarders like Saraqael set a miserable example. Only the prodigal are Godly. But does God know that?

Does God, in *that* sense – in the sense of being able to gauge how a spirituous value will look when it has flesh on it – know anything? It is a time-consuming business, keeping an eye on two worlds. And requires an intellectual flexibility, a capacity for agile mental dualism, which a God who by His own admission is unusually and irreversibly jealous, that is to say self-fixated, cannot fairly be expected to possess. Jealousy floods the system. It does not merely poison the mind, it confuses it with that which is not mind. It passes off electrical impulses as cogitation, the opening and closing of arterial valves as introspection, the sluicing of the heart as philosophy. Whoever heard of a jealous man who was capable of judgement? Or a jealous god?

Or a jealous brother?

I was envious, as I have not tried to conceal, and envy is not jealousy. Its greater coldness makes it more the friend of reason. I have heard it said, though I stop a little short of this myself, that envy is so far reasonable that it is a species of irrationalism *not* to suffer it. That envy is nothing other than a calibration, measured on the meter which is oneself, of the inequity of the world. And is therefore scientific.

Which is a claim I am at least prepared to make for the disgust I felt – no, the disgust I mensurated – in the company of the angel. He coaxed his name out of my mother, and then regarded her, in a slow unblinking stare, with the most absolute contempt. With my father, who was no less anxious to please, who in truth believed he had been pinched out of earth for no reason other than to please, he was more imperious still, not even bothering to pretend to smile when my father attempted innocuous sallies of humour, or tried to engage him in the man-to-man banter his heart yearned for, or threw up the occasional altar to his own designs, a sportive folly the height of a hundred angels.

'Pull that down,' Saraqael ordered. 'Dost thou think nothing is to be restrained from thee? An altar of earth shalt thou make unto the Lord, not a tower whose top may reach unto heaven.'

Very well, Saraqael.

All I knew of death was in his voice. It was without music, without colour, without desire. And yet it seemed to have an under-voice which seductively whispered: 'Come, come, I have music, colour, desire within me, if you can only find it.' And off they went every time, my poor gullible father and mother, haring after the angel's miserable mystery, only to run slap into his invariable rebuff.

'You only have I known of all the families of the earth,' he once said, eking out the messages he had been commissioned to deliver from God, ensuring we were always wondering what else he was holding back; 'therefore will I punish you for all your iniquities.'

And they shone upon him, my beggared parents, not curious as to who these other families were, then, that did not enjoy the favour they did, and not struck by the cruel logic that had them paying so high a price for this unique acquaintance. No, there was compliment to them in there somewhere, and they would suffer any humiliation to lay their hands upon it. Gladly suffer, for the punishment was the very token of His love. His, meaning God's; but also His, meaning the angel's.

Saraqael's.

I had to look away. It is no sight for a son, the pain-lust of his parents.

And it is no sight for a sibling, his brother's angelolatry.

On the face of it, Abel fared better with Saraqael than my mother and father did. He kept his distance more. Was more subtle in the means he used to wheedle appreciation out of the angel. He was of the angel's party in this, of course, being himself one who had to be coaxed, caressed, bathed into animation. Consequently the contest could almost be said to have been even – each giving only as much to the other as the other looked prepared to give to him. Watching them in the early morning in Abel's paddock, thinking about exchanging a salutation that would not on either side cede sovereignty, a passer-by (had we been blessed with passers-by) would have supposed them either to be stalking ghosts or to be the spirits of the dead themselves.

But this equality of tactical torpor did not extend beyond disconnected sociableness. The minute our working day began and Saraqael again fell to schooling us in the science and theology of sacrifice, Abel became the panting pupil, starting out of his skin whenever his teacher noticed his application, as eager to please, to be seen to be assiduous, to be praised for his virtues and punished for his iniquities, as the rest of us . . . I mean the rest of *them*.

So the offering is to be *of* the herd, *of* the flock, he said – repeating what he'd been told, wanting to be certain that he'd investigated every corner of every stipulation – does that imply selection over and above what is blotched or spotted?

Saraqael moved a muscle in his cheek to show satisfaction with the question. 'Yes,' he said. 'For obvious reasons, not every animal is suitable to be an offering.'

Obvious reasons?

'Yes. In the first place the beast must be your own.'

I asked why that was.

'Because that which you have not reared does not belong to you . . .'

And?

He didn't like me. I could see that his hackles were high, as high as was consistent, anyway, with his severe cropping; and that his whole plumage shuddered, not so much angrily as hypersensitively, whenever I spoke. 'And what does not belong to you cannot be given in sacrifice.'

I take that point to be covered, said Abel, by the use of the words herd and flock, so some further consideration as to selection must be intended.

'If a man's offering be a burnt sacrifice of the herd,' Saraqael instructed, 'let him offer a male without blemish.'

Why, I asked.

'Why no blemish?'

Why *male*.

'Because of the superiority of the flesh of the male and because of his greater value to the offerer.'

Does the value to the offerer affect the savour of the offering?

Did I detect a feathery flinch, a stiffening of the already stiff wing-carriage? 'It proves,' he said, 'the sincerity of thy devotion.'

And is that the matter finished, Abel wanted to be clear, as to limitation?

'Not quite,' Saraqael pronounced. 'An animal is not suitable for sacrifice upon which any sin has been committed.'

Any *sin*?

'Any uncleanness.'

That still didn't help Abel. His fingers fluttered at his lips.

'Any sexual uncleanness,' Saraqael spelt out.

My poor brother's face twisted horribly at this. And mine twisted horribly for him. It is a most painful thing to see the collectedness vanish from the face of someone you love. It is as though you are privy to the undressing of their soul. And you know you will never be forgiven for what you have seen. But why did Abel's soul undress itself just then? It could not have been that Saraqael's words reminded him of some guilt. No, nor even of an intention towards that which would end in guilt. He was too conscious of his beauty to think of wasting it on an unappreciative ewe. No, it had to be the fantasticality of the suggestion that shamed him. The vast scope for wrongdoing in his nature which he had not, until now, even begun to put his mind to. Sexual sin? Upon a burnt offering designate?

What a child he was, or what a narcissist, not to have long ago ticked this off the unending list of conceivable abominations. Was it possible that he carried in his head some other list, of crimes he thought he never could commit? Were we *that* different, even though we were brothers?

Saraqael read both our minds. An expression of the finest, most unadulterated angelic distaste passed over his features. Passed? No. The revulsion twitched and stayed. I was relieved that neither of my parents, off carving altar-stones and collecting frankincense respectively, was here to see it. Though in another sense I wished they had been. It would have done them no harm to learn what an enemy to themselves they had tried to please. 'Humans,' Saraqael as good as said – for it was his skin that spoke and not his mouth – 'inhabitants of this lowly sphere, will stoop, in fact or in their thoughts, to anything.'

If it is true that higher up the hierarchy there had been strong resistance to the initial creation of fruitful flesh down here, and the implantation therein of chosen seed, then Saraqael had assuredly been of the circle which had counselled against it. He was not Semyaza. He was not here in fulfilment of a raging desire to be among us. Abel caught his fancy, true enough, but his fancy was always passing. He intended soon to be gone from us. Departure had been in his eyes from the start. And we would vanish from his thoughts, Abel included, the moment he opened his shoulders and took off.

Speaking for myself, there was nothing in his travel arrangements I would have wanted him to alter. But nobody willingly contemplates his disappearance from another's mind. You want to lodge somewhere in the memory even of those you despise. *Especially* of those you despise. And I liked the idea of lingering a little longer in the angel's.

Which must have been why I decided to go on worrying at the edict against tainted flesh. So an abused animal, I said – nudging, nudging with my lowered horns – is no more savoury to the Lord than a lightly prized one?

He looked surprised that I needed to ask. No, not surprised – how could any of us surprise him? – sickened.

You see what I'm driving at, I drove on. You tell us that an animal which is not the offerer's own, and which on that account he values not at all, is unsuitable as an offering for precisely that reason. But now you also tell us that an animal which might be exorbitantly valued, which is very much the offerer's own, is unsuitable for *that* reason.

Angels think in prohibitions. Even Semyaza spent every waking minute preoccupied by moral law. Keeping it/breaking it – these are merely alternative forms of the same engrossment. Saraqael was so weighted with injunction it was a miracle he could fly. 'Whosoever lieth with a beast –'

Yes, yes, I knew that, I said. But I was not talking about the whosoever, I was talking about the beast. And why that beast should have been unsavoury unto the Lord, notwithstanding the likelihood that in any particular act of disqualifying impropriety he or she (or it) would have been the innocent party.

Here in the enlightened city of Babel – praise be to you all – where you show esteem for those of your gods you can remember by eating them and drinking them, my line of inquiry must strike you, at the very worst, as robust. But Saraqael was in the service of an indefatigable Proscriber. A rigorous Segregationalist. And a most fastidious Picker at food. Added to which there is the angel's own refined character to be taken into account. So it should not be considered surprising that he grew warm with me, fixed me with those coals through which his vision blazed, and unloosed, at last, his sooty pinions – unfolded them, let air and light into them, and shook them, rattled them at me in the way that a bird is sometimes to be seen flexing its feathers in an attempt to throw off something foreign, something unwanted, that has stuck to them.

It was an impressive and, honestly, a fearsome sight. When he extended his wings, it was as though a sea of fire burnt around him, as though he were the fire's core, its cause and its object, only it was black fire not red, jet not jasper, a great cloud of enfolded smoke and fire, out of the midst whereof a thousand tongues of flame, ten thousand times ten thousand points of feathery light, licked like demons at what they burnt and at what burnt them.

His countenance, too, suffered an eclipse; was like a sun blackened by lightning, incinerated; his coronal of clipped hair as dazzling as an exploding star, the stubble on his chin and above his lips glowing an empty interminable nigrescent blue, the blue-black of undisputed night, the colour chaos must have been when it was left to reign unchallenged.

In my dread I looked at Abel, wondering why he had not, if only out of brotherly solicitude, fainted clean away. But he was transfixed by the angel's iridescence. His mouth was open. He held his fists, clenched, to the fine bones of his cheeks. He was white of course – when was he not white? – but it was an opalescent whiteness, the whiteness not of pallor but of frost. In his fright he had frozen over.

But it wasn't only fear that possessed him. As surely as he was iced was he in love with what he saw.

And was not I?

Let me say it now and then have done with it. We fell out once and for all, my brother and I, over colour, over patterning, over – for want of a better phrase – the aesthetics of belief. In the coruscating spectacle of Saraqael's spread wings and flaming nimbus, Abel beheld the Deity, the Great Designer, with his own eyes and experienced an excitation, an astonishment, a seizure, which he chose from that time onwards to call wonderment and to keep alive with worship. If that was what God looked *like*, then he was predisposed by the composition of his temper, by the very tone and tincture of his soul, to reverence HIM. It was the Art that won him, just as it was the Art that lost me. I am not saying that I was not struck by the Originating Genius – I had marvelled at It many a time in the days when my mother was the one being wooed – only that It didn't find a path into my soul. I apprehended Its power, but my apprehension was ungodly. I didn't deny It, I just didn't like It. Whereas for Abel there was no disjunction between The Thing he saw and what he felt. There *could* be no disjunction. Since It was, he must adore It.

I saw the trance into which he'd fallen and knew there would be no waking him. I'd failed in that attempt before, when he cried his childhood away spinning mollusc shells in the dirt. And this was an identical order of insensibility.

The angel saw it too, and was satisfied. After all our efforts, all our Saraqaelizing, this and this only was the way to please him. Spiritual abjection. Suspension of disbelief. And my parents weren't even here to try it out.

But he was satisfied. Now he could go home. Mentally, he was as good as packed. He ran a hand over his cropped head. Lowered his plumage. Took the weight off his spine. Blew away the down that clung to his moist chest. There was still smoke coming off his wings, a fine, weeping, forest mist, and a rich, feathery barn-yard smell. He shook them, flapped them a number of times, protruded them in an angular half-broken attitude, allowing them to cool before shuttering them closed. No further demonstration of divine majesty was going to be necessary. He had landed Abel and had never expected, never meant, to land me. Not without annoyance, I must say, I grasped that nothing of what had just taken place, nothing in Saraqael's visit, had been devised with my capture in mind. There I had been, hanging out, as I supposed, for critical independence, shielding my senses against a terrible and very nearly irresistible assault, and all along I'd been labelled as a lost cause and earmarked for forfeiture. It hadn't mattered that I'd cavilled at burning off the first and the best, that's to say the first and the worst, of my fruit. The Nostrils of the Lord did not twitch to anything but meat anyway. It hadn't mattered that I'd found the angel gaudy. It was never going to matter how I found him. I wasn't the celebrant, Abel was. He had the temperament for it, I didn't. He was the sacrificator, I . . . I was the sacrifice.

I must have looked what I felt. Or else an angel can see a fallen countenance, can read it as a spiritual condition, even when the face is firm.

'Cain, why art thou wroth?' he asked.

Wroth? I waved away his concern, working wonders with my jaw.

'If thou doest well,' he continued, mellifluous now, mediative, melted, 'shall it not be lifted up?'

It?

'Thy countenance.'

It was as if I'd been kissed not by honeyed lips but by honey itself. I was the bee and he was the flower. Only the flower had come buzzing around me.

You must hold out against kindness when you are in a weakened state. This is the time when angels love to come visiting. They hear the ebb of life's blood; they see courage evaporating in a thin smoke from the roof-top; they sniff the sweet decomposition of resolve – and they drop, in a twinkling, to your side. Art thou lonely, my child? Art thou troubled? Art wounded? Slighted? Spurned? Piqued? Forfeited? Listen, listen: for out of our mouths will come words of deceptive hope and comfort. That which thou takest to be forfeiture – how if it is only watchful and patient love? How if it is only thy Father – with a big *F*, with a soft *F* – biding His time, waiting until thou art ready for Him?

So, they had not given up on me after all. 'If thou doest well,' they had promised – half promised, intimated – 'shall not thy countenance be lifted up?'

My countenance – how heavy it felt. But lifted up – how light it was!

Beware the angel when the blood in your veins is as weak as water.

And if I doest not well? I asked.

He came very close to me, and for a moment I thought he meant to unfold his wings again and embrace me in their fire. But there was no longer any heat coming off him, and no lightning in his face. For the first and for the only time he made me the object of his elusive charm; and for the first and for the only time I was no better than the rest of my family and could imagine no finer compliment to myself, no greater benefaction, than to see him smile.

'Ah, if thou doest not well,' he said, 'sin coucheth at the door; and . . .'

He shook open a wing, soundlessly, and grazed my cheek

with his feathers. I became weightless, as though I were a fish and he held me in his talons. A shudder ran through us both, but do not ask me whether its cause was the herring's impatience or the bird's cruelty.

And . . .? And . . .?

'And unto thee is its desire.'

I scanned his fiery eyes for explication, but there was none offered. Even this close up, nose to nose as it were – though I did not reach to anything like that eminence – he was the angel of the enigma.

I looked across at Abel who was listening, listening, mouth open, skin not yet thawed, but in whose expression I saw only a sort of pastoral absence, a soul out wandering in sparkling grasses.

'But,' said Saraqael, at last, and now he did smile – not extravagantly, not even warmly, more, I suppose, reflectively: reflecting Someone Else – 'thou shalt rule over it.'

Thou shalt? How did the grammar of that work? Was it an order? A prediction? A promise? Was the kingdom of sin being dangled before me as an enticement, a reward if I did such and such? Or had it been given to me, there and then, with no strings attached?

He must have looked into my mind and seen the riot he had caused, because he shook his head, rattled his feathers – I would say apologetically, except that he did not have apology in him – and corrected himself, or at least corrected a false impression. 'Thou mayest,' he said. 'Thou *mayest* rule over it.'

It was up to me, in other words. There was no order, no promise, no prediction. Only the teasing gift of liberty. The gift that was no gift. The liberty that was no liberty. For to be told that a certain obligation is to be fulfilled, but that one may, of one's own choice, fulfil it or fulfil it not, deprives one of all choice. Self-respect insists that under those conditions one fulfils it not. Had they delivered the kingdom of sin, repining and groaning, into my hands, I might have made a resolute and wise emperor. As it was, they merely left the gates open and I rode away. As they knew I would. As they knew I had to, the moment they changed their shalt to mayest.

Our eyes met over this diabolic transaction. It was the last time I was ever to look into the cunning labyrinth which is an angel's soul; and it was the last time an angel was to look into the undeviating track to ruin which is mine.

He touched me with his plumage, lightly, once, below my ear, then he turned to say his goodbyes to my brother. I watched him take Abel by the arm, high up, almost by the shoulder, almost by the almond-white neck, and lead him in the direction of the soon-to-be-slaughtered sheep. Something in the manner of their intimacy, boy and bird, moved me to tears. Something fleeting and frail in their confederacy. Perhaps it was the unequalness. Or the ungainliness of their gait as they tried to find a common step on the uneven ground. Or maybe it was just that accursed old sadness that capsized my heart whenever I beheld my brother's back. And then I saw, or rather I did not see, the angel vanish.

Whatever passed between them, this was the last time for my brother, too, that he was to share soul-searching, in his earthly incarnation at least, with an angel of the Lord.

14. THOSE LENTILS... THAT POTTAGE WHICH JACOB SOD...

I

'Those lentils,' Naaman remarks to Zilpah, stopping her in their perambulation and getting her to peer with him, father and daughter, into an open sack stowed in the doorway to a seed and spice merchant's, 'I hope I will not soon be having to breakfast on such for your sake.'

'For my sake? Since when have I had any influence over what you eat?'

'I am not speaking of influence.' He pauses. 'I am speaking of respect.'

She doesn't follow him, but like any child in the company of a parent, she knows that abstract nouns unfailingly herald trouble.

'Have I failed of it in some way recently?' she asks. 'I cannot think what I have said or done to you . . .'

He turns his eyes from the lentils and treats her to a slow scrutiny. 'You still misunderstand me,' he says – and she worries because it seems a long time since he has said anything playful – 'I am speaking of the respect *I* feel for *you*. I hope I will not soon be having to show it in lentils.'

Something comes back to her. In Babel, as in most Shinarite cities, lentils were once served as a funeral meal. The custom is now defunct, practised only in waywardly, wilfully traditional families, but she is alarmed and wonders whether her father intends some threat to her.

He stoops, too tall to bend easily, and slides his hand, palm downwards, into the sack. When he withdraws it, there are still a number of the little red seeds nestling like ladybirds in the hairs that grow upon his fingers. 'It is not their colour that is significant,' he says, 'but their shape. Their roundness suggests the universality of loss. The mortality that rolls through all things.'

'And why do you fear that I may be the cause of your having to breakfast on them?'

He continues to hold the back of his hand out towards her. Partly so that she should go on looking at the lentils, and partly because he has been told that his long, feminine fingers, with their beautifully tended nails, more violet than pink, and their silken yellow hairs, have a powerful effect on people. Zilpah's mother used to say that he had hypnotized her with his hands, and admirers of both sexes have spoken of dizziness and other ecstasies occasioned by the combined smell and silence of his fingers.

He would like Zilpah to hear their quiet.

'Because I am worried about your health,' he says at last.

'I am in good health.'

'That is not what I have heard.'

'Heard from whom?'

He flicks the remaining ladybirds from the back of his hand. 'You were seen lying on the road the other day.'

She senses her colour rising and knows that she cannot keep it down. She wishes she had something to hold or otherwise busy herself with. 'I was not ill,' she says.

'Not even temporarily indisposed?'

'Not even temporarily indisposed.'

'In a way I think that distresses me more.'

'You would prefer it that I'd been ill?'

'I would prefer it that you didn't lie down in the road.'

She cannot conceal her shame. Or rather, she cannot conceal her awkwardness, and that is a cause of shame. She is too light in stature to bear scrutiny. There is nowhere in herself that she can hide. She is not being fanciful, she is not thinking metaphorically, when she fears she can be seen through.

'I won't be lying down in the road again,' she says.

Naaman throws his head back, arching his neck like a swan, and emits one of his famous laughs. Few people in Babel who have heard this laugh do not want to acquire a similar one for themselves. It seems, somehow, to comprehend everything that is bright and brittle in the city – its temples to forgotten gods, its love of reflective surfaces, its equivocal antiquarianism, its serious unseriousness. Zilpah has been in flight from it ever since she can remember. And she shrinks from it now, as though she has been struck.

'You don't believe me?' she asks, although she knows that that is not the reason he is laughing.

'I have every confidence,' Naaman says, taking her by the elbow and hurrying her along, 'that you won't be lying in the road again. But there is the question of where else you will be lying.'

'You are still imagining me in my grave? I have told you, I am not ill.'

It is a brave try, but even she knows it will not succeed.

'I am certain you understand me,' Naaman says, 'but since you force me – there is the question of with *whom* you will be lying.'

A calm, quiet as devotion, falls with the feather-touch of fatality itself on Zilpah's narrow shoulders. It is good, now that there is no more colour left to rise in her, and no greater transparency that she can show, to have the unmentionable mentioned. It even releases some capacity for archness in her. 'You don't care for him, then?' she notices.

'Isn't it a question, rather, of his not caring for you?'

'Who told you that?'

'My dear, everyone who has observed you.'

She is silent for a little while, content to be propelled by her father at his speed. Then she says, 'We are all in accord in that case. You do not care for us together; he does not care for me; and I do not care for him.'

Another of Naaman's white marble laughs. 'You are not saying that for the sake of symmetry, I hope.'

She shakes her head violently enough for her plait to rise and flick the air, like a horse's tail. 'I don't think *caring* has ever been the issue,' she says.

Naaman sneaks a glance at her. In the unceasing war which irony and prudery play out on the wet terrain of his unsteady mouth, prudery appears suddenly to hold the upper hand. 'There are some things it is not necessary for a father to know about his daughter,' he says.

'This is not a conversation of my choosing,' she reminds him.

'I know,' he says.

'The lentils were your idea, not mine.'

'I know,' he says. Elegantly abashed.

'So, since you mean to attend my funeral, you should know what I might die of.'

He doesn't answer. Only tightens his grip on her elbow and works his lips into a kind of poultice of distaste.

'It won't be love,' she assures him.

He catches an unexpected bitterness in these last words, and this emboldens him to ask what it will be instead. 'Hate?'

This time she is the one who is able to find a laugh. 'Old age,' she says.

It's possible he is disappointed. What father does not want to hear his daughter confess an ugly and, if possible, un-requited infatuation? What father does not nurse the furtive ambition of having the old jealous dread – the humiliation of rivalry, the vicarious ignominy of rejection – realized just once?

But there are consolations to seek, no less than thrills. It can be as great a satisfaction to discover that your daughter is well, as that she isn't.

He stops and puts his beautiful violet fingers to her cheeks, so that she may find a little moment of peace in their immunizing smell; then, as though examining her for fever, he drops them lower and feels for her salivary glands. 'So it's all right?' he asks tenderly.

Here is exposure of another kind. She steps back from him and reaches for her plait. It is essential she have something she can pick at. 'Yes, it's all right.'

'You sound hesitant.'

She hesitates. 'It *will* be all right.'

There are to be thrills for Naaman after all. 'Do you want me –?'

She shakes her head. 'I don't wish him . . . harm.'

'But you wish him . . . away?'

She thinks about that, her eyes lowered, looking for her answer in the paving stones. 'No. Not away.'

Naaman follows her gaze, wondering whether she is finessing as to grammar, as to particles of place. If *away* is not exactly it, how about *below*? This frightens even him. 'You don't mean . . .?'

They stand solemnly, shoulder to shoulder, staring at the paved street and imagining what lies beneath it. It is not usual for them to be amused by each other simultaneously, but she reads his thoughts at the very moment he reads hers, and the coincidence leads to merriment.

They present a tableau which Preplen, observing them from across the street where he is sitting rehearsing imprecations over an infusion of bitter herbs, finds it easy to interpret. Another Shinarite conspiracy. Another whorish daughter of Babel confiding her secrets to the Shinarite whoremonger, her father. More laughter over a stranger – traveller from Nod or Eden, worshipper of Law and Y-H-W-H. More poison which will finally find its way to him, Preplen, and carry him off like

one of those rats whose extermination the civic authorities of
Babel have perfected.

Conspiracy theories never go far enough. It does not fall
within the compass even of Preplen's paranoia to guess that
Naaman and Zilpah, father and daughter, are at that instant,
if only for that instant, sharing the amusement of imagining
Cain laid out before them in unimpressionable earth.

'No,' says Zilpah. 'I do not mean that.'

Naaman rubs his chin in mock perplexity. 'Not here. Not
there. Not away. Not under. I am wondering where that
leaves.'

'Up,' says Zilpah. And because the pair are in high spirits
now, she adds, 'And I don't mean in smoke.'

'Up?'

'Yes, up. He dreams of being buried in a tower. Let him
build one.'

'My dear, are we speaking of immurement?'

'No, but he is. We are speaking only of loaning him an
architect.'

'And a thousand masons.'

'More likely two thousand. He dreams of building very
high.'

Naaman's lips again take on their poultice look. 'They
always have such extravagant ambitions,' he says.

'*They?*'

'He – the Edenite. By they I simply mean the type.'

She worries over, worries around, her father's proposition.
Do *they* have extravagant ambitions? Does *he*? Is there profit
in considering him a type? She had thought she had done
and felt something exceptional, but if he is a type then
perhaps she has merely done and felt something typical. Yes,
there is profit to her in that. She can easier forgive herself a
typical mistake. She can, perhaps, even look forward to
making it again, if there are more like him bound to show
up in Babel. Or she can generalize her hatred of him, dignifying

267

it with universal truths and comprehensive observations, for there is moral and intellectual honour, not to say duty, in despising what is hateful in the type rather than the individual.

Surprising, the room there is for conflict in that narrow chest. Watching her through the steam of his herbal infusion, Preplen thinks she is standing silent, with her head bowed, picking at her plait, because that is the attitude Shinarite women strike when they are plotting ways of inveigling dark-skinned strangers. Whereas, in truth, what she is revolving is the allopathic drama whereby a private wound turns into a public scar.

She meets her father's eye and signals that it is all right for him to release the twinkle he has been holding back. 'Well, then,' she begins, 'if the heavens are the only place that will satisfy them –'

'We should encourage their ascent? You are more wicked than your father. But will he stay there once he gets there?'

'He will never leave.'

'Are you the cause of that?'

'Me? No. Worms.'

'And you're sure you wouldn't, in that case –?' He gestures with his thumb in the direction of the place to which they had alluded earlier.

She smooths her plait, doing her father the credit of showing a long consideration to his offer. But, 'No,' is her decision. 'No, I don't think so. I know the type. They are primed for anything that looks like persecution. If you want to make them really suffer, you give them what they want.'

Watching, watching, through eyes that neither take in nor let out light, Preplen gratefully receives the thing he wants.

II

'I'm not acting for myself,' Cain tells his Anatolian masseur. 'I'm not here on my own behalf.'

The Anatolian has soft wet soles and is skilled in the art of spreading his weight. When he walks over Cain's back it is as though an army of jellyfish is on the move. 'There is no reason for you to apologize for yourself, sir,' he says. 'You are not the only gentleman who comes here more than once a day.'

If I had laughter in me, Cain thinks, I would spend it now. 'I am not talking about the baths,' he explains. He is flat on his stomach, able to use only one corner of his mouth. 'I am speaking existentially. Things are out of my hands. I'm out of my hands. Other people are deciding my movements. Other people *are* my movements. If I didn't exist they would invent me.'

'If you didn't exist,' the Anatolian replies, working at Cain's coccyx with his heels, 'You would *want* them to invent you.'

Cain winces. He is sore where his tail is reported to be – such is the power of rumour. He thinks about saying, 'If I didn't exist I wouldn't have any wants,' but this is not the sort of conversation he is after. Among the desires he comes to the baths to have satisfied is a desire to lie on his stomach, talk through one corner of his mouth only, not see the person he is talking to, not hear the person he is talking to, suffer no interruption whatsoever, in short, to a prone musing accompanied by dim physical pain but rescued from the sharper pangs of solitude.

'Mmmmmm,' he says, to remind the Anatolian of the conventions. 'Mmmmmnnnnn.'

The Anatolian climbs off Cain's back and rubs himself with

beeswax. The next stage in the treatment is a speciality of his and a particular favourite of Cain's. He uses his torso as though it were a rolling-pin, ironing out whatever tension is left in his clients' spinal columns after he has finished walking over them. Because he is as flocculent as Esau, the effect is of being finely punctured by a rotating brush. Cain can take no end of this, and sighs before the bristling masseur has climbed back on him. And sighs again. And sighs a third time, before registering that the Anatolian has pulled up a stool and is still waxing himself absent-mindedly.

Cain does the last thing he ever wants to do when he comes to the baths, and raises his head from the table.

Taking this to be an invitation to speak, the Anatolian pursues his theme. 'If I didn't exist I would make someone invent me,' he says. 'I could not bear to have missed this . . .' He holds his hands up like goblets and extends them, agitatedly, to all corners of the steamy massage room, as if afraid he may not catch the precious streams which are pouring forth. '. . . this . . . life!'

Cain looks at him. A young, fiery man, black as Nanshe's eye, thistled, stinging, a man of points and edges, a projectile. Who has thrown him? Setting aside his youth, they are not dissimilar, he and Cain. They are both travellers, they are both far from home, they are both stocky, firm in the leg like foot-soldiers, they both like to talk. But someone – Someone – has taken the Anatolian by his ankles or his crop and flung him, hurled him with such vigour into life – life! – that it is impossible to imagine him ever losing his velocity and landing. That's the way to leave; that's the way to turn your back on home. Fly like a stone out of a sling. Not slink, as he did. Not slope. Not sneak. Not snake.

But when did Yahweh ever reach out to any of His chosen children and fling them, just for the fun of it – just for *their* fun of it – through the firmament? When did it ever occur to Him that they might like it, to feel the wind rushing past their bodies, to see the earth, in all its colours and undulations, flashing beneath them, to smell exuberance, precipitation, power coming from their skin, instead of fear, hesitancy and obedience? A jealous God, angry every day, He could not confer what He had never Himself experienced. He nudged His way through the skies, and nudged Cain into exile.

I Am What I Am Not, thinks Cain. I am not a meteor. I am not a shooting star. I am not a missile. I am not a goblet held up to catch the precious streams of life. I am not an Anatolian masseur with soft flying feet.

I am a nudged man.

He must have said it aloud, because the Anatolian twists on his stool and allows perplexity to pass, like a spring shower, across his handsome, hopeful face.

'How would you answer the call of life if you were me?' Cain asks him. 'What does life say you should do when you are conscious of a light but persistent pressure on every side – to do this or to do that, to be here or to be there, to honour him or to honour her? How do you know where your life lives and what its voice is?'

The Anatolian laughs, showing his white teeth, his red mouth – something else Cain cannot do. 'Why do you worry about sides?' he asks. 'Why do you let yourself be pressed on this side or that side? Life understands only two directions – up up up or down down down.'

He is back on the table now, remembering his occupation. The human roller. The rotating brush.

Cain braces himself against the shock of the first fine puncturing of his skin. He is pleased to be flat on his stomach again, able to use only one corner of his mouth. 'I don't suppose it is necessary to ask you which direction your life understands,' he says.

Another laugh from the Anatolian, which seems to penetrate the entirety of Cain's ganglionary system. 'Up up up,' he cries. 'I'm going up up up up up. And you?'

'Me? I'm following you.'

'Up up up up up?'

'I don't know whether I can manage five. Up up up, certainly.'

But he can manage five, and is thinking down down down down down.

III

Those lentils . . . That pottage which would decide who went where and owned what in Israel.

Like many another crossed in love, Sisobk has become bookish and biblical again. Scholiastic. Disputatious. Talmudical.

Sisobk the No-Longer-Sentimental. Sisobk the Sophist.

He is not of a mind to adjudicate between the two opposing theories of that most famous and far-reaching of all thick soups:

(a) that it is the price Esau exacts for his birthright, proving in what low esteem he holds his inheritance;
(b) that it is a ritualistic business meal of the kind brothers may be expected to tuck into after closing a perfectly amicable transaction as to real estate.

The important thing, whichever way you look at it, is that Jacob – father of the Twelve Tribes – is a sodder of slops.

The rabbis know it too. This is why they worry at those little red seeds, as though they are beads threaded on a rival religion's string.

Now that he is, so to speak, back home again, Sisobk is not averse to whiling away the odd lonely hour in the company of those cacophonous Babylonian schoolmen. They are easy to summon. You don't need steam. You don't need entrails. You don't even need a trance. One hint of an interrogative and they're yours. Of all the foreshadowy company waiting, pacing, jostling in the small back rooms of time, they are the most vociferous, a passion for exegesis prevailing over all other passions – even the passion for righting wrong, even the passion for justifying the unjustified self.

'I'll ask, you answer,' says Sisobk, settling in for the evening. If he had a chair he would settle into that. But he must make do with his rat's nest of a bed. Some men write in bed. You can always tell. You can smell the sheets. Sisobk has no sheets, but he doesn't mind if the odour of rags permeates his symposium with the future.

'First question: Why is Jacob sodding pottage?'

Because it says: Jacob is a plain man, a quiet man – the word is *tam* in Hebrew – a man whose lips speak what his heart believes, a man of modesty and simplicity, not given to kitchen skirmishing, who would sooner prepare pap in his own pan than a banquet on another's brazier.

Because it says: Abraham gave up the ghost, and died in good old age, full of years; and Jacob is preparing lentils as funeral food for Isaac. Faint from the field, Esau comes upon his brother engaged in an act of filial, and grandfilial, devotion.

And by the way: the verb is seethe – *seething* pottage. Sod is the past participle.

Sisobk is disappointed. He had hoped to damn Jacob and the Sodomites together – drown them in the same sodding pottage. But invite the rabbis in and you can't expect to have everything your own way.

'Second question: Why lentils?'

Because we say: the roundness of the lentils symbolizes death – grief and mourning rolling among us, now from this person, now to that.

Because we say: lentils have no mouths, and so remind the bereaved of their obligation to observe silence, to be mouthless, except on the subject of their bereavement.

Because it is said: Adam and Eve ate lentils after the murder of Abel.

'I know his brother,' Sisobk says. 'He's a tourist here. But that's not my question. This is: Why seek a precedent for lentil eating in violent death? Abraham will pass away quietly. Is it not said: Abraham gave up the ghost, and died in good old age, full of years?'

Yes, though not so full of years as he might have been. The Lord laid him to rest in the Cave of Machpelah at the age of one hundred and seventy-five. That is five years short of the number his son Isaac is going to attain. The reason for this charitable curtailment being, that the *good* old age promised, the contentment he looked forward to, would have been denied him at the last had he lived to see the evil wrought by Esau.

'Third, no, fourth question: To wit?'

To wit:
The ravishing of an already betrothed maid.
The murder of Nimrod.
The casting of doubt on the resurrection of the dead.
The denying of God.
The lying publicly in his field with Canaanite women.
The lying privately in his bed with Canaanite women.

'The fricasseeing of a dead dog?'

That is a folk-tale At least in so far as it is dramatically predicated on a scene of supernatural barking. The Lord does not, even for the purposes of admonition, take up residence in a stew. But there is a further obvious evil to add to the list:
The scorning of his birthright.

This one vexes Sisobk, though his dissatisfaction with it is as hard to find as his moustache.

'If the occasion of Esau's selling of his birthright is the morning of his brother's sodding . . . seething pottage, and the pottage is in honour of the death of Abraham, then can't it be argued that the continued existence of Abraham would have denied Esau the occasion for selling his birthright? And that far from Esau's evil contributing to the demise of Abraham, the demise of Abraham contributes to Esau's evil?'

From the darkest corners of Sisobk's hovel comes the muttering of rabbis. Doubts, queries, counter-doubts and counter-queries, the unreasoning reasoning of men who read too many words. Then at last, a verdict:

You have not foreseen – O sciolist – how much the Lord foresaw.

Sisobk does not want to gloat, but he foresaw they were going to say *that*. He means only to be placatory, though. Scare away the rabbis and he has scared away his only company. 'So in a sense then,' he says, 'in six, or is it seven senses, Esau is the murderer of his grandfather. But that still leaves Jacob as an opportunistic burglar of brothers' birthrights.'

No, it doesn't.

'It doesn't?'

He isn't a burglar in the sense of hoping to secure material advantage to himself from what he takes.

'He isn't? Then what does he mean by saying, "Sell me this day thy birthright," the price having already been set at a plate of lentils?'

In the first place he means: You are, by your own confession, faint – faint in your pursuit of venison and pheasant, and faint in your pursuit of God – and therefore you lack the will to perform such priestly services as go with your inheritance; which services, my brother, I, being a gentle and quiet man (*tam* in Hebrew), am prepared to do in your stead.

In the second place he means: You speak frequently, my dear brother, of your expectation of death – 'Behold, I am at the point to die,' you say – which I take to be an enunciation either of the daily fear that hunts you in the field, or the terror you feel in anticipation of your priestly duties; the job appears to be wasted on you in the first instance, and a burden to you in the second. Why do you not free yourself of unnecessary anxiety and let me bear your fears for you?

In the third place he means: Given your disbelief, my beloved brother, in God's universal promise to resurrect the dead, and his particular provision of the Holy Land to the seed of grandfather Abraham, *alav ha-sholem*, what possible logic or profit can there be for you in your inheritance? Can a man inherit what is not to be? As I love you I would not see you the victim of moral subterfuge and theological sophistry. Permit me to wear the inconsistency for you, and pay you for that which, by your own reasoning, cannot come about.

Sisobk the Scryer laughs wildly. 'So in truth,' he exclaims to the familiar spirits of his room, 'Esau is doing rather well out of the bargain. Considering how little he has to sell, he can count himself fortunate to be paid in lentils!'

But a premonition of sooner rather than later time snaps his neck back and clears the room, on the instant, of every trace of ghostly scholar. Not a hair remains. Not a thread from a fringe, not a quill, not a quarrel, not a quibble.

Sisobk hears the sound of footsteps on the streets, ringed fingers tapping on a copper pan. The fingers stop, tap and stop, teasing Sisobk's hearing. Is he listening with his ears or with his heart? Is it now or is it soon? The tapping resumes, the ringed fingers no longer walking like feet but rapping like a fist. On the barred gates of the very building that hovels Sisobk. Soon. Sooner. Now.

'That will be Cain,' Sisobk remarks nonchalantly. And doesn't even bother to clean up.

IV

Has Cain come to the House of Hearsay and Hermeneutics intentionally, of his own free will? Or was it long ago settled for him in some other place that this was a visit he would have to make?

Has he fallen or was he pushed?

Ask Cain. 'I was nudged,' he will tell you.

He is disappointed that the House really is a house and not a cellar. Down down down down down should be down down down down down.

The building enjoys no particular eminence; it makes it to five or six storeys at best, but spreads, consuming whole streets, swallowing crossroads and corners, turning every edifice it touches, or looks at, into extensions of itself. It is plaguy and contagious. It is monumentally forbidding, great blocks of featureless grey stone laid one upon the other according to no principle except the order in which they were quarried. Like one of my father's constructions for the accommodation of a field-mouse, Cain thinks, it looks simultaneously everlasting and on the very point of collapse. An immutable geometric law threatens to bury it under the weight of its own sloping walls. It has been built without regard to regularity or harmony, without considerations as to light or prospect, its guiding architectural assumption evidently being that those it is meant to confine will receive their illumination and perspectives from internal sources.

'Like it?' Sisobk is already at the gate, wearing one of those expressions of fractious surpriselessness favoured by men who know the end of things and grow weary waiting for others to catch up. 'A wonderful invention of the civic mind,' he says, gesturing to the dead walls. 'Keeps light out and metaphysical rumour in. The authorities like to store all secrets of the heart under one roof, so they always know where they are.'

Cain has never seen him less subservient. This too, of course, is disappointing. No one enjoys losing an acolyte. But he was half expecting some change. Sisobk's last words to him, hurled at the unheeding back he had turned on Zilpah – 'You are just a holiday-maker in the Land of Shinar, Cain, and a tourist in the City of Woman' – clearly signalled some wavering in the prophet's devotedness. Is this another reason he is here? Has he come to win back lost esteem? Has he come to listen greedily to more rudeness?

How does he know? He was nudged.

Sisobk whistles, scratches himself, takes a keen interest in passers-by. It is cold in the shadow of the walls; a sharp, unseasonable wind blows up from beneath the flagstones, in protection against which Sisobk has lined his filthy robes with parchment. When he moves he rustles like a scroll. 'Want to go in?' he says inconsequently – indifferent guide to idle tour-

ist. He doesn't wait for an answer. Everyone knows what a
tourist is going to say. He puts his bear's shoulders to the
gate. 'Watch the puddles,' he says, 'and don't mind him.'

'Him?'

'There, near the rubbish. There . . . there. He cannot make
himself distinct until somebody believes him.'

In a black passage by the stairs Cain sees a wall stir with
the urgency of a man. The stones motion to him, clutch
vainly, like the stumps of fingers.

'Why does no one believe him?'

Sisobk knew this was going to happen. Questions, questions.
'Because he claims to have measured the toe of a god.'

'Any particular god?'

'No doubt yours – He's the cause of most of the trouble in
this building.'

'Do you know what dimensions he claims for it?'

'Ssh! Let him hear you asking that and he'll start considering
himself credible. The next thing we'll be having to listen to
what else he's measured. It never stops with the toe, you
know. Best to leave him. He's happy enough being indistinguishable from a wall. It lends him the distinction of in-
distinctness in this place where most of us aspire to be particles
of light or rivers of molten fire. But say hello to this one. He's
intensely curious about you. I don't know how often he's
pestered me to bring you here. Humour him. He's quite harmless. Just a touch literal, like all of us.'

Cain finds himself staring into the red eyes of a gaunt
figure, wasted by faith, standing by an open door with his
hands clasped not so much *in* prayer as *around* it. 'I will bless
the LORD at all times,' he says, in an easy conversational
manner, as though he would have said it even had Cain not
been passing, 'His praise shall continually be in my mouth.'

He gives Cain proof of this, opening his mouth wide, as if
for a doctor, letting his tongue hang out. It is broad and
rounded, a spoon, a spatula, and almost as red as his eyes.

'Now show him yours,' Sisobk urges. 'Humour him. See it as an act of charity.'

'Mine has not sung praise for a considerable time,' Cain says. 'Will that matter?'

Questions, questions.

Sisobk, sighing, does not think it will. The Lord's eulogist would like to exchange ahs! with a mouth that once did, not necessarily one that still does.

So Cain opens his, and for a few precious seconds experiences the singular intimacy, inveterate only among beasts, fowl and some species of fish, of breathing accommodatingly down a stranger's throat while the stranger pants necessitously down yours. Then, with a sound that resembles the gurgling of drains, the stranger begins to ferment further psalmody in his gullet. 'O taste and see that the LORD is good.'

Cain closes his mouth.

The gaunt man appears distraught, seizes Cain's shirt, stabs at him with his tongue. 'Thou hast seen and tasted the LORD?'

Cain pulls away.

But this petitioner is not trapped inside a wall. He grabs again. 'Thou hast seen and tasted the LORD – how was HE?' He is all maw now, alive only on the lips and in the gullet. 'How was HE to the palate? Show me again the tongue wherewith thou hast tasted Him. Describe to me how It was.'

Cain the homicide, the murderer of his brother, the rotten fruit in the First Gardener's eye, feels his stomach rise into his gorge. His jaw is clamped so tightly the whole building can hear his teeth grind.

From the mouth of the holy gourmet a more fluidal commotion – 'Like unto kid, was It? Like unto venison? Did It scald the skin from thy gums as the flesh of mortal woman's womb is scalded when she is penetrated by an angel? Did It smoke? Was there bone? Was there gristle? Was It like unto . . .?'

Only the intervention of Sisobk saves Cain from more of

this. Sisobk the Saviour. How the mighty . . . He leads the way, Cain following obediently, mouth shut, through blackened passages in which men cry 'Chaos!' or shudder from the Twelve who have become their persecution, or accuse the sun and moon of fornicating and dripping their lewdness to the earth in dew and honey; then up staircases, uneven and treacherous, where some cry out 'Murderers!' against those who swallow eggs, and others open and close compasses, calculating in a frenzy the geometry of the foundations of the earth.

Careful of his guest's distress, enjoying leadership, Sisobk hurries him along, like a father hurrying a son past an accident, past a killing, by a charnel house, through Gehenna. 'We are almost there,' he promises, although there has never been any mention of a destination. And at last they arrive at the wet and windowless cell in which Sisobk shelters from what is and starves himself into deliriums of what will be.

Although it is never closed, Sisobk kicks his door, to shoo away any ghostly rabbi or other textuist who may have thought to return in his absence, mad for more contention.

There is no light in the room and no provision for its manufacture. Grateful not to have to see anything, Cain allows himself to be led to Sisobk's rat's-nest bed – a rubbish dump of hassocks spitting straw, rags, flock, strips of rotting papyrus. Cain stretches out on it, thinks of Preplen, thinks of sticks, thinks of food and faith, and is asleep before his host can ask him if there is anything he wants. 'Just as well,' Sisobk mutters, 'because I haven't got it.'

He sits on the floor and listens. Like a father, or a brother. Like a friend. Like an assistant. Not any longer, then, like a disciple? He sits and watches, watches over, reading Cain's bad dreams, providing cold and melancholy sanctuary. It is not the honour it would have been, having Cain comatose in the corner of his room – it is not the honour he frequently and fantastically anticipated in the days before . . . *a certain matter*. But it is not nothing, either, to be privileged to sit and watch and listen. To watch over. To listen out for. To succour.

Sisobk the . . .

The very thought of himself in this protective role softens Sisobk's short-lived obduration. He goes over to the rat's nest and takes Cain's hand. Holds it gently in his. Pats it. Traces the whorls of hair on the knuckles. Puts the fingers to his lips. One at a time. So soft, so pliable, so *womanly* – you would never think they were murderer's fingers.

V

He gets the idea from Rebekah. If, despite the stink of goat-skins, she can pass off Jacob (who is white and smooth) as his brother (who is red and rug-like), then he, Sisobk (who is shambling and foul), can pass himself off as Cain (who is erect – when he is not prone – and fragrant).

It's easy to do. The sleeping, unresistant Cain comes out of his clothes as sweetly as lentils emptied from a sack. You hold his gown, and then his undershirt, by the ears, and literally spill him out. It takes the Scryer longer to undress himself. This is because his body has not been parted from its garments in such an age, he is not always certain which is which. Were he to hurry he would as like as not peel his skin off with his drawers.

And as Rebekah took the choicest garments, the goodliest raiment, of Esau her eldest son, and put them on Jacob her younger son, so does Sisobk put upon him the costly linen of Cain the elder and less loved son of Eve. He does not, though, reverse the process and put his own goodly raiment upon his unconscious guest. Why run the risk of waking him? Why

waste the time? Why multiply duplicities? He is only borrowing the outward form of Cain – taking it out on loan for an
hour – not usurping him. He might have got the idea from
Rebekah, but he is not Jacob. He is not his brother's thief.

Standing in Cain's clothes, Sisobk fancies he is owner of the
memory of every sin which, despite all the laundering, still
clings to them. He sees forwards as a rule, not backwards.
The past is a luxury to him. A feather bed. Now he understands why men are so eager to yield to it, and so reluctant
ever to let it let them go. Unlike the future, which fumes and
reeks, the past is placid, imperturbable, painful only as a
recollection of pain. You do not return from it with blood in
your eyes and foam around your mouth. Still to come, yet to
be, the drama of Jacob's jealousy must be boiled up like
pottage in a prophet's brain. Whereas Abel – already over,
never to be again – comes at the first summons, like a remembrance of youth.

As long as you are mantled in his brother's garments, odor-
iferous with wrongdoing, the lovely doted-upon boy glides
sociably before you, starts at you adorably from the fields,
whiter than his woolly sheep, or presents himself, shiftless,
shameless, in that scalloped rock wherein his mother worshipped him clean.

Sisobk holds him there, indifferent to the shapeliness and
becoming pallor of his limbs, intrigued only by the configuration of the boy's own desires, the thing he envied, not the
thing he was envied for. Envious? Abel? But of course. Is this
not the lesson of Jacob – that the good brother must always
covet the accumulations of the bad: the red hair, the mouthful
of milk teeth, the daughters of Canaan, the carcasses of meat,
the wherewithal to please a father, the wherewithal, on such a
scale, to displease a mother? The last especially. Who would
settle for being merely the apple of his mother's eye, when he
could be the arrow in her side, the thorn in her flesh, the
pestilence in her blood?

Envious? Abel?

The one-time prophet, turned historian, shudders and pulls his adopted gown around him. He likes the direction of his thoughts. Very soon, very soon now, he believes he will have achieved that moral reversal without which there can be no comprehending the affairs of men. Yes, it is good for him, borrowing the skin of a distinguished and proven fratricide. He can feel it charging him with light. Flooding him with goodness. He is ready, like a descended angel, to try his new-found footing on the streets.

He closes the door quietly behind him and goes down into the city. He does not know what he is going to find, or how it is going to find him, but he is serenely, superbly, angelically confident that by the time he returns he will have grasped the sense in which Abel can be said to have killed Cain.

VI

He wakes, the victim in question, without his clothes, in a cold room none of his senses recognizes. Foul tatters have been thrown around him. An appalling stench, glutted with the morbid discharges of mind no less than body, comes off them and off himself. Wherever he is, he has been here long enough to be impregnate with the place.

He waits for his eyes to make something of the darkness, then tries to find his way around the room. He reaches for the security of walls, but recoils from them at the first touch. They are wet with slime, slippery like the clay sleeves of a potter or the insides of his pot. He feels about him for his clothing, but nothing that sticks to his fingers is familiar to him.

He decides that he has been stripped and robbed and

dumped here. In which case I suppose I ought to count myself fortunate that they have left me with my life, he catches himself thinking, before he remembers that fortune doesn't enter into it. Hath not the Lord set a mark upon him, lest any finding him should . . .

He shakes his head fiercely, as a parent might shake a bad dream out of a screaming child, in order to dispel all recollection of that hateful hour when the Lord marked him with the shame of fatalism, branded him where everyone would see it, with an unresisting tragicalness which rendered any idea of doing violence to him otiose, since you knew you could take from him without it, and since you knew you could damage him the more seriously, anyway, by leaving him to damage himself. Only the pertinacious are worth murdering, the Lord calculated – proceeding from the knowledge of the murderer in Himself – and as a consequence lined Cain's face with restiveness but not resolution. 'They have only to look at me,' Cain feared, 'to see that I do not expect to prevail.' And because he feared it, it was so.

God's final rebuff to him: Thou shalt be unkillable.

No matter where the room, no matter what the hour, he has never mastered waking. When Zilpah woke with him, starting into consciousness wonderfully, the very second he did – 'See,' she would say, 'how finely we are attuned, how identically we are twinned' – she took the hopelessness of his expression, the abstraction in his eyes, to be the consequence of his having raised his hand against his brother.

'It will eventually pass,' she promised him, pressing her cold lips to his brow, or into the hollow sockets of his seeing, as though she would taste their weariness, swallow it for him, swallow it *from* him. 'The day will eventually come when you will not remember.'

But in this, as in everything else, she was mistaken. His

brother has nothing to do with the apparently contradictory sensations of universal worthlessness and personal insufficiency to which he invariably wakes. It was the same even when his brother lay sleeping unbruised beside him. All that has changed is that he is now without anybody close to him to punish for how he feels.

This has been the most lasting effect of his crime against his brother: he has once and for all denied himself the other side of his great argument with life. He has risen against his own yearning to quarrel, to be at variance, to enjoy and suffer disjunction, no less than he has risen against his own blood.

As with all those who take extreme measures to silence their rivals, who are literal enough to insist that their view must alone prevail, his punishment is identical with his crime – single-mindedness.

Single.

Mindedness.

But he does not wake to an immediate apprehension of this. He has to crawl towards it every morning.

He would like something to eat and drink. No man experiences futility in the act of devouring food. But he is not prepared to search for victuals in this room. He ties a rag around his loins and feels his way to the door. Like a dog scenting love or liver, he lifts his head and twitches his nostrils. And then it comes back to him, where he is and how he got here. The smell that does it is not the smell of damp timber and streaming walls, but the smell of visionaries and their unventilated hallucinations. Spectres always leave an odour behind, and the stairwell is choked with the charred oniony sweetness of their passing.

He is reminded of a whimsical expression of starvation commonly used by the beggars of Babel – 'I am so famished I could eat a ghost.' Which, for all that he detests whimsy, makes him hungrier.

He descends the stairs, disgusted by what he imagines the timbers to be oozing beneath his unsandalled feet. From a doorway on the half-landing a finger beckons him. 'Traveller,' a voice whispers, 'dost thou know how many sparks from the great One Spark lie trapped in every ear of corn? Canst thou count the brilliances imprisoned in a loaf of bread?'

I will not get what I want here, Cain thinks, and keeps descending.

On the next floor down he has to negotiate a group dressed like desert nomads, standing in a tight circle and holding candles. If he is not mistaken they are discussing his mother.

'Then Satan moulded the form of woman from the slumbering body of the man, and tricked an angel of the First Heaven into taking up abode within her. And when the angel saw that he was trapped in mortal flesh, he grieved sorely, shedding tears. And all the angels wept to see him weep. But Satan's heart was hardened all the more, and he filled the woman with a madness and a longing for sin that was unquenchable. And the woman's desire, brothers and sisters, was like unto . . .'

The speaker pauses. He is young in body but without colour in his face and without, as far as Cain can see, any openings in it either. A beard has grown over him, like grass over a neglected grave. Only a wandering tongue is visible – an alien soul, a lost fragment of primordial harmony, a fugitive with no mouth to go home to.

'. . . what was it like unto, brothers and sisters . . .?'

'A glowing oven!'

'A raging fire!'

'A flaming furnace!'

'A volcano that never sleeps!'

Would that my father were here, Cain thinks, to listen to this description of his wife. Then he changes his mind and thinks, praise be to heaven that he isn't. People cannot always be relied on to see the funny side of things. Like the angel who wept to find himself trapped in the flesh of mortal woman.

Although he is not dressed to be seen, Cain pushes through the rapt congregation. No one notices him. No one knows that the first ash from that sleepless volcano, the first bun from that glowing oven, is passing among them.

The catechist has begun again. 'And seeing the conflagration in the woman's womb, forthwith the devil in a serpent's form slithered out from the reeds and sated his lust on her with his . . . with his what, brothers and sisters . . .?'

Here it comes again . . . all they can ever think about! thinks Cain. The far limit of every believer's conception of original wickedness – the old slab of creeping coccygeal joint and muscle.

'Tail!' the brothers and sisters proclaim together.

'Tail!'

'Tail!'

'Tail!'

He turns his, but before he can make it to the next flight of stairs a voice blows warm in his ear – 'I know who you are, of course, being a scholar, and am honoured.'

Cain finds himself looking into the fine but swerving eyes of a man of middle height and middle years, but of more than middle respectability, judging from the sumptuous room – the sumptuous suite of rooms – that extends behind him, and the magnificently brocaded gown he wears open at the throat, where whitening hairs of unusual length and tenuity sprout like lady-fern, and where a stone, not unlike lapis lazuli, swings on a golden chain.

'My name,' the gentleman continues, 'is Raziel, though my ideas are circulated under the pseudonym, Antinomi. I don't suppose you . . .'

Cain apologizes. 'I have not long been resident in this country,' he explains.

'Of course you haven't. Of course. Of course.' An illimitable capacity for pain shows in Raziel's flickering grey eyes and in the nervous gestures of his hands. He is unable to control his fingers. One moment they are at his lips, then they are plucking hairs out of his chest, then they are up to his scalp where no hairs grow at all. He has removed those too, in his disquiet, Cain decides, imagining the absorption in self-cruelty, the Abel-like concentration of such a task.

He follows Raziel into his rooms. Yes, he will take wine. Yes, he would love cake. Yes, he will accept date wine. Yes, grape if it is superior. Yes, red is fine. Yes, white if it is more suitable to the time of day. Yes, cherry cake. Yes, syrup. No, not if it clashes on the palate with white grape.

While Raziel is in his kitchen, Cain surveys the drawing room which has been offered to him as an alternative to the library, and in which he has been given the choice of sitting or standing – sitting on cushions or on a stool, standing with his back to the fire or the door. The room is divided in the middle so that one half is an exact mirror image of the other, an identical reflection marred only by slight but deliberate distortions – an ivory statuette of a goddess looking back at a clay figure of a demon; the painted vine-trellis on the left half of the ceiling bearing healthy fruit while the trellis on the right bears only berries that are blighted.

'I am mortified,' declares Raziel, returning suddenly, unable to prevent his hands wandering to his chest. 'I have not offered you the loan of apparel. How do you like your sleeves?'

'How?'

'Long or short?'

'I will take either.'

'Aha,' says Raziel. 'Aha.' It is the sound of a small nerve snapping.

I am in a place, Cain tells himself, where not to choose is to be damned. 'Long,' he says.

'Short will suit you better. And your preferred goblet?'

'Large.'

'Aha.'

'Crystal.'

'Aha.'

'Cut.'

'Aha. And in the stem?'

'Squat.'

'Slender is more appropriate to white grape.'

'Then slender,' says Cain.

In the event he is offered carrot juice served in an ornamental gourd. And a bowl of fruit. And a copper patera – although his taste runs to pewter – of marshmallow.

It is while Cain is bent low over the marshmallow, trying to keep the sugar off the borrowed gown, that his host slips silently out of his robes. Almost silently. Perplexed by what he takes to be a susurration of draperies, a swoosh as of a tent flap blowing open, Cain raises his eyes just in time to catch, or just too soon not to miss, Raziel emerging prematurely from the chrysalis, still larval white, and quite bare except for a bangle around each wrist, a leather thong about his ankle, and the lapis lazuli humming on the end of its golden chain.

I am about to be required to make a choice again, Cain fears.

'I know who you are,' Raziel says.

'You have told me that,' Cain replies.

'You are numbered among the transgressors.'

Cain says nothing.

'You are reckoned with the sinners, and you bear the sin of many.'

Still nothing.

'You have trodden on the vestures of shame. How are they to the foot? Are they soft, or do they chafe you?'

Cain keeps his head in marshmallow. He is not going to be caught staring at Raziel's forelimb which, thanks to the orbed character of vision, he can peripherally discern – a thin, pointed pod, like okra, hanging as though it is a broken pendulum in the dead centre of the room, where each reflection meets itself.

'You have attained virtue through evil –'

'I must consider leaving,' Cain says.

'You have loved God by loving the devil –'

Cain rises. Because he cannot go on looking down and safely navigate the room, he must look up. Raziel is standing on one leg, like a water bird, and is shielding the back of his head with his arm, as though expecting – as though inviting – heaven itself to fall on him.

'Abase me so that I may know pride,' he begs.

'I don't hold with paradoxes,' Cain says.

Detecting threat, Raziel raps out a litany. 'Strike me down so that I may rise. Wound me so that I may heal. Murder me so I may live.'

'That would be no way to return your hospitality,' Cain says, recognizing, even as he says it, that he's wrong.

Raziel sways on his stalk. His handsome head, with its stern discriminating mouth and skidding grey eyes, astounded by the foreign body it surmounts, appalled by the strange importunings it speaks. The swaying is so precarious, one puff of wind would blow him over.

But the room is close and still, without draughts.

'At least steal something from me,' he implores. 'Take –'

'That you may be given?' Cain looks about to see if there is anything he has use for, and then remembers that the only thing he needs is round his shoulders. 'All right,' he says. 'I owe you for your kindness. I'll keep the gown. In return you may have the rag.'

A tremor passes over Raziel's body. Even where the hairs have been pulled out in agitation, he ripples like corn. 'Praise be to Thee, O God of heaven and hell,' he hymns, 'who permittest what is forbidden, who allowest the cruel to subdue the meek, and the wicked to teach their ways to the good. He robs me and – behold! – I am richer.'

Before he leaves, Cain notices that Raziel's pale, pointed okra pod has begun to stir and rise . . . like a ziggurat . . . godwards.

VII

Abstract and brocaded, he runs into Sisobk on the stairs.

Gleaming and in tatters, Sisobk drops to his knees and embraces Cain's feet. 'You saint,' he says, 'You martyr, you tower –'

'Get up,' Cain tells him. 'I see that in one night you have reduced my clothes to the condition of your own.'

'And I see that in one night you have raised mine to the condition of yours. Didn't I say we were the perfect complement to each other!'

'You should not have stolen my clothes. And you should not have inveigled me into this House.'

'I only invited you. You came of your own accord.'

Cain thinks: no, I didn't – I was nudged. But what he says is, 'And that is exactly how I am leaving it.'

'Not yet. Wait till you hear . . .' Sisobk pulls at the hem of Raziel's robe. 'Wait till I tell you what I've done.'

'Not if it involves watching you moving your mouth. I think I will not mind if I never see a human mouth move again.'

Sisobk is only too willing to cover his. Don't his fingers fly naturally to his betel-stain moustache anyway?

'Didtfyou,' he says, behind his hand. 'Didwayoudvdon. Iraisdmarm.'

'And not if it involves listening,' Cain says. 'I think I will not mind if I never listen to a human voice again.'

'Buisabouyou.'

'Especially if it's about me.'

He turns, trusting his feet blindly to the rotting stairs.

Sisobk follows, freeing his mouth, making a final lunge for Raziel's robe. 'I did it in your name, and in your clothes, and with your brother and your God goading me.'

A deaf man, Cain continues his descent, past the gourmandizer, past the twitching shadow, through a crowd arguing the sex of the Demiurge. 'Like unto a hermaphrodite He is . . .'

'I don't know how you stood it,' Sisobk calls out. 'Having those two dinning in your head. One too old and one too young. One angry every day and one grateful every minute. And both resenting you because you wouldn't play give-me-thank-you with them. How did you stand it for so long? How did you hold out? I couldn't. I *didn't*!'

But Cain has found the daylight and is off, breathing hard, and giving vent to some reflections of his own. 'Mould is metaphor,' passers-by on the sun-blanched streets of Babel are surprised to hear him muttering. 'Mould is monotheism. Mould is the One Model that all those *like untos* are like unto. Mould is whatever I do not mint new every morning for myself. Mould is mother's milk and Maker's mud. Mould is memory. Mould is what moulded me.'

'You are talking, sir, to yourself,' an elderly citizen observes, taking him by the arm for his own, and for the city's good.

Cain is obliged to him. 'I've passed an uncomfortable twenty-four hours,' he explains. 'But at least I now know what I've had growing on my skin.'

Sisobk the Scryer, meanwhile, sits on the hermeneutic steps and thinks: so these are the thanks you get!

You go out in the guise of another man – for no baser reason than that you would like to honour him by inhabiting his skin for one hour of one night; you are fallen upon by a madman with a twisted spine who believes the clothes you are wearing you have stolen from his friend; you are charged with being in the pay of the cursed Shinarites, accused of being a hired agent or an assassin; you are wrestled to the ground by this same contorted lunatic, who threatens you with a terrible vengeance, who promises that every Edenite is the ally unto death of every other Edenite; you find that when it comes to a trial he has even less strength in his body than you have in yours, and it is therefore given to you, in a quiet street, on a dark night, in a habit not your own, to take a head between your hands and bounce it – lifting it gently as though it is a pretty ball and you are a pretty child playing with it – and bounce it . . . catch and bounce, catch and bounce, on paving stone so hard that a man's sandal, let alone a man's head, rings from the contact like a bell.

And these are the thanks you get!

That's three things I've learnt about murder tonight, Sisobk concludes – it isn't difficult to do, it isn't really you that does it, and nobody is willing to say thank you afterwards.

Sisobk the Sagacious.

He gets up off the step and like a bear that has come in hungry from the country, blunders out into the street. He thinks he can see Cain's back retreating, always retreating, in the distance.

'Does this mean we're not going to Padan-Aram?' he calls out.

15. Cain Rectifies a Failing in His Brother

I hold my brother Abel so still in my mind – as though to disturb him would be to spill him – that he is more present to me as the small collection of phonetic sounds his name makes – two little vowels, a labial, a liquid – than as a thing of moving parts.

Was there a time, before he had become a rack of letters to me, when I grasped him as blood that flowed and bones that could be snapped? Was he company for me? Was I company for him? Did we do anything, go anywhere? Did we play? Did we run? Did we make? Did we destroy? Did we talk, ever?

I cannot animate my memory of Abel because I cannot animate *him*. He will not escape my affection for him, my watchfulness, my brotherliness. He will not move.

I have loved him into an abstraction.

We must have argued. My recollection of that offers him a partial release if he will take it, at the very least oils his joints and points him in his own, in a contrary, direction. But no sooner does he gather a momentum than I become rooted to my spot. There is room in my mind only for one of us to be in action at any time. This is how I avoid contemplation of antagonistic motion. We did not collide because we were not opposed. There was no rupture because there was no divergence. We didn't argue. We didn't separate. We didn't fight.

But we did, whether I permit myself to think of it or not.

We argued. Without our eyes ever meeting, without acknowledging we were at odds, without in the beginning raising our

voices, we argued over everything. We argued, if the truth be
told, the very existence of each other's souls. We queried, not
simply our individual right to be, but the palpable fact that we
actually were. Palpably, we said to each other, you are not.
There was nothing, as I now understand, unusual in that. For
love that originates in the binding coincidence of family, there
can be no other fate. Parties to family love cannot simply, like
participants in mere passion, run out of the energy that mutual
regard demands; they are not free to walk away until they've
obliterated where they've been; they do not move in a cloud of
pure differentiation until they've hacked at every likeness to
themselves. This is the common law of families. Where we
were unusual, Abel and I, was in our reluctance to admit
disaffection. Had either raised his voice to the other, neither
would have been able to bear it.

Raising a hand is another matter. Raising a hand can be
soundless, unadmitted, loving.

I loved Abel. Forty thousand seraphim could not with all
their love put together, not with their eighty thousand nostrils
opening and closing in unison to inhale the sweet smells that
issued from his offering, have loved him more. I even loved
him *while* he made his offerings, and felt protective of the very
sacrificial diligence that divided us. You do not have to approve
the service to feel tender to the servant. The very opposite may
be true: that you grieve and sorrow over the officiant in exact
proportion as you despise the ceremony. The more abominable
the paraphernalia of sacrifice became to me – the more I grew
to hate the punctilios of selection, the time and spirit expended
on precautions, the blood, the fires, the smoke, the charred
aroma – the more touching I found Abel's dedication.

I would have needed to be an animal myself not to have
been moved by the sight of him crawling among his flock,
feeling between haunches and through fleece for that taint or
blemish which, once found, disqualified the beast from God's
table. It is a test of love to see your brother on his back

beneath a ram, and I passed it. I watched him in the field, minding ordinances, and I wept for him. I could scarcely hear above the beating of my own heart when I caught him severing a carcass, not with any of that eager anticipation of pleasure that could make slaughter such a sociable activity, but in strict obedience to prescription – his lips pursed, his knuckles white, his whole frame tensed and tipped, as though the effort of concentration required to celebrate the glory of God in one act of meticulous butchery after another would at any moment prove too much for his balance.

Not that he ever did fall. That capacity for still, self-punishing stupor that had held him ensorcelled in his sea-shells as a child kept him faithful and upright now, no matter how much smoke was blown back into his blackened face.

You are changing colour, I warned him. You were not told you had to sacrifice your fairness to God.

It washes off, he said.

(Of itself, 'it' did not do anything. The washing-off was seen to by my mother.)

You are damaging your skin, I persisted. You are ruining your eyes. You are breathing in filth.

I don't feel damaged, he said.

I'm not talking about what you feel. I know what you feel. I'm talking about what I can see.

You're not, he said. You're talking about what *you* feel.

I was always proud of him when he was clever. And surprised by him. Had he been clever every day I would still have been surprised. He was younger than me. I had watched over him all his life. I had mounted guard over all his intellectual entrances and exits. Whatever was handed to him or taken from him had to pass by me. I checked everything in and out. Hence my surprise when he delivered himself of a thought or an opinion which I had not logged. Family surprise: that ultimately unshakable disbelief in the virtues and intelligence of those to whom you are related, by blood.

I was proud of him, I still maintain, though I can see that my pride was blemished – had it been one of Abel's rams he would not have selected it as an offering to the Lord.

Of course he was right: when I complained of the damage officiation was doing to his health, it was my own health I was thinking of. His conscientiousness made me ill. Not because I saw it as a reproach to my negligence, but because the repetition and monotony of it set up a sort of drone of drudgery around me. Every morning the same carnage, the same terror in his flock, the same roaring and bellowing, the same sour smell of intestines, and the same songs of adoration. Every morning the pall of incense funnelling to the heavens. Every morning the sounds of celestial inhalation, the sniffing of the spheres.

But this regularity of death and prayer, gore and gratitude, constituted only the tangible part of the turmoil to which I was subjected. Worse was the emotional agitation – the mental buzz of faith and worship. I mean the atmosphere of piety, the rapt expressions, the consciousness of grace, those vibrations in the ether – rhythmic and persistent enough to turn your brain – which tell you that spiritual exercise is in train, that callisthenics of the soul are being practised, thunderous in their silence, under your very nose.

So why did I stay to be unnerved? Why did I hover around the service when I could easily have found another and more remote garden to defoliate, and been about my business far from all knowledge, far at least from all witness, of his?

Because I was maddened by his concentration, and galled by how completely it negated my concerns. Do I mean I was jealous of the relations he enjoyed with Him – the great Separater and Divider, of waters and of men? No. Do I mean I was jealous of his freedom from jealousy? No. Do I mean I was jealous of his capacity to *feign* freedom from jealousy? Perhaps I do mean that. But it should be clear by now why I had to stay. Had I decamped in the circumstances that prevailed, it would have seemed like a banishment – him expelling me.

You are in danger, I warned him, of becoming mono-maniacal.

He couldn't hear me.

One of these days you will be sucked up, I said, in your own column of smoke.

He threw me a look, as though to ask, Would that be so bad?

Should I have answered, Yes, it would be so bad, because in that case I would miss you?

It was easy enough for me to imagine him rising, slowly spinning in the eye of a benign tornado. I had been preparing his departure ever since his arrival. There was no form of leaving that I had not rehearsed for him. I knew how he would look drowned, choked, charred, crumbled. I sank him in quicksand, hanged him, starved him, dipped him repeatedly in boiling fat. Ascent was simple to arrange. One, two, three . . . and he was up, his tunic billowing, the soles of his feet foreshortening, losing their definition, losing their graceful incurvations, entering the same plane as the rest of him before disappearing at last into cloud.

This I could do, yet saying I would miss him was beyond me. Ours was not a family that gracefully expressed intimacies. We were harsh, in the image of a God who didn't dare trust His affections.

Anyone would think, I said, that you keep animals only in order to burn them.

Anyone would think you have no sublunary obligations.

Anyone would think you have no one else to talk to.

Anyone would think you have something in particular to thank Him for.

Anyone would think He was the one that carried you in His belly and washes between your toes.

Anyone would think He was the one that watched over you in the night to be sure you were still breathing.

Anyone would think . . .

I kept it up for weeks, months. I squatted in the bloodied dirt, raking the never cold, always crimsoned ashes, pricking the ground with splintered bone, pricking him with the rage of my exclusion.

Anyone would think you were put on earth for no other reason than to spirit yourself off it.

Anyone would think you preferred There to here, Him to us (I didn't risk saying me), Death to life.

Life? The movement of his pale lips was clear in its meaning. Life? Since when was I a champion of that sentimental entity?

Since when? Since yesterday. Since morning. Since that very second. When you are in the business of goading a brother who goads you with silence and self-sufficiency, you have to be opportunistic. If I could rattle him with life, I would not let squeamishness stop me. Besides, I was a lifer in this sense: I abhorred the earth so violently that anything was preferable to the idea of a long lying in it. And life was the sole alternative to death that had so far been granted to our comprehension.

And I wasn't the one doing all the killing.

You have the right to make your own choice, I told Abel, but you oughtn't to be calling one thing another.

He shook his head and sighed one of Eve's dismissive sighs – meaning, I know none of this, and will *have* none of this. Perhaps a sigh is not the word. It was more a tut, a tst, an intake rather than an expulsion of air, a toothy click of habituated scorn which my mother had stealthily tricked us all into learning – a withholding of approbation from a universe that had withheld everything from her. There were sweltering, ungenerous nights when, as a family, we clicked contemptuously at one another, and the only sound to be heard above the hysteria of the hyenas and the chomping jaws of crocodiles was the uninterrupted tst-tst-tst-tst of human contrariety.

Don't pretend you don't know what I'm talking about, I said. One thing is not another. You understand that perfectly well when it comes to what you cook up on your holy altar. You don't lay a thigh of calf alongside a rump of lamb. You don't seethe kid in its own mother's milk. *Habdalah* forbids it. The law of separation says that one thing is not another. Admit that you are butchering not to celebrate life but because you are in the service of death.

I make an offering to express my thanks, he said.

Why can't you express your thanks some other way?

Such as?

Such as by begetting instead of killing. You could twist flowers between your goats' horns and encourage them to increase.

They don't need encouragement.

They don't need depletion.

He came very close to tutting me. Then wiped his eyes instead. I felt sure that underneath the smoke his usual pallor had paled a little more. Although he had set his jaw, his lips would not stay together. Although we never argued, we were arguing.

I don't believe, he finally calmed himself to say, that you are genuinely concerned for my flock. The welfare of my sheep is not what motivates you.

What does?

He didn't want to say. He would have liked to leave it at that. We disagreed. That was all. His mouth was so far out of his control that he all at once reminded me of the manikins my father had manufactured years before, to win back my mother from the shekinah.

I asked again. What does? What motivates me?

He still didn't want to say.

I arched an eyebrow. Small gestures can be as weapons between brothers. He choked me with his white, throbbing lips – those two recalcitrant slugs that could never bring themselves to mate. And I drew blood from him with my quizzing eyebrow.

Very well. All right. I'd asked for it . . .

Greed and envy, he said in a broken voice. And then, more sonorously – Envy and greed.

Greed? (I never saw the point of denying envy. One might as well have denied one breathed.) But greed! What am I greedy with? I asked.

How spiteful he suddenly looked. You are greedy, he said, with whatever's yours.

I laughed. What – my bits of grass and grain? My first-fruits, as our blazing angel of the personal enigma grandly called them? My wheat, my barley, my grapes, my figs, my pomegranates, my olive oil and my honey? Do you suppose I hoard them?

You do not offer them.

Why would I?

As a token that you understand they are His.

If they are His, then He already has them.

He does not have them. He has given them to you.

In order that I should give them back to Him? Here is a fine giving, if the receiver must –

These things are gestural, Cain. The meaning is larger than the act.

Then why are you so punctilious in the act's performance?

To show I value the meaning.

You mean, to show you value the meaning punctiliously.

He had been sharpening his knife on a whetstone the whole time we'd been arguing (except that we never argued), and now he drew the blade across the palm of his left hand. A faint line of red sprang up where it had been. He would sooner hurt himself, I thought, than hurt me.

Do you remember, I asked, how you used to spin shells?

He looked away. I must have too obviously signalled my intentions.

Do you remember, I went on, how you could never be drawn from them? No matter how late it was, or how tired

302

you were, or how much damage you had done to your hands? You were punctilious in the act's performance then. What underlying meaning was there? What lay beneath the act?

There was none, he said. Nothing did.

He was not as good an advocate for himself as I was for him. Of course there was an underlying meaning. He sat in the sand with his shells spinning and his fingers bleeding and the tears running down his baby-blue-veined cheeks because all in all that was a better way of consuming the time than any we'd been able to teach him. He had descended into himself early. I did not rule it out as a possibility that he had opted for his own company (over all others that were offering) in the opening seconds of his conscious life. He tried the muscle first of one misted gelatinous window, and then the other, and saw ... what? Saw me, flaming against his intrusion; saw my father, not knowing where to put his hands or how to frame the words or gestures that denoted welcome; saw – no, sucked upon my mother, and drank therefrom the alternating sweets and bitters of every woman's milk, the surges of wild pride in her instrumentality, the acrid loathing of having been fashioned functional; saw, and heard, the discomposure of the heavens, thrown into havoc by the fear that flesh might again prove devilish or, worse, angelic – saw, sucked, heard all this and plumped without further ado (as who would not?) for an inner rather than an outer life.

He had been absent from the start, that was all I wanted him to admit, no criticism implied. He had been absent from the moment he had decided against being present, and he was still absent, tending his altar, now. We were in a disagreement only over words. I called it absence. He called it worship.

In that case, I said, if the ritual you performed with the shells had no underlying meaning, was performed in the name of nothing but itself, and yet was performed so religiously, does that not lead you to wonder whether you aren't an incorrigible ritualist by nature and would do just as fervently by a pyramid of stones as you do by God, were the stones only to speak out and ask it of you?

He was very angry with me. Posed. Pretty. Sooty. A morsel for a monarch. A Giftling for a God.

You see resemblances where there are none, he said.

Resemblances are all we have to go on, I replied. (For I was young and mad for metaphor.)

Shells are not God, he said.

Then I am holier than you. I think God is everything.

And therefore nothing?

That must follow, I agreed. The earth was without form, and void, when He created it. Therefore He must have had say over the void.

Word games.

Words, too, are among the little that we have, I said. So why not play with them? What else are they for? You refuse the game only because you fear it will demean the object of your ritual. But you're wrong. My reasoning does not lower God, it elevates the shells.

Yes, but to the level of what? Elevate everything and you eliminate all difference between high and low.

What then? Is this not the last goal of worship – that we all aspire and ultimately rise?

If there were nothing base –

Aha, I said. I see, I said. If there were nothing base, there would be nothing noble. So it is still you who passes sentence on what is low in order to protect the status of what is high. You are the one with the poor opinion of the shells, not me.

Why do you keep returning to my shells? To remind me of the difference in our ages?

I couldn't look at him. His face had become pointed, almost like a snout. An animal face, shaped to sniff out insults to itself in loving conversation. I said, I recall the hours you spent spinning because I am fond of the recollection. It also reminds me of how you waste your mornings now. I'm glad you are able to go on abstracting yourself from matters with which you would rather not engage. I don't blame you. I wish I could. But don't speak to me of your thankful spirit or my greed. Compulsive and repetitive behaviour has nothing to do with vice or virtue.

After which there was not much either of us could say to the other for many days, or, if you prefer to count in carcasses, for the time it took to hack and dismember a whole family of spotless ruminants – father, mother, sons, brothers.

Although my parents' zest for helping out with offerings was no longer the eager thing it had been when Saraqael burned among us, keeping us fired with promises of praise that were never once fulfilled, they still welcomed any physical remission from the torpor their unpeopled existence had become. At its best their contribution had always been confined to the associated fuss of burnt-oblation – altar-building, secondary ingredient collection, unspecific all-round encouragement to the officiant (such as washing him) – and these duties they could pick up or leave alone as the fancy took them, without serious consequences for Abel's ministry. He kept brimming oil jars by his altar. And jeroboams of olibanum. And firewood stacked high like the ziggurats of Babel, out-topping conceivable need. He was a priesthood entire unto himself, and had my parents not attended him for a year he would have remitted nothing in his panderings to the Ever Hungry One. But they wanted to feel useful. If Abel noted that his store of flour was running low – that is to say, that in fourteen months, allowing for a plague of rats, it would be gone – my mother hastened to mill him another hundred homers. If he believed it was time to treat Yahweh to a fowl, he had only to mention it and Adam would be off and back again in a trice, with a young pigeon flapping under his great arm, or a turtle dove, which he pretended to have palmed clean out of the air, struggling for breath inside his gown. Off with its head, Abel would say, and my father, wreathed in the smiles of the effective, would attack the bird's neck with his finger-nail until he had severed through to its gullet and windpipe. So adept had he become at this that it takes me longer to say it than it took him to do it. Nip, shriek, smile – not the bird, my father – spurt, and off. By which time Abel was ready with his blessing.

There was not always, though, such a happy meeting of inclination and prescription. Some ceremonies bogged down, grew tense and even argumentative for the simple reason that Saraqael's instructions were not as foolproof as he'd intended them, and left too much scope for that individual interpretation which is the death of all religions. How big a handful, for example, did a handful of fine flour signify? A hand as my father understood and possessed such a measure was not a hand according to my mother's daintier comprehension of the term. And even when agreement had been reached or compromise conceded on the brute issue of size, that still left unresolved the question of whether a handful was a handful heaped or a handful flat.

Do words mean anything or not? my father asked. He sounded exhausted, at his wit's end before the argument had begun.

He took our silence as a signal that we concurred, that words did indeed mean something. Then if the angel had meant flat, he stormed, the angel would have said flat!

And if he'd meant heaped, my mother insisted, he would have said heaped.

My father held out his claw-hammer hands – behold, empty, a reasonable man. Full! he shouted. Hand full!

As a matter of course my mother winced beneath his empty violence. A hateful drooping of the neck and of the spirits, a dumb-show of weariness and martyrdom, but also an indication of adversarious stubbornness, fixed for all time.

Saraqael didn't say hand full, she countered, he said *handful* – there's a difference.

What difference? Show me how it's different.

You know it's different.

Show me – show me how it's different.

She closed her eyes, as though to blind herself to his shouting, since it didn't please the Almighty to make her deaf to it.

It's different, she said, because it implies what a hand can naturally hold, not what a hand can be made to hold. Saraqael – Saraqael, Saraqael, Saraqael: she still had not stopped naming him – Saraqael was not setting us a test. He was not asking you to prove that you can balance half the universe in your hand.

Adam looked to his younger son for a refutation of this. Tell her, his glance implored, tell her that she has never had a single true thought in her life.

But Abel never decided between disputants. He would sooner have plunged up to his shoulders in entrails. I agree with both of you, he said. The ruling's ambiguous.

Adam looked to me, positioned as was my wont now, at a suspicious distance from the altar and its attendants, like a snake outside a ring of fire, contemptuous but transfixed. It must have been an evening service because I remember the sun sitting like a bubble of blood on the point of the grassless mountain my father and I no longer visited. The Creator had taken to stretching out our evenings interminably, pleased with the succulence of what reached Him as long as it stayed light. Sometimes, in order to extend His enjoyment, He would halt the sun in its decline and hurl it back into the sky. On this occasion He kept it bouncing on the pinnacle while we quibbled over flour. You could hear the earth ticking with His waiting. The sky throbbed above us, flecked, taut, attenuated, like a stretched nerve.

My father was still waiting too. Go on – tell her, tell her, tell her she has never once been right . . .

I agree with neither of you, I said. Saraqael, may his name be soon forgotten, said the handful should be brought – that is to say, carried; but you cannot *carry*, without spilling it, an open palmful, heaped or flat. Therefore he must have intended us to understand, whatever can be carried in a closed fist. Not that I care.

A closed fist? My father had never heard anything so ludicrous. A closed fist? What – like one of these!

My mother saw no merit in the suggestion either. She clicked her teeth at me. Treated me to the family jeer. Showed me how my own mouth wanted to go. How it would go if I didn't move heaven and earth to stop it. Closed fist? I'm not having *that*, she said.

Ha, said Adam.

Tst, said Eve.

S . . . nap! went the sky.

Truly, I sometimes think I must have been a messenger from the God of Hymenaic Bliss Himself, so reliably did I harmonize my unhappy warring parents with themselves, with each other, and with short-tempered nature.

And yet they thought Abel was the loving one.

The important thing, he said to me, a week or two after the disagreement over greed and envy we never had – the important thing is to give something away.

I tossed a stone at him. Like that?

Something that's your own.

I plucked a hair from my head. Like that?

Something you value.

I looked about me. You have me there, I said.

I wearied him. He never once began a conversation with me that he did not ultimately regret. He must have vowed a thousand times that he would not speak, or at least not initiate a discussion, again. But I was always able to lure him into talk, though talk was not his medium, by seeming to have mended my ways, by appearing to be curious this time, finally, at last, once and for all, to hear what he had to say. Then the moment he opened his mouth I would look away, feigning boredom or disgust.

It was his discomfiture that I was after. Not because I was callous and enjoyed the sight of suffering, but because his distress was my excuse for remorse. This is what happens when you love your pretty brother to excess: you need to bruise him so that you can kiss him better.

And all the time *he* thought we were discussing God.

What I mean when I say it's important to give something away, he persisted, is that it's necessary to let something go.

What's the difference? (I could sound like my father when I needed to.)

You think I'm talking about making a gift, but actually I'm addressing the idea of release.

From captivity?

In a sense, yes.

Like this bullock you are dismembering –

The bullock doesn't enter into it. What matters is that I'm parting with something, allowing something to be taken from me.

And why does that matter?

Because it accustoms me to the idea that I will be taken myself.

So you're saying that you're practising.

He thought about that, narrowing his vision as though the thing he wanted to say hung like a spider on its thread at the very vanishing point of sight. Seeing how much it hurt him to think was one of the voluptuous pleasures I derived from these encounters.

In a sense, yes, he said. Though it's not dying, exactly, that I'm practising, but diminution. I'm getting used to going, bit by bit.

So young, I said, and yet so morbid. There was, I now acknowledge, flirtation in my tone: the sort of challenge that hopes both to conceal and to reveal admiration. So young and yet so morbid – I could not have wooed more frankly had my brother been my beloved. But then there was no beloved.

Did he flush? Did *this* bring colour at last into his face? It was impossible to tell, so blackened and gory was he from practising his own going on the carcasses of hapless animals. But he did not accept the charge of morbidity. Not at all, he said. It is not morbid to prepare for death in life. You're the morbid one, fearing dying so much that life which must end in dying disgusts you.

One thing is not another, I said. Like and unlike are better kept separate.

You said that last time. And you are right – life is not death. But neither are they complete strangers to each other. If we can allow a little death in life –

Then we may look forward to a little life in death? Is this why you burn meat – in the hope of striking an advantageous bargain? O Lord, who seest how I stalk among the dead in life, please grant that I may move among the living in death.

I saw him struggle with the disposition of his mouth, but there was nothing he could do against its ugly will. The corners dropped. The bottom lip skidded off the top. His jaw lurched. I wondered if he meant to daub me with the marks of greed and covetousness again, but he surprised me – instead, he dipped his reeking fingers into veins of family history that were never opened.

It's not your fault, he said, that the sin to which your birth is attributed is payable with mortality. It's not your fault. I don't blame you. You are a child of death and cannot bear what you brought into the world with you. It's not my connection to death that is morbid, it's yours.

I stared at him. Didn't I say he was clever? I stared at him for so long and with such admiration that the heavens began to fear seriously for their supper. The hills rumbled. The horizon, which had turned so blue recently with gratitude that we thought we could actually see sea beyond it, snapped shut against the sky, squeezing whatever clouds were trapped between into a grey dyspeptic dust.

A lick of flame, like a cat's tongue, passed across the face of the sun.

Thank your towers that you do not get to see much of the sun in the late hungry afternoon. We had no such protection. Short of lying belly down on the squirming earth and covering our heads with dust, we knew of no system for blinding ourselves to its voraciousness. We watched it boil. We watched it swell. We watched it pulse like an angry throat, or sometimes fall open, indolently, as though put to sleep, sent into a pre-dinner doze, by its own expenditure of heat and energy.

I was caught between radiances – my brother's cleverness, the sun's angry insatiable repletion.

I'll tell you what, I told my brother, I'll go and roast some grain . . .

But I put it in the form of a proviso. I'd roast some grain, provided he thought that was a good idea, provided he'd love me for it, provided he'd withdraw the charge of morbidity, provided he'd *ask* me to roast some grain . . .

Not a word from him. What I did I was to do for myself.

I'll tell you what, I told the sun, I'll go and roast some grain for you.

Heavenly bodies are not as proud as brothers. Hearing food mentioned, the sun flicked out its cat's tongue once more, and licked the blood that was running from its eyes.

Saraqael had been airy on the subject of grain-offering. Half-hearted, uncommunicative, mealy.

It hadn't seemed to matter to him whether the offering was roasted, baked on a griddle, poached, stewed or fried, so long as it was made of the finest flour, patted into cakes or wafers – he didn't say what size – and kept free of leaven and honey. I took the casualness to be a proof both of the contempt in which my produce was held – though I could scarcely argue against that, since it had been grown in contempt – and of God's overwhelming preference for flesh. I could scarcely argue against that either. Who would want to clog up his gums with grainy biscuits, lacking all pleasing consistency and sweetness, when the alternative was lamb or veal, spitted with adoration over charcoal – skin, fat, marrow, innards and all.

I had no argument but nor did I have any feeling for the job. You cannot cook enthusiastically for an unenthusiastic Diner. He – HE – didn't care, and therefore I didn't care. Was this not mutuality?

Of course it could be argued, and no doubt was argued, that He, who knew everything in advance, only didn't care *because* He knew I wouldn't care. Looked at from His point of view, what was the point of licking His lips in anticipation of oatcakes more succulent than the breast of dove when it was written in flaming letters across the firmament that nothing that came from my oven would be worth the eating? The argument goes on and on. Why should I have tried to care when I knew that He already knew that I would not succeed? On and on. It would have been better for Him, and better for all of us, had He relinquished His advantage and walled off the future from Himself as well. Had I not known I was predictable to Him, I might not at last have said, So be it, have it Your own way, I will do what You always intended me to do.

But nothing, I fear I must admit, would ever have changed my attitude to cake-making. We were not a family that made efforts around food. What fell from a tree we ate. If quail appeared out of the sky, at more or less the time we were getting hungry, and landed in our fire – well, we could persuade ourselves to nibble at the bones. Otherwise it was whatever happened to be sticking out of the ground within reach of where we sat. We weren't pernickety, we simply lacked – until

Abel's conversion – any instinct for personal ceremonial. We didn't know how to commemorate our daily existence and make it graceful for ourselves. We didn't value our functions sufficiently. But then how could we, given the small confidence we inspired in the Mind that had concocted us.

I wish I didn't have to say it, but not everything can be blamed on Him – the Big *F*. My smaller effed father must bear some responsibility. He fed himself standing up, ate and drank while he was building rafts or perfecting sleight of hand, and understood communality only as an opportunity for him to show the rest of us what he could do. And my mother was no better. She had had her hour of grandeur when the Divine Light had shone on her and posted feathered messengers to whisper ineffabilities in her ear; thereafter everything was stale and wretched. What daily beauty, other than Abel's limbs, did she have to solemnize? For her, too, the breaking of bread with dear ones was a tiresome rite, perfunctorily observed. A nuisance comparable with having to rise, bathe, dress and present herself to an empty world.

So I lacked example and training. And I lacked will. Any sort of manufacture that did not in some way diminish or deny God's plan for nature exhausted me. Making mutants in my garden was energizing; it filled me with the conviction of noble purpose: nothing less than the creation of an antithetic pygmy continent. I would have thrown myself similarly into the construction of a city, a Babel built above the very mud from which my father had been ignominiously pulled. As long as there was labour of contradiction to be done, I believed I could draw on almost limitless reserves of vitality. There was nothing contradictory, though – unless I poisoned them – about cakes. However plain and undelightful, however bitter to the tongue or tormenting to the teeth, a cake was still a celebration of God's foison. And, not being a poisoner, or a foisoner, I could not find the heart to bake one.

*

Abel looked amused to see me. Seriously amused. He had raked out his altar, laid a new griddle across it, and removed all traces of flesh from its vicinity. A cursory glance told me there were no spots of blood in the dust, no splashes on the nearby rocks. Had he gone down on his hands and knees to wash them off?

I knew who had gone down on her hands and knees to wash him. His skin still hummed from the friction. He was wearing one of his shorter, more skittish tunics – the sort that made angels blush – and I could see red blotches on his thighs, tell-tale signs that somebody loved him.

I was struck again by what a beautiful feature it was, how bewitchingly agonized it made him look – his lips being the same colour as his face. A vermilion mouth might be voluptuous, but a white one whispers of far subtler pleasures, far more excruciating pains.

Well? He was impatient, waiting for me to show him what I carried in my hands, the tray of sacramental cakes, hidden behind my back. Well?

Well? I mimicked, affecting not to understand his curiosity. Where was the harm in a little torment. Especially when the object of it was framed in every pore to be a tormentor himself. Wandering blue eyes. Lips not quite a pair. Skin so fine you believed you could kiss holes in it. Where was the harm. *Well?* Well what?

Would he approach and pull at my concealing arms? Would he run around and circumvent my surprise? Would we tumble to the ground, laughing? Did we have it in us, we two, to gambol?

He stood still. Colourless. Worn out with my teasing already, although I had hardly begun.

What a lovely evening it is, I said, nodding to the distant hills (because of course I could not point with my baker's hands behind my back), where God had chosen to flatter our seeing with the prospect of ocean. Ocean the colour of cobalt, and, on some days, if we strained our eyes, surf the colour of milk.

This softening of our landscape had been going on ever since the departure of Saraqael, and the erection of Abel's altar. We had gone to sleep with the smell of slaughter on the wind and risen to find the desert . . . lawn. Trees with scabrous, armoured bark vanished in the night; in their place more benign and musical vegetation – oaks and cypresses, as I was content to call them, having lost my zeal for naming at about the time I lost my foreskin. Beetles and reptiles were not to be got rid of so easily – at any time a new species more horrendous than the last would conceive itself out of urine and manure, snorting, crackling, feeding on its own obscene pupae – but gentler creatures began to appear too, crane flies and ladybirds and crawlers of such limpidity that you could see the sun and God's weightless beneficence through them.

All this because He loved praise.

Hear my prayer, O Lord, sang Abel, twice a day, as the spitting fat and the frankincense rose in an undeviating pillar. *O Lord my God, who coverest thyself with light as with a garment: who stretchest out the heavens like a curtain: who layeth the beams of his chambers in the waters* – and lo! the drapes of heaven parted with a movement like the billowing of Abel's vestures when I imagined him God-bound, and waters that had not been there the day before swallowed light as though it were a spring of crystal. Swallowed it and blew it back again, so that one could not say whether the beams fell or rose. There were moments when the sea, or whatever it was that teased us at the far blue edge of vision, seemed to flutter garments of its own, and thence send light streaming to the heavens.

What love between the water and the sky! What orchestrated reciprocity! Moved to melting, my father's mountain – my mountain – flamed yellow, caught its breath – though we'd been there and knew it had no lungs – and seemed to lose its head for heights.

O Lord, who laid the foundations of the earth – and lo! those foundations themselves swooned and tottered, and it was as if a golden light whose centre was the centre of the world would take us all – sea, sky, mountains, Abel, seasoned carcass, desert laid to lawn, even me – into an embrace of everlasting molten joy.

All this because He loved praise.

My praise – What a lovely evening – was as swoony as I could make it. Totterer's praise.

Abel said nothing, waiting for me to show my hands.

God's in his heaven tonight right enough, I sighed. Ecstatic. Transported. Out of my skin.

He turned from me, too pettishly, I thought, for one with oblation and psalm-singing on his mind.

I sighed a few more times – Mmm! Aaah! Well, well, well! – then said abruptly, Do you want these cakes or not?

He kept his head averted. Put them on the griddle, he replied.

In any particular sequence? Surely they don't just go *on* the griddle?

Just put them on.

You have to guess which hand.

Come on, he said, the sun is going down.

Does that matter?

It'll soon be dark.

Does that matter? Does God eat only what He can see? And cannot He see, anyway, as keenly as a cat at night?

This was your idea, he reminded me.

We . . . ll, I said, rocking the word in both our favours. It was my idea only to show you that I'm not morbid.

Then put them on the griddle.

Guess which hand.

He said nothing.

Pretend I'm my father! Humour me! Guess which hand!

Right.

Wrong!

Left.

Wrong!

This time he looked up and saw me with both arms outstretched and both hands open – behold, empty, a trivial man.

He shook his head, dispelling anger, sorrowing over me, trying to find some way to bring his lips together.

What man do you know – what boy do you know – who likes to be sorrowed over?

I'm joking, I said – but there was no laughter in my voice. I'm teasing you. Look. I have the dough here. Inside my shirt.

He wouldn't look. Enough jokes.

I mean it, I insisted. I have the dough. A big, fat, round ball of it. Here. Catch.

He swung around and something in the urgency of his movement, something in the clumsy desperation with which he made to catch, clutch, fumble, caused the blood to run cold in my veins. I froze at my extremities, watching him scrabbling in the dirt. Why did he care? What was there in a ball of dough, rolled in anger, thrown with contempt, that ought to have concerned him? A paste ball! What magical properties did it already possess for him, before a fire had been built beneath it, before a blessing had been crooned over it, before it had been smoked and sent on its demeaning errand, that he was prepared to roll around in the dust himself rather than let it lie there unretrieved, unsalvaged, unredeemed?

It is a vile thing to witness agitation, in one you love, caused by a matter you consider trifling. I dropped down with him in the dirt and fought for possession of the ball of oil and flour, besmirched now, blemished, fouled, made forever filthy and unfit. It was difficult not to overwhelm him. He wouldn't fight me. How could he? I had watched over his cradle, making sure his heart worked.

I left him on the ground, unharmed, and busied myself unnaturally at his altar. I didn't look at him. I prepared the fire, lit it, shaped what was left of my unleavened cake mix into ten round wafers and arranged them on the griddle.

When he came at me he had the advantage of surprise, but not strength. He was too finely made.

You mustn't, was all he said.

I held him off, my first concern being my offering which was now hallowed by struggle no less than sacrifice. Not only was it a gift against my nature, it was an offertory against my brother. We were both on that griddle. I hoped the gesture would be well received.

You mustn't, he said again. And this time put his hands on me. It had been years since I'd last been rough with him. And now that I was rough with him again I discovered that I'd missed it, that it was no way for brothers to be, keeping each other at arm's length, not touching, not fighting, not arguing, just silently denying each other's right to be. We should have got to grips physically more often. It should have been ordinary with us, commonplace, an unexceptional event. Then we might have known better how to go about it. Might have found the sensuousness of it more resistible, less of a luxury.

All right – *I* might. It was on me that the charm of novelty fell. I smelled his bathed skin. I smelled his fear. I smelled his likeness to me. It's always possible that I smelled his hatred and took it for something else. Hatred is the chameleon of scents and to survive must pass as bergamot or attar. When I pulled him close, I couldn't be certain he was not my father, not my mother, not myself. Get very close and you lose a person altogether. This is universally true, but in my brother Abel's case there is also his delicate framework to take into account. He almost fell apart in my arms. And when I began to punch him, not hard but persistently, first on one shoulder, and then another, first on this side, then on that, all that was ponderable in him, all that gave him weight – and all that lent density to his whiteness, all that was silver, all that was milk – fled his body.

I held him so that he shouldn't fall or float away, and so that I could go on rhythmically striking him. Getting the rhythm right seemed to be important. It needed to be the rhythm of speech. A duplication of the patterns which I knew dispirited him. This was just talk, I must have wanted him to know. A continuation of our argument. The argument we never had.

I had to take him round the waist at last, supporting his spine for fear that, as he could not fall on me, he might choose the other way to go and break backwards. His face was tight against mine. Or at least someone's face was. The lips twisted in what looked like the old family jeer – triumph when no issue had been contested, stealing what had been freely given – and more teeth showing than I cared to see. Marvellous, how teeth can express despair. The eyes were open but blank. No one's eyes that I recognized. A bad odour came from him, whoever he was.

I let him go and he fell easily, almost comfortably, crumpling from the middle, his ankles crossed. I turned to my unleavened cakes but they were black and fuming, like the droppings of those three-eyed amphisbaenae that used to groan and vomit themselves into being in the days when the Lord had even less control over Creation than He did on this wild flaming yellow evening, painted to harmonize us with Grandeur.

A bad odour came from the altar too.

I looked back to Abel. I wanted to say, I hope you are pleased with yourself. But was so ashamed of him for lying there without weight or pigment, without fight, only a grimace of absurd concentration on his face, as though he were taking advantage of this quiet time to make his devotions, to give thanks where all his senses should have told him no thanks were owing; I was so angry with him for his compliancy, and so humiliated by his exposure, that I began to shovel debris on him, just dust at first, just grit and pebbles that I could kick, but then shale and flakes of slate, flint, chippings from the clumsy slabs of stone quarried by my father in slavish obedience to Saraqael's instructions for a sacrarium and slaughter table.

A great dust rose from where he lay, as desolate as his altar. I could not penetrate it to see what damage I had done until the sun dropped like a stone itself into the earth, and a wind, smelling of salt desert, of drifting sand, of distance, blew the air from red to purple. I knelt by him and wiped the gravel from his eyes. His body had taken the main force of my attack; the only disfigurement to his face was a small cut running across his cheek like a broken vein. The idea that I had punctured his skin upset me more than any thought of what I had done to his bones. I couldn't *see* his bones.

I cleaned the cut and then sat him up, putting my head to his chest as I had done for nights without number, crouched over his sleeping form, listening to the evenness of his breathing, keeping him from harm – but on this night there was no breathing to be heard.

Not from him, not from anything.

16. A HIGH-MINDED OFFER

A short interval.

When they are greatly amused, or sorely distressed – and they are not always certain of the difference – audiences in Babel find that it settles their nerves to break, briefly, for refreshment and perambulation. A glass of iced water or sherbet, a turn beneath the steadying Babel moon, a quick exchange of pleasantries with friends, and they are once again ready to be entertained.

For those who prefer to stay in their seats and mop their foreheads with their sleeves, a divertissement is normally provided, not necessarily balletic, but always musical, light in spirits, and ironical if only by virtue of its incongruity to the main event.

Just like Naaman himself.

'Going well,' he says to Cain, off-stage.

Cain nods.

'Oatcakes!' Naaman shakes his head, has difficulty containing all the mirth that is in him. 'Oatcakes! Wicked!'

Cain stares ahead.

'So,' says Naaman, as though Cain's determination to make merry cannot be allowed to hinder the discussion of more serious matters indefinitely, 'So, you are almost finished. You must be relieved.'

'Were it not that the end is always a prelude to another beginning, I would be. As it is –'

'Of course, of course,' says Naaman. 'Goes without saying.

But presumably you'll be taking a rest. A deserved rest, if I may say.'

'I have no specific plans,' says Cain. 'Naturally, I mean to discuss further engagements and other locations with you.'

Naaman puts his hand on Cain's shoulder. A gesture implying willingness, concurrence, expansiveness beyond the scope of words. What he next says is so by-the-by, so much in the nature of an afterthought, that were he and Cain not such good friends he would probably not even bother to mention it. 'This tower of yours –'

'What tower of mine?'

'This temple or whatever that you have a mind to rent or build or ruminate a while in . . .'

Cain risks continuing with not knowing what Naaman is talking about.

'My daughter,' says Naaman, not hiding that this is difficult for him, and not hiding that he is not grateful to Cain for making it so, 'my daughter assures me that possession of an edifice enjoying elevation and solitude has long been an ambition of yours. I may have something that will answer.'

'It has never been my intention,' Cain says, 'to climb on another man's shoulders. If your daughter has told you I seek altitude for its own sake – to secure a view or to proclaim my eminence – she has either misled you or misunderstood me. I am not looking for a pedestal to perch on. I do, however, frequently think of a monument to my brother which will also serve as a resting place for myself.'

Naaman thinks Cain is too touchy for his own or for anybody else's good, and wonders how his daughter . . .

'I understand,' he says, 'I understand. A man cannot be too prudent or too premature in the arrangements he makes for his retirement. And as I say, I may have something that will answer.'

'My expectation has been to build my own.'

'I never knew,' says Naaman, 'that you were an engineer.'

'I am not, though of course my father –'

'Or a mason.'

'I am not.'

'Or an architect.'

'I am not. But expertise of these kinds can be bought.'

'Why bother? Why pay their prices? There is a ziggurat at the southern end of the city, on the road to Larsa, on which work has been languishing for a while – don't ask me why – priestly wranglings, I suppose. I can't recall which god it is consecrated to, if any, but there would be no objections to you making it over to your own, or to yourself if you prefer. We are easygoing about such things here, as you know. I can't vouch for what state it's in, but I'm told the foundations have been dug, and if I'm not mistaken there is even a storey or two completed. You do the rest. Build as high as your fancy or your ambition takes you.'

'I am not an engineer,' Cain reminds him.

'You don't need to be. The city's full of them. And one's bound to be on the site anyway. Asleep, but on site. All you'd have to do is see he stays awake.'

'I am to be a sort of foreman?'

'Nnnn . . .' Naaman squeezes his womanly lips together. Foreman is not the word he would use.

'Caretaker, then?'

Naaman still isn't happy. He likes to be precise about these things. Clear from the beginning. He lays a finger along the bridge of his nose, drops an eye, pops his cheeks. At last the imp of acuity can be seen dancing again across his face. 'I have it,' he says. 'Presiding genius.'

Cain decides against asking the reason for Naaman's liberality. Or his mirth. But he does have one question: 'May I take time to consider this?'

Naaman appears nonplussed. Is he not offering Cain the painless realization of the foremost of his desires? Naturally, he is too gracious even to think of pointing this out. 'Heavens, yes,' he says instead, after a pause. 'Tell me later this evening – after you have finished burying your brother.'

The briefest silence between them. Nothing threatening to good relations.

'By time,' Cain says, 'I did mean something more like weeks.'

Naaman's long, lovely hands, smelling of camphor and camomile, appear once more, as though they have flown there, on Cain's shoulder. Cain knows he must not inhale, must think of the smell of sea or snow, if he is not to swoon.

'I think things have to be settled sooner than that,' Naaman says.

Cain wonders where the hurry is, given that the ziggurat is and has been lying idle for some time, and no god is thundering for its completion. 'Things?' he queries.

Naaman sighs. It is the sigh of a man who would much rather smile. Why do you make me do this, the sigh says, when our natural medium, you and I, is laughter? Naaman himself says, 'This business over the poet puts pressure on all of us.'

Cain is aware of the business he is referring to. News of Preplen's mishap has not exactly ripped through the city of Babel like wildfire – Shinarite consciences would rather be touched by romance than reality, by princes than by poets who sing satirically of princes – but he has heard it carelessly brought up, sometimes as an example of the increasing hazardousness of the streets, sometimes with a fatalism he would feel to be callous, were he in the business of feeling anything about it at all. 'Too bad . . . but they come here to escape from worse . . . and given how fast they breed one less is hardly a catastrophe . . .'

Cain cannot swear that this is what he has heard. He fears it is not impossible he is hearing with Preplen's ears. The market places of Shinar rejoicing over his demise . . . the heathen populace of Babel deaf to the orphaned cries of Jabal, Jubal, Tubal, Gether and Mash, the widowed wails of Nanshe/Naomi, marooned without a helmsman in her furniture

... or worse, or better, bent on refilling his shrine to Law and Family with feathers, bones and partridge semen – why, not in his blackest, happiest hours could Preplen have arranged himself a more exemplary final outcome. 'See!' Cain can picture him rejoicing, his neck twisted away from a sky he no longer has to scan for ill-intentioned birds, 'see what I told you! Next time it'll be you. Since you don't intend to struggle, since you're convinced they love you really, at least be certain you're bathed and barbered for them when they come.'

It is in order not to attend to Preplen's vindicated voice that Cain remains unsure what sentences he has heard uttered in the streets. He would not want to swear that he has heard what he has heard. But then again he would not want to swear that he has not.

In this way he substitutes a lesser equivocation for a greater – concedes confusion of the senses rather than the affections.

But if he is unsure what he's sure of, he is at least sure of what he isn't. He isn't sure of the implication for *him* of Preplen's decease, and isn't sure of its bearings here, now, on Naaman's offer of a place of high retreat. Unless Naaman means to round up for their own safety those who may be thought to be in comparable danger of attack – Preplen's . . . Preplen's what? . . . Kind? . . . Tribe?

Cain shakes the idea from his mind. What's he to Preplen!

'I do not see,' he says, 'how the business of the poet affects me or the timing of my decision.'

Naaman does not want to enter into this. How can he communicate to Cain his extreme unwillingness and fatigue? How can he express his indifference to the niceties of detail and contingency? 'Look,' he says, falling heavily against Cain, as though himself pushed by the shoulder of confidentiality – 'you know what rumour is. You, above all people, know how stories start. If I tell you there are one or two abroad who think they saw you, or your shadow, at more or less the time, in more or less the vicinity, looking more or less intent . . .'

Does he have to go on? Does he need to say more about the variable surmises of approximate attestants?

'Saw me?'

'Saw you ... saw your shirt ... saw the soles of your sandals ...'

Something returns to Cain. A recollection he would as soon dispel, of waking naked in a filthy room, hungry in a house where there was only God to eat.

Even to himself he will not name Sisobk. And what then is he to plead to Naaman? The impertinence of the imputation? The wild irresponsibility of the slander? Is he to say, 'Who? Me? A murderer!'

Naaman is relieved to see that Cain has fallen quiet. He doesn't believe his nerves would stand for noisy protestations. 'As you must have noticed, we set no limits to ambition in the construction of our temples,' he says. 'You are welcome to build to whatever height you have a head for. Make a name for yourself. Pierce the heavens.'

17. Cain Accepts the Protection
of Y-H-W-H

The ravens came.

We sat so quietly, my brother Abel and I, that they dared approach us, their hop hideous, their eyes scorched with greed.

We had heard bad things of ravens. They had so little regard for one another, were so disgusted by the idea, let alone the fact, of their own propagation that they mated contemptuously, the male impregnating the female orally, by firing spittle in her mouth. They were also envious to their souls. Hence their foolish gait. Jealous of the graceful deportment of other birds, they had lost whatever was natural to themselves in a scramble of inept mimicry – now trying to strut like an ostrich, now trying to make an entrance like a swan.

Let the raven be a lesson to you, Saraqael had warned us bitterly, as though he were in competition with the birds himself: Be satisfied with what you have, however little, or you shall lose even that in vain hankerings and preposterous emulation.

With such words do angels of the Lord ensnare the ingenuous into contentment.

In corroboration of this truth, a raven met me, eye to eye. Envious bird to envious brother. Reluctant propagator to one who could not be certain he was meant to propagate at all.

Why, if my eye was open, the raven wondered, was I sitting quite so still?

In order, I answered, not to spill my brother.

The raven dropped his head on to one shoulder and eyed me with horizontal scorn.

He knew something about death I didn't. But then so did the meanest maggot I trod on in my garden. We had no experience of it among ourselves. No one had lectured us on the subject. No one had said whether we were built to go the way of Abel's flock – a bleat, a gush of blood, and then up in smoke to please the nose of God; or whether life would drip out of us, in a crimson trickle, like wine from a punctured wineskin. We had been left untutored in mortality. I held Abel hushed and moveless in my arms to keep the life steady and irreducible within him.

The sky would not progress into darkness. The sun had gone, but everything else – moon, stars, wind, the black that normally superseded purple – hung in a suspense that was more respectful than expectant. An evening such as this, perhaps this very evening exactly, had been long awaited. And eventuation commands deference. A ghastly, formal surprise-lessness spread inexorably into every corner of the night, like a last reprimand to doubters, like a proof too damning to be questioned, like the final reassertion of absolute power.

Only the ravens wondered what the long lingering of half-light held for them.

In time – although all usual measurement of time had stopped – the raven to whom I had confessed my ignorance of death began scratching in the soil. I took him to be after worms or shard beetles or some other vileness mirroring the mind of God, but conscientiously though he clawed, he never once looked to see what he'd unearthed, never once removed his gaze from mine. His expression was serious, reflective, fretful, not lacking in rapacity but requiring me to grasp that rapacity was not the first and last of his character. I also have it in me to be of use, the eye said. I am the enemy of angels, just like you. Learn, then, from me. Scratch, scratch, scratch as I do, and all may yet be well.

It was only then that it occurred to me that I had done something that needed to be hidden. Did I suppose, with the whole of heaven watching, that I could conceal my brother, as the bird advised, and go on as though nothing out of the ordinary had happened? Of course not. I knew how comprehensively I'd been observed. But I had at last to put Abel down. My arms were tired. He was tired. It was necessary that I lay him somewhere. And while I believed I was ready to withstand whatever questions the Holy Inquisitor was soon to hurl at me, I felt less confident about meeting the wailings of my mother and father. I could not say to them, as I could to Him, this is Your doing, for the reason that they were His doing too.

It was from them I had to hide Abel.

But I could not lay him in the earth.

The raven's eye grew more livid. Scratch, it said, scratch if you value your immunity. Scratch if you value your good name. But how was I to tell a raven that I could no more claw the earth with my fingers than I could receive spittle from his throat?

Scratch, scratch, said the raven.

I cannot, replied the man.

Then my friends and I will do it for you, coward, scoffed the bird.

We sat in unblinking silence, we two brothers, and watched the ravens excavate. Their envious natures made them competitive. Jealous of the sharpness of one another's beaks, they attacked the ground as though it were their enemy, perforating the soil with a ferocity that must have made the writhing worms beneath fear Armageddon had begun. We sat as still as owls, smelling dung and loam, listening to the breaking of beetles' backs, the splintering of shields and shells, the juicy skewering of slugs. Until at last there was a shallow trench the size – the length and depth, the shape – of Abel.

Lay him down, said the raven.

I shook my head.

Lay him in, said the raven.

I shook my head.

Lay him on his back, so that he can look up towards the sky, said the raven, and we will cover him, my friends and I.

Only if you promise he will always see the sky, I said. Only if you promise you will never turn him over.

Trust us, said the raven. Lay him down, lay him in, lay him on his back, and we will hide him.

And so I did. And so they did. But the moment there was no more of him above ground – not one straggling hair remaining, no cruelly broken bone, no gentle outline showing through impressionable soil – I remembered I had failed to show a brother's love, had not put my ear to his breathing in the one hour above all others when it mattered that my hearing should be infallible. Where had been the use of all those years of vigil if I were to prove careless now?

The ravens read my mind. Nothing is ever lost on the envious. For envy is the engine of intelligence. They hopped around the perimeter of the grave they'd made and dared me to unmake it. Scratch here, they said, and we will requite you, claw for claw.

I outstared and outwaited them. Disgusted by their own company, they grew impatient for the night that would not come, began to fear that elsewhere there were other birds doing better out of the interminable suspension of darkness than they were, and one by one – all except my bird – hobbled off, broken-footed and crooked-spirited, to sink their sight, if not their claws, into whatever thing they'd missed.

But when I raked the earth for Abel, he too was no longer there, and the soil was not warm from where he'd been.

Was this how we died? Did the ground below the ground open wide its mouth to receive our bones and swallow down our blood? Were we not available to be visited? Had I seen the very last of Abel?

The bird squinted at me, still astonished by how little I knew.

I called to God: Where is Abel my brother?

All at once the darkness which had been held in an unbearable abeyance, like thunder that would not break, fell around me. All shapes vanished. All solidity dissolved. There was no separating me from the blackness. It was as if space itself had been swallowed, just like my mother's other child, in a single gulp. Only the raven's eye gave out light.

I cried: What have You done? Where is my brother?

And God answered through the bird, saying: 'Wouldst thou dare call unto Me! What hast *thou* done? The voice of thy brother's blood have I listened to, and thy brother's generations which thou hast denied. For their sake have I done what I will never again do, and opened the earth's stomach to receive him. But thee will I not receive.'

Am I, of all people, not to be told what You have done with him? I demanded of the Lord. Am not I my brother's keeper?

The livid eye narrowed and flashed, like a blade piercing the blanket of the night. The beak snapped shut, as though upon a fly, and then creaked open – a rusted gate emitting rusted sounds.

'Thou couldst not keep what thou wert given, Cain. Instead thou didst what thou now must name. Speak it: What thou hast done!'

How far back, I wondered, how far back into the history of doing would He allow me to go. Against just such a question as He had put to me, delivered in just such a voice at just such an hour, I had long prepared my answer: Lord, I have done what You fashioned me to do. But I did not have the courage for it now, face to face with the dishevelled raven, blacker than the night wherein I stood and quaked, alone. Instead, I said: Lord of the World, for Whom the whereabouts of the finest grain of sand is certain knowledge, Who cannot be surprised by any thought, of whatever monstrous growth or vile complexion, that flowers in the mind of man – why do You ask to hear what You already know? You knew my deed before I did. Is it out of cruelty that You would make me name it?

'There is less cruelty, Cain, in owning to the crime than in committing it.'

There was no cruelty, I protested, in its committal.

'Thou wilt not dare to say there was kindness?'

Would I dare?

Towards him I did not feel anything that was cruel, I said. If there was cruelty in my heart, my brother was not the reason it was there.

'Thou wilt not dare to say he merely came, by ill-chance, between thee and thine unhappiness?'

Would I dare?

Lord, my unhappiness was great, I said, and had many teeth. But I loved my brother and always wished him whatever the opposite is of harm.

'Thou wilt not dare to say thou art a thing of love?'

Would I dare? I *was* a thing of love. The word itself had been my undoing from the moment I coined it. *Love* – it was giddying just pronouncing it. It did not even try to conceal its delusiveness. You tasted its hollowness before you tasted its fruit. That was its nature. That was its purpose. To put an illusion of substance around a sensation of emptiness. But did I dare to say this? No, I dared nothing. The argument with the Lord which I'd rehearsed a hundred multiplied by a hundred times did not proceed as I'd imagined it. He did not find my reasoning as incontrovertible in actuality as He had during practice. He took less time to weigh the gravity of what I said. Left no room, in His replies, for counter-retorts or controversy. And had the advantage of commanding a time and place that were His choosing, not mine.

As for the bird, here too He had the beating of me. Whenever I spoke, the raven fell into an attitude of derision: hopped from one leg to another, clawed its throat, or collapsed, as though its wings were broken, a misshapen thing with no life left in it, like my brother.

I dared nothing.

I am sorry, Lord, I said. I repent me, Lord, I said. I am nothing, Lord, I said.

A little of the tautness went out of the night. Infinitesimally, the hands that stretched the blackness loosened. There was contrition in the air, and God breathed it.

I postponed a bitter thought, for the hours of vacancy which were to come. It was: He is making me do with words what I refused to do with cereal. I have gained nothing, then, by my stubborness. Unless the loss of everything can be accounted a gain.

Another version, both more and less flattering to me, of that same thought: I am saying what I do not feel in order to escape the earth to which I have consigned my brother. If I can dissemble now, why did I not do it sooner?

I waited, cowed, thinking only of myself even as I denied myself . . . to hear my sentence.

'A fugitive and a wanderer shalt thou be.'

How bad was that? It did not *seem* bad. I had to repress a sudden urge to laugh. What, do You call this a punishment, I wanted to cry out. Do You mean to pay me out with fugacy and exile, even though my transgression was itself a sort of flight? Do You suppose that turning me from Your sight will hurt me, when I have never once found blessing or consolation in Your Shining Countenance? Will You visit me with like for like and call it vengeance? My laughter was ready to tip over into tears. Was this the only justice my poor brother could look forward to? Was this *all*?

The realization that had I been God I would have punished me more cruelly, emboldened me. It is hardly any time, I said, to You it must seem no more than the interval between sleeping and waking, since You expelled my mother and my father from eternal happiness. Out of a family of four, this is now three of us that You have exiled. Truly it will be said of You that You know no other way but to banish.

The raven twisted its neck and closed its eye. In the momentary extinction of its light I could just discern the outline of the bird, black as righteousness, more ragged than revenge. 'Dost thou tempt Me to another way?' it said.

I am in the great hand of Thy Mercy, Lord, I answered.

'What wouldst thou encourage me to do – shed blood for blood? Slay as thou hast slain?'

Your sentence, Lord, I said, amounts to as much. If banishment from my family does not kill me, then some strong stranger's arm, seizing the opportunity of my uncertainty and homelessness, surely will.

'I will set a sign upon thee, Cain, so that whosoever killeth thee . . .'

I waited for Him to finish. Inadvertently, speaking only the fears to which I was prey, I had laid a trap for Him, simple enough though it was to detect – faggots of brushwood merely, camouflaging a lime pit beneath. But a God when he stumbles falls as clumsily as a bear.

These whosoevers, I inquired, that may not smite me unless they would pay sevenfold for their guilt – where will they come from if Adam and Eve and their one remaining son are the sole inhabitants of this earth which You alone worded out of chaos? Are there then others who suffer the same delusion of exclusivity that we do? Is there another Abel, perfuming the air with olibanum? Another Cain, on his knees with grief? How many, O Lord, are the children of Thy Choice?

The little tautness that had gone out of the night returned to it. The fingers that stretched the blackness stiffened.

'Thou speakest jealously, Cain.'

I did not dare say: I acquired my jealousy from You.

'Thou art jealous even of those thou canst not see.'

I did not dare say: How is that worse, Lord, than being jealous of those of whom You know the beginning and the end?

'Thy jealousy will be a greater punishment to thee than thy banishment.'

I did not dare say: And there will come a time when the undeviating worship You jealously exact will sicken You; when the thousand times a thousand roasted rams will stink in Your nostrils; and the rivers of oil will drown every pleasure You once took in our vain oblations.

Where is the use of prophesying punishments? Man or God, we will die of too little devotion, or too much. Think punitively and there are no acquittals. Abel himself had not escaped, lying cradled in the earth for ever – lying cradled *somewhere* for ever – with the shame of being the first to inspire murderousness, and the shame of being the first to submit to it.

My own punishment, I told God, was already more than I could bear.

I was just beginning to understand it. The pleasure I had taken in my unknowing cunning, trapping a confession of moonlighting out of the Most High, had obscured the true import of His intentions for me. 'I will set a sign upon thee,' He had said, and only now did His meaning dawn on me. He would not emblazon a letter upon my brow – that would have looked too much like magic. His hatred of the necromantic arts saved me, likewise, from horns or tusks or other disfigurements spectacular enough to freeze the blood of an attacker or excite a dangerous curiosity in an audience. The sign He spoke of was itself a sign, a trick of speech to trick one who overvalued speech, a manner of speaking which, once spoken, could not fail to hold a dreadful fascination for me. I was marked, that was what it came to, marked out, marked against, marked down, a man of mark, a man beside the mark . . .

. . . a marked man.

He knew my nature. How could He not? He knew that one who had named himself apart would never be able to resist the lure of actual, spatial, geographical separation; but the naming, this time, had been done by Him, making me a thing separate from everybody, and everything, *but* Him. I was *His* – that was what the sign amounted to. I was to experience the circumambience of His supremacy as no one else ever had. I was to comprehend the preponderance of His Word as no one else ever would.

Did I think I knew anything yet of the inescapability of the Lord? I knew no more of it than the stones I'd kicked on Abel knew. This was His promise, His lenience to me:

'A wanderer and a fugitive shalt thou be, but I shall follow thee all the days of thy life; and it shall be in thine heart as though MY NAME burns across thy forehead.'

My punishment, I said, is greater than I can bear.

'Bear it,' said the bird.

A silvered light, as horrible as dawn, began to pull at the frayed edges of the night. Another day. All at once I was very tired. I needed to sleep or I needed to see Abel, or I needed to do both. My father would already be awake, dematerializing matter, working towards his illusion to end illusions, when the abundant breeding world itself would pass from his right hand to his left hand and thence melt away altogether. In no one's sight – for no one's pleasure – but his own. My mother would still be in her bed, coiled against the blow in certain expectation of which she expended all her days.

I sat upon a stone, holding my face between my hands, listening to her calling to me. *Cain ... Cain ...* My name round as a pebble in her mouth. My anger soothed before it had exploded. My crimes forgiven before I was a criminal. Had she ever called to me like this in reality, or was it a dream? Did I have a mother only in my head? Could I carry her with me, therefore, and by the same token leave myself behind?

'Cain ... Cain ...' This time a real voice spoke – jealous

God through jealous bird – saying: 'Arise and go.'

And I looked into the raven's eye, scorched with disgust and greed, and I arose and went.

18. LAST WORDS

'A hit!' exclaims Naaman. 'They all love you. That bird!'

'Just a bird,' says Cain. 'About the tower . . .'

'Yours,' says Naaman. 'All yours.'

'And I may build as high as fancy takes me?'

'Higher! The clouds themselves need not obstruct you. Punch holes in the celestial sphere if you have a mind to. Throw a ladder up to Shamash or whoever.'

'The celestial is not my goal,' says Cain. 'Neither is the sun.'

'Up to you. Up to you. Aim where you like. And don't ever come down if you're happy. Remember: nothing is withholden from you. Ask and it shall be given. Speak and it shall be done.'

'You sound like a god.'

Naaman laughs. 'You have gods on the brain,' he says.

* * *

No two witnesses agreed. Depending on which reports you trust, Cain's Tower – variously misattributed to Marduk, Nemo and Nimrod, mistaken for the House of the Foundation of Heaven and Earth (otherwise *Etemenenanki*), and misnamed the Tower of Babel, as though there were only one – rose seven and a half or seventy miles into the air, was five or fifty miles in circumference, and threw a shadow it took a horseman one or one hundred days to ride out of.

From the summit of the tower either you beheld the cities of Ur and Larsa and Erech, like wisps of white smoke from a single hookah, or you beheld nothing except your own reflection magnified in cloud. If we follow the calculations of some who made measurements with compasses and T-squares, a trowel dropped from the last tier to be completed is falling to this day; whereas others, marvelling less at the majesty of the building than at the mayhem it occasioned, described displaced masonry regularly showering the city of Babel, threatening the safety of anyone who took bareheaded to the streets, but especially those whose livelihoods depended on their performing augury or fairy-stories around the tower's base.

One eyewitness tells of an almanac salesman with raisin eyes, killed because the quantity of paper tied to both his feet hampered his escape from a flying tile. But it was also said of him that he deliberately stood his ground, while others fled, declaring that there was some fatality in his family, that the curse had come upon him, that it was written – 'Pass it on.'

As to how many masons and hod-carriers and plasterers and carpenters and surveyors and sculptors and mosaicists and mathematicians were employed on the edifice – no estimate bears any similarity to the next. By some reckoning the total workforce, not including wives and shuris, was five hundred thousand; but there were, and still are, those who maintain that Cain worked alone on his mausoleum, completing a storey every three months, performing single-handedly all the functions mentioned above, always without having recourse to materials that included earth and water in their composition, and always without recourse to wives or shuris.

Citizens of Babel fearful of the structure claimed they had irrefutable evidence that its atmosphere induced morbid retentiveness of memory, and forbade their children to go within a thousand royal cubits of its influence. But many workmen on the tower who returned to the community either because they had grown old in Cain's service, or because they had been fired for refusing to work twenty-four-hour shifts, or because they had suddenly lost their enthusiasm for elevation, swore that their powers of recall had deteriorated out of measure as a consequence of labouring close to the magnetic fields of other planets, and supported this assertion, in the presence of elders, by forgetting what they'd just asserted.

For obvious reasons, opinions have always been still more divided over what took place in celestial circles as heaven's guards and watchmen observed Cain's progress. The view most commonly held by scientific and rationalist commentators is that scepticism, and even pity, must have prevailed; since the most rudimentary assessment of likely danger or damage would have established the impossibility of Cain's posing any serious territorial threat had his life been extended to ten thousand times its expected span. Quite simply, the tower was never going to reach.

But those of more fantastical turns of mind imagine a God beset by petulant and panicked counsellors, who saw the zooming ziggurat as a symbolic if not an actual threat to their hegemony, and a promise that matter would at last, however long it took, assert superiority over spirit. They had opposed the original creation of Adam on just such grounds. True, they had softened when it came to judgement on the fratricide, because Cain's murderousness seemed then to be their own best hope for the future – matter, left to itself, would destroy itself. But now they insisted that he should be reminded of the sentence leniently passed on him: that he be a wanderer and a fugitive *in the earth*, not among the clouds.

Pull him down, was their advice.

At last, as everyone agrees, the decision was God's alone. There is evidence that He never did much care, aesthetically or practically, for buildings. The sublunary world was His idea, was put together after a blueprint of His own, and He knew how He wanted it to look. He was also familiar with the incidence, among city dwellers, of imploded humanism:

put a man within doors and he quickly comes to believe immoderately in himself.

This was reason enough to raze a pile capable of housing half the world. But when the hour finally did come for Him to wield His arm, He made no bones about the thing that had upset Him most. His mighty ear, upon which not the slightest or least formed thought was lost, had picked up an intention buried beneath the lowliest brick in the building. It was *to make a name*. Which does not mean merely to find fame, but to *speak* it. To *pronounce* sufficiency. To *word* itself abroad. To glorify *expression*.

Nomenclature had been at the heart of God's disagreement with His creatures from the start. He had foreseen evil as a problem, He had anticipated knowledge, pride, sex, snakes. But He was not prepared for names to come between them, forgetting how essential to His idea of Himself was His Own. I AM WHAT I AM – Cain's refusal to offer sacrifice was nothing other than an unwillingness to accept the obligations of obeisance inherent in That Name. YOU ARE, Cain as good as told Him, WHAT YOU ARE NOT.

And what God will tolerate a mortal telling Him Who He Isn't?

Height was therefore purely incidental to what ensued; it was the tower's tongue that Y-H-W-H, the G-d who had forbidden vowels, went down and severed.

'Come, let us descend,' He said, 'and there confound the thing they speak with.'

Th thng th spk wth.

As for Cain, return to spongy earth was a blow more terrible to him than death. Away from it for many years, he had forgotten its burial-ground smell, its longing for decay, its oblivious, incessant mulch-making. Insects had grown noisier in his absence; he could hear them scratching at their shells, pulling out their own feelers, even when he was far from fields. The maggots in his dead meat were plumper than they'd been before, quicker, hungrier, whiter. He didn't dare kick a stone, for fear of what he'd find underneath. For fear of its colour. It was the colour of life he most couldn't bear on his return.

At least the colour of death cannot be worse, he consoled himself.

The dispersal of language was a further setback to one who was more a story than he was any other thing, and who was therefore compelled to tell himself in the way that other men are compelled to raise a family or an army. He understood no one in Babel now, and relied on signs to secure him approximations of what he wanted. A shave became a hit or miss affair – they either cut him too close, or not close enough, they left the hot towels on his face longer than was comfortable. At the baths, the aches in his back that most troubled him, the pains he couldn't point to with his fingers, were the ones the Anatolians always forgot to assuage. Lacking language, he at last let his body go, let it fall back into nature like his father's, did not bother to distinguish himself from a berry.

But language came into being at the behest of wretchedness, marbled with misery, and eventually its loss was a solace to him. Where there is silence there is no betrayal. Now, no one could accuse him of apostasy or tourism. He excited no one's expectations and let no one down. He didn't nightly exhume his brother. He didn't expose his mother's muddy breasts to the curiosity of a well-dressed audience. He didn't open and close his father's hands.

Rendered to all intents and purposes mute, Cain found few pleasures in the hundred or so years of life that were left to him; but slept easily, without dreams, now that he was no longer naming names and had forgotten the word for God.